THE
OTHER
WOMAN

*You can choose your sin, but you cannot choose
your consequences. . . .*

THE
OTHER
WOMAN

HANK PHILLIPPI RYAN

FORGE®

A TOM DOHERTY ASSOCIATES BOOK • NEW YORK

THE OTHER WOMAN

A Forge Book
Published by Tom Doherty Associates, LLC
175 Fifth Avenue
New York, NY 10010

www.tor-forge.com

Forge® is a registered trademark of Tom Doherty Associates, LLC.

ISBN 978-0-7653-6913-0

Forge books may be purchased for educational, business, or promotional use. For information on bulk purchases, please contact Macmillan Corporate and Premium Sales Department at 1-800-221-7945 extension 5442 or write specialmarkets@macmillan.com.

First Edition: September 2012
First Mass Market Edition: July 2013

Printed in the United States of America

0 9 8 7 6 5 4 3 2 1

Everybody, soon or late, sits down to a banquet of consequenses.

—ROBERT LOUIS STEVENSON

THE OTHER WOMAN

1

"**Get that light** out of my face! And get behind the tape. All of you. *Now*." Detective Jake Brogan pointed his own flashlight at the pack of reporters, its cold glow highlighting one news-greedy face after another in the October darkness. He recognized television. Radio. That kid from the paper. *How the hell did they get here so fast?* The whiffle of a chopper, one of theirs, hovered over the riverbank, its spotlights illuminating the unmistakable—another long night on the job. And a Monday-morning visit to a grieving family. If they could figure out who this victim was.

A body by the river. This time, the Charles, down by the old dock. Her legs, black tights striped with mud, leather boots, one zipper down, splayed on the fallen leaves and slimy underbrush on the bank. Her head, chestnut hair floating like a punk Ophelia, bobbing and grotesque in the tangled weeds.

Too bad I can't call Jane. She'd love this.

Jake's yellow beam of light landed on that Tucker kid, notebook out and edging toward the body. Rubber boots squished in the muck of the riverbank, still soft from Boston's run of bad-luck weather. "Hey, you, newspaper kid. *Out.* This means you. You don't wanna have to call your new editor to *bail* you out."

"Is it a serial killer?" A reporter's voice thin and reedy, carried in the chill wind. The neon green from the Boston Garden billboards, the purple beacons decorating the white-cabled Zakim Bridge, the glaring yellow of the chopper's spots colored the crime scene into a B-movie carnival. "Are you calling it a serial killing? You think it's one person? Was she killed the same way as the other?"

"Yeah, tell us, Jake," another voice demanded. "Is two murders serial?"

"One a couple weeks ago, one today, that's two." A different reporter's voice. "Both women. Both by water. By bridges. Both weekend nights. Both dead. That's serial. We're going with that. Maybe . . . 'the River Killer.'"

"We are, too. The Bridge Killer."

"Have you figured out who the first victim is?"

"Outta here, all of you!" Jake tucked his flashlight under one arm, zipped his Boston Police–issue brown leather jacket. Reporters scrambling to nickname a murderer. Crazy. *What does Jane always say? It bleeds, it leads? At least her stories aren't like that.* A siren screamed across Causeway Street; then the red-striped ambulance careened down the rutted side street. Every camera turned to the EMTs scrambling out the opening ambulance doors.

No need for them to hurry, Jake thought. His watch showed 2:15 A.M. She'd been dead for at least three hours.

Just like the other woman.

Jane Ryland had thrown up after the verdict.

She'd twisted her damp hair away from her face, avoided the mirror, and contemplated how long she could hide in the Suffolk County Courthouse ladies' room. *Forever would be good.* Instead, she'd gritted out a smile for the scrum of cameras as Channel 11's defense attorney promised her television colleagues an immediate appeal of the jury's decision. The two then marched down the granite steps of the courthouse, the lawyer's pin-striped arm protectively across Jane's shoulder, as if a million-dollar damage verdict were the honorable cost of doing journalism business.

But soon after, Jane could read the counterfeit smiles, rescheduled meetings, abysmal story assignments. Her TV reporting career was over. She'd protected a source, but nobody was protecting her.

MILLION-DOLLAR MISTAKE, the headlines screamed. RYLAND NAMES WRONG MAN AS JOHN IN SEX-FOR-HIRE CASE. Indy rag *Boston Weekly* called her "Wrong-Guy Ryland."

Jane knew she hadn't been wrong. There'd been no mistake, but it didn't matter. Days later she was fired.

"And most incredibly bogus of all, they pretended it wasn't about the verdict." Jane had banged out a bitter and bewildered e-mail to her pal Amy. Once newbie co-anchors together in Iowa, Amy had landed a high-profile reporter gig in Washington, D.C., then Jane got a similar deal in Boston. Amy's star was still rising. Plus, as she never let Jane forget, *she* was married.

"After three years of promos, all those promises," Jane typed, "they said they wanted to 'go another direction' with their political coverage. Are you kidding me? There's an election coming. It's the biggest story since the Kennedy thing. What the hell other direction can they go?"

"I'm so sorry, Janey honey," Amy typed back. "They had to blame somebody. Everyone hates TV reporters. And everybody hates TV. I'm probably next, you know? We should have gotten real jobs, kiddo."

Now Alex Wyatt—*Register* city editor Alex Wyatt, of all people!—was about to offer Jane a real job. Such as it was. At least the *Register*'s headlines had been objective. GROCERY MAGNATE WINS SLANDER SUIT.

Jane closed her eyes briefly at the memory. Dad would take care of her, if it came to that, even urge her to come home to Oak Park. Then he'd probably urge her to go to law school, like younger sister, engaged sister, good sister Lissa. Dad would be supportive, at least try to be, but Dr. Ryland never approved of failure. She was on her own. And she'd be fine.

Perched on the couch in Alex's new and already file-strewn office at the *Boston Register,* surrounded by the clutter of his half-unpacked boxes, Jane was working hard at being fine.

She wished she could just say no. Leave town. Change her name. Forget the jurors, forget the verdict. Talk to her mom just one more time.

But reality included a hefty mortgage on her condo, payments on her suddenly extravagant Audi TT, looming utility bills, and evaporating severance pay. She'd once reported heartbreakingly headlined stories about the terrors of unemployment. Now she was unemployed. Jane knew she'd tell Alex yes.

"I vouched for you with the bigs on the fifth floor." Alex positioned a framed Columbia J-school diploma against one beige wall, raised his wire-rimmed glasses to his forehead, then marked the wall with a pencil, turning his back to her. "Told 'em you were nails on the street. Tough and fair. Beat me on a couple stories, that's for sure. The hospital thing last year, remember?"

I sure do. "The hospital thing" was an overnight stake-out of a politician injured in a suspicious hit and run. Alex and Jane, each refusing to leave while the other kept watch, shared the last of the murky coffee. Jane had secretly contemplated sharing a lot more than coffee. Luckily, as she later admitted to Amy, she'd checked Alex's third finger, left hand. *Taken.* At least she'd eventually gotten an exclusive interview with the victim.

Alex was still talking. "But here at the paper, we respect reporters who protect their sources. We don't fire them. Told 'em I figured your source threw you under the bus."

He turned to her, glasses back in place and pencil now behind his ear. "Speaking of which. About the case. Sellica Darden told you, didn't she? She had to be your source. Want to talk about it? Off the record?"

Not now, not ever. "Lawyers, you know? The appeal?" Jane smoothed her black wool skirt over her knees, carefully pulling the hem over her best black leather boots. Looking anywhere but at Alex. Why didn't life have an "Undo" button? She hadn't realized she was risking her career for Sellica. She tried to keep the sorrow out of her voice. "I can't. I really can't."

Alex narrowed his eyes. "There's nothing that'll hurt the paper, though, right? Nothing'll come back to bite us? All any of us has is our reputation, you know?"

"Right," Jane said.

Mortgage. Heat. Health insurance. Food. Mom would have said, "Jane Elizabeth, you should remember every closed door means another door opens."

"You can trust me, Alex. I know times are tough for newspapers. I'm grateful Jake—Detective Brogan—called you about me. I'm grateful, really, for the opportunity."

The room went silent.

Maybe Alex was getting cold feet, no matter what Jake had told him. Maybe no one would trust her again. The jury was wrong, not her. But how can you battle perception? Jane gathered her black leather tote bag, ready to be dismissed. Maybe it was too soon. Or too late.

Leaving his framed diploma propped on top of a peeling radiator, Alex leaned against the side of his battered wooden desk. He smiled, running a hand across its pitted wood. "They told me T. R. Baylor himself, founder of the *Register,* used this very desk back in the day. Brinks job, Mayor Curley, the Boston Strangler. All the Kennedys. They offered me a new desk, you know? But keeping this one seemed right."

Jane smiled back. "Wonder what T.R. would think about your Internet edition? And maybe there's a new Boston Strangler now, the one they're calling the Bridge Killer."

"Times change; news doesn't," Alex replied. "People sure don't. The *Register*'s covering it, but we're not calling anyone the Bridge Killer yet, that's for sure. Who knows if those killings are connected? But yeah, you can't understand the future if you don't understand the past. I'm hoping this desk reminds me of that."

He pulled a yellow pad from a pile beside him, flipped through the top pages, then held up a hand-drawn calendar. In several of the pencil-line boxes was written JANE.

"Anyway," Alex continued, pointing to the schedule. "You're dayside. We're all about teamwork, and saving bucks, so I have you sharing a desk with Tuck. Tuck's covering the 'bridge killings'—whatever you want to call them—always out, so you'll probably never see each other."

She was in. She felt a reassuring flutter of the real Jane. *I'll scoop the hell out of those jerks at Channel 11.* "Sounds absolutely—," she began.

"I have to give you a six-month tryout," Alex interrupted, gesturing "upstairs" with his notepad. "Fifth floor says that's the deal. Are you with us?"

Jane managed a network-quality smile. Even if "network" was no longer in her future.

"You got yourself a newspaper reporter," Jane said. She looked square into the city editor's eyes, telegraphing she was not only the right choice to cover the election and share a desk with Tuck, whoever that was, but a valuable addition to his staff as well. One who did not make mistakes.

His eyes, however, were trained on the screen of his iPhone.

"Alex?" she said. If he dissed her on day one, she had low hopes for the teamwork he promised. But, facts be faced, her hopes were fairly low to begin with. She was still navigating the raw stages of grief over her dismissal from Channel 11.

It had been a while since her heart was broken.

Jane had avoided all the good-byes. She'd gone to the station one last time, after midnight. Packed her videotapes, Rolodex, fan mail, and three gilt-shiny award statues; stashed the cartons in the musty basement of her Brookline brownstone. The next two weeks she'd wrapped herself in one of Mom's afghans, parked herself in a corner of her curvy leather couch, and stared at her television. A screen no longer her domain.

She hadn't gone outside the apartment. Hadn't answered e-mail or the phone. A couple of times, drank a little too much wine.

Dad had been brusque when she called to tell him. "You must have done *something* wrong," he'd said. It was okay. Even after all these years, Jane knew he was still missing Mom. She was, too.

Mrs. Washburn from downstairs had appeared with the mail, bearing her famous mac and cheese, Jane's favorite. Little Eli, the super's starstruck eight-year-old, tried to lure her, as always, into an Xbox marathon. Steve and Margery, once her producer and photographer, sent white tulips, with a note saying, "Television sucks," and suggesting beer.

"Television sucks" made her laugh. For about one second.

Week three of unemployment, she'd had enough. She had clicked off the television, cleared out the stack of empty pizza boxes, and popped open the résumé on her laptop. The next day she rolled up the blinds in her living room, dragged the unread newspapers to the curb, and had her TV-length hair—the stylist called it walnut brown—cut spiky-short. She savagely organized all four closets in her apartment and dumped her on-air blazers in a charity bin. She'd listened to every one of her voice mail messages, and one was Jake. With a lead on a job at the *Register*.

And now she had an offer. Such as it was.

"Sorry, Jane, had to answer that text. So? Can you start tomorrow?" Clicking off his blinking screen, Alex tucked the iPhone into a pocket of his tweedy jacket. He'd been promoted from senior political reporter to city editor in time for the *Register*'s geared-up election coverage. Once Jane's toughest competition, Alex Wyatt—"Hot Alex," as Amy persisted in calling him—was about to become her superior.

Jane couldn't ignore the irony. The up-and-coming Jane Ryland, award-winning investigative reporter. Crashed on the fast track and blew it at age thirty-two. Possibly a new land speed record for failure. Her smile still in place, she pretended she hadn't noticed her potential new boss had ignored her.

"You got yourself a reporter," Jane said again. Now she just had to prove it.

2

"You want what?" Jane struggled to keep her voice even. Day two of the new Jane, only nine fifteen on Tuesday morning, and her vow to be upbeat was taking a beating. Alex, leaning against his chaos of a desk and offering her a bulging file folder, was asking the impossible.

Find Moira Kelly Lassiter? *How?*

An hour earlier, Jane had bought a subway fare card at the Riverside T station, then grabbed a soggy cup of coffee from the instantly inquisitive guy at Java Jim's.

"Aren't you—?" he'd begun, his eyes calculating.

"No." She'd almost burst into tears. *Not anymore.* It seemed like everyone was looking at her. They all knew who she was from TV. And now they all thought she'd made a mistake.

"You are too!" he'd yelled after her. "You cut all your hair off, but you're the one who . . ."

But she was through the turnstile and into her new life. Through the newly opened door. She glanced skyward, at Mom. *Gotcha.*

Unfolding the *Register* as the train racketed through Brookline's yellowing maple trees and plunged into the subway underground, Jane tried to keep her elbows from poking the sleeping commuter beside her. Bridge Killer

stuff, of course, on the front page. *Wonder if Jake*—?
She wished she could call him. Get the scoop.

Her heart fluttered, tempting her. Maybe one call,
briefly, just to— *No way*. She turned the page. Pushed
Jake out of her mind. She was focused on a new job, not
on an off-limits relationship. Not on the only man in
the past year or so—*since Alex*—who'd made her wish
that . . .

No. Work.

Governor Lassiter was up in the polls, according to the
Register's latest. Election looming. Lassiter's wife cancel-
ing her schedule again. Gable campaign scrambling. No
issues. No depth. The *Register* needed her.

Jane had crossed the busy street in front of the *Register*'s six-story yellow-brick offices and yanked open the
heavy glass door, in the throes of a high-speed mental
pep talk. Her lawyers promised they'd appeal the verdict.
Maybe Sellica would change her mind. Jane would be
vindicated. Channel 11 would clamor to take her back.

And tomorrow she'd be extra nice to Java Jim.

Jane had beeped her new ID card through the security
reader, waved to the guard at the front desk, punched
the elevator button. Punched it again, for punctuation.
She'd tackle this newspaper challenge, same way she'd
tackled every tough problem. On her own.

Except now, hearing her first assignment—it seemed
semi-impossible. She reached up to worry her hair, a left-
over-from-J-school nervous habit, but her hair wasn't
there anymore.

"So, Jane?" Alex came from behind his desk, urging
the manila file folder toward her. In tasseled loafers, wire-
rimmed glasses, and loosened tie, casually attractive, he
still seemed more rumpled-preppy street reporter than
influential news executive. His wife—having removed
him from Boston's most-eligible-bachelor list—was some

corporate honcho. "Here's the background I had Archive Gus dig out for you. Lots of photos. Think you can find her?"

No, she wanted to say. *I can't "find" Moira Kelly Lassiter, because she's not lost. She's just—home.* Apparently not wanting to come out. Plus, Alex was assigning her the candidate's *wife*? Like some foofy society reporter? Hardly destined to make headlines.

"Alex, maybe she's tired." Maybe she could gently derail this idea. "Maybe Moira doesn't like campaigning. Not all political wives are willing to keep standing in the background, staring adoringly at their husbands." Jane pushed up the sleeves of her black turtleneck, glad that Alex also wore jeans. Newspaper work did have its fashion pluses. "I should look into campaign contributions, or that union thing. The crime bill. Profiling Moira Lassiter seems kind of—puff."

Alex had started shaking his head before she was halfway through her plea. "My other political reporters are covering those angles. But Moira, seems she's suddenly off the radar. What if it's a face-lift? Great story. Maybe rehab? Hell of a story." Alex ticked the ideas off on his fingers. "Exhausted? Bored? Depressed? Sick? Unhappy? All front-page stuff. You're with me on this, right?"

"Ah, sure, Alex," Jane said. She put her hand to her hair, took it down. She was the new kid now, and it was key to be a team player. "I'll make some calls, sniff around, see what I get."

"We'll play it up big." Alex held up two fingers at a harried-looking man who'd arrived outside his glass-walled office. *Two minutes,* Alex mouthed. He turned back to Jane. "All set?"

"I'll have to go through Lassiter's scheduling gorgons. If they say no—"

"That means another door will open, right?" Two red lights flashed on Alex's desk phone, his intercom buzzed, the man waited in the doorway. "We're counting on you, Ryland. Find out what's happened to Moira Kelly Lassiter."

3

Kenna Wilkes opened the maroon-lacquered front door while the doorbell chimes still echoed through the front hall. On the expansive wooden porch stood the handsomest man she'd ever seen. Elegant. Regal. Silver hair, expensive suit.

Holy shit.

She fussed with her skinny white T-shirt, tucking it into the low-slung waistband of her new jeans, then looked up into those flinty eyes. Governor Owen Lassiter. *Former* governor.

Over his shoulder, she could see his entourage. A guy wearing khakis and a green LASSITER FOR SENATE button on his oxford shirt hovered behind the candidate, clutching a metal clipboard. A sleek black car was parked at the end of the driveway, headlights on. A blue and silver van with an enormous crimson *11* painted on the side idled across the street.

"Kenna Wilkes? We'd like you to meet Governor Owen Lassiter," the young man was saying, as if announcing a state occasion. "He's—"

"Running for the Senate, as you may have heard, Mrs. Wilkes." Lassiter's voice, interrupting his campaign aide, came across honey and steel.

Kenna hesitated, then took his hand.

"It's my Tuesday tour," Lassiter said. "Hoping to meet registered voters who are still making up their minds."

He looked at her as if she were the only voter in Deverton.

Kenna had tied her tumbling blond hair away from her face with a thin white satin ribbon. Used a hint of pink lip gloss, a blush of color on her cheeks. Tanned skin peeked between her T-shirt and jeans. Her hand was still in Lassiter's.

"If you have a few minutes, Mrs. Wilkes, perhaps we can answer your questions about our goals for this state and for this country. Unlike the negativity and fearmongering of the Gable campaign, we want to be a force for good down in D.C." Lassiter squeezed her hand gently, a gesture she'd find patronizing if she weren't so fascinated. "With your help, of course."

She hadn't been prepared for this. His charisma. His power. She'd been told he'd arrive this afternoon, between three and four, as part of his "Lassiter for Your Neighborhood" meet and greet. She'd seen the candidate on television. But no screen was big enough to contain him.

"Who dis?" Four-year-old Jimmy, Tonka dump truck in one hand and a half-eaten peanut butter sandwich in the other, toddled into the entryway, then rested his head against Kenna's thigh.

"He must be the only one in Massachusetts who doesn't know," Kenna said, laughing. She took back her hand to tousle Jimmy's dark curls. She had to get herself and this situation under control. "Still, Jimmy's only four. Back when you were governor, of course, he wasn't born yet."

"Hey, gunner," Lassiter said. He leaned down, close to

both of them. "I'm Owen. Pretty nice truck you got there."

Kenna breathed a hint of citrus and spice. When he looked up at her, she couldn't read his expression.

"You're lucky, Mrs. Wilkes. My wife, Moira, and I don't have kids."

Lucky? Not exactly how I'd have described it. She turned on a welcoming smile. "Would you like to come in? It's not like you're a stranger."

"Thank you, Mrs. Wilkes," Lassiter said. "We won't stay long."

"Kenna," she said.

"Kenna," he acknowledged. He turned to his aide. "Trevor? We'll be—" He looked at Kenna, confirming. "—fifteen minutes?"

Trevor raised the clipboard, apparently a signal to an unseen person in the black SUV. The headlights clicked off. But the door of the Channel 11 van slid open. Kenna could see bare legs and black high heels emerging from the passenger side.

"Mrs. Wilkes?" Trevor said. "Channel Eleven is tracking the campaign today. Would it be all right if they came in?"

Not a chance. "I'd rather not. If it's not a problem? I'm not really comfortable having our picture taken." Kenna made fluttery gestures at her hair and jeans.

"No television." Lassiter frowned briefly at the aide, who performed an exaggerated thumbs-down at the news van. The stiletto-clad legs swung back in; the door slammed. "We'll talk privately. The two of us."

His expression softened. "And Jimmy." Lassiter paused at the sound of Trevor's jangling cell phone.

"Hold on," the aide said into the phone. "Governor? Your schedule. Maitland's found another problem with—"

"Tell Rory I said to deal with it. No more interruptions."

And he stepped inside.

"See her, Alex? Right there. The tall twenty-something in the red coat." As if dealing a hand of solitaire, Jane placed the glossy photos on the city editor's cluttered desk. She stabbed a finger at the fuzzy crimson image. "I found that woman in at least five of the recent photos Archive Gus gave us. I've been down in the archive room most of the day, looking for more. Every time she's behind the rope line, but right in front of the crowd. Look. Down in Cohasset. Up in Lawrence. Way out in Worcester."

Jane looked at Alex, checking for signs he was buying her pitch. *Funny to be on the same team with him, instead of battling for sound bites. Wonder why he was never a TV reporter. Those shoulders. Those cobalt eyes. All that hair.* She reached out a hand, trying to persuade him, almost touching his jacket.

"I'm telling you, Alex, it looks like she's—"

"She's another Lassiter groupie." Alex shook his head, dismissive. "Or some political activist. Wants a job in D.C. Wants Lassiter to vote for the omnibus bill. It's an election. Everyone wants something."

"But what if there's something between them? Look at the Cohasset shot. See how she's looking at him? That's—" Jane paused, analyzing the photo. "—it's lust. What can I tell you?"

"She *is* hot." Alex yanked off his glasses, held the photo under his desk lamp. His wide gold wedding band glinted in the light. "No mistaking that."

No mistaking? Was that some sort of crack? She didn't make mistakes, damn it.

Jane held up a different photo. "Who would wear this

slinky getup outside? In October? She's at least thirty years younger than Lassiter. And she sticks out like high beam headlights. You think she's just doing her civic duty?"

"You can be a knockout and still be a political activist, Ryland." Alex slid the photos into a pile, tamped down the edges, handed them to her. "These were to give you a sense of the campaign. Not to send you into reporter fantasy land."

"Two little words," Jane said, tucking the photos into her tote bag. "Monica Lewinsky."

"Three little words," Alex replied. "Leave it alone."

"But—"

"Jane. Listen to your editor. Don't go near this in print. This close to the election, it's ethical quicksand. And if he's having an affair? It's hardly even news. They all do it."

"But—" But Alex was ignoring her, swiping pages on his iPhone and almost turning his back. *Dismissed*. Fine. She had listened to him, exactly as he asked. But if "they all do it"? That simply confirmed there was a story. She was determined to find it.

4

"Jimmy never knew him." Kenna made an infinitesimal adjustment to the photo on the polished mahogany fire-place mantel, caressing it for a moment as she spoke. "He was a month from coming home."

The black-framed photograph of the marine, dark curly hair, desert fatigues, squinting into the sunshine, held the place of honor in the cozy Deverton living room. A folded American flag in a stark wooden box sat next to it.

"You must have been so proud of your . . ." Lassiter hesitated.

"Husband." Kenna finished the sentence, slowly sliding her hands into her back pockets, the toe of her silver ballet flat tracing a pattern in the pile of the creamy shag rug. A blond curl escaped from the ribbon, fell across one cheek. She looked at Lassiter from under her lashes.

"Yes. I still think of James every day. Jimmy was less than a year old when it happened. Three years later, I'm still working on explaining it to him. Why he doesn't have a father."

"You—," Lassiter began.

She turned to Lassiter, earnest. "No, please, this isn't about me. Or even Jimmy." She gestured through an archway toward a toy-littered playroom. "He's happy entertaining himself with his trucks. Today is about you. And your campaign, Governor."

"Owen," he said.

Kenna agreed, with a shy smile, then tapped her silver-linked watch. "I believe you said your schedule allowed fifteen minutes here, Owen. That means only twelve minutes left for you to win me over."

"May I speak to Mrs. Lassiter, please? This is Jane Ryland at . . . the *Register*." The new title snagged her. "Sure, I'll hold. I'm following up on the interview request from this morning."

About six hours ago.

The scruffy chair rattled over the murky once-gray carpeting as Jane swiveled to get comfortable at her new desk. Her *half* of her new desk.

Tuck—was he the flannel-shirted surfer-looking guy in the photo pinned to the peeling corkboard?—had graciously cleared off one of three adjustable wooden bookshelves and emptied one of four battered metal desk drawers. Someone's idea of sharing. He'd scrawled a note on a Post-it pad: "Welcome, Roomie." Someone's idea of camaraderie.

She thought of her old office at Channel 11. Sleek built-in corner shelves holding her kept-from-J-school tattered reference books. Lighted mirror. Huge bulletin board covered with dangling plastic-sleeved press passes, happy snaps, and souvenir campaign buttons. Mike the mailroom guy delivering fan letters, the occasional skeevy plea from a creepy admirer, sometimes even rants from hostile viewers. After the trial, she'd gotten a few particularly unpleasant ones, ridiculous, but she'd told Jake about them, just in case. *Where's the mailroom here, anyway?* Back then, she'd had a door that closed. And locked.

Good-bye to that. This was her new domain. Fabric-covered cubicles. Tops of heads of strangers. Fragrance of aging coffee. Buzzing tubes of fluorescent lights. Half an office.

Now some huffy press assistant was asking, could she take a message?

"No," Jane replied. "I prefer to talk to Mrs. Lassiter directly. Do you know when she'll be available? And wouldn't it be better if she took a break, as you called it, *after* the election?"

Silence. Then a tinny Sousa march as someone hit the Hold button.

Slipping the phone between her cheek and shoulder, Jane typed her password into the coffee-smudged beige computer on the desk, puffed the dust from the monitor. She pushed aside a haphazard stack of Tuck's file folders, the one on top marked LONGFELLOW BRIDGE, and clicked into the *Register*'s Web site. The front page of the latest edition appeared on the screen.

The "hold" music stopped.

"Jane?" The new voice was soothing, conciliatory. Sheila King introduced herself.

Another press secretary. And soon after, yet another refusal of the interview.

"Sheila? I'm confused." Jane leaned back in her chair, the heels of her boots stretching past the cubicle divider. "I'm simply looking for the standard-issue candidate's-wife interview. No surprises, no big deal. Just, hey, how ya doin'. How goes the campaign."

Jane stared at the dingy ceiling tiles as the press secretary spun out excuses and double-talk. *Give me a break.* She snapped her chair upright and clicked down the *Register*'s online front page.

The main headline, byline Tucker Cameron, read PO-
LICE CONTINUE TO DENY SERIAL KILLINGS. Below that, a
Tuck sidebar, POLICE INSIST NO "BRIDGE KILLER." *My
elusive deskmate is getting some big ink*. She clicked on
"Politics." There, the headline read GABLE GAINS IN
POLLS, LASSITER LAGGING. Maybe Alex was on to some-
thing.

"No, you listen," Jane said into the phone. "You're telling me Moira Lassiter's 'not available'? 'Not now. Not
tomorrow. Not next week.' That sounds a lot like 'not
ever.' Might I ask why?"

"Dump truck. Box truck. And what's this one?" Lassiter
had folded his soft charcoal suit jacket over the back of
the overstuffed couch and sat on the living room floor,
legs akimbo, surrounded by a convoy of miniature vehicles.

Kenna clicked red and green Lego blocks together
and apart, watching the man who wanted to be the next
senator from Massachusetts play with a four-year-old.
Fifteen minutes had long passed.

Over one cup of coffee, then two, she had drawn him
out about his campaign, his policies, his strategy. She
was fascinated, of course. Riveted. It was almost too
easy. Lassiter had answered a second phone call with a
terse: "I know what time it is. I'll call you."

"Dat is a oil truck!" Jimmy crowed. He grabbed the
plastic vehicle from Lassiter's hands. "I know it!"

"Maybe he can help with your Middle East policy,"
Kenna said, smiling. She uncoiled herself from the chintz
armchair, tossed two Legos into the rubber bowl. "Or
transportation."

"Absolutely. We can use a guy who recognizes his
trucks." Lassiter leaned back against the side of the couch,

stretching his legs across the oriental rug. "The campaign could also use a well-informed mom who cares about his future. Ever thought about volunteering? Work for the Lassiter campaign?"

With an insistent buzz, Lassiter's phone vibrated across the glass-top coffee table. The doorbell rang. And rang again.

"Your master's voice," Kenna said, looking at the phone. "I guess our time is up, Governor."

"Will you do it?" Lassiter clambered to his feet and punched off his phone. "Join our merry band?"

"You're a hard man to resist." Kenna stood, hands on hips. "But I'd better answer the door before your staff comes looking for you, don't you think?"

By the time Kenna returned, Trevor and clipboard in tow, Lassiter had rebuttoned his suit jacket and adjusted his tie. Jimmy, making *vroom*ing sounds, was running the oil truck up the side of the couch.

"Mrs. Wilkes has volunteered for the campaign." Lassiter pointed a finger at his aide, delegating. "Make sure she gets the information and paperwork she needs. Tell Maitland to expect her downtown."

He turned back to Kenna. "Right?"

She held out one hand, palm up, agreeing. "You got yourself a campaign worker. I like what you said about the environment. And your foreign policy is . . . well, James would approve, I'm sure." She saw Lassiter's eyes soften.

"I'm sure you're right, Mrs. Wilkes."

Standing in the doorway, Kenna waited until the entourage drove out of sight. She slid open a drawer in the foyer's mahogany desk. Took out a cell phone. Dialed. Waited for the beep.

"Slam dunk," she said. She paused, taking a deep satisfied breath. "Now. Come take this damn kid away."

5

Would anyone answer this time? Detective Jake Brogan stepped back from the front door, angling himself sideways on the concrete front steps in case the response to his second round of knocking was a bullet. He'd almost lost a partner that way, back when he and DeLuca were rookies.

Tonight DeLuca was on call, and Jake was scouting solo. Fine. Couldn't solve a murder, two murders, from the couch of his condo. He didn't have to touch the Glock under his shoulder to know it was there.

He strained to hear what might be going on inside the Charlestown three-decker, its white-vinyl façade a copy of the one next door and the one next door to that. Black shutters, random shrubs. Streetlights mostly working. Down the block, newer brownstones, carefully gardened, pumpkins on stoops, gentrified the neighborhood into class battle lines, townies versus yuppies, all in the shadow of the Bunker Hill Monument. The granite obelisk in the middle of Charlestown marked the slaughter that began the Revolutionary War. People around here were still fighting authority.

Code-a-silence, they called it. The townies never saw anything. Not much chance whoever was behind this door, or watching from the windows above, would admit to knowing what happened by the bridge last Sunday. Or would identify the victim, even if they knew her. Still, that's what cops mostly did. Ask questions. Behind every closed door was a possible answer. This time on a Wednesday night, people should be home.

Still no response. Holding his BlackBerry under the feeble glow of the dusty porch light, he checked the canvass notes he'd tapped in. No grimy spiral notebooks for him, though the other guys sneered. "Harvard," they called him. But he could type in the info, zap it to himself via e-mail. Instant filing, paperwork done.

"Boston PD," he said, knocking again. "Anyone there?"

This time he heard something. A scraping, a creak. Maybe someone on a stairway.

"Nothing's wrong," he called out. Which wasn't exactly true. "Just want to show you a few photos."

A shadow behind the glass peephole, middle of the door. Sound of a dead bolt. The door creaked open, two inches, maybe three. The length of the chain. Then a slash of blue eye shadow, a heavy-penciled eyebrow. A fuzz of carroty hair.

"Ma'am?" Jake guessed. "Jake Brogan, Boston PD."

"So?"

"Do you recognize this person?" Jake pulled postcard-sized sketches from his inside jacket pocket, held one up. The first was colored pencil, a redraw from the crime scene photos of Sunday's Charlestown Bridge victim, the girl found three blocks from here. The real thing— bloated, bruised, basically grotesque—was too gruesome to show on the street. The sketch, brown hair, brown eyes, trace of a smile, softened the girl into someone's college roommate. Anyone who knew her would recognize her.

"She had this on her leg." Jake held up another drawing, this one depicting the green Celtic vine tattoo on one thin ankle. Minus, of course, the weedy vines the river waters had deposited around her leg. The tattoo was standard issue, another dead end, but he had a cadet hitting tattoo parlors and piercing places. Jake decided not to tell the reluctant townie exactly why he was asking.

In the drawing she didn't look dead. "She from around here at all?" Jake asked.

"Zat the Bridge Killer girl?" The eye came closer to the chain.

So much for strategy. "You recognize her, ma'am? We could use your help here. Someone's missing a daughter, maybe."

"You people should catch that guy," the voice said. "Before he kills someone else."

And the door closed in his face.

Another campaign event canceled? Jane clicked through the swirling graphics of the Lassiter campaign's online newsletter, elbows on her desk and chin in her hands, weary, trying to focus. Trying not to listen as coworkers she didn't know said good night to one another and headed for bars or gyms or someone special at home. The sounds of the newsroom, tapping keyboards, cell phone rings, beepers, and the occasional peal of laughter, were familiar, and yet—not.

It had been a while since she'd been the new kid. Some people were trying to be nice, but breezy hellos and good-byes aside, she was the outsider. Maybe they couldn't believe Alex had hired her. *Everyone hates TV reporters.* Amy had reminded her of that reality. Nobody hates them more devotedly than newspaper reporters. Especially a television reporter who gets it wrong. And they all thought she got it wrong.

The Lassiter newsletter blurred with a twinge of tears. There was nothing she could say that people would believe. They thought she was defensive, or lying, or a has-been, someone to be pitied, or dismissed. She missed her old life. Missed the after-news postmortems at Clancy's. Missed the sneaked lunchtime manicures with Margery. Except for Margery and Steve, stalwart pals who'd persisted with dinner and movie invitations, none of her "friends" from Channel 11 had even called. As if being fired were a communicable disease.

Get a grip, she told herself. *Shit happens. You'll make friends here.*

If only the lawyers could win the appeal. If only Sellica would contact her. Decide to come forward and tell the truth. Then everyone would know Jane wasn't wrong. A moment of hope lifted her heart. Then disappeared.

"'Night, Jane." Two women's voices, almost in unison, called out as they passed her cubicle. Jane glimpsed the tops of two heads, blond and blonder, as whoever they were hurried by. She heard them laughing as they headed to the elevator.

Unable to stop herself, she clicked off the Lassiter newsletter and into the *Register*'s Internet search. Maybe it wouldn't hurt this time. Maybe something had happened. She keyed in her own name. Then, quickly, "Arthur Vick."

The headlines scrolled. Her name and his. Over and over. He was still the winner. She was still "Wrong-Guy Ryland."

Nothing had changed.

Holly Neff squinted at the wood-framed bulletin board. She'd strung a thin wire behind it, one end to the other, attaching it to the frame with two little round things.

She'd measured with a foldout yardstick, so the board would hang exactly between the scrolling vines of the green parts of the wallpaper. Like a frame in a frame. She'd been at Harborside, what, two weeks now? And the living room was on the way to perfect. When things worked, they just worked.

The bulletin board was smaller than she'd wanted, not covering the entire wall, but that had been a fantasy, she supposed. It would have been impossible to bring home such a huge—she tilted her head one way, then the other. Something was—

Ah. The corner of the third photo wasn't lined up with the second one.

Holly frowned, adjusting the white-bordered eight by ten. It had to be perfect. She had to start all over.

One by one, she pulled the clear plastic pushpins from the corners of each photograph. There were an even dozen, which was perfect. One by one, she placed each picture, aligned in an even row, across the pristine white cloth on her dining room table.

Picture number one. Black-and-white. Owen Lassiter behind a bunting-draped podium, announcing his candidacy for the U.S. Senate. Crowds surrounding him. That woman beside him, all blond and smiling. Like *she* had something to do with it. Maybe that should be picture number two. Not first.

Holly moved the Lassiter announcement photo farther along the tablecloth and replaced it with the new photo number one. Color. Lassiter's head shot, just him, gray hair, cheekbones. Charcoal suit, white shirt, red tie with little—what were they? She squinted at the photo. Flags. Massachusetts flags. Flags on his tie.

She paused, remembering. The love of her life. He'd be happier, so much happier, when he realized what she was doing. Yes, it was a sacrifice. But doing what was right often included sacrifice. That's what made it powerful. That's what love was about. Devotion. And persistence. And timing. Then, happy endings. You just had to be patient. And she was patient, patient, patient.

Her timer, a red plastic apple that you twisted to set your limits, buzzed a warning. *Hurry.* She had to hurry.

Photo number one: head shot. Maybe she should measure? *No. I can do this.* Photo number two. Announcement shot. Pushpins into each corner. Photo number three. One of her favorites. Cut from the newspaper with pinking shears, its zigzag edges setting it apart from the others. She was in this photo with him.

Holly stared at it, seeing herself, *herself,* caught on camera, wearing that perfect little outfit, her honey brown curls perfect, that perfect expression she'd practiced, in the same photograph as Owen Lassiter. That was just, just perfect.

And now she had to go to sleep. Tomorrow would be a very exciting day.

6

If she were giving advice to a friend, Amy or Margery or someone, she'd tell them poking the place that hurts is no way to make it heal. *Easier to say than do.* Jane ignored the blinking screen of computer newsprint on her desktop monitor. How had doing the right thing backfired so disastrously?

What if she'd been on vacation, or busy, or out on a story? Sellica might have called someone else, or decided to keep quiet.

But no.

Back then, Jane picked up her ringing phone. And back then, that ordinary move, that no-decision decision, landed her in journalism hell.

"Is this Jane Ryland?" The voice on the other end had sounded guarded.

"Yes. How can I help you?"

Silence.

"Ma'am?" Jane had prompted.

"It's Arthur Vick."

Jane frowned. The voice was a woman's, most definitely not the grocery store mogul calling, unless he was brilliant at disguising not only his gender but the trademark Boston accent he exploited in his ubiquitous television commercials.

"Arthur Vick . . . what? I'm so sorry," Jane said. "You lost me."

"They're all like, *he* didn't do anything wrong. Like I'm some kind of slut-bitch who trapped the guy into, whatever."

The voice spoke quickly, tense, the words rushed and crowding one another. "He promised me I could be in the commercials. Then, like, he was outta there. And now the judge is like, yeah, oh sure, Mr. Big Shot, we wouldn't want your wife to be upset. So we'll keep your name out of it. Seal the court documents. Like, that's supposed to be fair? I want what was coming to me. And you help people, right?"

Jane instantly knew what this was about. Sellica Darden, "the other woman" in a headline-grabbing sex case, was calling her. Why?

She gripped the phone, white knuckled. She couldn't record it: Massachusetts law made that illegal. If this woman hung up and disappeared, she would never find her. But if Sellica Darden kept talking, Jane predicted, it could make her career.

Jane Googled up a newspaper article as she listened. It had been a lead story, all lust and lies. Sellica had threatened to expose her high-profile big-name john to his unsuspecting wife if he didn't fork over big bucks. He refused, and ratted her out to police. She was arrested for extortion, her name plastered across the news—but the judge had sealed the john's name, even though he'd also broken the law. Even though the names of other men who hired hookers were often made public.

Back then, Jane had felt her fingers cross. *Please let it be Sellica*. "Miss Darden? Is this you? And yes, I can help you. It was—unfair, that the judge kept the man's name secret. And threatened you with jail if you told. Can we meet in person? As soon as possible? When?"

It had been Sellica on the phone. And she said "yes," and "tomorrow." Soon after, Jane had gotten everything she wished for.

And soon after that—everything she feared.

Jane's big story outed Arthur Vick. He sued, saying Jane had named the wrong guy. Sellica disappeared. Jane refused to give up her source. Vick won. The station lost a million dollars. And soon Jane was the one who was out.

Jane's shoulders sagged under the weight of the memory.

Someday Sellica Darden would reveal the truth. Give Jane her life back.

She had to.

Jane's cell phone buzzed.

Wouldn't that be funny if—? She grabbed it, clicked, fearing to hope.

Amy. Texting.

U not home? Called U! Even Brenda Starr went home! TTYL.

Amy's right, as usual. Jane clicked away the headlines, wishing she could as easily delete the past. Things would be better when she was reporting again. Jane brought up the Lassiter newsletter. It had a new headline.

LASSITER FUND-RAISER RESCHEDULED. Jane reached for her hair, worrying a strand over one ear. The Lassiter campaign was imploding. No wonder Moira was hiding. Probably shopping for a new husband, or a new life. Probably Lassiter was off with that girl in the red coat. *They all do it,* Alex had said. As if somehow that made it okay.

She paged through the file folder of archive photos Alex had given her. Was there something she'd missed?

Moira showed up in the earlier ones. Front and center. Owen's shadow. That ballerina posture of hers, salon-silver hair and nonchalant tailoring. Radiating wifely approval.

Jane bent over in her chair, sorting the photos chronologically on the gray carpet of her cubicle. And there it was. Suddenly, a month ago? Moira was missing. Jane stared at the images, trying to imagine. Had Jackie Kennedy known about Marilyn? Had Gary Hart's wife been told about that girl on the *Monkey Business*? Elizabeth Edwards suspected John and Rielle, she'd said, but rationalized it away. Until she couldn't anymore. What would Moira do if she discovered that her husband—in the midst of an election, in front of millions of the very voters he was asking to trust him—was cheating? Who else knew about it? And who was helping Lassiter hide it?

Someone's phone ringing. An elevator bell. The heat kicking on. *Back to reality.* Was she the last to leave? Wasn't Tuck supposed to be working nightside? No sign of him, except for the array of grisly eight-by-ten photos of the Bridge Killer bodies—where'd he get all those?— posted with multicolored thumbtacks across the entire bulletin board. She peered at them, interested in spite of herself. The Charlestown girl had a tattoo. The other victim didn't.

The other woman. Exactly what I'm working on, too. Jane smiled as she yanked her black wool jacket from the hook and cinched the belt around her waist. It was late, close to midnight, but her weariness was evaporating. She was beginning to feel like a reporter again.

They all do it. So what? Cheating was unacceptable. For anyone, much less a U.S. Senator. The public had the right to know about it. Before the election. And she would be the one to tell them.

No mistake about that.

What did he expect to find here, anyway? Jake stuffed his hands into the pockets of his leather jacket, scuffing his work boots through the layer of slimy leaves under the Charlestown Bridge. Where the body was found. The place was deserted at this hour. What was he thinking, some coked-up asshole would show up? Drawn back to the scene of the crime, confessing all as he realized super-detective Jake had him dead to rights?

He'd made his gold shield, younger than most. The public explanation, two years ago, was that a thirty-three-year-old detective might bring some street cred. Privately, the brass and the street cops understood Jake's being grandson of a former police commissioner was a powerful—and unavoidable—legacy.

Not what they usually mean by blue blood, Jake's mother always said, disapprovingly. She was a Dellacort, a real blue blood, and Dellacorts were not in law enforcement. She still sniffed—elegantly, of course—at Jake's "unfortunate" career choice.

But an adolescent Jake and his grandpa had watched every episode of *NYPD Blue* together on the plush sofas of the Brogans' Back Bay living room. Jake soaked up every nuance and every roll call and every takedown, and even at Harvard, he'd never wavered in his resolve. Grandpa had lived just long enough to see his graduation. Jake's financier father presented him with an extravagant post-college trek around Europe, a thinly disguised effort to dissuade him from his career choice, but the year after he came home, Jake aced the exam, powered through the academy, and got his badge and gun.

Now, though his parents reluctantly accepted his occupation, Jake still needed to prove he'd earned his spot on the squad. Deserved it, Grandpa Brogan or not. To do that, he needed to crack some cases. About this one, for now at least, he had no idea.

The lights of Boston glowed at him. Jake's flashlight scraped across the browning grass and broken weeds. The crime scene guys were long gone, taking their yellow tape with them. He had their report stored in his BlackBerry. Nothing left here. Nada.

It was night, same time as when she must have died three days ago. Things looked different at night. You saw things. The way the light hit. Where you could be invisible. Jake stared at nothing, letting his mind go. Reconstructing. Why would a girl be here, that time on a Sunday night? Monday morning, really.

Water in her lungs, the ME had confirmed. So she wasn't dead when she got here. Big bruise on her back, one on her shoulder. Clothing intact. Jake tilted his head all the way back, considering the Erector Set structure of the bridge above. Headlights, creeping along then surging by, headed into the labyrinth of Boston's North End. Could she have jumped? Thrown herself off the bridge because . . . because of what? To kill herself? Escape?

Wouldn't someone have seen that? He looked at the cars, playing out the scene, screening a movie of the crime in his head. Someone would have seen that. Someone would have reported it.

But if she jumped, where did she leave her purse? Her car? How did she get here? If she was trying to get away from someone, who?—and why?

Wouldn't someone have seen that, too? Who was she? Why hadn't anyone reported her missing?

Maybe it wasn't about the bridge.

A sound.

Jake snapped off his flashlight, easing into the shadow of one of the ramshackle lean-tos townies used as fishing shelters. His left hand snaked under his jacket, feeling for the holster and his weapon inside. He waited. Heard the sound again.

Then—a flash of light. And another. *Christ.* Someone was—taking photos?

"Boston Police. Hands in the air. Now. Now. *Now.*" Jake took a step forward, then another, commanding. Weapon aimed dead ahead. Flashlight in the other hand, same direction. Then he lowered the weapon.

"Tucker, dammit." Jake holstered the Glock, adrenaline still rushing. He clicked off the flashlight, wiped a hand on his jeans. *I'm gonna kill that*— "Lucky I didn't kill you, ya know? What in hell are you doing out here?"

Tucker snapped another photo, the flash right in Jake's face. "Might ask you the same thing, right? You out here looking for the Bridge Killer? You ID the victims yet? Care to comment?"

"You're over the line, Tucker." *Unbelievable. These reporters think they're*— "Use that photo, any of 'em, and I'll nail you for trespassing on a crime scene. See how you like being the big reporter from the Nashua Street Jail."

"Okay, off the record, then." Tucker stashed the camera in a pocketed canvas bag and started toward him.

Jake crossed his arms over his chest. Holding his ground. "There's no off the record. There's no on the record. There's nothing. There's no Bridge Killer. And you're on your way outta here. Now."

"I'm just saying," Tucker persisted. Talking and walking backwards at the same time. "If you don't know who the dead girls are, and you don't know why they were killed, how ya gonna stop the Bridge Killer from killing again?"

7

"**Mrs. Lassiter? It's** Jane Ryland. Do you remember me?"

Jane sat in the damp chill of her apartment basement, perched on a plywood riser in her cramped storage space, holding her ancient Rolodex between her knees and her cell phone up to her ear. A bare bulb in the ceiling, string extending a too-short metal pull, gave just enough light. Lucky she'd kept her stuff. Lucky Moira Lassiter's personal phone number still worked. *Sorry, PR types.* She'd tried playing by the rules. But too many doors kept slamming. It was eight Thursday morning, certainly not too early to call a candidate's wife. Jane hoped.

There was a moment of silence. In the textured static, Jane could almost hear Moira Lassiter deciding. She couldn't let her make the wrong decision.

"Mrs. Lassiter?" Jane persisted. Hoping the candidate's wife would not hang up. Hoping being this pushy wouldn't blow her chances for an interview. She had to reclaim her life, one story at a time. If Moira was hiding because her husband was having an affair, that was front-page news. No matter what Alex thought. She simply had to prove it.

"You and I last saw each other, remember, at that fund-raiser for the Home for Little Wanderers? We had such a great talk that night. You told me all about—"

An intake of breath on the other end interrupted her, mid-pitch. "Yes, of course, I remember, Jane. And I've always admired your work. I'm sorry for what happened to you. It seems—unfair. What can I do for you?"

Moira was cutting to the chase. Skipping further niceties. Jane followed suit, fast-forwarding through her new job with the *Register* to her new assignment. She assured the candidate's wife the interview would be nonconfrontational, no surprises, and exactly what the readers wanted to hear.

"Voters, I guess I should say, not readers." Jane, wrapping up, reminded Mrs. Lassiter what was at stake. "People love you. But your staff tells me—you're taking a break? Just talk with me on background, maybe. If you decide to go on the record, we can discuss that later."

Jane squinched her eyes closed, hoping. Maybe she'd be able to give Alex some good news. Maybe, just maybe, there would be a story.

"Jane?"

"Yes?" Jane felt her stomach flip. In a split second, she'd know.

"Maybe. Let me think about it."

Damn. "So when—?"

Jane heard the unmistakable click as Moira Lassiter hung up.

Flash. No, no flash. There was certainly enough light in her apartment to take the photo without the flash, Holly knew, but it might look more perfect *with* the flash. She could try both ways, of course, then see.

The green LASSITER FOR SENATE balloons caught in

the eddies of the apartment's aluminum heating vent, bumping and floating across the photos pushpinned to the bulletin board. Holly had tied a three-foot-long green satin ribbon to each balloon, then attached them all to the bottom left corner of the bulletin board.

Then the heat came on, blowing the stupid balloons right in front of the pictures. Now she couldn't see the Lassiter announcement, or the shot of the front of his campaign headquarters.

She huffed out an impatient sigh. It shouldn't be this difficult.

Leaving the camera on her new tripod, she crossed the living room and slammed down the thermostat. She didn't need heat. She needed the balloons to stay in place for the photo to be perfect. It wasn't perfect. She needed one more shot. Could she get it today? She had to get it *today*.

Taking a deep breath, she counted to five and thought about happy endings. A kiss in a corridor. A promise made.

A promise broken.

The timer apple dinged.

Time to go.

"What is it about politicians, anyway?" Jane sat in the lumpy upholstered swivel chair outside Alex's office. His door was uncharacteristically closed. She could see through the window that he was on the phone. She'd wait. Her thumbs moved swiftly over her BlackBerry keyboard.

I mean, Ame, is everyone in DC sleeping with anyone who walks through the door? Are wives blind? Bored? Off with other men?

She could picture Amy at her desk in D.C., probably holding a phone to one ear, sending e-mails on her computer, and texting with Jane at the same time. Jane wished she lived closer. It was difficult having your best friend five hundred miles away. Especially recently.

"LMAO," Amy texted back. "We got a guy, state rep, sleeping with his secty. Until wifey got wind. Now husb in doghouse sted of statehouse. Said he thot she'd never know. Moron. What up with Hot Alex, sistah?"

"How they think they get away with it? And the other woman. What's in it for her? Sex? Power? Thrill of deception?" Jane hit Send. The screen stayed blank. Amy was probably talking to a real person. Then more green letters popped into view.

Avoiding question, Janey girl. ☺ Hot Alex? All work and no play. . . .

Jane smiled. She should never have mentioned him to Amy. Why did everyone on the planet think she should be hunting for a husband? She'd have one. Someday. Probably. "Married. Big time. He's my boss, remember? End of story. Gotta go. xoxo"

The office door clicked open just as Jane tucked her phone into her tote bag. Good thing Alex—*Hot Alex*—hadn't been reading over her shoulder.

"Sorry, Jane," he said, gesturing her into his office. He used his heel to click a doorstop into place, keeping his door open.

The job must be getting to him, Jane thought as she stepped inside. She noticed bags under his eyes, had never seen those before. He wore the same tweed jacket as yesterday. Maybe even the same brown turtleneck with his jeans. Stacks of file folders threatened to topple off his desk. A sleek white laptop, open and humming, sat in the center. Next to it a big PC showed the flickering *Register* home page.

Alex flipped the laptop closed, then flopped into his chair. He swiveled toward her, keeping his left hand on the laptop cover. "What can I do for you? Moira say yes?"

Jane stared at his hand.

"Jane?"

"Uh, yeah, matter of fact. Kind of. Maybe." Jane looked at the diplomas on the wall, looked at the two still-unpacked cardboard boxes in the corner, looked anywhere but at Alex's left hand.

Which was no longer wearing a wide gold band.

"So what'd she say? She give you a time? Wait a sec. Here's a—" Alex thumbed through a pile of manila folders on one corner of his desk, then stood, reaching for a stack of papers stapled at one corner. The rest of the folders slid to the floor, scattering white pages across the mottled gray carpeting. "Shit. I mean—sorry." Alex glanced at Jane, apologetic. "Sorry. Way to start the day."

He organized them back into a stack, then gave a little shrug. "Anyway. So. Moira?"

"You okay?" Jane risked the question. Maybe she'd seen too many movies, but that missing wedding ring had to mean something. The messy desk, the repeat clothing, the tired eyes. Maybe the wife was having an affair. Or. Maybe *he* was. Maybe there was another woman, and Alex's hotshot wife threw him out. None of her business, sure, but maybe that was why Hot Alex was trying to derail her Lassiter affair story idea.

Alex blinked, silent for a beat. He sat back in his chair, crossing one ankle on his knee. "Okay about what?"

"Forget it. Just—anyway. Moira." She filled him in on the morning's conversation, painting in brisk strokes how the candidate's wife had seemed sympathetic and left the door open for an interview. "She's always been 'the good wife,' you know? Every time I've seen them together, she's as doting as Nancy Reagan. Lassiter can do no wrong, say no wrong. That's why I'm still thinking there's more to this."

"More?"

One more try. "Yeah. You think something's going on with Moira, said that from the beginning. Now I think you might be right. But it's not about Moira. It's about Owen."

"How about the other woman?"

"The other—?" Was he changing his mind on her story? She smiled, eager. "That's what I meant. Exactly."

But Alex was shaking his head. He picked up a stack of papers, handed them to her. "No. I mean Eleanor Gable. Here's a background file for you. While you're waiting on Moira, put together a takeout on the glamorous Ms. Gable."

He held up his hands, bracketing his words like a scriptwriter pitching his next big-screen story. "'Can a gorgeous rich girl from the North Shore parlay her family's wealth and her crowd-pleasing style into a seat in the U.S. Senate? Eleanor Mead Gable like you've never seen her.' Something like that. You can handle both, right?" Alex nodded at her encouragingly, as if trying to get her to nod along with him.

She didn't. When did Alex-the-journalist turn into a tabloid headline-hunter? Maybe that's what happened when a reporter went management. Now he was obviously trying to sell papers. All that cheesy POLICE DENY BRIDGE KILLER stuff. Maybe he wasn't as attractive as she'd thought.

"Well, I figured this would be a good time to do some research on Moira." She tried for a positive spin. "Background. Check out her roots, her background, what she did before signing on as a politician's wife. Get inside. You know?"

"Get Gable," Alex said. He stood up, looked at his watch. "We done?"

8

It was disconcerting to feel so anonymous. Here she was, in the midst of hundreds of Lassiter supporters, all from Boston probably, and not one of them recognized her. With her hair chopped, without the Channel 11 TV camera beside her, and wearing her cropped Levi's jacket, black turtleneck sweater dress, and flat black boots, Jane could be a professor stealing a break from her classes at Emerson College. Or a Back Bay art collector, shopping the Newbury Street galleries.

The light turned green. Jane and the Lassiter crowd crossed Beacon Street, trooping up the steep ramp to the pink stucco pedestrian bridge over Storrow Drive. College-age kids, mostly girls, some wearing green LASSITER FOR SENATE baseball caps, iPod buds in their ears. Young mothers pushing complicated strollers, one carrying a crayoned sign reading LASSITER 4 YOUR KIDS. Beacon Hill matrons with heirloom hats and predictable shoes. Everyone with LASSITER FOR SENATE buttons, some more than one. So far, no gorgeous woman in a red coat.

Jane checked her watch. The rally was scheduled to start in half an hour. She'd called Gable HQ, as Alex instructed. They hadn't called back. Plenty of time to scout.

The crowd began its descent from the arched bridge

onto Boston's Esplanade, a verdant stretch of still-green grass and fading willow trees on the banks of the Charles River. To the right rose the Longfellow Bridge with its salt-and-pepper shaker-shaped turrets. To the left, the Boston University Bridge. Across the whitecapped water, past the sailing J-boats and mallards, the pillared halls of MIT.

Jane felt a hard jab at the small of her back.

"Don't move. Or it'll be the last thing you do. And do not scream."

She felt the man's soft breath in her ear. Then his hands clutched her, hard, holding both her shoulders. His body pressed insistently against her. The crowd around her blurred into a mass of color. All she could see was the Longfellow Bridge on one side, the BU Bridge on the other. The Charles in front of her. *A river, by a bridge.*

No one was noticing them.

Is this how he began?

In the middle of a campaign rally?

She clutched her pen and whirled, trying to escape his grasp, ready to poke and kick and—and why not scream? She saw his face.

He was laughing.

"You incredible idiot." Jane stamped a foot, then softly kicked Detective Jake Brogan in one blue-jeaned shin. "I thought you were the stupid Bridge Killer. I could have stabbed you, or screamed, or, or—"

"Yeah, but I'm a cop. Who you gonna scream for? I'm already here." Jake smiled, the same caught-in-the-hall-without-a-pass smile that successfully extricated him from annoyed females and detention halls ever since he'd been the preteen heartthrob of Boston's tony Back Bay. Jane was first exposed to his wattage at a Boston Police Department news conference, where she'd pushed him for details of a murdered city councilor's financial skullduggery. He'd avoided the question. And after the news conference, he asked her out to dinner. She declined. He continued to ask. She continued to say no. Until, one night, when she didn't.

"And now I might have to arrest you for assaulting a police officer." Jake tucked her arm through his, just for a moment, holding her close. "Taking you into custody might not be a bad thing, come to think of it."

Jane whapped him with her notebook and untangled herself from his grasp as they walked toward the rally. She pulled her jacket back into place. "Like I said, you're an idiot. First, there's a million people here. You know we agreed about this. We're friends, only friends. Second, I'm working. Third, well, there is no third. We discussed this. I'm a reporter, and you're a—"

"We discussed it on my couch," Jake interrupted again. A squawk from the loudspeakers brought a groan from the crowd; then the Sousa blared again. "After a few glasses of pinot and my famous burgers. Before you decided to keep your clothes on, if I remember correctly."

As if she could forget. He was verging on irresistible— tawny hair, green eyes, leather jacket, his own gorgeous cop cliché. Harvard education. Prominent family. Devoted to his work. He'd even rescued a golden retriever, Diva, whose tawny fur and cajoling eyes made them copies of each other.

Jake and Jane. She'd thought about it more than she liked to admit.

But Mr. Perfect's job was the deal-breaker. Dating a potential source? She couldn't believe she'd let herself come so close to such a career-complicating decision. One minute more on his couch, *one second more,* and she'd never have been able to change her mind.

If they were . . . together? Both their careers would be over. She'd never be able to cover the crime beat. No one would believe he wasn't feeding her confidential stuff. He'd know things he couldn't tell, and so would she. They'd never quite trust each other.

So they'd agreed—reluctantly, longingly, as one magical summer night became the reality of the next morning—that they'd have to remain just pals. And, because appearances mattered, to the rest of the world they'd be acquaintances. Professional. Separate.

Even though she could still feel his touch, there'd be no Jake and Jane.

"Thanks again for calling me with the lead on the *Register* job," she finally said. She turned to him, drawing a finger, gently, briefly, down the front of his jacket. The battered cordovan leather was sleek and soft. "Thanks for calling *them*. You saved my sanity. I was pretty sad there, for a while. And hey. Thanks for sending all the pizza. And for staying away while I was trying to figure things out."

"You took a huge hit, Janey. Pizza. Least I could do." He gave her that twinkle. "And even with your clothes on, we're still friends."

Jane rolled her eyes, hit him with her notebook again. "Enough with the clothes."

"But listen, seriously," Jake went on, ignoring her. "Sellica ever call you? Admit she was your source? I can't believe she walked, and you're the one who got nailed. Any more ugly letters from—whoever it was? I know you think it was Arthur Vick. I also know *you* know you should hand them over to us."

"Good try, Sherlock. You know I can't talk about that." No letters had arrived recently, anyway. And TV reporters always got mail from cranks and wackos. If you didn't, you weren't doing your job.

Jane scanned the crowd. Realized she was looking for Sellica. *Stupid.* Sellica Darden would call her, get in touch, someday. *She has to.* "But, Jake. How'd you know I'd be here?"

"I didn't." Jake waved toward the Charles, waggling his fingers as if announcing the title of a bad horror movie or a tabloid headline. "Bridge Killer."

"You think there's a Bridge Killer?" Jane's voice changed, all business now. Jake was pretending to kid her, but this was new. News. The cops never said *Bridge Killer*. They'd dodged every question about *serial* and *pattern*. But if Jake was assigned here, even calling the guy the Bridge Killer, that meant the cops knew a whole lot more than they were telling.

Jake was walking again, toward the river. Jane trotted to keep up with him. "Jake, wait. You think he takes his victims during the day? You think he'd do it here, with all these people? All these cameras?"

She grabbed his sleeve, stopping him. "Do you guys have pictures of him? At political rallies or something? How do you know it's him? Are you getting photos from the Lassiter people? Is he connected with the campaign?"

"Hey. Since when are you covering this story, Miss Jane? I thought it was that Tucker kid. And listen, since it's your paper now, tell your editor for me—it's a cheap shot, all that crap about 'police deny serial killer.'" Jake looked down at her, his face now shadowed with annoyance. "The more they play up how the brass denies it, the more it looks like there's some cover-up. There's no cover-up. Why can't the truth just be the truth?"

"Jane Ryland? Are you Jane Ryland?"

Jane took a step back, startled at the interruption. She saw Jake do the same thing, in one quick move, keeping a respectable distance. *Acquaintances.*

"I'm sorry?" She looked at the newcomer, a handsome-enough guy, her age, with a briefcase. A jacket and tie. No overcoat. Lawyer, maybe.

"Aren't you Jane Ryland? I'm Trevor Kiernan from the—"

"See ya, Miss Ryland," Jake said. Professional. He stepped farther away from her, backing up, raising a hand in good-bye. "Off to keep Boston safe."

"Hang on, *Detective Brogan*. Please." Jane took a step toward him, needing him to stay. She turned to the stranger, trying to juggle the two men. She couldn't let Jake leave.

"Can you give me a moment, Mr., um, Keerman? Yes, I'm Jane Ryland, but I'm so sorry, I just need to finish a quick—"

"It's Kiernan." The man picked up his phone, reading the screen as he talked. "From the Lassiter campaign. Did you call our office about an interview with Mrs. Lassiter?"

What? "Oh, I'm so sorry," she said again, flustered now. Damn. She hadn't recognized him. Trevor Kiernan. The campaign mogul. Kennedy School wunderkind. Insider. He'd orchestrated Lassiter's vaunted neighborhood meet and greets. She looked where Jake had just been. Gone. *Dammit.* Why did everything good have to happen at the same time? "Of course, yes, sorry, I wasn't expecting—"

"Ladies and gentlemen, and Lassiter supporters, a big Boston welcome to the Lassiter for Senate . . ." A booming voice paraded through the loudspeakers, cutting Jane off midsentence. She moved closer to Kiernan, straining to be heard over the escalating clamor.

"—I wasn't expecting to see you here. Yes, I'd love to interview Mrs. Lassiter. Can we do that? Can you—?"

"In five minutes . . ." The loudspeaker voice now competing with the cheering crowd and the trumpeting music and the whicker of a helicopter hovering over the Esplanade. "In just five minutes, Lassiter One will be landing right behind us, and you'll all be able to . . ."

"Listen, Ms. Ryland." Kiernan leaned in, his voice insistent. He'd put his briefcase on the grass, straddling it. "You've been around long enough to know the drill. You want an interview? You gotta go through our press office."

"But I did." Didn't the left hand know what the right, et cetera? If they couldn't even communicate about a simple interview, this campaign must be in more disarray than she'd figured. "I mean, yeah, I did call Mrs. Lassiter. But I absolutely talked to Sheila first."

"Sorry? Can't hear you." Kiernan moved closer to her. "You what?"

The chopper was buzzing the crowd, dropping confetti in a multicolored snowfall across the green. Billows of red, white, and blue caught the wind and floated onto hats and hairdos, covering the picnickers with color and sending the crowd into a crescendo of cheers.

"Called. The press office. Sheila." Jane moved as close as she could and still be polite, their heads almost touching. They stood eye to eye, his intensely brown, the same chocolate as the faint pinstripes in his suit jacket. A snippet of red and white landed on his shoulder. Jane waved away confetti as she tried to talk, raising her voice over the escalating commotion. "Sheila said no. That Mrs. Lassiter was taking a break. What's that about, anyway? Where is she?"

"Taking a break?" Kiernan's eyebrows went up. Still straddling his briefcase, he pulled out a white card from a jacket pocket. "Here. Call me. After the rally. She's not 'taking a break.'"

"O-wen Las-si-ter!" The voice reverberating through the public address system might have been introducing a conquering hero, or world champion of something.

Jane and Kiernan turned, catching glimpses of the now-spotlighted stage through dozens of waving signs.

The candidate, both arms raised in victory, strode to his place behind the flag-bedecked podium. A massive VOTE LASSITER FOR SENATE banner unfurled behind him. He tipped up the microphone, as if he were taller than anyone predicted.

Then with a *how can I resist?* grin, Owen Lassiter went to the front of the stage, leaning over the edge to shake hands with the delirious supporters who'd pushed to the front row. Blue-uniformed police, arms linked, tried to keep the crowds back, but Lassiter waved them away.

"You going to win this?" Jane watched Kiernan watch his boss work the crowd.

Without taking his eyes off the candidate, Kiernan cocked his head toward the stage and took Jane's arm.

"Come with me." He moved them quickly through the crowd, bringing her with him, dodging through the crush of supporters. "Up close. Watch what'll happen in about five minutes. Then *you* tell *me* if we're gonna win."

Kenna could wait. For as long as it took.

"Mr. Maitland?" The rabbity woman behind the desk on the third floor of the Lassiter campaign office spoke into her headset. "She says she's a 'Mrs. Kenna Wilkes,' insists she has an appointment." The woman turned pages in a spiral notebook. "But there are no appointments on the daily."

Today Kenna was all soft curls and wispy tendrils. Under her trench coat, a demure pink sweater set and a not-so-demure black pencil skirt that stopped just north of her knees. She figured Maitland would appreciate her expensive boots. Any man loved high heels. Oh, yes. She could wait.

"He's not answering, Mrs. Wilkes. Mr. Maitland doesn't see anyone without a—"

The door behind the secretary's desk swung open.

Standing in the doorway, a pudgy, middle-aged guy in a rumpled off-the-rack suit held out a hand, gesturing Kenna toward him.

"She's fine, Deenie." The man crossed in front of the secretary, eyes only for Kenna. "Mrs. Wilkes. The governor said you'd be arriving today. Welcome. I'm Rory Maitland."

Kenna watched him look her up and down. "Delighted, Mr. Maitland."

"Deenie, this is Mrs. Wilkes, a—" Maitland paused, as if searching for the right words. He rubbed a hand across what was left of his hair. "—a special friend of Governor Lassiter. She's volunteered to help on the campaign. And the governor has asked us to make her feel at home. Mrs. Wilkes, this is Deenie." He pointed to the nameplate on her desk: DENISE BAYLISS.

"Oh, please call me Kenna," she said. Flicking a glance at Maitland, she targeted the receptionist with a dazzling smile. "I cannot wait to get started. I hope you'll help me?"

"Help you? Get started?" Deenie turned to Maitland, questioning. Back to Kenna. Then back to Maitland. "Get started with what?"

Kenna touched a newly French-manicured fingernail to her single strand of pearls. "Oh, I'm so sorry. I thought Governor Lassiter had promised I could—"

Maitland interrupted. "And the governor would be delighted if you could start today. How about trying the welcome desk, downstairs in the main lobby? Sit right up front. Meet everyone who comes in."

"I'm ready as I'll ever be," Kenna said. "The welcome desk sounds lovely."

"The welcome desk is not as easy as it looks, Mr. Maitland." Deenie was frowning.

"You know what, Denise? I'll just take her downstairs myself," Maitland said. Case closed. "I'd like to get Mrs. Wilkes in place before everyone gets back from the rally."

Maitland approached the door to the corridor. He turned to Kenna. "Ready? You'll be the first person everyone sees when they arrive at campaign headquarters. Hope you don't mind being the new girl."

The new girl? That was one way of putting it. "Actually," she said, "I'd love to run over to that rally first. See it all firsthand? Then come back later?"

She looked at Maitland expectantly. Deenie must be beyond confused.

"Wonderful." He beamed, as if Kenna had the most brilliant idea ever. "In fact, here's an idea. I'll walk over to the Esplanade with you."

Maitland gestured Kenna through the door, then turned back to the secretary.

"Mrs. Wilkes will be back after the rally." He stabbed a stubby finger toward the girl, now barricaded behind her desk. "Remember, Deenie, the governor says we're to give her anything she needs."

9

"Hey! You two. Ya don't see the ropes?" The cop, a tank in sunglasses, waved off Kiernan and Jane, shepherding them away from the Esplanade stage. "This is as far as the both of you go."

Clutching her tote bag under one arm, Jane was banged and buffeted by Lassiter supporters grabbing their chance for an up-close moment with their political choice. They'd pushed themselves against the metal-stanchioned rope line, where a row of officers in blue, arms linked, stood between them and the huge wooden platform. A lofty half dome, intricately paneled, formed a partial ceiling over the flat of the stage.

Mammoth video screens gave a larger-than-life view to the people stuck far in the back. Sousa marches at mega-decibels blasted over the sound system.

Lassiter himself, his head and shoulders leaning precariously over the left edge of the stage, reveled in the spotlight, waving, using one hand to shake the out-stretched palms of the increasingly demanding crowd.

Impossible to get any louder. "Crazy," Jane whispered. She was only half joking. The event was verging on out of control. "Maybe we should—"

"Campaign staff!" Trevor Kiernan stepped in front of

her, almost shouting to be heard, showing the scowling blue uniform a collection of plastic-laminated badges on the lanyard around his neck. "I'm good to go through. And she's press. She's with me."

He turned quickly, drew her forward. "Jane! Got a pass? Show the man."

"Lass-i-*ter*. Lass-i-*ter*." The crowd's chanting grew louder as a crush of bodies pressed toward the stage. A few toddlers rode high on their parents' shoulders. One pinafored girl, her little Lassiter baseball cap askew, dissolved in tears as her dad pushed to get closer.

Jane held up the new bright blue plastic badge she wore on an aluminum-linked chain. It showed her photo and the insignia of the Massachusetts State Police. "Channel— I mean, *Boston Register*. Okay?

"Yikes," she said, trotting after Kiernan. "Is it always like this?"

He hurried her past a bank of temporary wooden risers, television cameras on tripods lined one end to the other, set up to hold the reporters covering the event. She tried to pick out Channel 11's camera, see who they'd assigned, but couldn't. *Well, tough. Now I'm getting even closer than they can.*

She followed Kiernan up three concrete steps at the side of the stage. He punched in a passcode on an electronic lock, then led her through a door hidden in the black-painted wall. The backstage entrance led to a shadowy concrete-walled corridor. Up a few more narrow stairs, around a corner, and—the daylight blasted her, so bright and surprising, she stumbled backwards. Hidden behind the curved proscenium wall, they had the candidate's eye view of the crowd. And that view, Jane realized, must be intoxicating.

The colors. The signs. The cheering throng of voters.

Adoring. Pulsing closer. Demanding attention. Calling his name. Some held their cameras high above their heads, capturing whatever memories they could.

"Watch," Kiernan said. "I'll stay right here. Off the record, right?"

"Ah, sure," Jane replied. *What the hell?*

Above her head, lofty metal poles held banks of spotlights and draping loops of wires. Thick cables, wrapped in duct tape, snaked across the concrete floor. It was darker here, the explosive light outside turning backstage into background.

People stood in groups of twos and threes. Campaign workers, Jane figured, insider enough to have special passes. Most clutched files or clipboards, plastic water bottles. Some wore suits and heels, others jeans. All wore Lassiter buttons. All eyes fastened on the candidate.

Jane could see only Lassiter's back, moving slowly to the other side of the stage. The police linked themselves in a wavering blue line.

"Hey, Trev, goin' great, man. Almost time. Gotta love it." A harried-looking man with a clipboard gave Kiernan a thumbs-up, then disappeared behind the flashing red and green lights of the elaborate sound system.

Kiernan pointed to Lassiter. "Okay, Jane. Any second now."

"'Scuse me, 'scuse me, 'scuse me." She was late, she was late. The subway ride had taken too long and the walk from Park Street station had taken too long, and her darling new kitten heels kept catching in the Esplanade's thick grass. Would she be *too* late? How did this happen? She'd planned it so perfectly.

Holly elbowed her way closer to the Esplanade stage,

hardly noticing the bodies surging around her, her eyes on the prize.

Owen Lassiter. On the stage, hand outstretched, that smile. She promised to be here. And now she was. Everything would be okay. Happy endings.

"Sorry, sorry, sorry." She forced a smile of her own, relieved, needing to stay polite as she edged through, some guys looking her up and down, as always. She ignored them. As always.

The wooden reporter's thing was set up to the left of the stage this time. Perfect. She aimed herself in that direction, propelled toward the cameras. Still photographers were posted there, too, she knew. Good. She had her own camera, out and ready to go. Too risky to leave it in its pouch.

Almost there. Almost time.

"Lucky you could get away." Kenna slid her hand through the crook of Maitland's elbow as a black-suited security guard waved them toward the back entrance to the big stage. "I'd never have gotten up here this close without you."

"No problem." Maitland guided her past a phalanx of rent-a-guards, then up close to one side of the stage.

"We going up there?" Kenna asked. The sun was hot, almost too hot to keep her coat on. Should have left it with Deenie. "Could we go backstage? Maybe I could chat with Owe—the governor—when he's finished."

Maitland looked at his watch, then seemed to listen. He smiled. "It's already 'Yankee Doodle Dandy,'" he said.

"Huh? Yankee—? Come on. You can get me closer."

"We're too late to go backstage." He draped his arm

across her shoulders, guiding her. "But come this way. You'll see."

"What?" Jane asked. Trevor stood next to her, elbow to elbow, backstage. "Watch what?"

"Now," Kiernan repeated.

She heard a roar from the crowd. Suddenly Lassiter was gone.

She couldn't take it in fast enough, had to stand on tiptoe, craning her neck to see. The music so loud, so thundering that Jane could feel the stage beneath her vibrating, had changed to a bass-pounding "Simply the Best." Cameras flashed. The crowd cheered, erupting in delight. More blizzards of confetti, this time spewing into the air from containers circling the green. TV photographers yanked their cameras from their tripods. Reporters dashed forward, jumping down from the wooden risers of the press pen, pushing toward the action.

Lassiter had leaped off the stage onto the grass. No longer above the people, he was now part of them. One of them. On their level. Blue uniforms surged to surround the candidate, linked arms in a protective circle, Lassiter in the center, moving away from the stage, deeper into the crowd. Every arm reached for him; every camera aimed at him. Every person wanted him.

She and Kiernan stepped to the edge of the stage, watching the spectacle. She stole a quick look at him. "You kidding me?" she said. "Isn't that dangerous?"

He smiled, one eyebrow raised. "Couldn't resist, I guess. Such a man of the people. Gotta give 'em what they want, right?"

Jane could catch only glimpses of Lassiter's face, smiling, radiant, accepting their devotion, embracing the rush. The crowd was in love. The candidate must know it. And he'd just proved he loved them back.

"Now. You tell me," Kiernan said. "We gonna win this?"

Jane dug into her tote bag, eyes still on the crowd, scrounging by feel for her camera. *Found it.* She brought it out, and in one motion aimed and clicked.

"Hey, you can't use that." Kiernan put a hand on her forearm. "No unauthorized photos. You're here off the record. Remember?"

"Had to try," Jane said. She dropped the camera back into her bag. With a dramatic flourish, she zipped it closed. "See? All gone."

She probably hadn't gotten anything usable anyway. And someone else must be covering for the *Register*. Lassiter's ring of blue moved across the green. The people around him surged closer, some ducking under the police to snag a photo with the candidate. A sea of red, white, and blue. And Lassiter green.

And then, red. A red coat.

Jane didn't need to check Archive Gus's photo to make sure. That was her. Heading steadily toward Lassiter. By herself? *If I try to get down there, through all those people, I'll lose her. I'd never make it.*

"Hey, Trevor—" Jane couldn't take her eyes off the crowd, but maybe she didn't need to get any closer. Damn it, why had she zipped her camera away? She yanked open her bag. *There's no more off the record.*

Where was Kiernan? She risked a look behind her. In a backstage corner, deep in conversation with a clipboard guy. She called his name, waving. "Trevor! Can you come here? For one second?"

Jane looked back at the crowd. The red coat was moving toward the candidate.

Back at Trevor. Walking, seemed like slow motion, toward her.

Back at the crowd. Jane squinted through the sun's glare, as if the very desire to see would make her vision stronger. And there was the coat. *Yes.* And then—the girl was—taking it off? Now she was just a woman in a white—

"Jane? What's up?" Trevor appeared at her side.

"See that woman? In a . . . a white blouse? At about ten o'clock from Lassiter? Curly hair? Youngish? Tallish?" She pointed at the spot—*I can't lose her*—looking at Trevor for only a brief second, then back at the crowd.

Trevor was laughing. "You're kidding me, right? There are thousands of women." He touched her shoulder, getting her attention. No longer smiling. "Is there a problem? Jane? Do we need to—?"

"No, it's fine, just look, really." Jane jabbed the air with a finger. "Now she's right next to him. Holding up a camera? See?"

Trevor leaned forward, following the direction of her finger. "Yeah, I see her. So?"

"Ever seen her before? Do you know who she is?"

"Why?"

"Just—do you? Know her?"

Trevor shaded his eyes with both hands. Shrugged. "Ah, not as far as—"

"I'll call you about the Mrs. Lassiter thing," Jane said. Maybe it wasn't too late. She waved over her shoulder. "Thanks so much, Trevor. Talk soon. Gotta go."

Jane raced down the three steps, slinging herself around the corner by holding on to the railing, slammed open the stage door, and headed into the daylight and onto the Esplanade grass. Then skidded to a stop. Suddenly she wasn't four feet higher than the crowd. Suddenly the swirl of people who'd been individuals from her lofty stage-high vantage point became an impassable mass of shoulders and faces and hats and signs and blue uniforms and impenetrable motion.

She stood on tiptoe in desperation. Ridiculous. She couldn't even see tops of heads. She tried again. *Nothing.* She looked longingly at the stage behind her—and the locked door with the unknown passcode. Her shoulders sagged.

Come on, she said to herself. *You can find her.*

In a flash, she hopped onto the wooden riser of the press platform, now empty of everything but left-behind tripods and canvas equipment bags. She shaded her eyes, scanning for the pack of TV cameras certain to be following Lassiter. They were already way down the green, past the gingerbread-decorated ice cream stand, almost to the river.

Leaping off the riser, Jane dodged through the edges of the crowd, turning and sidestepping like a wide receiver headed for the goal line. "Come on, Red Coat," she muttered. "Be there. Be there. *Be there.*"

10

Gotta love it. Less than a mile from Charlestown, but everything is different. Here on Beacon Hill, cobblestones and gas lamps, home of money and privilege and history, people actually answered their doors. Opened them. Offered Jake coffee. Like this one, the eleventh this morning, they wanted to chat. Wanted to help the police find the Bridge Killer.

Damn. There was no Bridge Killer.

"We don't think the killings are connected, Mrs. Connaughton," Jake said, putting his glass of ice water carefully on the dark leather coaster she'd scooted in front of him. Ten A.M. Friday, he'd already had enough coffee. Growing up just a few blocks away, he'd seen a million of these Beacon Hill brownstones: seasonally decorated living rooms, too-long curtains pooled on hardwood floors, fresh flowers.

"No matter what the *Register* says this morning, ma'am"—he smiled conspiratorially—"there's no 'Bridge Killer.' I'd stake my job on it. They're trying to scare you into buying papers."

"Well, they're succeeding." The woman, navy trousers, white shirt, heavy necklace, reading glasses on a gold chain, took a sip of whatever filled her teacup. She tapped the newspaper folded on a mahogany side table. "You must admit, it appears to be more than a coincidence, two poor girls killed, both by bridges, both left in the water. Honestly, when was the last time—?" She tilted her head, eyeing Jake. "You really don't know who they are? Is it true, they weren't wearing shoes?"

Jake shifted on the leather couch, unbuttoning his tweed sport coat, pulling another sketch from his inside pocket.

"Ma'am? That's why we're asking for your help." He placed one of the colored-pencil sketches, the head shot, facing her on the coffee table. Brown hair, shorter than the Charlestown girl. He called this one the Longfellow girl, since her body was found near the Longfellow Bridge. She was listed on the squad's case board as "Victim One." Didn't seem right, though, to make her just a number.

"Do you recognize her? Brown hair. Dr. Archambault, the medical examiner, says it was professionally colored. 'Walnut brown number 16,' apparently, if that means anything to you?"

The woman stared at the drawing. "Have you checked beauty salons?"

Everybody's an expert. "We're in the process, ma'am. But meanwhile. Anyone you know have a daughter, supposed to be at college? Maybe she was expected home, never made it?"

The woman was shaking her head. Using one tentative finger, she pulled the drawing toward her, then picked it up, adjusting her reading glasses. "I'm so sorry." Almost as if she were talking to the drawing. "It's very sad, isn't it?"

She handed the sketch back to him. Interview over. Jake turned toward the front door, and she followed his lead.

The woman touched his sleeve as he stepped across her threshold. "Do you think the Bridge Killer will do it again?" she asked. "Are we in danger? Should we all stay home?"

"Jane Ryland! How fantastic to see you. Do come in! So glad you could make it this early in the day! You're calling me Ellie, okay? And you're Jane."

Eleanor Gable, dripping exclamation marks, greeted her as if they were long-lost sorority sisters. And what was that accent all about? Locust Valley meets London. Far from the Massachusetts North Shore.

"Thank you, Ellie." Jane edged through the door into the spacious, window-lined office in Boston's West End. Gable's elaborate, expensively framed campaign posters displayed on cream-colored walls looked like Norman Rockwells. Dinner tables. Kids with cops. Ice cream parlors. American flags. Then, still in Rockwell style: Wind farms. Recycling centers. Skateboards and bicycles.

"Nice to see you, too," Jane added. "I—"

"Sit, sit." Ellie, interrupting, waved her to a puffily upholstered sofa, caramel colored and elegantly feminine, angled in front of an antique-looking desk. Ellie took the dark wooden desk chair, its cushion covered in crimson silk. "Coffee? Can you believe how well this election is going? We're so excited about what a difference we can make."

To the left Jane saw an American flag, ceiling high, set in a brass post. Next to it, the ocean blue and white flag of Massachusetts. On a narrow wooden table, an array of photos. Gable with at least two presidents. A general. Gable arm in arm with a T-shirted little boy. A beach scene, a rainbow of umbrellas on a stretch of white sand. Nantucket?

"Big, big changes," Gable continued. The soft collar of her tangerine bouclé jacket—Chanel, no question—barely touched the ends of her ash blond pageboy. "That's what the voters are looking for. Don't you think?"

Jane flipped open her notebook. She hoped Alex was happy. *She* sure wasn't. Eleanor Gable's office was the last place she wanted to be. After yesterday's sighting, her mind was still on red-coat woman. At least she'd seen her. But the woman had disappeared. Vanished. Jane had lost her.

So, now, she *should* be scoping out Lassiter headquarters, showing Archive Gus's photo, asking if anyone recognized Red Coat.

Jane sneaked a look at her watch. She had to get out of here.

"Interesting, Ellie. No coffee, thank you. My editor at the *Register* hopes you can give me an in-depth interview. Later." Jane looked around the room. "Maybe at your home on Beacon Hill? Would that be possible?"

Holly held up the padded brown manila envelope, making sure the address label was aligned exactly between the top and the bottom. Neatness counts. Perfect. She laid it on her dark green blotter, giving it an appreciative pat.

She slid the rest of the padded envelopes into the upper right-hand drawer of her desk, carefully keeping the shrink wrap intact as much as she could. Maybe she should put some clear tape on it? *No time.*

The left-hand drawer was full of hanging green file folders, each one tabbed, labeled, and dated. She slid them forward, one by one, not giving in to the temptation to look at each and every photo again. When she reached the date she needed, she withdrew an eight by ten, put it into the padded envelope. Her thin white cotton gloves made picking up the glossy paper a little difficult, but she'd never thought it would be easy. It wouldn't be worth it if it were easy. And it was going to be so worth it.

She paused, one hand on a green file folder, daring, allowing herself to imagine what it would be like. Knowing what it would be like.

Oh, he would say. *You did this for me? You've loved me all along, and I never knew it? And now you were ready to sacrifice. . . .* She closed her eyes to keep the vision from escaping.

He'd reach out and touch her face, using one finger to trace her cheekbone, move her curls aside, looking at her with those eyes. *Ah, my beautiful Hollister,* he'd say—he always called her that, Hollister—*how could I have let you leave? And how did you know what I needed to be truly happy? My deepest desire?* And now, she could actually hear his voice. *You're here, you've solved my problem, you're my deepest—*

The apple timer dinged.

Holly blushed, feeling the warmth as she touched her own fingers to her face. Oh, no. *No.* Now she'd daydreamed her time away. She'd have to make up for it, somehow.

She selected the final photos, quickly, perfectly, with the one on top the newest.

From yesterday. That nice man had offered to use her camera to take the photo she'd been struggling to get on her own. So it really looked just right; they looked so happy *together.* It must have been obvious—she could see the flashes from other cameras, and even those bright television lights, as she smiled her perfect smile.

She felt her mouth practicing it, even now. Oh, yes. It

was just right. He could not fail to love her. And very, very soon.

Now she had to make two final decisions. Which mailbox. And when.

11

"**It's green, idiot.**" Jane glared at the driver of the Jeep, who'd ridiculously honked at her as she trotted across the striped pedestrian walkway at the corner of Merrimack and Causeway.

"No, not you, Alex. Some driver. Never mind. Anyway, we need to talk. I saw the red-coat girl yesterday." She confirmed she had the walk light, still talking into her cell phone.

"I'm on the way to the paper now. Almost to the T station. Yes, I went to see Gable. She said yes."

Jane put her head down, listening with half an ear to Alex's instructions. Causeway Street was a wind tunnel, the chill blasting across the river. The white cables of the new bridge, spiking up like the rigging of some huge sailing ship, glared in the noontime sun. *Poor Jake,* she thought. *He sees that bridge, he thinks about murder, not colonial schooners.* The subway station was a block or two away, just past the—

"Hey, Alex? Listen, I'm right by Lassiter headquarters. I connected with a great possible source yesterday, a guy in the campaign, who says he can maybe hook me up with Moira. Okay if I stop by there first? See if he's there? Great. See ya."

She pushed through the revolving front doors of Lassiter headquarters into the spotlit lobby of a political photo gallery. Lassiter with a president. Arm in arm with at least three senators. Lassiter, hand on a bible, sworn in as Governor of Massachusetts. Moira beside him, elegant even with her Hillary headband and '90s shoulder pads. A FedEx guy in shorts and a backward baseball cap wheeled an overloaded cart of packages behind her, retrieving a few that slipped over the edges, and hurried through as the elevator doors were closing.

Place is a zoo. Blaring Sousa music. Messages squawking intermittently over a PA system. Two metal tables covered in patriotic bunting, heaped with multicolored campaign brochures. TIME TO TRUST, one said. ENERGY FOR ENERGY. Jane stashed a few into her tote bag. She'd post them on her "half" of the bulletin board, if Tuck's morbid photos didn't take up all the room.

Now to find Trevor. But the reception desk was empty. A green notebook, obviously a sign-in sheet, lay open in plain view. A can of Diet Coke, lipstick-ringed straw inserted, sat abandoned next to an elaborate telephone console. Lights flashed as phones rang, unanswered. Someone sure wasn't doing their job. No wonder the campaign was in disarray.

Jane reached into her tote bag for her phone to call Trevor. But it was already buzzing with a text.

"Call me, roomie," it said. *Roomie? Tuck? What does he want, another shelf?* Ah, sure she would call. Later. She found the white business card Trevor had given her and dialed him instead.

"There's no Bridge Killer, Supe. I'm telling you, there isn't." Jake placed a manila file folder of his printed-out canvass notes onto his boss's desk, then plopped into the ratty padded seat of the chair beside it. Boston Police HQ was new on the outside, limestone and double-tall glass, but they'd moved in all the old furniture from downtown. Even the superintendent's office, prime territory, looked furnished from law enforcement yard sales.

"There's however many bridges in Boston, and the Charles River runs from Beacon Hill out to Newton," Jake continued. "The harbor. Fort Point Channel. Water and bridges, hard to have a murder here that's not near one or the other. Or both. But they're not connected. You know? Sir?"

Superintendent Francis Rivera had opened the file, looked at it briefly, tossed it back at Jake. "So what I'm hearing is, you're nowhere," Rivera said. "And your partner DeLuca is nowhere. Correct, Detective?"

Jake started to answer.

"I'm not interested in files of nothing, Brogan. You're a murder cop, right? You're supposed to be about answers. That's why I called you in here. Answers."

"Yes, sir." Jake knew Rivera's bad-cop mode was SOP. The supe was a good guy, up from the ranks, born in Roxbury, football, debate team, West Point, Desert Storm, Boston's second black superintendent. Knew his stuff. "Let me run this by you. Remember the ME findings. Doctor A says the Longfellow victim was well taken care of. Good teeth. No tats. No piercings. Professionally colored hair. Manicure. No bruises, nothing. No defensive wounds. *Nothing*. I'd put her—college kid. Maybe older. Sir."

"So? And that means?" The supe laced his fingers behind his head, waiting.

"The Charlestown, not so much," Jake said. "Bruises. Big-time. That ankle tattoo. Another on her thigh. She's older. Like, thirty-something. Missing some back teeth. And Dr. A says—" He paused, scanning through his BlackBerry notes.

"You're killing me with that thing," Rivera said. He pretend-scratched his sleek-shaved head, dramatically dubious. "You got something against paper?"

"Easier for me, Supe," Jake said. "Anyway—"

"You think hookers?"

"I suppose. Seems kind of—" Jake made a skeptical face, shrugging. "—made-for-TV movie, you know? But like I was saying—" He clicked his BlackBerry, scrolling through his notes. "—ninety-three homicides last year in Boston. Eighty-one so far this year. It's a big city. People get killed. Sometimes two in a row. It makes sense there'd be two in a week and a half. Mathematically, there'd have to be."

"All closed," Rivera said, raising one finger. He tilted back in the worn leather of his big chair, stared at the ceiling. "By murder cops who did their jobs. Bad guys put away."

"Yes, sir."

"Except for these two. IDs unknown. And you're saying there's no connection."

"Yes, sir. No, sir."

"Tattoo parlors? Beauty salons? Colleges?" Rivera was looking at Jake again. "Anybody missing a student? A client?"

"Nothing yet. We're on it, though. DeLuca's out there now."

The superintendent reached into his wastebasket, picked out a folded copy of the *Register,* the same issue Jake had seen this morning on so many Beacon Hill coffee tables. With a quick sidearm throw, Rivera tossed it across his desk.

Jake, startled, caught it with both hands.

"What the hell is this, Brogan? Who's talking? Look at that headline. 'Police Deny Bridge Killer'? The more we deny something, the truer it seems."

"Hold on, Supe." Jake put the newspaper back on his boss's desk. Was this why he'd been called in? "That's not me. That's *your* guy, Laney Driscoll, in the press office. I told you, that Tuck kid was lurking at the Charlestown location. Trying to take photos. A bottom feeder. But none of what's in the paper is coming from me."

"What if it turns out there *is* a Bridge Killer?" Rivera, on his feet now, all six-five, was talking right over him. "Then what do you think 'my' Officer Driscoll is supposed to say?"

"But—"

"But, hell. You have no idea. We have two dead girls. No identifications. No suspects. The damn newspaper is scaring the shit out of people, saying we're covering up a serial killer. What's more, we got nothing proving there isn't one. And you, Detective Brogan, are giving me that nothing. Am I wrong?"

A quick knock, then the office door opened. Behind it, a lanky brunette Jake didn't recognize, wearing the orange webbed shoulder strap of a police cadet. "Superintendent Rivera? Sir? Cadet—"

"What is it, Kurtz? Detective Jake Brogan, this is Cadet Jan Kurtz. From intake."

"Sir," Kurtz said again. "They told me Detective Brogan was here. There's another body, sir."

Jake looked at his boss. Rivera was back in his chair, rubbing both hands across his wide forehead. Jake had a dozen questions he needed to ask. He was almost afraid to.

Instead, Rivera fired, "Bridge? Water? Woman?" His voice sounded dark with certainty.

"North Street, yes, sir."

Jake stood, his mind racing. The newspaper headlines taunted him.

"ID?" Jake had to ask, though he knew the answer. He knew, like the others, there would be no identification. And when Cadet Kurtz said no, as she certainly would, he'd be facing an impossible possibility. That maybe there *was* a serial killer seeking out single women, or students, or hookers, or whoever they damn were, stealing their purses and wallets and anything that had their names, and murdering them. And Jake would be screwed.

"Yes," Kurtz said. "We have ID."

12

Lucky she checked her voice mail. While she'd been leaving a message for Trevor, Alex left a message for *her*. Now she sat in a row of empty chairs outside the closed door of the *Register*'s fifth-floor conference room. *What on earth can this be?* She'd told Alex about the girl in the red coat. Was it something about that? Her interview with Gable? Maybe Alex had gotten caught in his affair. Maybe because he'd hired her, she was going to be fired. But that didn't make sense.

The door opened. "Jane? Can you come in?" Alex had his hand on the doorknob, his eyes on hers. He looked—worried?

She widened her eyes, silently inquiring. *What?* She thought he held up a finger, as if to say, *Everything is fine.* But she couldn't be sure.

He gestured her inside. At the head of an oval table she recognized Taylor Burleigh Reidy, the paper's executive editor, in pinstripes and black-framed reading glasses. Another suit she didn't recognize was flipping the pages of a green leather-covered volume. Next to Reidy sat a—fashion model? Even with her dark hair yanked into a stubby ponytail, no makeup, wearing a denim jacket and black leather skirt, she was cover girl material.

Twenty-something, hip, gorgeous. A stick. Next to the girl, an empty chair.

Everyone in the room was looking at Jane.

"I'm Tay Reidy, Jane. Please. Take a seat." He stood, indicating the empty chair. His trademark silver hair slicked back from his aristocratic forehead, his suit impeccable. A braided rope bracelet circled one wrist. He smiled, waving a hand over the group. "We're so pleased to have you on board. Right, Alex?"

Alex nodded.

"But we must ask you a favor," Reidy continued. He pointed to the man beside him, giving him the floor. "And Ethan Geller here, our legal eagle, says it's legally— how'd you put it, Ethan? Appropriate. Beyond reproach."

Jane pulled out her chair as Reidy talked and sat down, frowning. *Beyond reproach? Appropriate? What is?* Every one of her nerve endings turned to high. *Everything is fine* was so not true. Under the table, her foot tapped.

"Whatever you decide, Jane," Ethan said. "But you're not in violation of any law. Either way."

"It's an incredible opportunity for us," Alex said. "And of course, since you're on our team now, we want to get our show on the road before anyone else calls you."

"She doesn't know, Alex. Look at her. She doesn't know what we're talking about." The brunette swiveled her chair to face Jane, then leaned forward, hands on her bare knees. "There's another Bridge Killer victim. That's why I texted you, roomie."

Jane's heart dropped. Then raced. *Roomie? This girl? Is Tuck?* Her bewilderment could not be more complete. *Another bridge victim?* No, she didn't know. How would she know? And why would they think she'd care?

"Alex?" Jane said. "Did Lassiter's campaign—?"

"Tuck, why don't you tell her," Alex interrupted. "Tuck's the one who's breaking the story."

"It's Sellica Darden, Jane." Tuck's voice was even, almost compassionate. "Her body was found by the Moakley Bridge. The Bridge Killer's new victim is Sellica Darden."

13

"**She was your** source, correct?" Tay Reidy leaned his pin-striped elbows on the conference table, fingers laced, eyes riveted on Jane. "Sellica Darden was who you were protecting. The one who could prove the john was Arthur Vick. This changes everything, of course. You see what a major story this is."

"You can tell the whole truth," the lawyer said. "You wouldn't reveal your source in court, understandable, but now you're free to do so."

"You're the only one who can write it, Jane." Alex was out of his chair. "You know the facts, you know the background, you know the inside story. Like Mr. Reidy says, you're on solid legal ground. Sellica's dead now. You're fine. You're free. Right, Ethan?"

Fine? Free? Sellica's dead? The Bridge Killer? The room was buzzing around her, all these people talking at once, almost as if she weren't here. How was she supposed to process this? Sellica was dead. And Jane's life was irrevocably ruined.

"Oh, most assuredly." The lawyer opened his book to a place marked by a yellow sticky and traced a finger down the page. "Your agreement to keep her name confidential has no power of law, so as a contract issue, it's not even . . ."

Jane knew the lawyer was still talking, something about protections and dissolution and shield laws and termination of confidentiality, but her mind, struggling for equilibrium, was full of Sellica Darden. Sellica very much alive, in room 2306 of the Madisonian Hotel.

Odd place to meet, a sleek high-rise in the bustle of downtown Boston. Jane had protested at first, suggesting they find an out-of-the-way coffee shop, or take a walk in a suburban park. She could almost hear Sellica's insistent voice, its hint of amusement.

"I have friends at the Mad," she'd told Jane on the phone. "And I'm all about discreet, right?"

The next morning, a key card had been left at Channel 11's front desk in an envelope marked JANE and PERSONAL in purple Magic Marker. An hour later, Jane, in sunglasses and a baseball cap, had used the key card to click open room 2306. Sellica, voluptuous even in silhouette, had been standing in the window, looking out at the Boston skyline.

Have I ever met a hooker before? The question had crossed Jane's mind, surprising her. *Hooker* was probably inappropriate. What did Sellica call herself? Jane realized she hadn't known what the woman looked like. The photos in the paper had been either mug shots or blurred, and in the snippets of TV video, Sellica was always more sunglasses than face.

The woman in the window had turned, offered a hand. Her narrow charcoal skirt, white shirt, sleek suede pumps, and horn-rimmed glasses looked almost prim, from the dress-for-success handbook. Her chestnut-frosted hair was pulled back, severe. Her lips pale pink. Chunky gold earrings and matching necklace. Jane looked around the room briefly, wondering if Sellica had sent her lawyer instead of showing up in person.

"No, it's me," the woman said. She lifted one perfectly plucked eyebrow. "Not what you expected 'the other woman' to look like?"

Jane had fumbled a greeting, trying to cover her embarrassment. Jumping to conclusions was hardly the way to build confidence. But that day had ended with promises.

Promises Jane knew she had to keep. Even now.

Even now that Sellica is dead. The *Register*'s conference room seemed to go cold. Jane crossed her arms in front of her, hugging herself against the chill. Sellica was dead. And now, so were Jane's chances for redemption. She could never prove her story. She would always be Wrong-Guy Ryland. *Arthur Vick wins again.*

Arthur Vick. Could he have killed—? Jane played out the possibilities, fast forward.

"Jane? You with us here?" Tuck touched her lightly on the shoulder.

Jane blinked, back in the present. *Ridiculous. Arthur Vick didn't kill Sellica. The Bridge Killer did.*

"Think it's doable?" Tuck was saying.

Doable? Jane scanned their faces. Tuck, eyes shining. Tay Reidy. That lawyer. Alex, dressed up for some reason in a dark blazer and striped tie. Everyone seemed to be waiting for her to answer something.

"If you two get started now, we could have it for tomorrow's edition. Here's the plan." Alex gestured with his chunky ballpoint at a list he'd scrawled on his yellow pad. "Jane writes the Sellica backgrounder, Tuck writes the Sellica murder story. Photos, bios, excerpts from the trial transcripts. Recap the other Bridge Killer victims in a sidebar. And we'll have to get reax from the cops."

He abruptly stopped his high-speed instructions.

"Gotta wonder if the other victims were hookers. You know?"

"You got it, boss," Tuck said. "Cake."

"Are you with us, Jane? I'll take you off the Lassiter thing, of course. Just for a day. Moira hasn't called, right? Or Gable?" Alex clicked his pen, eager for her answer. "You've got police sources, too. Right? You know Jake Brogan. That works."

"I—" Jane's voice wasn't working very well. Her brain was full, churning. Was Sellica a random victim of the Bridge Killer? Or had someone sought her out? And if so, who? And why? *Would Arthur Vick kill Sellica?* "I think—"

Every eye in the room focused on her.

"Perhaps Jane would prefer to write the story herself?" Tay Reidy interrupted the silence. "Jane, is that why you're hesitating? It is, after all, your vindication. Proof you were telling the truth, all along."

"Ethan, that reminds me." Tuck turned her back to Jane. "What happens to that million-dollar judgment against Channel Eleven when it comes out that Jane *was* telling the truth?"

The lawyer nodded, picked up his yellow pad. "Yes, indeed. The appeal process. Could be probative. I did some preliminary research on that, and it appears—"

Jane stood, slowly, balancing herself, palms down on the table. The lawyer stopped, midsentence, pad in the air. Tuck pivoted to face her.

"No one knows who my source is. No one. Not even at Channel Eleven." Jane took a deep breath. She had to sort out her secrets. Her responsibilities. And her future. "I never said it was Sellica Darden."

"Well, no, but . . ." Alex was frowning. So was everyone else. "I mean, if not Sellica, then who? It's pretty obvious. And listen, Jane, promises end with death."

"They don't." Jane collected her notebook and her tote bag, then looked at the door. This decision was going to cost her another job. Perhaps her career. Her father would not believe this. "I promised I would never reveal the name of my source. The fact that Sellica Darden died—was murdered—doesn't change that. Never means never. If it doesn't, no one will ever tell me anything again."

She paused. Good-bye, *Register*. Hello, unemployment.

"You'd do the same thing," she said, trying to keep her voice on track. "You would."

The air went out of the room. Tay Reidy, eyes narrowed, rolled his pen between two palms, the metal clinking against his wedding ring. The lawyer closed his laptop and seemed to be studying the grain of the conference table. Tuck swiveled her chair back and forth, her eyes on Alex.

No one looked at Jane. And then, in an instant, everyone did. And everyone began talking. Alex's voice was the loudest.

"Are you kidding me?" Alex tossed his notepad onto the polished table. It slid across the glossed surface, stopping, pages splayed, against the law book. "So you'd rather keep this secret? A secret about a dead hooker? Even if—"

"Hey, that's not fair, Alex." Jane tried to keep the edge out of her voice. Failed. "I don't have a choice. You know that."

Alex dragged his fingers through his hair, then shrugged. "Okay. I'm sorry. I know, it's—difficult. But, listen, you see our position."

"Not to mention, of course, it could be critical evidence in a murder case." Reidy's voice, arch, cut into Alex's apology.

"Interesting call, Jane," the lawyer said. "Unnecessary, I must say."

Tuck raised a hand, as if asking for permission to talk. "Listen, though. Storywise? Whether Sellica's the source or not, I mean, does it really matter?"

Alex thumbed the edge of his yellow pad, flipping the pages. Did it again, then again. When he finally looked up, he was nodding. "Okay, I hear ya. I suppose—it doesn't. We know Sellica was involved in the sex extortion case. She hit up a bigwig for money; he ratted her out. And Arthur Vick sued Jane for saying it was him. So for us to do an inside story about Sellica's murder? I suppose . . . we don't need to know Jane's source."

From the depths of Jane's tote bag, her cell phone trilled. Maybe Moira Lassiter was calling, since the universe loved irony. Or Dad. It rang again.

"Pick up," Tuck said. "Might be the cops."

"Or a friend of Sellica's," Alex said. "Maybe she left you a note. We're pushing deadline here."

The phone rang again.

Tay Reidy nodded at her. "Might as well."

Maybe it's Jake. I need to talk to Jake. Jane mentally crossed her fingers as she pawed through her bag, searching for her suddenly too-small cell. Found it.

"This is Jane," she said.

Everyone leaned forward, eyes wide, waiting. Jane sat back down, the cell clamped to her cheek.

She needed to talk to Jake. But this wasn't Jake.

"Yes," she said. "I know that."

She paused, her lips pressed tight together, her spine rigid, as a wheedling voice from her too-recent-employment past made her an offer.

"You're kidding," she said. Her head was shaking *no,* as if the voice on the other end could see her. "You must be kidding."

"What?" Alex whispered.

"Who is it?" Tuck reached out a hand as if to bring Jane closer.

"Please don't ask me to do that. And please don't call me again." Jane clicked the phone to black, slamming the door on her career and on her dreams. All to protect a sex-selling criminal who'd lied and cheated and ruined a marriage and was now lying dead in the city morgue.

"What?" Everyone in the room asked it at the same time. Then everyone waited.

"Channel Eleven," Jane said.

She swallowed hard, then slowly walked to the sideboard at the end of the room. She carefully selected a plastic bottle of water from a silver ice-filled container, twisted off the cap. Turned back to the table.

"They want me to come back. 'Do the Sellica story,' they said." She took a sip, leaning against the sideboard. She didn't trust her knees.

"But you said you didn't tell them your source." Alex took a step toward her, brow furrowing. "You said they don't—"

"Alex. Stop. They don't know who it is. But, like you—" She waved her water bottle at the room. "Anyway. They said if I talk, do the big reveal, maybe the court will reverse the ruling, and reverse the million-dollar judgment. If that happens, they said, they 'might even have an opening for a new reporter.'"

She tried to smile.

"All I have to do, they said, is tell."

14

Sellica Darden's murder could mean only one thing.

Maybe two. And they were both disasters.

He needed to talk to Jane.

Jake drummed his fingers on the steering wheel of the police department's undercover Jeep and watched through the windshield. The streetlights, most of them working, barely made a dent in the late afternoon gloom of Hampstead Street. Struggling chrysanthemums made a last stand in the cared-for houses. In others, forgotten bicycles sprawled on crabgrass or frost-heaved driveways. The trees, municipal afterthoughts, had already lost most of their leaves.

At Leota Darden's house, one of two porch lights allowed Jake to see the faces of those arriving to pay their respects. Surprising that Leota's daughter had used her real last name. Surprising they hadn't moved out of town after the Arthur Vick mess. Wonder if the neighbors came to visit after *that* hit the fan.

Jake watched as the afternoon turned into evening.

Maybe there are three possibilities.

More people arrived at the Dardens' triple-decker: a man in a Celtics cap and a woman teetering on ridiculous heels, holding hands.

Three possibilities. And all disasters.

Jake slid back the front seat in a futile attempt to get comfortable. The radios glowed, pinpoint lights flashing, their squawk turned down.

Sellica's body had been found by water, by a bridge. Possibility one, damn it, meant he was 100 percent wrong. There was, in fact, a Bridge Killer. Sellica was his third victim. Which meant some maniac was stalking random women—random?—and killing them. Getting away with it. *Holy Christ, a serial killer on the loose in Boston.*

But serial killers had patterns. Processes. Habits. Their killings had similarities. And Sellica was an outlier. At least, not the same. He'd spent hours at the crime scene. Looking for something. Anything. Looking for similarities to Charlestown and Longfellow. Hoping there weren't any. Hoping there were.

Knowing that cops aren't supposed to hope. They observe. Connect. And find answers.

Sellica's body lay at the ME's office, autopsy still under way, but Dr. A's prelim had found roofies. Maybe it had nothing to do with her job, but why would someone give a hooker a knockout drug? Had some john flipped out? Or was there another reason? Charlestown and Longfellow, tox screens there showed no drugs. *Different*. Sellica was different.

No bruises—so, yeah, that was the same as Longfellow. But not like Charlestown.

The same. And different.

Possibility two, he was right. No serial. Maybe there were *three* killers. Three separate incidents. That would be a huge piece of crap to solve.

Possibility three was why Jake had to talk to Jane. Possibility three meant Charlestown and Longfellow were killed by the same person. Fine, he was wrong, there was a Bridge Killer. Which sucked. But possibility three meant Sellica was a separate deal altogether.

Maybe she'd finally hit a john who'd gone too far, doused her with roofies, freaked, pushed her into the water and booked. Or—and here was the biggie. Or, Arthur Vick had decided it was time for a big payback.

A payback bigger than a million dollars.

That's why Jake had to talk to Jane.

This isn't across the boundaries we set, because this isn't personal. This is part of the investigation. Maybe Jane is also a target? I'd want to call her, even if she wasn't . . .

He grabbed his phone, then stopped. The call would be on his cell log. And the supe, clearly unhappy with him, must suspect he was the department leak. His shoulders sagged. Jane would be safe for now. No one was getting killed tonight. And the supe was waiting for an update. If he solved the damn case, no one else would get hurt.

Jake opened the Jeep's front door and stepped into the October evening. Time to visit the victim's mother. Maybe she'd know something.

Someone sure did.

15

It can't be. Matt stared at the photo on his desk computer. He was reading the *Boston Register,* online, as he did every day. A Red Sox fan since he was a kid, he imagined he remembered his dad talking to him about Yaz, and Eck, and Carlton Fisk. Now, a thousand miles away and twenty-some years later, Matt couldn't shake the Sox habit.

Today it was political news, not sports, that skidded his work to a halt. A picture of a woman at a rally. One face in the crowd. It hit him as hard as a wild pitch.

It was only a couple years since he'd seen her. *If that was her.* Matt clicked the arrow in the center of the picture, zooming in. Closer.

Crap. It's her. Is it her? He placed the plus-sign directly over her face, his heart racing. Clicked his mouse, making the photo bigger. Her face blurred from black-and-white to gray. No help.

Her attitude. Her stance. That wild hair, knockout body, curves obvious under those almost too-tight skirts she always wore. She'd wanted to be a model, she'd admitted, but the big agencies told her she was too short. *Maybe I can just model for you . . . privately,* she'd teased him. With that same smile he now saw in the photo. Back in B-school, after the library closed, walking by the river, she had—he remembered it, perfectly— thrilled him. Then terrified him. He thought she was out of his life.

The bustle and buzz of his office faded. He vaguely heard see-ya-tomorrows, saw lights flipping off in the glass cubicles down the hall, the ticker go dark. The markets were closed, the gang headed home. Not him. Not now.

Maybe there were other photos. Maybe it was by chance. Maybe it was someone who looked like her. His keyboard clattered as he typed in the search.

Lassiter. Rally. Boston. Search images. *Click.*

A gallery of wide shots popped up on his flat computer screen. He'd have to check one at a time. But even if he could tell, what would he know?

Damn it. This would be fricking impossible.

Matt yanked at his tie, pulled open the collar button of his pale blue oxford shirt. He felt the prickle of sweat at the back of his neck. Why'd he ever thought this day wouldn't come?

What the hell is she doing in Boston? If she *was* in Boston. He calculated the possibilities. And there were only two: It was a coincidence. Or it wasn't.

And if it wasn't, he was screwed. And he wasn't the only one.

Why had he told her? A couple of brews, the sun on the river, that striped blanket. It had been hot for May. She'd stripped off her top, laughing, thrown it across his shoulders, drawing her to him. Surprising him with that little bathing suit thing underneath. They'd come here to study, he reminded her. Marketing finals, big stuff.

She'd teased, pouted, yanked off his Sox cap and tossed it into the river. When he protested, she'd retrieved it, returning dripping and slick, the sun glistening on her wet skin. "All I want is you, Mattie," she'd said. "I know I can change your mind. We're meant to be together. Let me show you."

And how could he have said no? Even though it wasn't her, it never had been, it never would be. It was almost the end of the school year. A month or two before B-school graduation. Why not?

Later, afterwards, he was—whatever. Wiped out. Might as well have been on drugs. And he'd told her, told her why they couldn't be together, told her why he couldn't love her, or anyone. Grief over his mother still raw, he'd told Holly everything. Even about what happened.

"Your poor mother," she'd said. Consoled him. "But I can wait. However long it takes." He remembered her drawing one finger, slowly, down his bare chest, remembered how the finger continued, remembered he couldn't stand it. And she knew it. Christ, he'd told her. *I told her.* Even though he'd promised not to. He made her vow to keep their secret.

"You'll change your mind about me, when you're ready," she whispered. "That's what I'm promising you."

When the semester was over, they graduated, she went—wherever she went. Two frigging years ago.

He stared at the computer screen, cursor flashing, the pixilated image taunting him. *But maybe it's not her.* It was his secret to tell. When he wanted to. *If* he wanted to.

A rustle at his doorway. He swiveled his chair, annoyed. The intern took a tentative step into his office. "Matt?"

Matt raised one hand, waved her away. Pointed to his headset. *I'm busy.*

Made another gesture. *And close the door.*

"Boston," he said into the phone. "Round trip. Open

return. When's the next flight? Tonight? First thing to-morrow?"

Do not turn around. Do not turn around. Jane leaned her forehead against the chilly window of the subway car as it motored up into the night landscape of bustling Kenmore Square, racketing her home. She pulled her black wool coat closer, sliding her gloved hands under her sleeves. Absurd, wanting to look behind her. No one was there. What could be safer than the Green Line?

Arthur Vick was not on the train. She was spooked, that was for sure. But Arthur Vick, with all those grocery stores and TV commercials, picture in all the papers, would never take the T. He didn't send the letters. He didn't kill Sellica; he was not the Bridge Killer.

Right?

Boston hurtled by. Beacon Street front porches, lights switching on. Rows of brownstones, a spate of restaurants, cars playing beat-the-trolley across the intersections. Friday night, beginning of the weekend rituals. She was almost home.

Sellica was dead. *Her* secrets were safe. Jane was alone.

"There you have it," she whispered to the window. Her breath made a little fog place on the glass.

Alex, for now at least, had let her off the hook. *Maybe he'll even turn out to be a good guy.* Tuck was assigned the Sellica story. Jane, fighting off stomach-clenching memories, had agreed to give some color from her trial days. No byline. Tay Reidy acquiesced, even giving Jane a regal pat on the back as he made his exit, lawyer in tow.

Tuck had already added a photo of the Sellica crime scene to the macabre collection tacked to her more-than-half of the bulletin board. *How'd she get that, so quickly?* Jane had tried to avoid looking.

Channel 11 hadn't called back.

All in all, another fun day in Jane world. And the prospects for tomorrow were no better. In fact, they might be worse.

She forced a smile. She would go home, put on sweats, have a glass of wine, turn on some Diana Krall. Watch a movie. Call Amy. Go visit Eli for a game of Psychonauts; maybe his mom, Neena, would be up for a chat. See if Mrs. W had some leftovers. Almost home. She was not afraid.

But Jake. He would go ballistic over tomorrow morning's headlines. Jane had hung around the newsroom for a while, still bemused over the identity of the real Tuck, who seemed driven but friendly enough. At some point, BRIDGE KILLER CHANGES TACTICS popped up as the headline in the dummy edition. The press room had held the front page for Tuck. As long as there were murders, Miss Tucker Cameron was queen bee.

The train's doors hissed open, jolting Jane back to reality. Her stop. Corey Road. She grabbed her purse and tote bag from the train's gritty floor and clattered down the steps to the street.

Her mind spiraled around Sellica's murder. Was there anything she knew that Jake should know? If there were, should she tell him? Could she? She really wanted to talk to him. She really, really wanted to find out what he thought about Sellica. Maybe she could just call him, all business, totally reporter, and say—

Jane jumped as her cell phone rang. She clutched a hand to her throat, then burst out laughing, the sound disappearing into the night. Lucky no one was here to see how jumpy she was. She looked around, spooked. A police car on patrol, lights off. Sidewalks deserted. Safe. And maybe it was Jake calling.

The phone rang again. She clicked it on, stepping into

the protective glow of a streetlight. It better not be Channel 11 again. *Jerks.* She missed TV. Missed her old life. But that door was closed.

"This is Jane."

"Jane Ryland?" A woman's voice. Low, not quite a whisper.

"Yes?"

"This is Moira Lassiter. I apologize for phoning so late."

Good news? About time. "Oh, Mrs. Lassiter. Thank you for calling. And it's not so—"

"Jane?" Moira Lassiter interrupted. "I can't talk now. About that interview. Let's do it."

16

"**May I help** you?"

Holly Neff stared at the beauty behind the desk. That woman should be, like, on television, not answering phones in some campaign office on a Saturday morning. Maybe she was someone's daughter, had the job because of who she knew or how she looked. It didn't matter. Holly had to get inside. Upstairs.

The lobby was completely decorated for the campaign, lots of posters and photos. The music was pretty loud. Groups of people hurried by, holding up badges hung around their necks. Miss Beauty Pageant hardly looked at them.

Elevator bells dinged, doors opened, people came out, others elbowed their way inside. She *had* to get upstairs.

Oh. The woman was waiting for her to answer. Lots of lipstick.

"Thank you so much," Holly said. She felt a little strange with all her hair pulled back, and she wasn't used to not wearing makeup. She'd never go out looking like this, so dowdy and plain—except today. And she wasn't used to wearing the geeky glasses. Well, it would all be worth it. Holly zipped open one pocket of her carryall, feeling for the folder inside. Her camera was there, too, safe in its pouch. She pulled out a little spiral notebook she'd gotten at the drugstore. It had a picture of an American flag on the front.

"I'm a very enthusiastic Lassiter supporter." She held the notebook up so the woman couldn't miss it. "I've been to all the rallies. And I think it's time I got involved."

She looked for a nameplate or a name tag, since you were supposed to call people by their names, but there wasn't one.

"I'm—" She paused, remembering her plan. And her secret name. "—I'm Hannah," she said. Bright smile. *Hannah*. Then she waited.

The woman didn't introduce herself. Whatever. Didn't matter. Holly knew from her phone calls that the volunteer office was on the third floor. So was the communications department, where the press people were. Owen's office was the only one on the fourth floor. Holly-Hannah simply had to get upstairs.

"Do you have an appointment?" the receptionist asked. The phone rang, and Holly waited while she answered it, saying, "Lassiter for Senate." The woman pushed some buttons on the phone console, then looked at Holly again. It seemed like she didn't love her job.

"Oh, well, no, I don't, but this is such an important election, you know?" Holly had practiced what she would say, and it seemed just right. "I do the neighborhood newspaper? I'm like, kind of a neighborhood reporter? I write while my kids are at school. And I'd love to do a story about Governor Lassiter. Maybe I could get a quick tour of headquarters? See what it's really like inside a campaign?"

She watched the woman look her up and down. *Well, fine, go ahead.* Holly looked perfect. She tried not to smile. *Perfectly awful.* A coat she'd gotten at a cheapo store, an acrylic scarf, stretchy wool gloves. The blonde behind the desk, all that chest showing even under that sweater, hideous. She'd assume she was seeing some nerdy housewife, trying to get out of the house and have a life. *As if.*

"If you'd like an interview with the governor," the woman was saying, "you'll have to go through our press office. I could take your name and number."

The woman yanked a sliding shelf from under the desktop. Holly could see a list of names and phone extensions taped to it, but it was too hard to read upside down. "Or you can contact Sheila King directly. She handles press. Extension 403." The woman looked up at her. "Do you need to write that down?"

The blonde's lipsticky mouth went tight, as if Holly were bothering her. Pretty snippy for a receptionist. The phone rang, then rang again. Holly waited, so patiently, while the woman answered the calls.

"Lassiter for Senate. Please hold. Lassiter for Senate."

It made Holly smile to hear his name.

"Oh, I don't need an interview with the governor, gosh no." Holly tried to look as if the thought had never crossed her mind. "Can I call Sheila King from here? Maybe someone could show me how it all looks, and I could maybe get some shots of it for the paper?"

Another call came in, then another. The phone woman kept answering, looking more and more annoyed. Another group of somebodies talked as they waited at the elevator, comparing pieces of paper, voices bouncing off the marble walls.

The woman behind the desk stood up. She was smiling, patting her hair, adjusting that sweater. But she was looking past Holly, beyond her shoulder. The people at the elevator stopped talking, every one of them, and turned the same direction. So Holly had to turn, too.

And there was Owen Lassiter. Striding through the revolving door and into the lobby. The bustle of the evening swirled into the building with him, the clatter of traffic, the wind, sirens peeling down Causeway Street. His hair was blown, cheeks ruddy, white shirt so white. She could almost feel the force field around him. Two men in suits trotted to keep up, one of them, a youngish man not far behind, carrying a stack of papers.

Holly's hand went to her heart. Owen Lassiter. *I needed to find him, but he found me!* She tried to remember to breathe.

"Mrs. Wilkes." The candidate was talking to the woman at the desk. He took her hand in both of his. "Welcome, Kenna. Rory told me you'd be here."

Holly thought she saw Mrs. Wilkes blush. *Huh.*

The phone rang, but the Wilkes person ignored it, she was so locked in to Lassiter's greeting. When he let go of her, finally, she didn't seem to know where to put her hands.

Then Owen Lassiter himself turned to her. To her! He held out his hand, smiling at her, drawing her in with those eyes. "And who do we have here?"

Holly almost blushed, seeing him. He would never recognize her.

Not until she wanted him to.

"I'm Hannah," she said. "I'm so delighted to see you." See you *again,* she was careful *not* to say.

She could almost feel the camera in her bag.

Perfect.

When things worked, they just worked.

17

"**Is it the** Bridge Killer? Is it? Oh, Detective Brogan, I'm not sure I can do this now."

"Take your time, Mrs. Darden," Jake reassured the woman on the couch. The low-slung coffee table between them could not have held one more doily-covered plate of cookies or little muffins. "Let me know when you feel up to continuing."

Jake sat in the striped wing chair, pretending to read over his notes, while Sellica Darden's mother composed herself. Leota Darden had made it through about five minutes of Jake's questions, poised and polite, even offering Jake tea, answering carefully.

She'd been too distraught to talk last night, so they agreed he'd return first thing this morning. He hoped that wasn't a mistake.

Wearing a flinty gray silk dress that ended below her knees and what his mom called sensible shoes, Mrs. Darden had shooed all but one of her other Saturday morning callers down the hall. The woman now sitting beside Mrs. Darden, pinched face and bright red fingernails, gave Jake a dark look. He'd seen it in many other living rooms. It meant, *Get out, cop*.

He wished he could. But this was part of the deal.

Death. Trying to explain it. Trying to understand it. Intruding on grief. Sitting in people's living rooms, bringing up exactly what grieving families didn't want to hear.

The scent of flowers, heavy-headed dark red roses and masses of carnations, mixed with the fragrance of brewing coffee and burning candles. A black-framed photo of a sleekly stylish young woman wearing a white turtleneck and ropes of pearls was displayed on the mantelpiece, a single white lily in a slim crystal vase beside it.

The ME's photos of Sellica that Jake had studied last night were not so attractive. He hoped her mother would never see those.

He had started with the easy questions.

Yes, Mrs. Darden told him, her Sellica kept in touch. Yes, she knew what her daughter did for a living. No, she hadn't mentioned being afraid of anyone.

He'd ignore her question about the Bridge Killer. But that's what was haunting him, too.

What's more, the newspaper sure as hell isn't ignoring it. Tuck's story this morning was total bullshit, speculation and psychobabble. The "Bridge Killer" cases aren't exactly the same—and that proves they're connected? That girl never let the truth get in the way of a good story.

"Did Sellica ever mention trouble of any kind?" Jake asked. "Anyone who threatened her? Bothered her? Followed her?"

But Mrs. Darden was deflating, collapsing, fingers to her forehead. "It is, isn't it. The Bridge Killer."

"I won't lie to you, Mrs. Darden." So much for ignoring it. "But I don't think there's a Bridge Killer. And that's why I need to—"

The other woman sniffed. "Ridiculous. Of course there is. I read the newspapers. You people couldn't stop him, and now—" She stopped, giving her head a fretful shake. She clutched at Mrs. Darden's arm. "Oh, I'm sorry, Leezey. Honey. I'm so sorry."

"I'm all right, Neesha." Leota Darden patted her friend's hand, then rearranged herself on the couch. "It all started when she talked to that reporter. I told her she shouldn't talk to her. I said to her, 'Sellica—' "

"Jane Ryland, you mean, right? Did you ever meet her?" Jake had to interrupt. Jane had never admitted Sellica was her source. But never said she wasn't. And if Jane's story had something to do with Sellica's murder somehow . . . Jake's thumbs flew over his BlackBerry as he continued his questions, looking up at her as he typed. "Mrs. Darden? Did you ever meet Arthur Vick?"

"I most certainly did not," she said. Her back stiffened. "That man—"

"Ruined Sellica's life." Neesha finished the sentence. She turned to Mrs. Darden. "Well, he did, honey. You know he did. But she's in a better place now."

With that, Leota Darden lost it. She collapsed onto her friend's shoulder in a flood of sobbing. Neesha glared at him again.

Can't you go? she mouthed.

Probably should have questioned her alone. Too late now.

"I'm sorry, no, I can't," he said. This sucked. But he had no choice. "Take your time, though. It's okay, ma'am."

Jake scanned his BlackBerry screen, letting the women comfort each other, trying to give them some privacy. He scrolled his Google search results into view. Arthur Vick, owner of the Beacon Markets grocery stores, megabucks, big political donor, wife in hiding post-scandal, she was some kind of artist apparently, million-dollar judgment, yadda yadda, Wrong-Guy Ryland.

Poor Jane. But it wasn't so much Jane who was the key. It was Arthur Vick.

"See if L and C"—Jake's shorthand for *Longfellow* and *Charlestown*—"connect with A Vick." Jake banged out a reminder e-mail to himself, and hit Send. Maybe the other victims worked at grocery stores. He'd have the guys do a photo array at Beacon Markets. Maybe Arthur Vick used his employee files to track down his victims. *Possible.*

Maybe Arthur Vick's grocery stores were not the only place the victims worked for him.

"Detective? I'm so sorry." Leota Darden dabbed her reddened eyes with a shredding tissue. "I know you're doing your job. I'm better now, thank you."

"Tea?" Neesha stood, edging between the couch and coffee table. "I'll go get you tea."

She did not offer any to Jake.

"Arthur Vick," Jake said as Neesha left the room. "We were talking about Arthur Vick. Did Sellica mention anyone who was missing? Someone she knew from her—work?"

"You're thinking of the other Bridge Killer victims? You think they did what she did? No, Sellica never mentioned anything like that. Poor things." Mrs. Darden leaned back against the softly flowered cushions, closing her eyes for a moment. Then she sat up straight, planted her hands on her hips.

"Detective Brogan. Arthur Vick promised my Sellica she could be in his grocery store commercials. She counted on it, with those other girls, thought it was a way out of the life. All she wanted was what he promised her. He promised her! Then he turned on her. Dragged her into court. And she, she . . ."

"She fought back by talking to Jane Ryland. Correct?"

One white candle hissed as it sputtered out, a wisp of smoke rising toward the ceiling. Jake leaned forward, needing to hear what would come next.

"Sellica was ordered by a judge not to tell," Mrs. Darden whispered. "But she did. She did tell. Now she's dead. Now Arthur Vick is even richer."

"Ladies and gentlemen, please make sure your seat backs and tray tables are . . ."

Matt tuned out the staticky voice coming from the plane's public address system. His fingers worried the iPhone in his hand. The flight attendant had caught him using it during takeoff, almost confiscated it. Now he had to wait till the damn plane landed till he could call. He'd already programmed in the number.

Resting his forehead against the window, he peered at the whitecaps on Boston Harbor. He could feel the plane descending. *Almost there.* One hand curled around his phone. *Almost time.* He had to be here in person. He'd call first, because he was curious, then get up close and personal. See her. If it was her. And find out what the hell she was doing in Boston.

Do not ever, do not ever, *ask about your father.* He could hear his mother's voice, words interrupted by puffs on those cigarettes. Picture her, so beautiful and so sad, sitting across from him at their kitchen table, one of her hands, thin and drawn, covering his smaller one. *Do not look for him, do not go to him, do not ask me about him.*

It had been one of her rituals, almost like their grace before meals. His sister Sarah—he called her Cissy—had been too young to understand. But he remembered enough to miss his dad. Couldn't understand why he was gone. Why his mother felt so bitter about him. Why she'd tried to erase him from their family.

And then, while he was in grad school, she'd erased herself. Cissy always blamed their father. Hated their father. Before their mother killed herself, hate was what she taught them.

Do not look for him, do not go to him, do not ask me about him. But how could Matt resist? It was his father. And eventually, he learned everything he could about him. Then that day in B-school, he had stupidly revealed all of it.

The rumble of the landing gear jolted Matt from his memories. He slugged down the last of his second Bloody Mary, wincing at the pepper, then hid the two little empty bottles in the seat pocket in front of him. Even the drinks hadn't helped him calm down. Eyeing the overhead rack where he'd stashed his coat, he calculated how quickly he could yank off his seat belt. He had to get out. He had to know.

If she was in Boston, there had to be a reason. And it could not be a good one.

18

Sitting in her car, just outside the gated entrance of the Lassiters' asphalt expanse of a driveway, Jane adjusted the rearview mirror and leaned across the steering wheel, checking her lipstick. Then reality hit. This interview was for a newspaper, not TV. Didn't really matter what she looked like.

This is easier, right? No lights, no cameras, no wires or microphones or cranky photographers. Those days were over. All because of Sellica Darden. Jane blew out a breath, her memories crashing into one another. Forgetting about lipstick, she stared out the windshield, unseeing. Sellica's funeral was later this afternoon.

Why did she feel so guilty about Sellica's death?

A lone car trundled by on the street behind her. PRIVATE DRIVE, the sign down the block warned. The Lassiters' white-columned Georgian stood almost at the end of the cul-de-sac.

If she attended Sellica's funeral, out of respect, would it telegraph that she'd been Jane's source?

It would. Wouldn't it?

First things first. Moira. Five minutes till her one o'clock interview.

Maybe she should go inside, whip out Archive Gus's

photos and say: *Mrs. Lassiter? Do you know this woman in the red coat? She was photographed near your husband at this rally, and this one, and this one. Does this concern you at all?*

Jane laughed out loud, imagining it. Played out the whole impossible scene, making dramatic faces in her rearview. "Well, yes, Mrs. Lassiter. The reason I ask is that from my research, it appears your husband may be—"

She scratched her head, pretending to consider. How would she put that? *Having an affair? Being unfaithful? Seeing another woman?*

She'd also have to ask if the affair was why Moira was suddenly off the radar. "So, Mrs. Lassiter, is that why you've been hiding? And oh, by the way, who else knows about the affair?"

Obviously there was no tactful way to bring this up. Plus, Alex would kill her.

Mrs. Lassiter opened one side of the double front door herself, before Jane even touched the brass lion's-head knocker. Wearing a white jewel-necked sweater, white cardigan tied around her neck, and sleek black pants, she was a silver blond lady of the manor, framed by the white-trimmed moldings and the still-green ivy twining up an arched trellis.

Jane knew from her research Moira Lassiter was an ex-ballerina, small company, but still. That took training, and devotion, and self-restraint. Single-mindedness. And a solid sense of her own body. She'd reportedly met Owen at a—

"Jane? So nice to see you again." Moira Lassiter reached out a graceful hand, then stepped back into her entryway, ushering Jane in. No hovering servants or housekeepers. A well-kept but low-key foyer, with a not-quite-extravagant display of all-white chrysanthemums in front of a gilt-edged mirror, polished black and white tiles on the floor. Not ostentatious. Confident. Established.

Moira herself took Jane's coat, draping it over the back of a cream-on-white wing chair beside an arch in the entryway.

"We have tea in the living room." She pushed the sleeves of her sweater to her elbows, revealing a triple-strand pearl bracelet and tanned arms. Her fingernails were polished but pale. "I'm glad you could see me this morning on such short notice."

Jane followed her through the archway. *I'll let her make the first move.* "Of course, Mrs. Lassiter. I'm so happy you decided to chat."

The book-lined living room, fire crackling in a white-brick fireplace, polished white baby grand piano, dozens of photographs in silver frames, looked as if someone had just plumped all the white-on-white couch pillows and disappeared. A flowered china tea service, delicate and gilt edged, lay jewel-like in the center of a mahogany coffee table. Lemons, pumpkin-glazed cookies, honey. Two diminutive silver spoons.

Jane perched on the edge of a sleekly white club chair.

Moira settled directly opposite her, centered on the pillow-lined couch—so slight, she barely made a dent in the cushions. Her gold wedding ring, with a modestly massive diamond engagement ring above it, glittered in the firelight.

She didn't say a word.

Jane's spiral reporter's notebook was burning a hole in her purse. But now was not the time to get it out. She couldn't figure this. Maybe Moira was waiting for her to begin?

"So shall we—?" Jane began

"So, Jane," Mrs. Lassiter spoke at the same time.

"Oh, sorry," Jane said. Not an auspicious beginning. "Please. Go on."

But Mrs. Lassiter seemed to be studying her hands. If there were a clock, Jane could have heard it tick. A cinder popped against the fireplace screen. Mrs. Lassiter looked up.

Is she on the verge of tears?

"So, Jane," Mrs. Lassiter said again. "This is somewhat difficult. But I know I can count on your discretion. I've followed your investigative work from the beginning, and I've always felt—your heart is in it. You authentically care about doing the right thing. That's why, even under all the pressure, you protected your source in that prostitution case. Your station was hit with the million-dollar judgment, correct? But you never told. Isn't that true?"

"Yes, I never—" Jane paused, thought for a second. "I mean no, I never revealed my source."

"That proves you're trustworthy," Mrs. Lassiter went on, nodding. "And that's why I called you. Because now I—I need your help."

Jane waited, blinking. *She needs my help?*

"Can we be off the record?" Mrs. Lassiter continued. "You don't use this in the paper until I say you may?"

Just what I need. Kiss of death. I can know something that I can't use. Of course, if I say no, she won't tell me, and then I won't know it. At least it's not another source thing. Whatever she tells me, at least I can discuss it with Alex. So here we go again.

"All right, Mrs. Lassiter. Off the record. But let's have an understanding of what that means. I'll go with the story only if I can confirm it on my own. I won't do that without letting you know. I won't connect the source of the information with you. And I'm going to tell my editor. Are you comfortable with that?"

The other woman took a sip from a crystal glass of ice water, carefully put the glass on a coaster. She moved the spoon on the right closer to the one on the left. Moved it back.

"Here's the problem, Jane," she said. "I think my husband may be having an affair."

"Black. Two sugars." Jake slid across the cracking black wannabe-leather upholstery of the corner booth at Cuppa Joe's. *Why is the guy behind the counter wearing a—? Oh. Halloween coming up.*

DeLuca now had about three minutes before he was late. Why'd he always cut it close? Today wasn't the day to push it. Sellica Darden's funeral started in two hours. Jake needed to get there early and grab a parking spot in the front of All Saints so he could check out the arrivals. For whatever that was worth.

The vampire-waiter sloshed a pale cup of coffee in front of him, then pointed with a black-polished fingernail to a crusted container of sugar, kernels of rice sprinkled inside it. *Lucky for him I'm not the health squad, Halloween or no.* Jake tipped a flow of sugar into his coffee, monitoring for rice.

Sellica's funeral. Did the Bridge Killer attend the funerals of his victims?

Dammit. Jake stirred so hard, coffee sloshed into the saucer. *There is no Bridge Killer.*

Even so. There was no way to know whether the bad guy would show up for the first two victims. Because there had been no funerals yet. Because the cops—his guys—had gotten exactly nowhere, still waiting for ID. The victims were waiting in the morgue. In a couple of days, someone'd have to make a decision.

Jake took an unrewarding sip.

But Sellica, she had ID. Her face. Oh, sure, her purse was gone, like the others. Anyone else, it'd be another investigation to figure out her identity. But Sellica Darden, her fifteen minutes weren't up. Had the killer realized Sellica didn't need a driver's license for her name to be known? Or did he hope she'd be anonymous, too?

"Yo. Harvard." Paul DeLuca slid into the booth, opposite Jake. DeLuca was all points—nose, elbows, cheekbones, ears. Everything too long, too sharp. His beat-up leather jacket hung on him like a deflated basketball. He examined the bottom of the salt shaker, which dumped a pile of salt on the table. He threw some over one shoulder, swiped the rest onto the floor.

"Yo, dropout." Jake completed their now-ritual. He let his language slide a bit with DeLuca. Can't beat 'em, join 'em. They'd been partners two years. "Whatcha got for me?"

"Well, funny you should ask. I got—" DeLuca pulled a tattered spiral notebook from inside his jacket. Thumbed a few pages, then stopped. Gave Jake a look. "Guess."

"Gimme a break," Jake said.

"Amaryllis Roldan."

"What?" Jake looked at his partner. Baffled.

"*Who,* you should say. Amaryllis Roldan is a who."

"Who what?" Jake said. This was not funny.

"She's Charlestown, Jake. Bridge Killer number two. The tattoo? Some moke in a Hyde Park shop recognized it. From that, we snagged her address. Outta town, but they knew she'd come to Boston to make it big, whatever. No family connections here. They knew of, at least."

"You sure? It's her? Amaryllis—"

"Roldan. Yup. ME's confirming now. But it's a sure thing."

"Motive?"

"Zip."

"Family?"

"Checking."

"Job?"

"Yeah," DeLuca said. "That, we got."

DeLuca flipped through the pages of his notebook and consulted something. Scratched his nose, as if seeing his notes for the first time. "Clerk at Beacon Markets. The one in Brighton. Started, like, a week before she was killed. How a-friggin'-bout that?"

"Holy shit."

"Yeah. Good call, Harvard. Second store we hit."

"Supe know?"

"Yup. He says keep a lid till it's confirmed. Gotta dig up next of kin. All that."

Jake paused, processing. *Amaryllis Roldan.* The victim had a name. It was a start. A good start. And she was connected with Arthur Vick. Had to be.

"Harvard?" DeLuca was sliding the salt shaker back and forth, like a hockey puck, between his palms. It scraped across the pockmarked tabletop.

"Yeah?"

"So now what?" He caught the shaker in one hand. "We gonna pick up Arthur Vick?"

19

"Your husband may be having an affair?" For a billion dollars, Jane could not have predicted that Moira would be the one asking *her* about it, not the other way around. Moira Lassiter's bombshell landed square in her lap, and now she had about zero seconds to figure out what to do with it. But there it was. Even off the record, it couldn't be unsaid. "Mrs. Lassiter? Ah—I'm so sorry. I'm not quite sure how to respond."

Moira's hands seemed steady as she poured steaming golden tea into one delicate cup, then the other. She gestured one of them to Jane. "Sugar?"

"Mrs. Lassiter?" Was Moira—in denial? On medication? Crazy? If she was blurting out stuff like that to strangers, no wonder she was home. Maybe the campaign bigwigs had grounded her. Perhaps not a bad plan.

But what was Jane supposed to do with this? What they don't teach you in journalism school.

"Please, call me Moira." The candidate's wife smiled and reknotted the soft sweater draped around her shoulders. Ignoring her tea, she took another sip of her water. "Now that I've given you 'the scoop.'"

"Well, that's, ah, an understatement," Jane said. Questions jockeyed for the front row. Red-coat woman?

Someone else? Moira didn't look nuts. But certainly the biggest question of all was her motive. Why on earth would she divulge such a suspicion? To a reporter? "Might I ask—why would you tell me that?"

"Because—because I'm not sure it's true. But how am I supposed to find out? It's not like someone's sending me photos. I can't ask Owen, of course. Because true or not, he'd deny it. They always deny it. And the more they deny it, the truer it seems."

Jane took a sip of tea. Moira had a point.

"I've seen those other wives. Hillary. Jenny Sanford. Silda Spitzer. Maria. You can picture them, all those news conferences and awkward interviews," Moira went on. "My heart went out to them. They'd believed in their husbands. Trusted them. Supported them. Devoted their lives to them. And then, in one headline, or one video clip, it's all . . . just over."

Jane nodded. Kept silent. *Maybe this will make sense in a minute.*

"But it always comes out, doesn't it?" Moira fiddled with her pearl bracelet. "They all think they're the ones who'll manage to keep it quiet, manage to have their careers and their women, too. But they can't. They can't. If my husband is having an affair, you media people are going to find out sooner or later. And it's not only Owen's life that'll be ruined. *My* life will be ruined, too."

She narrowed her eyes at Jane.

"After being married almost twenty-two years, giving up my career, being the candidate's wife and the governor's wife and then the businessman's wife and now the candidate's wife again, and always in the background, my life becomes the footnote. Well. I won't have it." She took a sip of her water, seemed to be considering.

"For instance," she went on. "Where is Owen now? His campaign schedule has him out in Springfield. Until recently, I'd have been there with him. The crowds loved me. Loved our marriage. Loved us together. But oh, somehow, not anymore. Now, according to Mr. Rory Maitland, I'm no longer needed."

"The campaign consultant? Told you—?"

"Oh yes, in no uncertain terms. Rory told me the polls showed I'm 'unpopular.' 'Too reserved.'" Moira closed her eyes briefly. "He said their internal poll numbers showed I interfered with Owen's female demos. As Rory so delicately put it, I was 'in the way' when it came to women voters. So he told me he'd handle it all, but it would be best if I 'had the flu.' Or was 'tired.' This is off the record, remember, as we agreed. But that's ridiculous. He's lying to me. He's covering something up."

"And that's why you've been off the campaign trail? You were told to stay home?"

"Owen and Rory are inseparable," Moira replied. She stood, picked up her water, edged past the coffee table, and stood in front of the fireplace, arms crossed. Almost a silhouette in the already-darkening afternoon, the fire glowing behind her. "He's new to the campaign. A hired gun, here for the duration only. And Owen relies on everything he says. I think Rory knows about her. He's helping Owen hide her. Until *after* they win, of course. Then they'll go to Washington. What if I wind up as another one of those poor wives, pushing their redemption books on TV talk shows?"

Over my head. I'm in over my head. Even if Jane ran out of the room with her hands over her ears—*la la la, I can't hear you*—Moira Lassiter already started the dominoes falling. It's what Jane suspected all along. What the holy hell was she supposed to do now?

Jane had to ask.

"Who?" she said. "Who is this other woman? Would you know her if you saw her?"

Moira shook her head. "No. But when you called, asking why I wasn't making campaign appearances, I knew the sh— Well, it was about to hit the fan. As they say."

"But . . ."

"Sheila King, the press secretary? Knows Rory is insisting I lie low," Moira went on. "But I found a phone number in Owen's jacket pocket. The phone was disconnected. Another time, I found a matchbook from some hotel. I'm putting two and two together. As you would. You weren't going to let go of your 'Where's Moira?' story, correct? And that's the problem I had to solve."

"But I never said—," Jane tried again.

Moira kept talking. "Erase me from the campaign? No. Rory's not going to get away with it. Cover-ups don't work. We have to get in front of this." Moira jabbed her palm with a finger. "Face it. Handle it. That's why I need you to find out what's true. Find her. Stop this."

Crazy. Nut city. Over the edge. There is no reason—

But there was. A reason that took Moira's whole unbelievably twisted story and twisted it back the other way.

Jane had to ask.

"Forgive me, Mrs. Lassiter," Jane said. "But if your husband is having an affair, and it becomes public knowledge, Eleanor Gable's campaign would instantly cash in on that. It's likely your husband would lose the election. So I need to ask you. Are you hoping Gable wins? Do you *want* your husband to lose?"

20

"You were so patient with her, Governor Lassiter. Don't you think so, Rory? No wonder you're doing so well in the polls." Kenna Wilkes turned to the candidate, smiling as she closed his office door behind that Hannah person. *Gone at last.* Now it was just the three of them. Hannah'd asked some pretty ridiculous questions in what she called her "interview" for her pitiful neighborhood paper. But all good, actually, since Rory had suggested Hannah interview her as a typical volunteer. Brilliant. He'd taken her picture with the governor, too.

"Always happy to spread the word, Kenna," Owen said. "And happy you could join us for the interview." The governor was concentrating on a stack of papers Rory placed in front of him. Not on her. Still, there was time.

Lassiter signed something, closed the folder. "So, Maitland. Weren't we going to Springfield later this afternoon? It's what I told that young woman."

"Still on, Governor, but postponed a bit. Snafus with the hotel, but it's all fine now." Rory shot Kenna a look. "In fact, Mrs. Wilkes volunteered to help with the event. To get a feel for the campaign. Right?"

"Happy to," Kenna said. *Understatement of the century.* "Jimmy's at his grandparents' this weekend for Halloween. I'd adore to come."

Rory was still talking. Didn't wait for Owen to respond.

"She'll pass out name tags, flyers, that sort of thing? She can ride with us. We'll leave as soon as you're done. It's gonna be a late one, Governor. Maybe too late to get back to Boston tonight. We should stay over."

Rory lifted his briefcase onto the governor's desk, pushing a hefty leather-bound book out of the way. Snapping the locks, he took out a sheaf of papers. "Our internals show we can hit it out of the ballpark in Western Mass. See? Here, and right here. What I'm hearing, the Gable people are ignoring it."

But Lassiter seemed to remember she was in the room. Now, instead of focusing on Rory and his poll numbers, Lassiter focused on her. Kenna felt him raking her with those eyes. What was he seeing? What did he want? He stared at her, hard, as if he were about to say something.

What would it be? As she waited, her mind sampled the possibilities, one delicious idea at a time.

Maybe he would finally send Rory away. And she'd get what *she* wanted. It wouldn't take long; then everything would be different. She crossed her arms in front of her, holding in her hopes, trying not to smile.

A buzzer sounded on Lassiter's phone console. Startled, he pretended he wasn't staring at her.

"Sir?" The receptionist's staticky voice came through the speaker. "You need to leave for Springfield soon."

Kenna glanced at Rory. He rolled his eyes at the phone console. "Under control, Deenie," he said, raising his voice at the speaker. "Mrs. Wilkes will be joining us."

"I should call Moira," Lassiter said. He patted the breast pocket of his pin-striped suit jacket and pulled out a flat silver cell phone. "She's expecting me for dinner. No hope of that now, right?"

Did he chance another look at her? Kenna touched her hair, allowed herself the trace of a smile. *Oh, yeah. Call Moira. Just do it.*

"Good idea, Rory. Let's stay overnight in Springfield," Lassiter continued. His cell made a soft trill, turning on. "I'll let Moira know I won't be home."

"Jane!" She couldn't hear him, not from this distance, but he'd recognize that walk anywhere. Bundled in her black coat, that gray scarf she loved flying out behind her, her head down in the darkening Saturday afternoon. *She must be here for Sellica's funeral.*

Jake threw a BPD placard in the windshield, banged open the door of his unmarked cruiser, and took off after her. She was already across Cumberton Ave. Headed for All Saints Church, had to be. Question was, *why*.

"Jane!" Getting closer now, headed up Harrison Street, almost to the crosswalk, Jake called her name again, raising his voice. A chunky city bus wheezed between them, erasing Jane briefly from view. A siren whirled in the distance. *Damn.* He would never catch her before she got to the church. He took off, in a flat run, then stopped. In the middle of the crosswalk. *Wait a minute.*

He stared at her vanishing form. Maybe he could learn more if she didn't know he was here. He hated to spy on her, but that was why she'd put the brakes on their relationship, right? Insisted their jobs would get in the way. Maybe she was right. Like now.

Jake hung back, letting her get ahead. He felt like an idiot, tailing Jane. But Sellica Darden had been murdered. Maybe Jane knew something she wasn't telling.

She was a block from the church. Long black cars

pulled up to the front, exhaust pluming from their tail-pipes. Clumps of dark-clad mourners gathered on the far street corner, some walking arm in arm. Detail cops in orange webbed safety jackets stopped traffic, allowing people to emerge from their cars unhurried, unthreatened by the busy street. A huge wreath of white flowers and some kind of greenery hung on the front doors.

Jake kept to the shadows. He had a perfect view. What did he expect to see? He'd know when he saw it.

Now Jane was trotting up the wide front steps. She stopped to talk with a woman in a black coat, her face hidden by her broad-brimmed black hat. He saw Jane take the woman's hands, lean forward. *Leota Darden.* Did Jane know her from before? Had Jane met Sellica's mother? Leota had never answered him directly about that.

If Sellica was Jane's source, maybe she'd told her more about Arthur Vick than Jane reported. Maybe that was key.

Another big question: What if Sellica knew Amaryllis Roldan?

DeLuca was on it now, checking. And if his partner found a connection, it meant there was a Bridge Killer.

And that meant they were all screwed.

Dammit. Arthur Vick? He could picture Vick killing Sellica in some testosterone-fueled revenge move. Maybe an accident, a mistake. But the others? Arthur Vick as Bridge Killer? No. No way. Too much to lose. Too public.

If there was a Bridge Killer, whoever it was, he was nuts. Arthur Vick wasn't nuts. An egocentric asshole, but not nuts.

Probably not nuts.

Jake checked his watch. The five o'clock funeral didn't start for another twenty minutes. He watched more mourners arrive and stop to speak with Mrs. Darden,

THE OTHER WOMAN 117

Jane seeming to stand aside. Keeping his eye on the front steps, he hit speed dial.

One ring. Almost two.

"DeLuca."

"D? About Arthur Vick."

"You come to your senses, Harvard?" DeLuca's sarcasm was punctuated by bells ringing and what sounded like—cash registers? Of course. Grocery store. "Gonna let me pick him up?"

"Not yet," Jake said. "Listen. On the down-low. Let's check Vick's alibi. For Longfellow and for Charlestown. I mean, for Miss Roldan. And for Sellica Darden."

"By 'let's,' you mean me."

"Ten-four, good buddy." Jake smiled. D was a good guy. "You getting anything at the grocery?"

"Nada."

"Anything on Sellica? More on Roldan?"

"Nope. And nope. Like I said. Nada. Roldan's a no-body at Beacon Markets. Passing through."

"She know Arthur Vick?"

"Oh. Yeah, they were boyfriend–girlfriend. I just forgot to tell you." DeLuca paused. "Like I said. Nada. No connection so far."

"Keep me posted."

"Will do."

Jake hung up the phone, then scrolled his BlackBerry for the notes from this morning's interview with Leota Darden. The green screen glowed against the glare as the corner streetlight popped on. Something Leota had said. About her daughter and Vick. About the money. He rolled the ball with his thumb, squinting at the screen, working his notes into view. *Found it.*

"She counted on it, with those other girls, thought it was a way out of the life." Word for word what Leota said.

What other girls?

Clicking off his BlackBerry, Jake eased closer to the church. Two men in black robes opened both front doors. Golden light from the vestibule spilled out the entryway and over the front steps. He could hear the low murmuring of organ music.

He could go inside. Stand in the back. See who arrived. See if anyone looked like a Bridge Killer. *Right.* Jake ran his jacket zipper up and down, thinking. Was there someone else Jane hoped to talk to? Who would she come here to see?

He could watch and wait. He reached for the Black-Berry in his jacket pocket. *Or.* He could ask.

21

Jane felt guilty as hell.

Guilty about Alex. Guilty about Sellica.

But right now, standing on the steps of All Saints waiting for a funeral to begin, she had to ignore her cell phone's insistent vibration. It was certainly Alex, certainly reacting to the voice mail message she'd left him about the Moira Lassiter bombshell. Moira, intense and persistent, sticking to her story, insisted she was in love with her husband and wanted only to "uncover the truth" to prevent him from making "a career-ending error."

The fact that Moira divulged her suspicions was almost a bigger story. And if that was vodka in her glass instead of water? Did that make her story more true? Or less? It would sure explain why she suddenly became a nonperson in the campaign. Jane was dying to get into the newsroom. Confer with Alex. Plot their strategy. Figure out how to confirm it all.

Alex would have to admit that her instincts about the other woman had been right, which would be really gratifying. And if it was a drinking thing, fine, *his* instincts had been right, too. But now Jane had to be here at the church. Guilty or not.

A few TV stations had sent crews to Sellica's funeral,

vulture patrols, looking for mourner-video to "human-ize" their coverage of the murder. This part of TV she didn't miss one bit. Intruding on strangers' grief to tape a few moments of video sorrow. She watched as a stern-faced minister allowed TV to get a few exteriors, then banished them to across the street. Eventually they gave up, headed off to some other tragedy.

Two black-clad arrivals hugged Mrs. Darden, then entered the church, leaving her alone next to a tall ar-rangement of pine branches and white chrysanthemums. Jane approached her, took the woman's gloved hand in hers. Mrs. Darden was all shades of black and soft gray, a fragile sparrow.

"Mrs. Darden, I'm so sorry for your loss," Jane said. She struggled for the appropriate words. "Sellica was . . . you must be . . ."

It was only the second time she'd met Mrs. Darden. The first time, Sellica was alive, and had told her about Arthur Vick. Jane had been pumped for the scoop. As-sured Sellica she'd never reveal her as the source. Assured her mother she could keep the secret. It had been excit-ing, knowing she'd be able to change their lives. As it turned out, change was exactly what happened. Jane got fired. Sellica got killed.

"I'm so sorry, I don't know what to say," Jane started over, trying not to lose her composure. Sellica's death had nothing to do with her, logically, but somehow it felt as if it did. Everything bad happened after Super Jane stepped in to make things right. "It's just—"

"She trusted you, Miss Ryland, and don't you worry that you let her down." Leota Darden wore a single white calla lily pinned to her black coat. She touched it briefly with a gloved finger. "My Sellica got herself into trouble. We tried, we all tried, but none of us could help her. Now she's in a better place. I appreciate you're here."

Mrs. Darden's eyes were rimmed with red, tears threatening, lines on her face deeper than Jane remembered. She clutched Jane's wrist, pulling her closer. Jane picked up a faint scent of roses, maybe vanilla. Mrs. Darden's hat brushed Jane's cheek.

"But, Jane. I need to ask you . . ."

Jane leaned down, calculating. *Ask me what?* Maybe Sellica told her something. *Dammit.* The cell phone. It vibrated again, fuzzing against her thigh. Lucky she'd turned off the ringer. Alex again, no question. She had to ignore him. Had to hear what Mrs. Darden was about to say.

"Will the police care?" Mrs. Darden whispered. Her slim fingers tightened around Jane's wrist. "Will they find who did this? Or will they think my Sellica deserved it? For the life she had? And what if it *was* the Bridge Killer?"

Jane almost burst into tears. How could she be so selfish, so self-centered? Of course what Mrs. Darden wanted to say had nothing to do with the Vick case. Nothing to do with her. This poor woman. First, seeing her daughter's disreputable profession put in the spotlight by a lying, manipulative jerk. Then learning she was murdered, maybe by a serial killer. And today, at her only daughter's funeral, the grieving mother actually had to worry whether the police cared.

Sellica had trusted Jane. Now her mother was trusting her, too. Despite everything that happened. Jane owed them. This time, she would make things right.

"Of course the police care. Of course they do." Jane held Mrs. Darden's eyes. Promising. Meaning it. "Listen. I know someone on this case. Pretty well. A detective. I'll see what I can find out for you."

"The police already came. A young man, to my house." Mrs. Darden leaned closer, whispering. "He said there was no Bridge Killer."

That was Jake. Had to be. What if Mrs. Darden told him about her and Sellica?

"Leezey? Honey, we're so sorry."

"Sweetie, we're here for you."

Two women, Mrs. Darden's age, gray hair, tweed coats, both in hats with fabric flowers and elaborate feathers, arrived at the top of the steps. One at a time, murmuring their condolences, they hugged their friend.

Jane retreated, grateful for the moment to collect her thoughts. If Mrs. Darden told Jake that Sellica was her source—that might solve her problem. If Jake knew, but not from her, she could talk to him about it. *Right?* Without breaching a confidence. That could change everything. The lawyers, the appeal, the million-dollar judgment.

Maybe Mrs. Darden, not Sellica, was the key to her redemption.

Jane's cell phone vibrated again. The women were still deep in conversation, so she reached into her pocket. A text. From Alex.

Where U? Yr Moira story hot. Big. Need U to go to Springfield. By 7. Lassiter rally. Staying o-nite. U right maybe. Got camera? Call me.

She stared at the screen. Alex was sending her to Springfield? Where Moira said the campaign event was scheduled. They were staying overnight? Of course she had her camera. Of course she was curious, and of course she wanted to see if Moira's suspicions were true. And Archive Gus's photos were still in her car, though she knew the face of the woman in the red coat perfectly, even without them.

What to do? Springfield was straight out the Mass Turnpike, maybe an hour and a half from Boston. If she left now, drove fast, she'd get there in time. But she'd miss the funeral. Which meant she'd miss talking to any-one who might be on the lookout for her. Whoever that would be.

"Jane?"

She looked up, startled at the hissed whisper from behind her, almost dropping her phone. Who knew her name? Was this the person? Someone who had come looking for her? She whirled toward the sound, squint-ing in the semidarkness. A shape came closer, stepping into the light. Jane smiled, stashing her phone. She'd know that shape anywhere. She kept her own voice low, not quite a whisper. It was a funeral, after all.

"Jake Brogan. You've got to stop sneaking up on me. What're you doing here?"

"What are *you*?"

He came up right beside her, standing shoulder to shoulder, closer than an acquaintance should. She loved how his hair curled over his chunky black turtleneck. Loved how he smelled of citrus and pine. Loved how his jeans . . . *Shut up*.

"Just paying my respects," Jane said. Though no one was watching, she edged away, putting some space be-tween them. For her own good. "I'm leaving, actually. I have to go to Springfield. A work thing."

He moved forward, closing the space, eyeing her. "I can't get used to your hair, Janey. But I think I like it. Anyway, I was phoning you. What work thing? You still following Lassiter?"

Jane waved a dismissive hand. She couldn't tell Jake about the Moira thing. But now she had to find out if Jake knew about her and Sellica. How could she ask without giving herself away? *And even if he knew . . .* "No biggie. So, like I said. What're you doing here?"

Jake shrugged back, imitating her.

She narrowed her eyes. Adding it up. "Oh. You're

doing the Bridge Killer. *Oh*." She took a quick look to see if anyone was aware of their conversation. Kept her voice low. "You think Sellica is a victim, don't you? Does that mean now you think there *is* a Bridge Killer? And he—might be here?"

She looked around again. Seemed unlikely, unless the Bridge Killer was a middle-aged woman. Someone's grandmother. Or a priest.

"Jakey?" She dared to touch the sleeve of his leather jacket. No harm in that. "Really. Tell me."

"Listen. I bet I can get you to Springfield on time. Want me to drive you in the cruiser?" Jake covered her hand with his, held them together against his jacket. "Lights and siren. Very sexy. Very fast. You know you love it."

"You're an idiot." *I do, though. Love it. Wish we could . . . but no.* She took her hand away, laughing. "No thanks, bub. I'd like to get there in one piece. Plus, you're working. I'm working. I have to go."

"Jane. Hang on a minute. Listen." He turned to her, straight on. His face had hardened. No more teasing. "Can we go off the record?

Jane laughed again, couldn't help it, poked him in the side with a finger. "What else is new? Our whole life is off the record."

"Seriously. Walk with me." Jake gestured toward the sidewalk.

"Okay, I'm walking. I'm walking seriously." Side by side but separate, they walked together down the steep front steps. No more mourners arriving. The detail cops had gone.

She heard a sound, saw a change in the light. She turned, and saw the church doors closing. The service must be starting.

"Jake, it's—" She stopped. "Do you need to go in?"

"Nope. I'm done here. Listen. Like I said. Can we go off the record?"

At the bottom of the steps, they stood on the sidewalk, alone. From inside the church, a spotlight bloomed, illuminating a multicolored rose window. Splotches of crimson and indigo appeared on the lawn and pavement and parked cars, coloring the twilight.

"Fine. Okay, *Detective Brogan*. Off the record." Jane rolled her eyes, all drama. She shoved her hands into her coat pockets. It was getting colder. And much darker. She was grateful for the streetlights. She wished she could stay with Jake, maybe sneak a dinner, talk awhile, someplace where no one would notice them. But there was no choice. She had to leave. "What's up?"

"Ever hear of an Amaryllis Roldan?"

"Who's that?" Jane flipped through her mental address book. "*R-o-l-d-a-n*? I'm pretty sure I don't know an Amaryllis anything. Who is she?"

"Just do this my way, for once. Sellica ever mention that name to you?"

"Why would Sellica and I have talked?" Jane looked up at him. "Listen. I lost my bosses a million bucks for not telling my source, and now they're my ex-bosses. Why would I discuss it with you?" She paused. They were alone. "Adorable as you are, Jakey. So who's Amaryllis Roldan?"

Jake smiled, acknowledging, but his mind was obviously somewhere else. He fiddled with the heavy metal zipper of his leather jacket, zipping one side up and down as he always did when thinking. The zipping stopped.

"Here's the deal: I know Sellica was your source."

This is it. Jane opened her mouth. Then closed it. *No.* It didn't matter what he knew. She'd made a promise.

Plus, if Jake really respected me, he shouldn't be trying to get me to break that promise. Right? This is the essence of the "Jake and Jane" problem. Proof that a relationship can never work. I'll never know whether he really cares about me, or about his case.

"Jake. I don't care what you say you know." Jane unwrapped her gray silk scarf, doubled it, then looped it back around her neck. "Or what super-secret cop methods you think you can use to get me to say something. I'm done talking about Sellica Darden. Done. I'm going to Springfield. And you should go find the Bridge Killer, or whatever it is you're really supposed to be doing."

She adjusted her shoulder bag, half turned, ready to walk away.

"Janey."

"*What?* Why are you pushing me? You know I can't talk about this. Why are we having this conversation?"

"Think, okay? Why am I here? Why would I care about Sellica being your source?"

Jane turned all the way back, considering. She felt her eyes widen. "Arthur Vick," she said. "You think it's Arthur asshole Vick."

Jake nodded. Barely. But that was a yes.

Jake is the one telling secrets. "Yeah," Jane whispered. "I think it's him, too."

22

Bat out of hell. That's how fast Holly had to drive to get to Springfield in time. She winced, apologized to herself in the rearview mirror as she waited for the stoplight to change. But *bat out of heck* didn't make sense. Besides, there was no one to tell on her for saying bad words. At least she looked like regular Holly again. New makeup, no geeky glasses, her hair puffed up, as it should be. *Much better.* Except she had to hurry. She had to really hurry.

She should have left sooner. But she had to pack and she had to organize and she had to get ready and there was no way to make it happen any faster.

The light must be broken. It had been red too long. Way too long. She clenched her fingers around the steering wheel. Other cars zoomed across the intersection in front of her. *They* were getting to go where they needed to. Why wasn't it *her* turn? She wanted to honk her horn, but that would draw attention to her, and she didn't want that. But what if the light was broken? Maybe she should—

The light changed. Green, thank goodness. Holly shifted into Drive and pushed the accelerator, lurching her rental car through the intersection. She always put it in Park when she stopped, especially on a hill, just in case. This car also had a little digital clock on the dashboard; she loved it, the little numbers changing as she drove, like having a timer. But now her timer showed she would be late.

"Drive. Drive. Drive." She said it out loud. The words sounded reassuring. Owen himself had told her he was going to Springfield. Obviously he told her that on purpose. He wanted her to join him. It was an invitation. Owen invited her. And she was accepting.

Yes, he thought she was Hannah, the little housewife. And that made it even better. Owen was going to be so surprised.

"So very surprised." She said that out loud, too.

Both hands on the steering wheel, ten o'clock–two o'clock, she rounded the curve onto the entry ramp of the Massachusetts Turnpike. *Just keep going straight,* the man at the gas station told her, *all the way to Springfield.* The New Englander Hotel, where Owen told her the event would be, was right by the highway.

She had her camera, safely in a black patent leather bag. She had her best coat and a very cute hat.

She'd mailed the first parcel. The second one was wrapped and ready to go. She'd already left her little gift in Owen's office. They'd find it soon enough.

It had been so easy to get inside the campaign office. Like playing dress-up. Who would ever think frumpy little Hannah was not who she seemed?

She caught a glimpse of herself in her mirror. She looked happy.

Soon, everyone's lives would be very different. Owen Lassiter's, that was for sure. For sure, for sure. Eventually, her own, too. Soon her life would be perfect.

23

"We can't talk about this in front of the church, Jake. It's creepy. And I have to go to Springfield. Like, now. Walk with me to the car, okay? It's over there in the lot."

Jane pointed across the street and took a step off the curb. Fallen leaves padded the pavement, still slick and shiny from the overnight rain. Jake stayed on the sidewalk.

"Jake? You coming?"

"Crosswalk," he said.

"You're such a cop," she said. "You going to arrest me?"

Jake didn't budge. "Aren't you late already?"

Jane hesitated, then stomped back to the sidewalk. As they walked to the corner, it was all she could do to keep from tucking her arm through his. Holding on to a cop seemed like an especially good thing. The darkness. The funeral. The Bridge Killer. *Arthur Vick?* She knew Jake had a gun in his shoulder holster. At this moment, she was grateful for that. She had such a feeling of— wrong.

Lights winked on inside the modest houses lining the street. Some had jack-o'-lanterns on their front porches, candles within showing off exaggerated grins and jagged teeth. Scary was funny on Halloween. But in real life, scary was just plain scary.

"So, listen." Jane kept her voice low. "You actually think Arthur Vick killed Sellica? Or d'you think Arthur Vick is the Bridge Killer? I thought you said there was no Bridge—"

"There isn't." Jake interrupted her. "I'm convinced of that. But I keep thinking about those threatening letters you got after the trial. And it's crossed my mind that—"

They waited for a lone car to pass, its tires hissing through the damp leaves. Then he gestured, *let's go,* and they crossed the two-lane street. The church parking lot was almost full, a waist-high chain-link fence surrounding it, a row of tall metal spotlights down one side cutting through the increasing darkness.

"Jake. You're scaring me. Crossed your mind that what?"

Jake looked around as they entered the parking lot. Peered through the thick plastic window of an obviously empty attendant stand. Checked behind them.

"What are you looking for? You're kind of freaking me out." Jane scrabbled for her keys as they walked. "Here's the car."

Jane aimed her keychain at her car door. It clicked open, the inside lights beeped, the headlights popped on and off. Then her phone rang. She turned, her back to the car, facing Jake head-on.

"Jake? That's gotta be Alex calling. Probably wondering where I am. I don't mean to push, but what are you trying to tell me? You're kind of—stalling. I can tell."

"Okay, listen." Jake's eyes swept the parking lot again, then came back to Jane. "We know Sellica was connected to Arthur Vick. Thing is, now we also know he's connected to another victim." Jake stopped. His head came up. He put out a hand, reached around her for the door handle. Clicked it open.

"Get in the car," he said. "Turn on the engine."

Before Jane could move, the parking lot suddenly got brighter. Lights glinted off the chrome of the outside row of parked cars. Headlights. Jane heard the low rumble of an engine. Getting louder. Closer. Arriving. Slowing.

Jake whirled, facing the street. His hand went inside his jacket. A car pulled into the parking lot and stopped, headlights full on them. He edged in front of Jane, moving her behind him. Her tote bag pushed against her car door, closing it.

It's a parking lot. Jane tried to make sense of what was happening. *Of course someone's driving in. Who does Jake think this is?* If she looked straight at the car, she saw only the glare of headlights. Aimed at them.

She heard the car's door open. Saw someone, a shadow, getting out. The engine kept running, punctuating the dark.

"Boston Police," Jake said, his hand still under his coat. "Stop right there, please."

"You sure no one named Holly Neff has been in here? I'm pretty sure she works for the Lassiter campaign. *N-e-f-f.* Maybe a volunteer."

Matt put both palms on the campaign headquarters reception desk and leaned toward the woman behind the phone console. He was pissed he got here so late. Couldn't believe he'd fallen asleep in the damn hotel room. He'd meant to watch the news only for a minute, figuring he might see her in some story about the Senate race. Next thing he knew, it was almost dark out. He lost, what, four hours? After getting on that early plane? *So* pissed. Luckily the Lassiter campaign office was still open.

The woman's face was redder than her turtleneck. Like some Time–Life operator, she wore a flip-up microphone attached to her telephone headpiece. For someone who was supposed to be working the reception desk, she was far from receptive. After a few worthless minutes trying to convince her, Matt was about to lose it.

"Don't you have a staff list or something you can check?" He patted the pockets of his down vest, pulled out the folded newspaper clipping from his wallet. "I have a photo of her. Maybe that would help."

The woman held up a hand, stopping him. "Sir? Our staff list is private. Our volunteer list is private. I'm sure you can understand it's all for security reasons." She offered him a piece of paper, some campaign flyer thing. "If you'd like to volunteer for the campaign? I can help with that. If you'd like some literature on Governor Lassiter, I'll provide that. But I cannot give information on someone who may or may not work for the campaign. I'm sure you understand."

The woman, Denise, if that was her nameplate on the desk, was trying to get rid of him. *Well, I'm not ready to go.*

This was too important. To him. And maybe to Owen Lassiter.

The phone rang. "Excuse me, please." Then, into the phone, "Lassiter for Senate. May I help you?"

Matt jammed his fists into his vest pockets. He had about ten seconds to make this work. He had to find Holly. He had to stop her.

If the woman in the picture was Holly. It was possible, of course, she wasn't.

What if he just told this Denise the truth? For a moment, he imagined the endgame. *No*. The truth was never gonna fly. Shit. She'd think he was a mental case.

But the woman really didn't seem to recognize Holly's name. Was she using a phony name? *Shit*. Of course. That would make this even more impossible.

On the other hand, he'd seen Holly in that campaign event photo, and a few others he'd dug up online. Maybe to find Holly—he just had to find Owen Lassiter. No problemo.

The telephone rang again, a green light flashing. Then another. "Lassiter for Senate, please hold," the woman said. "Lassiter for Senate, please hold."

She looked up at him, flustered. "I need to handle the phones now. There's no one else to help me. They're all in Springfield at the rally."

"Great." *Exactly.* "Where?"

"Lassiter for Senate, please hold," she said again, then covered the phone. "It's on our Web site, sir. But it starts in less than two hours. You'd never make it."

"Thanks," Matt said. He pulled out his iPhone. Punched up the Internet as he headed for the door.

Never make it? Denise was so wrong. He'd make it. He had to.

24

He had to move Jane out of the way. Get her out of the headlights. What if Arthur Vick wanted to scare Jane, make her miserable? What if he'd sent her those ugly letters, and now . . . what if Vick thought Mrs. Darden had told Jane something about him and Sellica?

"If I say get down, *do* it," he hissed. He eased in front of her, his hand on his holster. So close to Jane, he could feel her body tremble. "I mean it."

At the parking lot entrance, the new arrival was still a shadow. Car engine chugging. Headlights blasting. Whoever it was could see them. No way out of that. He couldn't see them for shit.

The person took a step toward them. Both hands out. No gun. *Probably.*

Jake clicked his weapon another fraction out of the holster. "Boston PD," he said. "State your business. Now."

"Don't shoot, Jake," the silhouetted voice said.

A woman? Laughing? His mind struggled to process it.

"You'd never live it down if you killed a reporter," the woman said. "Tell him, roomie."

"Oh, my god," Jane whispered. "It's Tuck."

"Tuck?"

"Tuck!" Jane's voice cut through the darkness. "You kidding me?"

Jake felt Jane's body relax. He tried to take a step forward, but she had grabbed the back of his jacket. Shaking loose, Jake stomped out from between the cars, one finger jabbing the air. "Tuck, you incredible moron. I could have—" Jake stopped. Slapped his hands against his sides. "What's the matter with you? You got a death wish?"

"Hey, I'm just covering the funeral, and I'm late." She gave an elaborate shrug, both hands in the air. "Trying to park. Is that suddenly illegal? Whoa, you two. You look like— Am I missing something here?"

"Holy crap, Tuck." Jake was shaking his head. "You're the last person I thought . . ."

"Holy crap, Tuck," Jane said at the same time. "I about had a heart attack. How'd you know we were here?"

"Didn't," Tuck said. "What're you doing here, anyway? Alex thinks you're on the way to Springfield. To the Lassiter thing."

"Just came to pay my respects," Jane said. She looked at Jake. "And I met up with Detective Brogan. By chance."

"I see," Tuck said. She looked at him, then at Jane, then back at him. "Gotcha."

Her headlights had clicked off, and now he could see her, jeans and a leather jacket, slim leather boots, a black cap yanked over her hair.

She walked to him, almost a swagger, slung one arm across his shoulders. As if he hadn't just come close to shooting her. *A real piece of work.*

"And how about you, Detective Brogan, might I ask?" Tuck said. She lined her body against his, enough so he could tell. "You just here to pay your respects, too?"

He took a step back, surprised.

She laughed softly, her voice barely carrying. Hands on hips, she narrowed her eyes at him. "I'm wondering what to make of seeing you here, Jake. Something I should know about the Bridge Killer? That why you're all on edge?"

"Tuck?" Jane approached them. "I'm leaving for Springfield now. Just got Alex's page. I'll talk to him from the road." She aimed her key-clicker at her car door again. "*Detective Brogan,* thanks for walking me to my car."

"Yeah. No problem." Jake wanted to signal her somehow: *Call me.* He needed to warn her, at least get her guard up. Plus, he'd never told her the deal with Amaryllis Roldan. With Tuck in the picture, that was no longer an option.

Jane'd be okay in Springfield. She had to be. The Bridge Killer was in Boston.

Somewhere.

25

"What was that name?" Jane said it aloud, willing her brain to remember. She eyed the stupid eighteen-wheeler she was trying to pass. He was hogging the fast lane on the Mass Pike, and if he didn't move his ass to let her by, she'd be late. She checked the digital clock on her dashboard. *Ouch.* Even later than she already was.

A huge latte in her cup holder and a last-resort drive-thru burrito in her lap—dinner—she watched for her chance. She tapped a finger on the steering wheel, replaying the conversation. Jake had said a name, a woman's name. She even spelled it. And he had told her the other victim was connected to Arthur Vick. She had to remember.

Hitting the accelerator, she eased her TT into the middle lane, gunned it to eighty, then zoomed in front of the truck. The big rig behind her got smaller and smaller. Oh, yes, she'd make it in time.

So. *The name.* Amber something. Amber Rowan. No. Not exactly Amber.

Maybe she should call Jake. He'd tried to tell her something, she could tell, but she bet he couldn't say it in front of Tuck. If only they'd had time to finish their conversation.

Jane took a bite of burrito, not bad, actually, since she was completely starving, then peeled down the paper wrapper with her teeth. She knew she could dredge up the name. It was in there somewhere.

What was it? And what did it mean?

From the depths of her tote bag beside her on the front seat, she heard the trill of her phone. *Jake, maybe.* She laid the burrito back onto its waxed paper wrapper, flipped the yellow cheese bits off her coat, then hit the hands-free button on the center console.

"This is Jane."

"Alex." His voice squawked through the speakers. "You in the car?"

"Yup," Jane said. Thank goodness she was on the way. "I tried to call you, right? You got my message?"

"Yup," Alex said. "You almost there? You get the info about the event? At the New Englander Hotel, Gus says. You know where that is?"

"Yup." Jane had taken a bite of burrito, forgetting she was on the phone. She tried to talk around it. "What's the scoop?"

"Huh? You're breaking up."

"Yeah, sorry." She swallowed. "Headed west on the Mass Pike. Reception stinks." She regretfully moved the burrito to the seat beside her. It would be inedible cheesy glue in about ten seconds. "Anyway, what's the plan?"

"There's some kind of rally, I have Gus checking on the deets. Apparently the candidate's staying overnight. Moira tell you that? She's still home, right?"

"Yeah, far as I know, she's home. No, she didn't tell me that. Pretty interesting."

"That's what I thought, too. Gus made you a reservation at the hotel, just in case. Hope you have a toothbrush."

A toothbrush? Whatever. She'd manage. It wasn't like she was going to Siberia. "Sure. No prob. So—"

"Hang on, my other line. Can you hold a sec?"

Jane reached for the burrito. "Sure."

Alex had a point about the overnight thing, although if Lassiter were trying to hide some assignation, he'd cook up a big plan, right? Make it all look plausible? No surprises? Or maybe surprises were good. How would she know what a cheating husband would do? Maybe she should ask Alex. He was the one who might be having—

"I'm back. Sorry." Alex sounded glum. "Where were we? Oh yeah, Moira didn't know."

Jane swallowed again, quickly. "Yeah, well, what do you think someone having an affair would do?" Lucky he couldn't see her face. Then again, maybe it was Alex's wife who was cheating. Not him. That's why he was so upset these days. Maybe that had been his wife on the phone, telling him she had to be out of town, suddenly, overnight. Although this was not the time to be thinking about Alex's marital problems. "They'd have some elaborate explanation set up, right? Not tell the wife at the last minute they suddenly had to be out of town."

Alex didn't answer.

"Alex? You there?"

"Yeah, someone at the door. Hang on."

Jane strained to translate the sounds coming over the speakers. Frustratingly, the transmission was all fuzz and muffle. And some jerk driving a souped-up Dodge took that very moment to honk at her. Jane gave him the look. *Idiot.*

"So, Jane." Alex's voice, back on the line, sounded different. "You were at Sellica's funeral? How come? I had no idea you were going. Tuck's here. Says she saw you."

Did she, now? Thanks, sister. "Ah, yeah, just paying my respects."

"Why?" Alex asked. "That's not your assignment, Jane. You wanted nothing to do with it. Since she's not your source, of course."

Jane could do without the sarcasm. Time to change the subject. Get back in Alex's good graces. Her "six-month tryout" at the *Register* had barely begun, and newspaper jobs were disappearing faster than . . . "Listen, Alex. I'm getting close to Springfield, so gotta wrap up. But Jake was there at the funeral, too. And he's on the Bridge Killer thing."

"Yes, I already know that. From Tuck. Because Tuck is covering the Bridge Killer case. Just as she was assigned. And Jake told Tuck—"

Alex's voice disappeared. Then returned. "But we're going with it anyway. Tuck says she's sure Sellica's a Bridge Killer victim."

"Sorry, Alex, my call waiting beeped in. The voice mail picked up. I missed what you said."

"I said: Jake's telling Tuck that Sellica's death is not connected to the others. But Tuck thinks the cops are lying. Water, bridge, female, no ID. So the *Register* is going with Sellica as the third victim. The only one who's identified. Not that it has anything to do with you. As you'd be the first to say."

If she was a reporter in her next life, she was never ever having anything be off the record. Never. Or maybe, in journalism hell, everything was off the record. Journalism hell, where you knew a bunch of amazing stuff that you could never tell anyone. Maybe that was now.

"Jane? You hearing me?"

"Yes, I'm hearing you. Listen, Alex." She crossed her fingers, hoping this wasn't a mistake. But Alex was clearly angry with her, seemed to have already forgotten she was the one who brought him the Moira scoop. Anger was not good for her job security.

A quarter mile till the exit. Now or never. *Never* was probably the wiser choice. But *now* was what she decided.

"Let's put it this way. I hear there might be an ID on one of the Bridge Killer victims."

"Yeah, duh. Sellica," Alex said.

"No, Alex. Not Sellica." Jane paused. "The other woman."

Roldan, her brain announced. *Roldan. Amaryllis Roldan.*

"An ID? What other woman? Which one?" Alex demanded. "How do you know? Who's the victim?"

Jane yanked the car onto the exit ramp, sloshing latte through the narrow hole in the cup lid. The burrito rolled onto the floor. The New Englander Hotel was around the next curve, barely visible behind a stand of giant pine trees.

"I don't know," she said. And she didn't really, she only knew Amaryllis Roldan was a name that Jake told her, off the record. She didn't know who that was. Or why Jake asked her about it. But he'd said the name, and the word *victim,* and the name *Arthur Vick,* and it was all connected. Somehow. "Get Tuck to ask someone at the cop shop about it. But not Jake, okay? Not Jake."

She pulled into the hotel parking lot. Searched for a spot among the wall-to-wall cars, many plastered with Lassiter bumper stickers. *I've gotten into trouble before for not telling. Will I get into trouble now for telling?* This was exactly why she and Jakey couldn't be together. It was impossible to sort out responsibilities and priorities and—sure, Jake had said "off the record."

But why would he tell her in the first place, if he didn't want her to do something about it?

She was going to tell. And hope she wasn't blowing up her life.

"Amaryllis Roldan," she said. A chill went down her back. "But remember, Alex. The name didn't come from me."

26

Holly rolled the waistband of her black skirt once, to make it shorter. Why not? She checked her handiwork in the full-length mirror attached to the bathroom door of her room at the New Englander. She'd gotten the last room, she was told. They were full up now. "Lucky you," the hotel clerk had said.

Exactly.

Holly nodded, approving, as she assessed herself in the glass. The rally was inside. Perfect. Black skirt, black tights, bright *bright* green silk blouse with a lacy camisole underneath. Lassiter campaign button on her wide stretchy belt. She flipped her head from side to side, watching her hair, all curled and shiny now, swish back and forth like one of those TV commercials for shampoo. Nice. Nice new Holly. No more drabby old Hannah. Tonight she was pretty Holly.

She tried putting her hair behind her ear on one side, one curl twirling down her cheek. No. Maybe one side up? With a green ribbon? No. It was fine. There wasn't time to change it again. She was perfect.

Camera. All set. Battery charged. Flash good to go. Into her purse. Everything else, ready.

She slid the flat key card into a side pocket of her bag,

checked again to make sure it was still there, then headed down the hallway to the elevator. She was supposed to go to the ninth floor, then take the special Skyview elevator to ten, where the rally was about to begin. She pushed the button, and pushed it again, her heart lifting with what she hoped would happen.

Owen would be so surprised.

She just. Could *not*. Wait.

"The rally is where? Tenth floor? Inside? Really? I thought it was outside." Jane slid her credit card across the hotel reception desk. The lobby was buzzing with Lassiter supporters, if funny hats and WE GO OWEN signs were any indication. Looked like a snafu of some kind at the elevators. One was marked OUT OF SERVICE, roped off with plastic tape. A crowd of impatient-looking rally-goers elbowed for space in the two still operating. No one looked happy.

Jane raised a hand, waving, recognizing that cute guy from the campaign—Trevor. Trevor Kiernan. But he didn't see her. He focused on his clipboard, checking something. Assigning people to elevators. Seemed like a mess.

"Miss Ryland?" The desk clerk, a wiry young woman, all slicked-back hair and empty holes along each ear-lobe, wore a gold plastic name tag reading HI, I'M GINA ORTICELLI. She handed Jane a folder of papers and a blue key card. Whispered, "You're room 916."

"Oh, thanks, and—"

"Um, are you covering this for Channel Eleven?" The clerk's eyes were wide, admiring. "I'm such a fan of yours. I completely love your new hair. I'm Gina. I hope you don't mind me saying."

"Oh, well, I—" Did Jane have to explain it? Which

was worse, having to deal with the looks of pity? Or having to explain when they didn't know the whole sad story?

Gina leaned over the desk, one hand above her mouth, conspiratorial. "I'm a Gable person, I don't mind telling you. Ellie's such a rock star. And I'm thinking I might have a story for you. This whole Lassiter thing has been disaster city. Can we go off the record?"

Jane almost burst out laughing. *Off the record?* What was this, everybody thought they were on *60 Minutes*? On the other hand, hotel clerks were privy to some inside stuff.

"Sure, Gina, off the record," she said. She stepped closer to the desk, giving Gina 100 percent. "I'm so flattered you recognized me."

Gina turned, checking behind her. A door marked ADMINISTRATIVE OFFICES was closed. At the other end of the counter, Jane saw another clerk, arguing with some red-faced guy wearing a Lassiter button. Fifteen minutes until the rally was supposed to begin upstairs. And the lobby still teeming with Lassiter people. Not good.

"Okay," Gina said. "Hand me back your registration papers. We can pretend to talk about that."

Jane struggled to hide her smile. Cloak and dagger in Springfield, Mass. Well, you never knew.

Gina pointed, dramatically, to something on the papers in front of her. "First of all," she said, her voice low. "This rally thing was so last minute. That guy over there? End of the counter? He's insisting they reserved a block of rooms, and the Special Pavilion for an afternoon rally today. But they didn't. Reserve anything. Anyway, now the opticians have the Pav, and the Lassiter people have to go upstairs. That guy, Maitland or something, is making a huge stink. Like it's the hotel's fault. But it isn't. The Lassiter campaign never reserved anything."

"So that's why it's now at seven o'clock? Upstairs?"

"Yeah, they had to change everything. It's already running late. And then the room reservation mess. We gave Lassiter the presidential suite, lucky that was open. Campaign types got the other vacancies. And you got one of the last regular rooms. We're completely full up now. I mean, if they can't set up a simple rally, how can they run the country?"

Rory Maitland, Jane thought. Hotshot consultant. A supposed insider who didn't seem too clued in to reality. The big question was, who else was a last-minute overnight guest?

"You're so observant," Jane said. Gina looked proud of herself. Exactly what Jane was going for. "The campaign does seem somewhat disorganized. Did lots of Lassiter people show up at the last minute?"

Gina cocked her head down the counter. "Maitland, for sure. Maybe a few others. And a secretary type. They were all so mad, you know? The guy with the clipboard?" Gina stuck a thumb toward the elevator.

Trevor.

"He's taking the heat," Gina said.

Holy moly. A secretary? It couldn't be this easy. *How to phrase this*—"Ah. So eventually there were rooms enough for everyone?"

"Yeah, barely. Like I said, you got one of the last ones. Most of the Lassiter people are on nine. We had to give the campaign the Skyview for the rally. Smaller, not so accessible, but that's what we had."

"I know Governor Lassiter, of course." Jane tried again. "And Mr. Maitland, and the guy with the clipboard. But the secretary? A woman? Like, a press secretary? I'm trying to figure out if I know her. Is her name Sheila King?"

Gina glanced around again. Gave Jane a fleeting wink, then tapped on the computer keyboard in front of her. "Of course, Miss Ryland, I'm happy to see whether we have availability at our other location." Her voice was louder, as if wanting to be overheard.

Jane watched the clerk's fingers move across the keyboard. The computer screen faced Gina, so Jane couldn't see what the desk clerk was actually looking up. With one quick move, Gina flipped the screen around.

"As you can see, Miss Ryland." She tapped the screen with a silver pen. "Does this look like the type of accommodations you had in mind?"

Jane peered at the monitor. It looked like a registration form, like the one she just filled out. But this was for room 981. And Gina's pen was tapping at the name of the person registered to stay there. Kenna Wilkes. *Mrs.* Kenna Wilkes.

Commotion at the other end of the counter. The door marked ADMINISTRATIVE OFFICES opened. A man in a navy blazer emerged. Frowning.

Gina twirled the monitor away, tapped the keyboard, looked up at Jane. "Will there be anything else, Miss Ryland?"

Not Sheila King. Kenna Wilkes. Mrs. Kenna Wilkes. *Mrs.?* Was there a Mr. Wilkes?

Was Kenna Wilkes the woman in the red coat? One easy way to find out—show the very helpful Gina the archive photos. But they were in the car, and Jane had to get to the rally. Still, if the red-coat woman was at this rally, too, it made sense that Jane had just discovered her name. She could always show Gina the photos later. *Thank you, journalism gods.*

"You've been so helpful, Miss Orticelli," Jane said. She had to call Alex. Figure out what to tell Moira. Figure out who the heck Kenna Wilkes was. And what she wanted. "Are you working later tonight?"

"Nope," Gina said. "But I'll be here in the morning."

Damn. Jane eyed the crowd at the elevator. She had to go. She looked at Gina, then waved a hand around her own head. "Curly hair? Semi-gorgeous?" Jane hoped the clerk would understand what she was asking.

"Totally," Gina said. "You got it."

27

"Inside? This thing is inside?"

Kenna could tell Owen Lassiter was not happy. She'd heard about his temper, of course, wondered if she was about to see it in action. *That'd be educational.* Edging into the corner of the elevator, she pretended to read the restaurant ad on the dark-paneled wall, as if giving him and Maitland some privacy. Whatever chaos was already under way at this rally, she didn't care. She was here, and Owen was here, and exactly where some event was being held was hardly the point. Her plans were the same.

She sneaked a look at the two men. So opposite. Owen all pinstripes and foulard, silver and tall. Looking down at the stubby, bumbling Rory.

The elevator pinged on four. The doors opened. Three or four people tried to step in, but Rory stuck out an arm. "Sorry, folks, take the next one," he said. "Thanks so much."

Kenna could hear protests fading as the doors swished closed. The elevator continued up. Poor Owen seemed even angrier.

"Christ, Rory. What the hell? What happened to our

security? We're running so late. This whole thing is a nightmare."

"Governor, frankly, I'm not sure what happened. Trevor Kiernan booked the place, then I followed up. We were supposed to have the venue called the, uh—" Rory checked some notebook, gave her a fast look. "—the Pavilion. This afternoon. But the jerks at the desk insist it was rented already. I'll ream Trevor a new one—excuse me, Kenna. But for now, we're gonna have to make do."

The elevator stopped on five. More passengers attempted to join them. Rory hit the button, closed the door in their faces. "Thanks, folks," he said.

"What gives with these elevators?" Owen grimaced, clearly annoyed. "I hate to keep people out."

"Security, Governor," Maitland said. "They understand. These folks are hardly undecideds, after all. They're Lassiter do or die. Big givers. A-listers. Or they wouldn't be here. And—"

"All the more reason. Kiernan said people were still lined up in the lobby. If they don't make it to the rally, we don't get the campaign dollars." Owen was full steam ahead, ignoring Rory's explanations. Kenna had never seen him like this. Annoyed, brusque, demanding. Maybe the campaign stress was getting to him. He'd napped during the car ride from Boston. So she and Rory had gotten to chat a bit. Carefully, so they didn't wake him.

"The place is full of opticians, a national board meeting or some such," Owen went on. "Not even all from Massachusetts, for godsake. Why the hell did we come here? Maybe do more harm than good. This close to the election. Waste of time. Maitland, you called Moira, right? I never got through."

"Governor, do you mind if I stop at the suite?" Kenna stepped forward, pushed the button for nine. "Rory gave me a key. I need to pick up one more batch of campaign literature."

"Ah, Mrs. Wilkes. I fear you're not seeing us at our best." Owen turned to her with a rueful smile. "But Rory said you wanted the inside look. That's certainly what you're getting. In a campaign, anything can happen."

The elevator stopped with a shudder; the doors slid open. Empty hallway.

Kenna laughed, head back, then touched the candidate on the arm of his suit jacket. "It'll take more than some rally to get rid of me, Governor. I'll see you soon."

She knew she saw his eyes light up as the elevator door closed behind her.

Jane dragged herself around the last stairway landing, grabbing the railing and puffing for breath. Eight floors up, then nine. If she waited for the elevator, she'd never get there. Someone said the campaign commandeered one of the elevators, leaving only one to handle the entire buzzing pack of Lassiter supporters. Some, she saw, had taken off their buttons and funny hats and headed for the parking lot. Gina was right about this. *A mess.*

Into the hallway, following the painted arrows toward the Skyview Room, almost at a run. One of the silver elevator doors swished open. And there was Owen Lassiter. Looking pretty unhappy. And Rory Maitland, if she had it right.

Perfect timing, for her at least. Something finally worked.

"Governor Lassiter." Jane stopped, hand outstretched. She gulped, catching her breath. "I'm Jane Ryland from—"

"The *Register* now. Yes, I know," Lassiter said. He shook her hand, using both of his. "We've met before, of course. Great to see you. You know Rory Maitland? Power behind the—"

"Hey, Jane," Maitland said. "So we're looking good here, right? Up in the polls, your paper says? Eleanor Gable's campaign collapsing?"

Not exactly, Jane thought. *And this rally fiasco ain't gonna help.* Jane looked around. No sign of Kenna Wilkes. She was probably arriving at the event separately. The prudent thing to do.

"Mrs. Lassiter joining you here?" Jane aimed her question at the candidate. Risky, maybe, but Lassiter didn't know what she knew. What his own wife had told her.

Maitland stepped between them. He held up a cell phone. "Governor? Time to go in. We'll use the front door tonight. Not the back entrance. It'll look terrific. Man of the people. We're going in to 'Yankee Doodle Dandy.' Security is all in place, no worries. You set?" Maitland took the candidate by the arm, escorting him away. "Sorry, Jane. Any scheduling questions, call our press office. Sheila King. You know the drill."

A roar of applause and a blare of music. Jane scurried behind Lassiter and Maitland as they entered through the double doors marked SKYVIEW, but two blue-jacketed guards, rent-a-cops, stepped in front of her, blocking her way as soon as she tried to follow them. The music was already deafening, bouncing off the walls. People elbow to elbow. Everyone talking.

"We're full up," one of the guards said. "Fire regs. No more room. We have to keep the doors closed. Sorry, miss."

"Press," Jane said. She held up the plastic pass she'd clipped to a webbed lanyard around her neck.

"Good for you," the other guard said. "We're still full."

No way. *No way. This is all I need.* Jane's stomach

clenched as she panicked for a solution. She could picture telling Alex, *Oh yeah, I was there, but I arrived too late to get in.*

"Ow-en Lass-i-ter!" A voice bellowed through the PA system, even louder than the music. "The next senator from the Commonwealth of Mass-a-chu-setts!"

"Maitland!" Jane pushed forward, trying to grab the consultant's sport coat. "They're saying the room is full!" she yelled, waving to show Maitland the situation. "But I have to—"

The crowd, shoulders touching, was cheering, waving, vying for access. Hands reached out to touch the candidate, shake hands with him, get his attention. Silver confetti and green balloons floated from the ceiling.

The blue-jacketed obstacle in her path threw out a gloved paw. "Miss, I told you, we're full." He rolled his eyes at Maitland. "Sorry, sir."

Maitland waved him off. "She's with us." He indicated a small riser on the opposite side of the room. "Press over there. You owe us, Ryland."

Lassiter and Maitland were consumed by the throng of cheering supporters, almost carried toward the stage in a surge of green and white. Soon, all Jane could see were Lassiter's pin-striped arms in the air, waving in political salute to those who swarmed around him.

Jane snaked past the guards, the doors clicking closed behind her. She couldn't cut across the room to the press section. Much too crowded. She remembered all the Lassiter supporters still waiting downstairs. How annoyed were *they* gonna be? What a mess.

Edging along the wall, she held her breath to squeeze by. *Red-coat woman would certainly not be wearing her coat in this oven.* Luckily Jane had dumped her own at the bell desk. Elbows poked her, bodies pressed against her, jockeying for position. *And if one more person steps on my feet . . .*

" 'Scuse me, 'scuse me," she muttered. Maybe on tip-toe she'd go faster. Using the wall for balance and hugging her purse to her chest, she edged closer to the press platform. Lassiter was onstage, palms down, trying, not terribly hard, to quiet the continuing cheers.

It was way too hot. *Way too crowded.* Jane made it to the end of the first wall. Took a deep breath. The press riser was just ahead, only about a million people blocking her way there. Three television cameras on tripods poked up from the wooden platform, logos from the Western Mass stations. No one from Boston. At least it was a foot or so off the ground, so once up there she could get a better view. Maybe even breathe.

"Ladies and gentlemen, I'm so proud to be your candidate." Lassiter's voice boomed through the speakers, making the one mounted in the corner above Jane rattle with the volume and intensity. Cheers erupted—so loud, the wall behind her started shaking.

Spooked, she turned, stepped away. And backed into someone.

"Oh, sorry," she said, voice raised, almost tripping on her own feet to turn around. She pointed to the press riser, then her press pass, apologizing. "It's so crowded. Just trying to get to the—"

A young woman in a Lassiter boater, too much jewelry, and a row of multicolored campaign buttons looked her up and down. "You're still on TV?" she said. "I thought you—"

"C'mon, Melissa, we need to get closer." A prepped-out young man, also in Lassiter hat and button array, grabbed the young woman by the arm, drawing her through the crowd.

No red-coat girl. No one she recognized.

"Thank you so much for being here," Lassiter's voice picked up again. "I know you agree with me, this election . . ."

Two more steps to the riser. She dumped her tote bag on the platform, then, grateful for her flat boots, hauled herself up. Three camera guys grabbed their tripods and turned to her, glaring. "Watch it, we're rolling tape," one scolded. "You're shaking the whole thing."

"Sorry," she said again. *Damn.* "My bad." She tried not to move as she dug into her tote bag for a notebook and pencil. As long as the cameras were rolling, she was stuck up here.

And there was the woman she'd been searching for. *There she absolutely is.*

Smack in the center of the crowd, head bobbing, arms raised in applause, edging toward the front. There was no mistaking that curly hair, that high-wattage smile. Even without the coat, Jane knew that face from the photos.

And now she also knew her name. Kenna Wilkes. The other woman.

Jane jumped from the platform, ignoring the hostile yelps from the photogs behind her. "Sorry," she called out. Not looking back. Headed across the room, eyes on the curly-haired prize.

"Sorry, press, sorry, sorry," she repeated, not caring, squeezing behind some people, in front of others. Everyone else was focused on Lassiter. She focused on the curly hair, moving forward, toward the podium. Jane scrabbled in her purse, unseeing, trying to get at her little camera.

She wasn't losing her this time.

"Recalculating. When possible, please make a legal U-turn." Incredible, in-frigging-credible. For fifty cents,

Matt would throw the frigging GPS and its robo-voice out the car window. No doubt the rental company would charge him out the ass for it.

Matt yanked the steering wheel, floored the accelerator, and swerved his midsize across three lanes of the Mass Turnpike for the exit. The traffic had been total hell, some moron had a flat in front of him, a lane closed, construction, every friggin' possible obstacle. A blast of horns behind him protested his abrupt move. He flipped them the finger. Assholes.

How hard could it be to get to Springfield, for godsake? *You can't miss it,* the rental car kid told him. Straight out the Pike, get off when the GPS tells you. He'd gotten the last car in the lot, the kid said, and Matt had hardly listened to the rest of the spiel about insurance and return policies as he signed the papers, grabbed the keys, hit the road. Now it was pitch dark, he'd been driving for frigging hours in the boonies, and the GPS was sending him god knew where, anywhere but the New Englander Hotel.

"Recalculating." The GPS voice, taunting, sounded like something from a bad spy movie. Like the universe was trying to keep him from doing what he had to do. Trying to keep him from protecting Owen Lassiter.

But the universe was not gonna win. *He* was. It was his turn.

28

"She's his wife. She's not gonna tell the truth if it's gonna get her husband nailed for murder." Jake yanked open his cruiser door and stepped into the Beacon Market parking lot.

"True dat." DeLuca tossed his coffee cup in a trash can, then followed Jake toward the entrance of the store's Brighton location.

Nighttime, spotlights, metal shopping carts scattered like tumbleweeds across the yellow-stenciled pavement. Not many cars at this time on a Saturday night. But Arthur Vick's grocery stores were always open. "We're here for twenty-four and, if you need it, more," his chorus of store clerks sang in those annoying ads.

"But she says her husband was with her on the nights of both murders," DeLuca continued. "Plus Sellica's. That's Patricia Vick's story. And she's stickin' to it."

"They always stick to it." Jake shrugged. "Until we prove they're lying. Then it's adios, hubby, nice to know ya."

The glass double doors swished open. Tinkling buy-me-now Muzak and a wind chill factor of forty hit them as they entered. Glaring fluorescents, buzzing, made it instant daytime. That stale meat smell. Vegetables. A guy with a mop pretending to do the stain-streaked flooring.

"See why Vick's such a moneybags," DeLuca muttered. "Low overhead."

"He gonna be here? Or who?" Jake looked around. Glad he got most of his food from the pizza place near his apartment. *Jane loves pizza.* He shook off the thought. She'd be fine. Especially if Vick was on his way here. "What'd he tell you?"

"He said eight P.M. Here. That's now."

Jake waved toward the counter. "After you. But I don't see Vick."

"Maybe this lovely young lady will know." DeLuca cocked a thumb at a clerk with almost-orange hair. She was leaning against a cash register, black-rimmed eyes staring at the empty aisles.

"Miss?" Jake flipped his badge wallet open, closed it, put it away. "I'm Detective Jake Brogan, Boston Police. This is my associate, Officer DeLuca. And you are?"

She touched the name tag on her electric blue smock. "Olive."

"Olive. In a grocery store." DeLuca smiled at her. "You get that a lot?"

"Don't mind him, miss," Jake said. Good cop. "We're looking for Mr. Vick. Have you seen him tonight?"

"Is this about the change machine?" the girl said. Almost a whine. A silver ring pierced her lower lip. "It's broken, that's all. Sometimes it doesn't work right. I only know because—"

"Miss?" Jake interrupted. He could hear DeLuca trying not to laugh. "It's not about the change machine, okay? It's about Sellica Darden."

Jake saw the girl's face go wary. She even took a step

back, away from them. DeLuca cleared his throat softly. Jake shot him a glance. *I get it.*

"So you know her." Jake scratched an ear. Casual, casual. "How? She work here, with you? How about Amaryllis Roldan?"

Olive looked between them, back and forth. Settled on Jake. "I don't know," she said.

"Don't know what, Olive? Don't know if you know her? Or don't know whether she worked here?"

"Nothing," Olive said. "I don't know anything."

"I think that's unlikely, Miss—? What's your last name?" Jake took out a notebook and clicked open his ballpoint. "And I'll need your current address."

"How long've you worked here, Olive?" DeLuca took a step forward, getting in her space, one hand on the counter. "You like your job? You think you're gonna keep it by covering up for your boss?"

"Am I under arrest?" The girl's eyes went hard.

"You got some experience with that, miss? Being arrested?" DeLuca was doing bad cop. "Easy for me to find out."

"Don't mind him," Jake said. Good cop. "Listen, Olive, you need to answer our questions. Truthfully. About Sellica. About Amaryllis. You can talk to us here, or down at the station."

"Or she can tell you to get the hell out of here."

The door had opened behind Olive. Arthur Vick held on to the knob with one hand, his other propped against the doorjamb. Tie loose, French cuffs hanging, one lock of dark hair falling over his forehead. His shirt pocket was monogrammed with an elaborate *AV.*

Guilty, Jake thought. Of something. Vick looked just like his TV ads. Only—guiltier.

"You hear me, Officers? Think I didn't hear everything

you said? You're out of line, you two." Vick waved a flat palm, dismissing. His gold wedding band caught the light. "Miss Parisella, you can go. You're done here. You don't have to say a word to them."

"Thank you, Mr. Vick," she said. She half lifted a partition in the counter and started to duck underneath it.

"Not so fast, Miss *Parisella*." Jake raised a hand. The girl stopped, still bent over, and backed out from under the counter.

She looked at Jake, *daggers*. Then at Vick, *pleading*. She kept one hand on the semiraised partition. Half in, half out.

"Arthur Vick? I'm Detective Jake Brogan. And this is my associate, Paul DeLuca. We had an appointment, I believe?" Jerk thought he was Mr. Big. Jake would let him have it, both barrels. What was true didn't actually matter at this juncture. "I assume you'd be eager to have your staff help us catch a serial killer. Before he strikes again. Before he kills another one of your employees. Like Miss Parisella here."

Olive gasped. She dropped the partition. It clunked into place and she jumped at the echoing sound, putting both hands to her mouth. Now Jake could see only her eyes.

This girl was terrified.

29

"Kenna! Kenna Wilkes!" Jane could almost reach out and touch her. She could see the ringlets in her cloud of shining hair, the sparkle of her just-too-big chandelier earrings as they caught the lights. Lassiter had chosen this moment to do his man-of-the-people, down-into-the-crowd move. Which, Jane now knew, was not so spontaneous as it had appeared when she first saw him try it back in Boston. Lassiter's sudden proximity made the rallyers explode into another wave of adulation. Kenna couldn't possibly hear Jane's voice, not even yelling as loud as she did. One more time. "Kenna!"

But the woman was moving, weaving steadily forward through the audience of boater hats and signs on sticks. No matter how Jane almost-pushed into the churning crowd, she couldn't manage to get any closer than three people away. *When she reaches the stage, she'll be trapped. I'll catch up, and I'll nail her. Game over.*

Odd, though, Jane thought, heading toward her quarry. Almost too easy. *Moira drops the bombshell. I get sent to Springfield. Gina tells me about Kenna. And there she is.* The old "too good to be true" thing they warned you about in J-school. No valuable story came easy. And this one—well, almost had.

I cannot be wrong again.

Damn it. Not wrong *again.* Just wrong.

The music blared; the crowd sang along, some locking arms, gleeful, almost marching in place. *If I hear "Yankee Doodle Dandy" one more time . . .* And there she was. Kenna. Almost close enough to—

"Kenna!" Jane yelled, and felt her voice get swallowed by the din.

The woman kept heading for the stage. *Not so fast, sister.*

Jane took two quick steps forward, found an open space, powered ahead. She reached out and touched Kenna on the shoulder. "Hey!"

Kenna whirled, turned to face her. She was, as Gina said, totally gorgeous. Luminous eyes, high cheekbones, all lip gloss and big lashes. A pear-shaped diamond nestled at her throat. She looked at Jane, skeptical, a flash of annoyance darkening her porcelain features. Then it disappeared, replaced by a blazing smile.

"Jane? *Jane Ryland?*" she said. She moved toward Jane as if coming in for a close-up. "From TV? I can't believe you're actually here. How perfect!"

Well, well, Jane thought. *She recognizes me. And if she thinks I'm still on TV, fine.*

"Yes." Big smile. "I'm Jane Ryland. How lovely of you to recognize me. Are you Kenna Wil—?"

The woman leaned closer, her mouth almost touching Jane's ear.

Jane's nose wrinkled at her dense perfume, Opium, maybe, or Angel.

"Isn't Owen Lassiter wonderful? I mean, wonderful? I've seen him a million times. Look at him, oh, now he's way over there! I can't wait to vote for him. I wish I could vote for him a million times."

I wish I had my notebook out, Jane thought. *And my camera. But there's time. This girl's all mine now.*

"Well, that's so interesting, because—" Jane took a step back from her, assessing. She'd expected some level of pursuit, not to have the elusive Kenna latch on to her like some local news groupie. But that could be useful.

"Are you covering the rally? Where's your photographer? Do you need a sound bite?" Kenna actually fluffed her hair, and though her glistening lipstick was flawless, she swirled her tongue over her upper teeth. Suddenly she paused, mid-preen. She blinked a few times. "Um, Jane? Wait. Were you looking for me?" She tapped her own chest with a pink fingernail. "Why?"

"Why was I looking for you?" *Okay, then.* Jane was going to have to face this sooner rather than later. "Well, I— Ow!"

"Here he comes, here he comes!" Some guy with a sweat mustache jabbed Jane in the back, gesturing and pointing as he yelled. She turned. So did Kenna. So did everyone else.

All eyes focused on Owen Lassiter. His elegant face was flushed with heat but radiating confidence, one hand raised, the other manhandled by voters needing one more handshake or one more autograph. The swirl of people ebbed and flowed around him as the pod of security, candidate in the middle, crabbed across the floor. The crowd seemed to change shape and density, swelling and pushing, cheering and noise and outstretched arms, heat rising from the pack. Bodies jockeyed for position, for access. Jane stood her ground, ignoring the shoves and the shoulders and the jostling.

The candidate was heading right for them. What would he do when he got to Kenna? How would he greet her? This was about to be a real moment.

No way could they keep some look from their eyes, no matter how they tried to fake it. *Monica Lewinsky.* You could tell from that photo, the one with the beret and the rope line, she had a secret. They had a secret. You could tell how excited she was, touching her fantasy man in front of a crowd with the whole world watching. Only the two of them knowing what was really going on.

Exactly what was about to happen now. A charade.

Jane felt for her camera—*where was it?*—keeping close watch on Kenna. This was a shot she could not miss.

Kenna whirled, raising her hand in the air, waving. "Governor!" she called out. She looked at Jane, eyes shining, color high on her cheekbones. "He's coming this way, Jane! Isn't it perfect?"

With a quick motion, the woman unzipped a black patent leather shoulder bag. And pulled out a silver camera. She clicked a button on the top, checked a reading, then held the camera out to Jane. "Will you take our picture?"

"Take your—?"

"Now!" Kenna said. She pushed the camera at Jane, then grabbed Lassiter's arm, tucking her hand through the crook of his elbow. Looked up at him, all eyelashes and adoration. The security guards didn't seem to mind. Probably knew all about her.

"It's so hot, isn't it?" Kenna's voice turned innocent-sounding, as if she were merely commenting on the stifling room. "Do you have time for just one picture, Governor? This is Jane Ryland taking it!"

Wow. They're good at this. Hot? Puh-leeze.

"Hello again, Governor," Jane said. "This is quite a—"

A security guard, pushed too hard by Lassiter's sea of admirers, lurched forward, pushing Kenna into the candidate's arms. They both laughed, tipping into each other, clambering for balance.

Jane clicked the shutter.

And clicked it again. *Got it.*

Then she swore. *Damn.* This was Kenna's camera. She jabbed it into her blazer pocket, yanked open her bag, grabbed her own camera. *Hurry.*

Kenna regained her equilibrium, still clinging to the governor's arm. Looking up at him. Lassiter was smiling, indulgent, patting her arm. Jane aimed and clicked. And one more time. It would be something, at least. And maybe she could get Kenna to e-mail her a copy of the laughing picture. Kenna seemed to like the spotlight well enough.

Jane watched, fascinated, as Kenna uncurled herself from the candidate. Did she whisper something, too low for Jane to hear? Did she slip something into his pocket? Is this how they communicated, maybe? How they arranged their next rendezvous?

The entourage moved on, leaving Kenna, face flushed and lifting the mass of curls off her neck, watching after Lassiter and crew as they paraded through the rest of the room.

"Jane!" she said. She let her hair down, held out a hand, moving closer. Urgent. "Did you get a good picture of us? You did, right? You have my camera, right? I need to get one more shot."

"Sure, Kenna," Jane said, holding it toward her. *Yeesh.* This girl was kind of—out there. Jane struggled to keep the amusement from her face, though Kenna, riveted on the entourage, would never have noticed. "But could you—?"

Kenna grabbed the camera, locked on Lassiter, and began to move across the floor toward him. Jane zigzagged after her, determined. She needed to talk to this gal, and she was not going to let her get away again.

And then, she couldn't see her at all. Or anything.

Someone screamed, back of the room, and so did every-one, everyone, as the sweltering room went pitch black. A Klaxon, something, wailed, some alarm, shrieking, ear-splitting. Insistent. Jane blinked, blinked again, terror rising in her throat. The crowd, spooked, stampeding, pushing her forward in the dark. She stumbled ahead, trying to keep her balance. Why weren't the lights—? The music was still blaring, how could that be? The en-trance doors must be closed, because there was no light. Shouldn't they be open? Should she try to get out? Or stand her ground? What were you supposed to do? What if it were worse outside than inside?

The screams, high-pitched, terrified, sounded louder than the music, louder than the alarms. "Call nine-one-one!" someone yelled. "Doesn't work!" someone else shouted. "We gotta get out of here!"

She couldn't see anything. Not anything.

Was there another way out? Maitland had said some-thing about the back entrance—Jane whirled, squinted in the darkness, tried to get her bearings. *Nothing*.

"Governor, Governor, this way, this way . . ." A new voice called out, insistent, commanding, "Everyone, stay calm! It's fine, it's fine, it's just the lights. . . ."

This is a story. Possibly a big story. Jane held up her camera, clicked and clicked the flash. For a split second each time, she could see terrified faces, people shoving and pushing. She clicked again, caught a woman crying, people with cell phones out, their greenish glows giving a weird phosphorescent light. And why wasn't any-one—? Didn't the TV cameras have battery lights? Why were they still off? She looked both ways, as if there *were* both ways, but nothing existed except a chaos of arms and hands and bodies, and heat and screaming and dark-ness.

30

Jake made a show of turning on his BlackBerry, languidly scrolling through a page or two. Olive, hands still clamped over her mouth, hadn't budged. Vick, arms crossed in front of his chest, Psych 101, hadn't budged. DeLuca turned the pages of a broadsheet of colorful supermarket coupons as if fascinated by the latest grocery bargains.

"So, checking my notes," Jake drew out his words, contemplative, all the time in the world. He scrolled some more. It was just the *Register*'s online edition, but Jerk would never know that. "According to your wife, oh, wait, excuse me, her name is . . ."

He looked up from the screen, smiling. "Bear with me here."

"Call my lawyer," Vick said.

Jake couldn't hear him. "According to your wife, ah, Patricia, it says here, correct?"

"Lawyer," Vick said.

"You're not under arrest, Mr. Vick," Jake said.

DeLuca looked up, right on cue. "Yet," he added, then went back to his circular.

"So according to your wife, *Patricia*," Jake continued,

"on the night of the murder of Amaryllis Roldan, you both were—"

Olive made a little sound, like a squeak.

Vick glared at the girl. "I told you, go."

She made it just half a step. Her once-white sneaker barely crossing the threshold to freedom.

"*I* told you, no," Jake said. No more Mr. Nice Guy. He turned to the girl. "Please give Officer DeLuca your contact information. And please don't walk to your car alone. Or go anywhere alone. Understand?"

Olive squeaked again.

"Is all this necessary, Detective?" Vick turned back the cuffs of his shirt, revealing a watch that was probably Olive's salary for a year. Manicured fingers. "It's late, it's Saturday night, I still have work to do before I can leave. Can't this wait until business hours? Call my secretary and I'm sure we can—"

"We're talking now," Jake said. "And we'll be talking for a much briefer time if you simply answer my questions."

Vick's face went to ice, then stone. "Here's how I'll answer your questions," he said. He thrust a hand into a pocket of his dark slacks.

DeLuca's head came up. Jake's hand went to his side.

Vick smiled, but only out of one side of his mouth. Change jingled inside his pocket. "Lawyer. That's my answer."

"One more question," Jake said. *Lawyer, shmoyer. What an asshole.* "If you're not interested in helping, why'd you agree to meet with us?"

Vick barked out a laugh. "Huh. Why? Just curious, *Officer.* Just wanted to see the faces of the *gentlemen* who think I'm the Bridge Killer. One word about me in the papers? You're toast. Both of you. And I'll sue the city-a-Boston, too. I don't like it when people lie about me. I've got a business to run."

"Don't leave town, *Mr. Vick,*" DeLuca said. Supremely polite. "You either, Miss Parisella."

"I'm going to ask you to leave now, Officers." Vick gestured toward the door. "This is my territory. You are now officially trespassing. Do I make myself clear?"

"Like I said." DeLuca took the circular, crumpled it, and made a two-point toss into a metal wastebasket. "Don't leave town."

"Just one more . . ." Jake looked at the screen of his BlackBerry, which had flickered, refreshed, then changed. For a moment, what he read didn't compute. Then it did. Suddenly, Jake couldn't wait to leave.

"We'll be in touch," Jake said.

Out the door, into the parking lot. Headed for the car.

"You know that French guy? In the foreign flicks?" DeLuca sauntered toward the cruiser, in no hurry. "The one the chicks love, but who always did it?"

"Something's happening in Springfield—it's on the *Register* Web site." Jake panicked through his Black-Berry screens, scanning for info. "Get on the radio, D. See what's going down."

"Springfield what?" DeLuca clicked open the passenger door, slid into the front seat. "What are you talking about?"

"The Lassiter rally," Jake said. He turned his entire focus to his keys, *turn the key in the ignition, get the car started, get going.* Springfield was impossibly far away. What if Jane wasn't okay? "Just call in. See what they know at HQ. See if Springfield has people at the scene."

"Scene of what?" DeLuca yanked down his seat belt, turned to check for oncoming traffic as Jake gunned the blue and white cruiser out of the parking lot. "The Lassiter rally? This about—Jane?"

Jake glared at him but didn't bother to deny it. He paused, fraction of a second, at the exit. Hit the accelerator. "Yeah," he said. "Jane."

Kenna Wilkes crossed her legs, luxuriating in the plush upholstered sofa in the ninth-floor presidential suite. She touched the pile of glossy Lassiter brochures stacked beside her. After all, that's what she'd said she came here for.

She looked at her watch, wondering how it was going at the rally. It would be hot, and crowded, and Owen would be occupied with his campaign routine. She felt the beginnings of a smile, composing her face for the coming performance. She'd tell him he was wonderful, brilliant, compelling. *Best ever.* He'd believe her.

Her cell phone buzzed. Showtime.

She grabbed the brochures, tucked a little notepad labeled PRESIDENTIAL SUITE into her purse, patted the couch cushions flat, opened the suite's front door, gave the room one last appraisal. She clicked off the lights and stepped into the hallway. Looked left, looked right, no one there. Trotted down the corridor and into the ninth-floor stairwell.

Leaning for a beat against the cool gray concrete blocks of the stairwell wall, she clutched the slick campaign brochures to her silk blouse and closed her eyes briefly, calculating. So far, so good.

"I'm walking down the steps, Alex. Fast as I can. In the stairwell of the hotel. I'm on floor—" Jane glanced at the painted concrete bricks beside her, saw a green-stenciled number. "—floor six."

Jane's heart was still beating too fast. One hand holding the railing, the other her cell phone, she tried to hurry down the stairs and talk at the same time. She pushed closer to the wall, letting a pack of still-buzzing rally-goers elbow by her. "Yeah, it's nuts here. The stairwells are packed with people trying to get out. They've stopped the elevators, even though everyone keeps insisting there's nothing majorly wrong."

"So what the hell—Jane, are you okay?" Alex's voice buzzed over the iffy connection, but the concern in his voice came through. "Is Lassiter okay? The wires said the lights just went out. In the room where the rally was? Or all over the hotel? Why? What's the story?"

Floor five. "Yeah, well, Alex, I have no idea yet. Sorry, sorry." Jane stepped out of the way as another group of people, all wearing Lassiter buttons, shoved by her. "No, not you, Alex, people on the steps. Anyway, I don't know. All the Lassiter people were gone by the time the stupid TV types realized they could click on their battery lights—gosh, it must have been, like, a minute? It seemed like an hour. Terrifying. I mean, people went crazy. I've got to admit, it was pretty scary. Everything goes through your mind, you know?"

"Yeah, I bet. So is Lassiter going to have a statement? A news conference or something? Can you get to him, get reactions? And the hotel's? What did Lassiter do, anyway? Calm everyone down, be a hero?"

Floor four. Jane thought back. "Hardly. I mean, who knows. It was pitch dark. He was in the middle of the ballroom floor, doing his meet and greet thing, rent-a-cops around him, people pushing to get close and— damn." *Kenna Wilkes. Gone again.*

"What?" Alex said. "Jane, you sure you're okay? You'll be able to get us info and file a story, right? There's no one else there to cover it."

"Yeah, yeah, of course," Jane said. *Kenna Wilkes is still in this hotel. She can't just disappear.* "I'm fine. Thanks. I'm—listen. Do me a favor. Look up the name Kenna Wilkes, okay? *K-e-n-n-a.* Wilkes with an *e.* There can't be many people with that name. She'd be like, age twenty-five-ish. Curly hair, blue eyes. Just see."

"Speaking of *look up,*" Alex said. "Nothing on that Amaryllis name. Who is that, anyway? Tuck is freaking."

Ah, problem. Jake. Dead girls. Arthur Vick. "Alex? Later, okay? Let me do this first. I've gotta track down the Lassiter people."

"Great. Call me when you're ready to file," Alex said. "I'll check that name for you. Who's Kenna Wilkes, anyway?"

Third floor. As Jane swung around the corner to the concrete landing, the stairwell door flew open. She jumped back, barely missed getting slammed by the metal door and run over by the man racing through.

It was Trevor. Trevor Kiernan. He'd know exactly what happened.

"Trevor? Hang on, Alex. Hang on, okay?" Jane recognized the dark-rimmed glasses, the tousled hair, the clipboard. She caught up to him, grabbing his shoulder. "Trevor! It's Jane Ryland."

Trevor turned, looking up at her on the step above him. His tie was loose, the collar of his jacket askew, a smudge of what looked like black ink stained his white shirt.

"Jane?" he said. "Jane. Holy crap. You were there?" He paused, adjusting his glasses. Took another step down. "Do you know what happened?"

"Do *I*? Know what happened?" Jane pointed to herself, taken aback. "That's what I'm supposed to ask *you.*"

Trevor shook his head, mournful, staring down at the concrete steps.

"Trevor? You okay?" Jane put the cell phone back to her cheek. "Hang on, Alex. Trevor? Is Lassiter okay?"

"Lassiter's—fine. Security took him back to his suite. I'm hoping he'll make a statement soon. We have no idea what happened. The lights just—went out. Then that crazy alarm starts shrieking. *Blam*." Trevor flipped a switch in the air, demonstrating. "Blam. Out. Across the entire floor, apparently. The rest of the hotel was fine. Christ, what a friggin'— This completely sucks. A disaster."

He twisted the corner of his mouth, rueful, then gestured imaginary headlines. "Lights Out for the Lassiter Campaign," he said. "Can you see it? Gable's gonna love this. And that's off the record."

Jane nodded, listening. *Wonder if Alex can hear this?*

"Was it like some transformer thing?" she asked. "Or power outage?"

"We don't know," he said. "Call me, say, in fifteen. I'll let you know where the governor is speaking. I'm sure we'll have something."

"It would look pretty bad not to." Jane couldn't resist. "Lassiter bailing in the middle of chaos, people freaking out. I mean, if it was an accident—"

"It won't matter what the truth is, you know? It sucks," Trevor said, interrupting. "If we can't run a simple rally, I mean, how can we run the country? That's what they'll say. You think we're gonna get any donations after tonight's fiasco? And Rory's trying to make Lassiter—"

He stopped. "Never mind. I gotta go."

He turned and headed down the stairs, waving his clipboard at her. "Fifteen minutes," he called out. "Or so."

Jane waited until he was out of sight. "You hear any of that?" she said into the phone. She continued downstairs slowly, wanting the privacy.

"Kind of," Alex said. "So I'm thinking—it was some

random accident? Or like, electricity overload? A circuit thing? You said it was really hot in there."

Jane shrugged. "The TV guys weren't with their cameras at the time. Didn't get any shots. I did, though. With my still camera. I'll check 'em out, ASAP. See what I got. This whole rally has been a total mess from moment one. I'll put it all in my story. And there's a bunch more. But—"

Jane's phone beeped, an annoying little whine. "Shoot, Alex, low battery. My charger's in my room. I'll call you when I get plugged back in."

"Jane?" Alex said. "Can you still hear me?"

The cell phone blurped out another warning. "For about two more seconds," she said. She swung open the door marked LOBBY.

"You said to look up Kenna Wilkes." Alex raised his voice, as if talking more loudly would solve the battery problem. "Who is she?"

Jane paused, considering. She knew the answer, but had zero time to explain it. "She's the other woman," she said.

And the phone went dead.

31

"**Governor Lassiter, are** you all right?" Kenna, wide-eyed and oh-so-concerned, called out to Owen as his entourage trooped down the stairs from the tenth floor. Two security types, both sweaty and worried looking, led the way, scouting as if some danger lurked on the stairs. Rory trudged two steps behind Lassiter. Both men's jackets flapped open, Rory's shirt coming untucked. Even Owen's tie was askew. His silver hair mussed. Each looked beyond annoyed. Enraged, more like it. Kenna fluttered even harder. "I was so worried. . . ."

"Ah, Mrs. Wilkes. I see you made it out safely." Lassiter gave a half smile as he took the last few steps down to the landing. The security guards had opened the door and were already in the hallway.

Probably looking for the evildoers, Kenna thought. Happily, Owen wasn't focusing on *her* whereabouts. "Are you all right?" she asked.

"Well, you're having quite the introduction to the campaign, I must say. Yes, we all survived the—" He paused, then looked at Rory. "What are we calling it, Rory?"

"We're calling it nothing at this point," Rory said. "The hotel people are already all over this. They're alleging *we* must have done something. Plugged in too much. Had too many people. They're insisting nothing was wrong with the electrical system. No circuit breakers, no blown transformer. How they know all that so fast is beyond me. Although . . ." He frowned, then stopped as he reached the landing. Rory crossed his arms in front of his chest. "Although."

"Although?" Owen turned.

Kenna waited. This was going to be good.

"Say it was the Gable campaign. You know? Sabotage," Rory said. "All you'd have to do would be—I don't know—find the main light switch. Turn off the lights. Pull an alarm. And *blam*. Chaos. Campaign dirty trick 101. And we're semi-screwed."

"Sabotage?" Owen's lips pursed, as if he'd never tasted the word before. "But by who? That guest list was vetted, correct? We know everyone who was there. A-listers, you told me. *Damn it*. Excuse me, Kenna. We didn't even get to make our final money pitch. Now we're talking in a damn stairwell. And the damn press is going to want some answers."

He called me Kenna. Finally. She waited. It'd be interesting to hear what would happen next. She'd take her cue from—she recomposed her face, remembering to look concerned.

"Do you need some privacy?" she said. "This sounds important."

Rory waved her off. "We trust you, Mrs. Wilkes," he said.

"And now you're calling it sabotage?" Owen, ignoring their exchange, adjusted his paisley tie, then did it again. "You're theorizing someone in the crowd—or someone with the hotel? What does Trevor Kiernan say? Where is he, anyway?"

"I don't know, Governor," Rory said. Then seemed to make a decision. "Look. This hotel has been snakebit from moment one. The whole room thing, the elevators, the GD lights. Let's get you out of here. Before who knows what else goes wrong."

"Ah, Rory, we need to make some kind of a statement to the press." Owen, frowning, made the time-out sign with his hands. "I can't just—"

"I'm afraid I insist, Governor." Rory took out a cell phone. "We'll get your stuff, get it downstairs, get on the road. We can make a statement tomorrow. From Boston. When we know the facts. I'll call Sheila to put out the word that you're fine. Then call for the car."

"I'm not sure. . . ."

"Governor? I insist. This kind of thing only gets worse. Although I don't see how it can be worse than this. Mrs. Wilkes? Can you be ready in twenty, thirty minutes?"

"Faster than that," she said.

"Use the service elevators. I'll tell security. Mrs. Wilkes, we'll meet you at the car in—"

"I need some food," Lassiter interrupted, frowning. "And a drink. And possibly a shower. I'm not leaving until after that."

Maitland raked his hands through what would have been his hair. Looked at his watch. "It's quarter till nine. We'll leave at ten. No later," he said. "Kenna, call room service if you want. Governor, come with me. Christ. I've had it with this place. We're done here."

Kenna followed them into the hallway, watched Rory use his key card to open the door of the presidential suite. She trotted down the corridor to her own room, passing a fully loaded maid's cart—towels, soap, little shampoos, trash bags. She looked both ways, then swiped two plastic bottles of body lotion with curlicue labels saying PRESIDENTIAL SUITE, tucking them into her pocket. She looked at the campaign brochures she was still holding. Thought for a second. Then shoved them into the trash.

32

Holly could barely wait to see the pictures. Maybe she could take a quick look at them, for one second, here in the hotel corridor? *No, no, no, I need privacy.* She found her blue key card in the pocket of her purse, just where she'd put it, and clicked open her hotel room door. She'd left the lights on, of course. Her heart was beating so fast! Almost like when . . . She felt herself blushing, remembering. *A kiss in the hallway, a promise made.*

She practically fell against the door as it closed behind her. Her knees felt almost weak. She had touched him, he had touched her, they had . . . had connected.

And Jane Ryland! Actually there! In person! Taking the actual pictures, which was so unexpectedly perfect. She would be so happy when she got the photos. What a perfect, perfect night.

The silly lights had gone out at the rally and the alarm was scary for a second, of course. But even that was so funny. Owen Lassiter, with her, in the dark. She could smell him still. So funny. Owen Lassiter in the dark.

And she had pictures.

She pushed the oval silver button on the camera. Pushed it again.

No. *No.*

The stupid camera was taking too long to power up. Broken? Jane Ryland broke her camera? No. No. Maybe it was out of batteries. *Out of batteries?* Holly hit the silver button again, praying. The camera made a little sound, like a mean whisper, like, *No, I'm not showing you the pictures. You were bad.*

No, she wasn't bad! She was good and she was right and it was just a stupid camera and it couldn't talk and it was a stupid battery and all she needed was the charger.

Had she brought the charger? Oh, no no no. She didn't have the charger.

Maybe I do. She yanked open her black wheelie bag, unzipped all the pockets, one at a time, jamming her hands inside, exploring every space where maybe she had been smart enough, good enough, to put the charger. Nothing. Nothing. Nothing.

The charger was at home in Boston. Hours away. *Maybe I just have to—*

She pressed her lips together, very hard, trying not to cry. She needed the pictures. She had to see the pictures. Had. To. See. Them.

Tonight.

It doesn't matter if I missed the rally. He didn't need to hear some speech. Matt felt one fist clench, and that muscle in his neck twitch again. He simply needed to see if Holly was there. This was about stopping her. And protecting Governor Lassiter from whatever the hell she was planning.

The campaign probably didn't even know anything was wrong. Yet.

He eased his car into the New Englander parking lot, scanning for a spot. Still pretty crowded. A good sign.

If Holly was following the campaign, which is exactly

what she would do, she'd still be here as long as Lassiter was here. Would they stay overnight, this far from Boston? He should have asked that Denise girl, but she was already spooked. He was here; he could find out. Not a problem. *It is what it is.*

If Holly was following the campaign, she'd be on it like—like she was on him back then. Started out signing up for the same classes. At first, he'd thought it a coincidence, and she was pretty cute anyway. He'd been nice to her, why not? His first mistake. It took him a while to get the real picture. They'd studied together, gone out a couple of times. No big deal. She was so damn hot. So willing. So what was he supposed to do, say no, go away? He'd kissed her, so what? It was grad school, for godsake.

Then, she'd be in the hallway every time he turned the friggin' corner. Cookies left at his apartment door. Flowers. Showed up with a whole dinner that time, all jazzed, saying it was their anniversary. *I mean, anniversary of what?*

And he was just too—too what? His mother had taught him to be polite, to treat women with respect. She'd drilled that into him every day. And to watch out for the bad ones. He simply hadn't realized Holly was a bad one. He couldn't let her hurt the governor.

Matt turned off the ignition, grabbed his overnight bag, pushed through the revolving door, made a beeline for the registration desk. A little after nine o'clock, the lobby was still crowded, and the bar, too. Maybe campaign stuff was still going on upstairs. Maybe Holly was still up there. Maybe she was in the bar. If the governor was there, she'd be there.

Some wimp in a navy blazer, name tag, and plastered-on smile waved him over to the end of the counter. Matt took a hotel brochure and a red apple from a big glass bowl. Why not. He'd be a paying guest soon enough.

"Reservation, sir?"

Matt took a bite of the apple, held up his hand, *wait a sec*. He swallowed, then said, "Nope. Just want a room for the night. A single. One night."

The guy looked pained or something. Shaking his head. "Oh, I'm so sorry, sir, we're fully booked this evening." He waved a hand across the lobby. "Convention. And the Lassiter campaign. As you can see."

Matt scowled. Hotels always had another room. This asshole just didn't want to give it to him. He put on his nice guy look and reached into his pocket.

"Oh, gee, well, that's too bad. I really do need to stay here tonight." Matt opened his wallet, folded two twenties, and put them on the desk, his palm not quite hiding them. "I've stayed in your hotel chain lots of times. I'm a gold card holder. Isn't there any way you could ... check again?"

The clerk looked even more pained. And looked at Matt's hand like it held a winning lottery ticket. "Yes—no, sir, we truly are full up. I'm so sorry. There's just nothing—"

Matt tossed the apple over the counter. It splatted on the wall behind the clerk, landing on a deep bluish swirl in the ugly patterned carpet. "I doubt that, asshole."

"Sir! I—"

Matt stuffed the two bills back into his wallet. Gave the clerk a look like, *You're lucky it wasn't you I threw against the wall*. Not that it would have helped. Plus, the guy had already darted behind the office door. Wimp.

Out the door, into the freezing night. He slammed on the ignition, cranked the heat. There was another way to handle this. He yanked out that brochure, then his cell phone, and dialed the hotel.

"I'm looking for a guest, a Holly Neff?" He disguised his voice a little, in case wimp clerk answered.

"One moment, please, sir." A woman's voice, so no prob.

"Sir?"

"Yes?" He'd get the operator to put the call through, hear her voice—he'd know it—then say, *Wrong number.* He'd come back at the crack of dawn, stake her out. Or hell, sleep in his car. Done it before. It'd be worth it.

"She's checked out, sir."

Checked out? "Checked out?" He tried to keep his voice calm, but he couldn't believe this. She had been here. And he'd missed her.

A rock sank in his chest. The clerk had unknowingly answered another question. The woman he'd seen *was* Holly Neff. She *was* in that photo. She was back in his life. And maybe, as a result, back in Lassiter's. They were all in trouble. Big, big trouble.

"Yes, sir. I'm so sorry."

Not half as sorry as I am. Shit. Shit on a freakin' . . .

"Can you tell me . . . when?" He put a smile into his voice, hoping it would work as well here as it did with his sales calls. "It would be so helpful if you could tell me—when did she check out?"

There was a pause. *Come on, honey.*

"Well, actually, just a few minutes ago."

Matt needed to think.

"Sir?" The voice on the phone.

"Yeah, thanks." Matt tried to control his breathing. It was fine. If she was with the campaign, he had a handle on this. He didn't need to find her tonight. He was cool. He just needed to confirm it.

He squinted through the rental's dirt-streaked windshield toward the hotel's glass-fronted doorway. "She was part of the governor's campaign, right? She's with the—"

And there she was.

Holly Neff. His worst nightmare. Shiny as a bad penny. Standing in the hotel's front doorway, walking out the doorway, nodding to the bellman. Walking into the parking lot. Walking his way.

Matt slammed off the phone.

His turn.

33

"**Dammit**," Jane muttered. She couldn't get the cell phone cord to reach the bathroom. "Alex? Me again. I'm in my hotel room. Plugged in." She looked around, remembering. "All the lights are working fine. I skulked around the main offices to talk to the hotel people, but they were 'unavailable,' some corporate lackey finally told me. I'll hit 'em again, later. Anyway, let me bang out a story—"

"Fifteen inches," Alex said. "It's for the morning edition, print version. Deadline's at three, so chop chop. It's so awesome you were there. Wish I had seen it, though. I mean, not seen it. You got pix?"

"We'll see," Jane said. It was odd not to worry about getting video. *Take that, Channel 11.* This newspaper stuff was much easier. "I just held the camera up, didn't aim. How could I? It'll be pretty cool if they turn out, very cinema verité. But I'm still waiting to hear from the campaign guy. He said Lassiter would have a statement in fifteen minutes, but now it's been more than an hour. I'll call him, soon as we get off. But I can write the lede without it and plug in the statement at the end. You know, Lassiter explains the blackout was—whatever they say it was."

"Cool if it were sa-bo-tage." Alex gave the word a spy-movie accent.

"You've watched too many thrillers," Jane said, eyeing the bathroom. Darn this cord. She tried to yank off her boots, toe to heel, without putting down the phone. No luck.

"I'm serious," he said. "What if it's a Gable thing? You know? It could be—'Lightgate.'" Alex was laughing. He could actually be pretty funny, though she hadn't seen him smile much recently. Maybe his wife was back. Or gone. *Bathroom.*

"Alex? I'll call you, okay?"

"—to know what Lassiter thinks," Alex continued.

"Alex? My call-waiting just kicked in. Missed what you said. Gotta go. This might be Trevor."

"—is that? And don't let me forget to update you on the Gable interview. It's gotta be soon. This week, they're saying."

"Alex? I'll call you." She clicked. "This is Jane."

"Janey?"

"Jake? Are you okay?"

"Am *I* okay?" Jake was almost sputtering. "You're the one who was in the—what the hell was it, anyway? Were you there? Are you okay? I tried to call you earlier, but you didn't answer. So I figured—not good."

He was truly wonderful. Maybe they could just ... Jane plopped on the edge of the flowery bedspread, stared at the tight-woven shag of the unfortunate carpeting. Here she was, goofy over a gorgeous cop who was totally off-limits. Reluctantly intrigued by a married man, her boss, also totally off-limits. Waiting for a call from a professional contact, kind of adorable, ditto totally off-limits.

Her source was dead, her reputation battered, and a bad guy—who might be a serial killer—hated her. She was in a cookie-cutter hotel room with unreliable electricity and no toothbrush, and she had a story to write. Welcome to Jane World.

"Yeah, Jakey, I'm fine. My phone died at one point. My guess? Someone turned out the lights. A mistake, maybe? Or—I don't know." Jane quickly filled him in on the rest. "But at least I get to write it for the paper. My first story, right? Once I find out the deal. Where are you, anyway?"

"Mickey D's. HQ confirmed Springfield was no problem. So DeLuca and I are getting—hang on." Jake paused. "He's back in the car. Says hi. Anyway, all good. I was only checking."

Jake's voice had gone professional. He must trust DeLuca somewhat, though. And Jane had to admit, Amy knew about Jake. Whatever there was to "know." Amy was doing her best to wean them apart. *It's a lose–lose, sister,* she'd warned. *Other fish in the sea.*

Okay, Jane could be professional, too. Even though she liked *this* fish. "Can D hear me?" Jane asked.

"Unclear at this point," Jake replied.

Ah. So Jane whispered. "Amaryllis Roldan."

"Yup, I can hear her." DeLuca stashed the two mediums, light, two sugars, into the molded black plastic cup holders between them on the console, then backhanded Jake's leather jacket. "Not at all 'unclear.' She wanna whisper sweet nothings?"

"I'll tell you what's clear, brother," Jake said. Then, into the phone, "Talk to you later, Jane."

That was close. Jake pulled out of the lot, heading back to HQ. Then again, maybe there was one more place they needed to check out.

DeLuca leaned in, punched on the car's radio. "News," he said.

A staticky radio-announcer voice blasted through the cruiser.

"Hey!" Jake said.

"Gimme a break," DeLuca said, turning down the volume.

"—and now, a very annoyed Governor Lassiter and his campaign team, just beginning to struggle in the polls, have left Springfield for the night. In other news—"

DeLuca punched off the radio. "So Lassiter leaves town," he said.

Jake glanced at him, then back to the clamor of Saturday night traffic. Boylston Street and Mass Ave.—the busiest intersection in Boston. Coffee shops, music stores, fast food. Kids in packs, cars honking, some guy playing the sax on the corner, nobody in the striped crosswalks.

He hoped no one would walk home alone tonight across the Mass Ave. Bridge.

"So?" Jake said.

"Ver-ry senatorial."

"Yeah, hardly a profile in courage." Jake stopped as the light turned yellow, watched three cars accelerate from behind him and bang through it.

"Wanna hit the lights and siren?" DeLuca asked.

"Just about," Jake said. The light turned red. One more jerk went through. "But listen, we know where Arthur Vick is, right?"

"Huh? He's at his store. 'Working,'" DeLuca added, making air quotes with his long fingers. Difficult, because he was also holding his coffee. "Probably banging—"

Jake hit his turn signal, rolled his eyes. "He's at the store. And that means Mrs. Vick is home alone."

"Or dead."

"Which would give Vick a pretty good alibi, wouldn't it, wise guy? So what I'm saying," Jake continued, watching the light and feeling for his coffee, "is maybe it's time to pay Patricia Vick a little surprise visit. At home."

"It's like, almost ten o'clock at night."

"I have a watch," Jake said. And the light turned green.

"It's almost ten o'clock at night! You kidding me, Trevor?" Jane wailed into the phone, peering out the window of her hotel room at the spotlit parking lot, half-thinking she might actually see the governor's car, *the courage mobile,* heading away from any news conference, official statement, or responsibility-taking. "He's leaving? Not going to say a word? I've been waiting here in my room, all this time—I gotta tell you, Trevor, that seems—"

She stopped. Gave a mental shrug. She was a reporter. Whatever happened, that's what she'd write. "Okay. Are you gonna have a statement, at least?"

A car *was* pulling out of the lot, she noticed, almost at the road. Then another set of headlights came on in a parking space near the hotel. Two cars leaving. Campaign cars? But she could hardly run down and stop them. On the phone, Trevor Kiernan was still in full-blown excuse-making mode.

"Listen, Jane, I'm so sorry, what can I tell you, it's out of my hands. But, yeah, we do have a statement coming," he said. "Call ya back in thirty seconds."

The phone went dead.

Jane pressed her forehead against the chilly window. The first car was booking toward the highway, the second car now at the stop sign. Lassiter types who'd been at the rally, probably. Off to spin their yarns of the disaster of an evening they'd witnessed firsthand.

Now she had to go back downstairs, hope people were still in the bar hashing it over, get some eyewitness sound bites. She raised one forefinger, correcting herself. Not sound bites, interviews. And demand reaction from the hotel management. Lucky her boots were still on.

It'd be fun to tell her dad about her first newspaper story. And Amy. Steve and Margery. Wonder if the other Channel 11 people would notice it? Come to think of it, they couldn't put this story on the air. They hadn't sent a crew. She felt the beginnings of a smile. She'd scooped them. The new door was opening. Score one for Team Jane.

"This is Jane." She clicked on her phone before the ring even finished. Tucking it between her cheek and her shoulder, she yanked her laptop from her tote bag so she could take down Trevor's certain-to-be-weasly statement. She eyed the glowing numbers on the bedside clock. She'd better get a move on.

"Jane?"

Woman's voice. Not Trevor.

"Yes? This is Jane." *Like I said.*

"This is Moira Lassiter. Do you know where my husband is?"

34

"Where the hell are we? What time is it?"

From her vantage point in the backseat of the campaign's SUV, Kenna Wilkes saw Owen Lassiter's head jerk awake. He looked across the front seat at Rory, driving, then back at her, then squinted ahead into the blackness of the Mass Pike unspooling in front of them. Seat-belted into the darkness of the backseat, she didn't have to hide her smile. This could be interesting.

"Ah, Governor, you're awake," Rory said.

"How long was I sleeping?" Owen rubbed his face with both hands, then blinked, looking at his watch. Three cars, high beams switched on, zoomed by. Passing them going east toward Boston, one eighteen-wheeler, lights dotting its double-long trailer. They had a long way to go. "It's almost two in the morning?"

The glow from the dashboard readouts spotted Owen's face with flickering shadows. A car went by, and for an instant, its headlights illuminated him, full view. He looked confused. Exhausted. Older.

"Kenna. Mrs. Wilkes. You're okay?" Owen said.

Kenna raised a hand. "Just fine, Governor. How about you? You've really been sleeping."

"Rory? What's the deal here?" Owen looked around,

a baffled owl in pinstripes. He peered at his watch again. "Two? How'd it get to be two?"

Rory kept his eyes on the road. "Well, you fell asleep soon after we left Springfield. Perhaps that scotch you—"

"Damn. That rally. Any word from the brain trust at the hotel?"

"Nope. Told them we'd call in the morning." Rory flipped a hand. "But let's write it off, Governor. What are we gonna do, sue? Farther away that whole fiasco gets, the better. At least Boston TV wasn't there."

"That Jane Ryland was, though. From the newspaper." The governor leaned back in his bucket seat, propped one foot on the dashboard. "But I guess she's—"

"Yeah," Rory said.

Jane Ryland. Reporter. Kenna tucked that name away.

"Anyway, I fell asleep? We should have been home hours ago."

"Well, you were so peaceful, and frankly I was a little tired myself, so we pulled over at a rest stop, Kenna got us some coffee, and I worked on some campaign stuff, lost track of time, I guess till the caffeine kicked in. All we need, the next senator from Massachusetts in a car accident because his driver fell asleep. Right? So we're running a little behind, timewise."

"Moira will think—," the governor began.

She sure will, Kenna thought.

"No, she won't," Rory interrupted. "If she picked up my message, it only confirms you're in Springfield. If she didn't get the message, she'd check your schedule and find out you were in Springfield. And after—what happened, it was too late to call and tell her about your, uh, change of plans. It's not like there's anything she could do."

"She might have seen it on the news, Rory. She'll be a basket case, worrying. Why'd you let me fall asleep before calling her?"

"Governor, listen. You know she doesn't stay up for the news anymore. She'll sleep blissfully until tomorrow—when you'll surprise her by arriving so early. She'll be delighted. What does it matter if you were sleeping in a hotel in Springfield or in a car on the Mass Pike?"

Owen patted his pockets. "I'm going to call her now. Tell her what's going on."

"Sure, do that," Rory said. "But you'll scare the hell out of her when the phone rings and wakes her up."

Owen stopped his search. "I suppose that's true."

Rory drove a few moments, then yawned. Hugely. He put one hand over his face, and gave his head a quick shake.

Owen put a hand on his arm. "Want me to drive?"

"Lord no, you're more tired than I am." Rory yawned again. "I'll be fine."

"Dammit, Rory, this is dangerous. Silly. We're scheduled to be out of town, so let's find the next reasonable place and catch some sleep. You're exhausted. I'm exhausted. Here's a Worcester exit. There's got to be a, whatever. Hotel. Motel. Mrs. Wilkes? What say you? You're certainly having an adventure."

Kenna yawned, eyes wide over the prayerlike hands that covered her mouth. "Whatever you say, Governor." She lowered her hands. "I must admit, the idea of bed is very, very tempting."

Maybe Arthur Vick killed Sellica, Amaryllis Roldan, and "Longfellow" merely as practice. As a setup. All to get ready for his real goal—to kill his wife.

To get her to stop talking.

Jake managed a straight face as he watched Patti Vick—Patricia Auriello Vick, age fifty-three, born Charlestown, Massachusetts, housewife, married to A. Vick for thirty-three years, no living children, no registered pets, according to Sergeant Nguyen in the Records Department—tuck into her second supersized single malt. It was the only thing that interrupted her blow-by-blow recitation of the years of "blissful" marriage to the "self-made" "wonderfully generous" guy who was her "first love" and "best friend."

DeLuca hadn't been cool with the "let's chat with Pat" program as they knocked on the Vicks' front door, warning, "It's so late, she'll probably shoot first and we won't be alive to ask questions later." Mrs. Vick had at first gone pale, asking if there was anything wrong. After they assured her they were only night-shift detectives who needed to ask her a couple questions, Patti "with an *i*" had acted as if the late-night arrival of two cops on her almost-suburban doorstep was exactly what she'd been waiting for. "I never sleep," she told them. Now, here the two of them were, facing a tracksuit-wearing fireplug on a triple-wide sectional. Listening to Patti Vick tell all.

Not that she was saying anything relevant. But Jake took another sip of his second water on the rocks. The enough-rope theory. Let them talk. Sometimes they talked too much.

And, Jake reminded himself, he believed—because Jane had sworn it under oath on the witness stand—this woman's husband had been paying Sellica Darden for sex. And a few days ago, probably killed her. And probably killed Amaryllis Roldan before that.

Mrs. Vick was living in some kind of dreamworld. Or she was a pretty good liar. Or a drunk. Or all three. He'd let her talk.

"Interesting," DeLuca was saying. Not that Patti-with-an-*i* needed encouragement.

It did seem that she worshipped at the altar of Arthur. After Jake's initial foray into Sellica Darden territory—which Patti had dismissed as "all lies and televisional sensational stuff" from "that horrible girl on Channel Eleven," Mrs. Vick's commentary about her husband had been all positive. He could do no wrong. Anything she ever wanted, she got. Yes, he was busy, but there were rewards. Now she was showing off the huge and incomprehensible oil-painted canvases hanging frame-to-frame on the living room's too-crowded walls.

"All mine," she said, jabbing her chest with a manicured finger. Her husband let her "do her art." She was an insomniac, she revealed. But he let her "have an atelier" so she could "find herself."

"Yes, I know, there's a bit too much of myself to 'find' these days." Patti poked one dark red fingernail into an ample thigh. "But that's what happens when your husband owns a grocery store, right? Artie always told me, even in high school, he liked that I was big-boned. 'Not some little fairy girl,' he'd say. 'You're my real woman.' He'd say."

DeLuca took a dramatic sip of water, waving the floor to Jake.

"You ever hear the name Amaryllis Roldan?" Jake said. Might as well get this wrapped up. They could always come back.

Patti's eyes went up, searching from one corner of the ceiling to the other, then back. "Ah, no. Why? Who's that?"

"Who chooses the women in your husband's commercials?"

"Aren't they great?" Patti perked up. "We're here for twenty-four and, if you need it, more."

"Ma'am?" Jake prodded her. The wife of a murder suspect singing TV jingles in the middle of the night. What they don't teach you at the academy. "The women?"

"Oh, my goodness, no idea. That's all business stuff. At Artie's office."

"So, finally." DeLuca looked at his watch, then at Jake. "Your husband has a habit of working this late, ma'am?"

"Even on Saturday nights?" Jake put in.

Sunday morning, really. When "Longfellow" and Roldan had been killed.

"Oh, yes, he—" Patti stopped, then looked at Jake, wary, like, *wait a minute*. She took a sip, then wagged one finger at him, midswallow. "Oh, I know what you're *real-ly* asking, Detectives. Is that why you're still here? Well, I can answer that one, easy peasy. The nights those poor girls were killed, my Arthur was most certainly not working late. In fact, he was with me."

35

"Do I know where your husband is?" Jane's eyebrows went up, trying to figure out exactly what to say to Moira Lassiter. *I mean, why not call him and ask him, you know?* The nightstand clock taunted her. She had expected this to be the call from Trevor, dictating the campaign's statement. What was taking him so long? She had to write her story. But she couldn't dump Moira. And why didn't Moira know where her own husband was? "Mrs. Lassiter? I mean, I saw him at the event, of course, earlier this evening. Here in Springfield. Did you try to call him?"

Jane had a thought. "Oh, I get it. You're worried about the rally situation. Did you see something about it on TV? It's all fine. Nobody hurt, everyone accounted for." *As far as I know.* Jane checked the clock again, semi-panic setting in. "I'm actually still waiting for a statement from the campaign. I could call you directly, if you like, when I find out more. After I file my story."

"The 'situation'? At the rally?" Mrs. Lassiter's voice lost its usual confidence. "What situation? I've been asleep since nine. Is something wrong? I tried to call, of course, but Owen didn't answer his—"

Jane's call-waiting beeped in. It *had* to be Trevor. She had to make her deadline.

"Mrs. Lassiter, I'm incredibly sorry. Nothing's wrong. Hold on one second, though, okay?" Jane clicked the button. "This is Jane."

"Jane? Trevor. Sorry to take so long, but—"

"Listen, Trevor, ah, do you know where—?" Jane paused, thinking of Moira on the other line. She could simply have Moira talk to Trevor. On the other hand, wouldn't Trevor wonder why Moira was calling *her*? And what if Trevor were in on whatever was happening? If anything was happening. No. She had to keep everyone and everything separate until she figured out whose side everyone was on. "Never mind. Do you have the statement?"

"Yup, I'll read it to you. Ready? 'We are deeply—'"

"Trevor? Hang on. One second. I've got to . . . ah, hang on." She didn't wait for a reply. Clicked back to Moira.

"Mrs. Lassiter? Please forgive me, I'm on a crushing deadline. Governor Lassiter is fine, I last saw him with his entourage—" *And the other woman you're wondering about,* which she didn't say. "Now Tre— Someone from the campaign is calling me with a statement. I'm completely sure it's fine. Do you want me to ask them to have the governor call you?"

"But what happened?" Moira Lassiter pleaded.

"The lights went out. During the rally. They're back on now." Jane was talking as fast as she could. She couldn't afford to lose Moira. But she couldn't miss her deadline. "It was briefly, you know, surprising. But nothing big. Really. Listen, let me promise to call you back, in the morning. Hang on, okay?" She clicked. "Trevor? One second."

Back to Moira. "I'll call you in the morning. Don't worry. But—why don't you just call your husband?"

She heard Moira sigh. "I'll try his number again. But this isn't the first time. You need to know that. It's not the first time I've not known where he is. Call me tonight, Jane. Tonight."

"Absolutely, Mrs. Lassiter. I really—"

"I'll wait for your call." And she hung up.

Jane held out both arms, head back, briefly pleading with the universe for a tiny break. "Trevor, I'm ready," she said. She scooted up against the bed's wooden headboard, arranged a pillow behind her, adjusted her laptop, and clicked open a new page. Jane Ryland, newspaper reporter. *Take this, Channel 11.* "Okay, go."

The next time the phone rang, Jane jerked awake so quickly, her head hit the slats of the headboard.

"Huh?" she said. The sky was pinkish outside her window. . . . Oh, Springfield. The hotel. The rally. She'd sent her story, just in time, she remembered that. Alex loved it, and then— The phone rang again. Her laptop was still on, but flashing a silent slide show of Jane's photos of her mom and the Emmys and a funny shot of a pigeon eating a piece of pepperoni. She grabbed for the phone, still bleary and half-confused.

"This is Jane." She squinted at the digital clock. Her eyes were stinging—her contacts were going to be impossible to get out. Hotel. No contact lens solution. *Five A.M.?*

"Jane? This is Moira Lassiter. I was waiting for your call."

Jane clapped a palm to her forehead. Trying to force her brain into gear.

"Oh, my goodness, Mrs. Lassiter." She licked her lips, wished for some water. "I must have fallen asleep after I sent the story. I'm so—"

"What are you keeping from me, Jane?" the woman interrupted. "Are you in on this cover-up, too, now? The

THE OTHER WOMAN 199

hotel told me Owen—and his 'staff,' as they so carefully put it—left there hours ago. If he were coming home, he'd already be here with me. But it's now five in the morning. Owen is not at the hotel in Springfield. He's not answering his cell. And he is most assuredly not home."

"I'm not keeping anything, Mrs. Lassiter. Of course not. As I said, I meant to call you, but I must have . . ." Jane took a deep breath, trying to adjust to the bitterness in Moira's voice, her own lack of sleep, and the impossibility of figuring out what was going on. She tried for diplomacy. "When you called the governor's staff, what did they tell you?"

"Call who, Jane? That Maitland person, who only knows the truth as he creates it? Sheila King, who informed you so erroneously that I was 'taking some downtime'? Which of his minions would you suggest I trust to tell me the truth?"

"Well, I—" It was on the tip of Jane's tongue to cut to the chase. To outright ask, *Do you know the name Kenna Wilkes?* But it seemed precipitous, to name a name that would forever, no matter what, true or not, taint the woman's reputation, and the candidate's, and Moira Lassiter's. But Jane could barely get in an "uh-huh" as Mrs. Lassiter kept talking. The woman couldn't possibly be drinking at five in the morning. Could she? Isn't this what Martha Mitchell had done back in Watergate days, drunk-dialing reporters, ratting out her Attorney General husband? But that wasn't about another woman.

"They're all covering for him," Moira was saying. "No point in my calling any of them. 'Yes, Mrs. Lassiter, I'll check, Mrs. Lassiter.' It's like calling a bunch of bobblehead dolls. All bobbling to whatever Owen and Rory tell them. So, Jane. Did you see anyone suspicious? Did you see the other woman?"

36

"Detective Brogan? Brought you a coffee. Don't get used to it."

Jake looked up from his computer. Paperwork almost done. His Sunday-morning habit, alone time in the Homicide office, catching up. He was tired from last night's interview with Patti Vick. *She* may not need sleep, but *he* did. He needed answers more.

"Hey, Pam. Back from your honeymoon, huh?"

The homicide squad's part-time clerk put a steaming paper cup on his desk, then held up her left hand, waggling her ring finger. "I'm now officially Pamela O'Flynn Augusto," she said. "Back from Maui, extra blond, extra tan, and extra ready to help you keep the peace."

"That's some handle," Jake said. A red light flashed on his desk telephone. From out in the reception area, he heard Pam's phone ring. An inside ring.

The supe? "Pam, can you handle that for me? I'm in a meeting or something. Unless it's the supe. You know the drill."

"Sure, boss." Pam picked up Jake's phone. "Homicide."

She plucked a pencil out of Jake's BPD-issue mug, held the phone against her cheek, and pulled a white notepad toward her. "Well, he's in a meeting right now. . . ."

Jake made a "score one" in the air. But Pam was holding the notepad in front of him. On it she'd printed, *Tucker Cameron*. Register. *Front desk. Urgent.*

Doomed, as Jane would say. Tuck had blatantly circumvented the required PR protocol. Why had Tuck risked calling him directly? Maybe she knew something. He pointed a finger-gun at his temple, pulled the trigger.

"Fine, bring her up," Jake whispered. He held out splayed fingers. "Ten minutes. Then call me."

Tuck appeared at his door two minutes later, tight jeans, knee boots, black puffy vest. Laminated visitor's pass clipped to one pocket. Notebook sticking out of the other. Pencil through her ponytail. *A regular Lois Lane.* Without the experience.

"You're working some big OT," Jake said. He kept one finger on the report he was reading, signaling he planned to return to it as soon as possible. "What can I do for you?"

Tuck pulled out the notebook, yanked the pencil from her hair. "Hey, Jake. I'm a twenty-four–seven kinda gal. But it's what you can do for *you* that brings me to your neck of the woods."

Jake gestured to her, *go on*. He didn't offer her a seat.

Tuck sat in the frayed swivel chair across from his desk. Planted her feet. "Okeydokey. Here's the scoop: We're putting together a big takeout on the Bridge Killer investigation. You know, the search for—"

"There is no Bridge Killer, Tuck. No matter how big the *Register* makes the font on your headlines."

"Yeah yeah, as you keep saying. But I just came from talking to Arthur Vick, and he told me—"

"Why'd you do that? Talk to him?"

"Well, hey. Victim three? Gotta start somewhere interviewing friends and family. Vick knew Sellica Darden, right? Talked to his wife, too. Anyway, Vick says you guys think he's the Bridge Killer. Whoa, Jake. That's huge. I would think you might have wanted to warn the frightened citizens of Boston about that. But, since you have not seen fit to do so, we at the *Register* are happy to take care of that little item for you. That's why I'm here."

"'You at the *Register*'? Will 'take care' of it?" Jake assessed his options for dealing with this potential nightmare. He arched an eyebrow and took a chance. "You sure you're comfortable putting Arthur Vick's name in your paper as a suspect? You're going to call him a serial killer suspect?"

"It's true, isn't it? Are you denying it? Is that an on-the-record denial?"

Jake gave an elaborate shrug. "It's an on-the-record nothing, Tuck. But you might want to think back a bit, think about what happened to Jane Ryland when she accused Mr. Vick of hiring a prostitute. Not a happy occasion. For anyone involved."

Tuck blinked at him.

"You might want to leave the police work to the police," Jake continued. "We'll determine what the truth is. And when we're ready to tell you, you can print it. Without fear of a million-dollar lawsuit."

"Well, you're not doing a very good job of it," Tuck said. Almost pouting. "Police work."

Jake smiled, benign. "How do you know?"

Tuck consulted her notebook. "Is one of the victims a Kenna Wilkes?"

Jake frowned. Then he stood up, fingertips on his desk. "Kenna—? Miss Cameron, is there something you care to tell me? As you are no doubt aware, if you have information about an ongoing case, you're required by law to tell us."

"Bullshit I am." She crossed her legs, leaned back in the chair. "As you are no doubt aware. So. Nothing on Wilkes?"

"Let me clarify. You're asking me to comment on some name you pull out of the blue, but you're not gonna tell me why you're asking? I don't think so." Jake looked at his watch. "Anything else before we say good-bye?"

"Actually, yeah. Let me float another name. Amaryllis Roldan."

Jane? Had she told Tuck? She was the only one outside of the cops who— Well, no, she wasn't. Arthur Vick knew that name. And Patti Vick knew it. And Jane wouldn't have . . . or would she? *Was I wrong to have told her? I can't think about it now.* Whatever the source, Tuck was figuring Roldan as a victim. And yesterday the supe had said to keep that under wraps until next of kin was notified. Which, as yet, had not happened.

Tuck prints that name, and I'm fricking toast.

"What's this about, Tuck?"

"Say we ignore the Arthur Vick thing for the moment," she said. "We're definitely going with the name Amaryllis Roldan as a victim—"

Jake gave her two thumbs up, nodding. "Do that. Really, do. But if it turns out she's actually a suspect, wouldn't that be a mess for you? Of course, I'm sure you're sure of your story. You don't put stuff in the paper if you're not sure. So, hey, no comment from me. On this. Or on anything. But I'm sure you know best."

Jake watched the emotions evolve over Tuck's face. Doubt. Caution. Fear.

Time to seal the deal.

"I mean, just saying—and this is one hundred percent off the record, background of background. Consider whether perhaps we want Arthur Vick to *help* us. If he knows her, and maybe she hates him, who knows, and maybe has some kind of a motive your little brain has never even considered. What if she's the bad guy?"

This was complete idiocy, Jake making it up on the fly, but he could see Tuck weighing it all. She was smart, no doubt, and a good reporter. But at some point a new kid simply doesn't have the stuff to keep up. He hoped.

Tuck yanked off her Red Sox cap, relooped her ponytail, jammed the cap back on. She stood up, batting her notebook against one palm.

"Keep your seat, if you need a moment," Jake said. Magnanimous. He sat down again at his desk, tried a sip of coffee. "Otherwise? I have work."

Jake's BlackBerry rang. It would be Pam, right on time. "See?"

He waited for Tuck's reply.

"I'll call you," she said.

"Contact Laney Driscoll in PR," Jake said. His cell rang again. "As you are no doubt aware. And Tuck? I'll forget to tell him you showed up today ignoring protocol. He hates when that happens. Tends to forget to return calls. We done?"

Now Tuck's pout was full blown. "You—"

"And don't forget to return that visitor's pass." The phone rang again. "Brogan, Homicide."

He watched Tuck turn to leave. Walking ever so slowly.

"Cameron," he called. "Close the door."

She did.

"Perfect timing, Mrs. Augusto," he said into the phone.

"Mrs. Augusto who?" DeLuca said. "What aren't you telling me, Harvard?"

Now Jake's desk phone was ringing. Pam's extension number on caller ID. He pushed the speaker button.

"Thanks, Pam," he said. He clicked off, went back to DeLuca on the cell. "Hey, dropout. What up?"

"We may have an ID on the Longfellow victim," De-Luca said. "Not confirmed. But a solid lead."

Jake's stomach lurched. He'd just tossed Tuck from his office. Could she have known the Longfellow victim's name? Before he did? How could that happen? Maybe she was more connected to the story than he'd given her credit for. If that was true, this was going to suck.

"Is her name Kenna—" He grabbed his coffee, gulped, tried again. "—Kenna Wilkes?"

37

Matt yanked the black watch cap down over his forehead, though it was unlikely anyone would recognize him later, even if they did see him in this parking lot outside Holly's building. Only one person in Boston would know his name, anyway—well, two—but say Holly Neff walked right up to his rental car window. So what, really? He would play it by ear.

Wonder why she'd left Springfield at ten o'clock last night?

She had a nice spot here, by the harbor. Boats and stuff. Seagulls. He'd driven all the way to Springfield, finally gotten to the hotel, bullshit bullshit, then had to drive all the way back. Tailing her, keeping a couple of cars between them. Once he'd even passed her. Luckily it was dark. Luckily she hadn't seemed to notice. Now, she was inside. All he had to do was wait.

If he didn't die of starvation. Last thing he'd eaten were two bites of that apple at the hotel. And maybe he could take a piss in the bushes or something.

He'd kill for a—

And there she was.

She had her hair stuffed under some sort of stretchy cap, and some black tracksuit with red stripes down the legs. Running shoes. A pair of iPod buds in her ears, the white wires trailing into a pocket in her jacket. A brown mailing envelope or something under her arm.

Shit. If she was going running, she'd be hard to follow. He could get out of his car and kind of stroll behind her. Follow her on foot. If he was lucky, she wouldn't notice. But she was such a wack, or used to be at least, maybe it wouldn't matter if she did see him.

She'd see him soon enough.

But Holly was reaching into a pocket and pulling out—keys. *Sweet.* He watched her walk to her car, that Honda Accord, get in, and back out of her space.

Matt ducked as she went by him. He counted to five, slowly brought his head up, and peered out the window. She was waiting at the stop sign. He turned on the ignition. Maybe she was going to a coffee shop or something? He played that one out. Lots of possible scenarios there. She was clearly not going to church in that getup.

All could have been settled so long ago. My life would be so different. I miss my mother. I miss my family. I miss the life I should have had.

Holly was on the move.

He watched her turn left, blinker on, into the sparse Sunday-morning traffic. Her white car showed through the railings of a rusting metal bridge. Matt shifted hard, banged out of his space, semi-ignored the stop sign, and eased into the flow a couple of cars behind her. She was easy to spot, putting on her turn signals way before she needed to. She turned left, and so did he. Waterfront, more harbor, more boats. He focused on her, but tried to keep his bearings. She turned left, then right again into a parking lot. He slammed on the brakes, hard. Waited, even as his light turned green. The parking lot didn't look that big.

Some jerk behind him honked. Matt flipped him off.

Then, creeping his car forward, he turned into the lot. South Station Post Office, open twenty-four hours, seven days a week, the sign said. Meters not in effect on Sunday. Why did Holly need a post office?

She parked in a metered spot along the fence by the water. Matt hung back, watching.

Holly got out of the car, crossed the alley, stepped up on the sidewalk. No one else in sight. Lots of empty parking places. She pulled the package from under her arm, stared at it. Touched the front. Turned it over, then turned it over again. Checked something on the outside. He was so close, he could see her frown.

She turned, as if going back to her car. Stopped. Tossed her head. Then, with a long stride and hips swinging, she marched through the glass doors of the building.

Ten minutes later she came out. Without the package.

By then, Matt had a plan.

38

Jane couldn't stop looking at the front page of the online Sunday *Register,* her story front and center. Sitting cross-legged on her bed at the New Englander Hotel, laptop balanced on her knees, she had to admit it looked great.

Nothing about the Bridge Killer, she noted. Take that, roomie. *Jake,* she thought. She needed to talk to him about Amaryllis Roldan. Whoever that was.

She zoomed in on the article. Her byline. Her name on the cutline under the photo. A pretty good photo, too, showing a chaos of blurry arms and heads, features mostly blasted out by the flash, but you could see one woman who seemed to be in tears, and someone else who seemed to be laughing. A red, white, and blue Lassiter banner was somehow in perfect focus in the background, though you could read only LASS.

She needed to show Alex the other shots, the ones with Kenna Wilkes. She could do that when she got back. They showed the same person as in Archive Gus's photos, anyway, so no biggie. They were good backup, though. Evidence. Proof.

She read her article one more time. It had the hotel's mealymouthed "we're investigating" statement. And quotes from a couple of eyewitnesses she'd found in the lobby. In the newspaper's version of "balance," she used one guy criticizing the Lassiter campaign for its "lack of preparation and inability to organize a simple event" and another saying "it was a prank or a mistake, who cared, no one was hurt and it all had a happy ending."

The Lassiter statement was a study in political rope-a-dope, essentially meaningless, about the "fog of campaigning in these exciting times leading up to election day" and "enthusiasm and understanding of the Lassiter supporters" in his "increasingly successful campaign."

Jane had pushed a reluctant Trevor about the possibility of a dirty trick, some kind of ploy by the Gable campaign. Sanctioned by them, or some renegade trickster. But he'd clammed up. She put that in her story, too. "Lassiter campaign staff refuses to speculate on questions about opposition sabotage, saying, 'The lights went out. It could happen to anyone.'"

And Alex had headlined it LASSITER RALLY DISRUPTED. Not Lightgate.

She saved the story to her laptop's hard drive. Jane Ryland, newspaper reporter. She still had the right stuff. Now, time to go home.

Jane jumped into the shower, then, wrapped in the hotel's fluffy white terry cloth robe, brushed her teeth with the toiletries she'd gotten from the front desk. She scrabbled her hair dry and checked her reflection in the mirror. Tired. But curious. Curious about Kenna Wilkes.

Jane had flat-out lied to Moira Lassiter the night before. She turned away from the mirror, leaning on the marble bathroom counter, replaying that episode. What was she supposed to say? *Yes, Mrs. Lassiter, I did see a bombshell woman, she checked in at the same time as your husband, and I saw them together at the rally, cooing double entendres at each other. I even took their photos.*

Jane knew a good story when she saw one. But she was still so—what was the word?—skittish. What if she was wrong? Her chest tightened at *wrong*.

She'd reassured Mrs. Lassiter that she was on the lookout, understood her concern, and would talk to her when she got back to Boston. Seemed like Moira bought it. That gave Jane time to think about Kenna Wilkes before she—

Wait. Maybe Kenna was still here. It was only nine thirty in the morning.

She picked up the phone, punched zero.

"Front desk. Good morning, Miss Ryland. What can we do for you?"

That still creeped her out, how they could tell who was calling.

"Is Gina on this morning?" Jane asked.

"One moment, please."

Good.

"This is Gina. Good morning, Miss Ryland. I trust you enjoyed your stay."

Her voice was guarded, formal. Jane followed suit.

"Yes, lovely. I'll be checking out momentarily, if you could prepare my bill. May I ask, did—'my friend' check out, too?"

Jane heard some keyboard clicking.

"Yes, ma'am, that appears to be correct. Around ten last night."

A moment of silence.

"They all checked in together," Gina continued, whispering. "The big guy. The other guy. And your friend. They all checked out together, too."

"We should drop Mrs. Wilkes off at that lovely home in Deverton first." Owen Lassiter, rested and chatty, sat in the front seat of the SUV. Kenna occupied her usual spot in the back. Watching. Listening. Taking it all in.

They were two exits away from Boston, midmorning Sunday, after coffee and baskets of pastries in the dining room of the Worcester Sheraton. He'd shaken fifty hands during breakfast, Kenna calculated. Signed autographs, gotten fawned over by hotel workers and guests. He'd introduced her and Rory as "campaign staff."

"When's little Jimmy getting back from his grandparents'?" Owen asked her.

Kenna wondered if he'd called Moira. Didn't matter. There was the truth-truth, and there was *her* truth. Poor Moira would never be quite certain which was which.

"Governor, that's so kind of you. But your home is closer, isn't it, than mine? Jimmy's fine, still at his Gran's. Please don't worry about me." She prattled ahead. "And I know Mrs. Lassiter will be happy to see you. Finally. After all the commotion."

Rory gave a thumbs-up, agreeing. "We're taking you straight home, Governor. You told Moira ten thirty. We don't want to keep her waiting. We don't want her to worry, right?"

Kenna fingered her newest acquisition, a sleek pink plastic bottle of shampoo from the Worcester Sheraton. *You never know*. She fluffed her hair and slid on her tortoiseshell sunglasses, very Jackie O.

Moira stood at the front door, waiting. Kenna could see her silhouette behind the glass, framed by white crown molding and curling ivy. As they pulled into the curve of the driveway, Mrs. Lassiter stepped outside. That icy blond hair, somehow coiffed perfectly even on a Sunday morning. White turtleneck, some kind of fuzzy white vest. Fuzzy boots. The woman looked like frosting on a cake. Like meringue. Like money. She held a mug.

She raised it, saluting their arrival, as the SUV stopped.

But she didn't move from the porch. Didn't come out to meet her husband, not even halfway.

"Thanks, Rory. Thanks, Kenna. You're both good sports," Owen said. "Ror, you'll call me about the rest of the day. And any update on the developments in the lights thing."

Rory started to say something, but the governor stopped him with a palm.

"Check it out. I don't like it. And then we're clear till tomorrow, right? Monday morning meeting, then—"

"It's all good, Governor," Rory said. "Go in. The election's coming. It'll be your last day off for a while."

"If we win."

"We'll win."

The governor clicked open his door, and Rory popped the hatchback where the overnight bags were stowed.

Kenna hopped out, came around behind the car. Why not? No reason for her to sit in the backseat after Owen was gone, right? She smoothed her jeans over her rear, then gave a little stretch, making sure her black turtleneck came just a bit untucked. *Oh, such a long car ride.*

She waved at Moira, breezy and casual. And closed her door. She glanced over to see what Moira and her husband were doing. Moira was gesturing at her. Kenna put a hand up to her cheek, as if to hide her face. Why not.

"All set?" Rory asked, turning on the ignition.

"Oh, yeah," Kenna said. "Set and match."

39

"Score one for the new kid," Alex told her, making a mark in the air. "Fifth floor loves it."

At work on a Sunday. He was taking his job seriously, Jane figured. Or maybe it was easier for him to hang out here in his office than at home. Maybe he was using work as an excuse. Or an escape.

Today he was weekend casual in a black T-shirt under a cashmere-looking zipper-neck black sweater. His usual jeans. *Hot Alex,* Jane thought. He was, indeed. Especially now that he was praising her story.

"Oh, terrific. Thanks," Jane said, taking a seat on his couch. She was tired, but never too tired for pats on the back. Soon she'd be home. "Remember, I've got those other photos of Kenna Wilkes. When I get to my desk, I'll download 'em. Send 'em to you."

"Great," Alex said. "But right now you need to— Well, wait. Let me confirm. Your pictures are definitely of the same woman who's in Gus's archive photos, right?"

"Yes, no question." Jane nodded. "Kenna Wilkes is her name. I'm pretty sure . . . well, yeah, it has to be. You know? She was there, at the rally, the woman in the photo. That's what my source at the hotel said her name was. And my source also confirmed Kenna Wilkes checked out the same time the governor checked out. Question is, who the heck is she? I Googled, and Zaba-Searched, got pretty much nothing. Did you?"

"Well, not me, I didn't have time to do it myself. But I told Tuck to look into it." Alex moved his wireless silver mouse across his desk. Jane couldn't see what was on the computer screen. At least she was learning not to take his multitasking personally. Workaholic or not, why was he here on a Sunday? She glanced at the third finger, left hand. Still no ring. But he didn't seem unhappy. No way, of course, to ask what was going on in his personal life. She rewound to what he'd just said.

"You told Tuck?" Jane tried to follow his reasoning. "To check on Kenna Wilkes? How come?"

Alex stopped his mouse and looked up at her, surprised. "On the phone yesterday, you told me the name Amaryllis Roldan. And later, Kenna Wilkes. Since I knew you'd talked to Jake, I thought they were both connected to the Bridge Killer stuff. So I asked Tuck to run them by her sources."

Jane thought back. "No, Alex. I was at the rally, remember? And I told you, Wilkes was the other woman."

"Yeah, I know. But I thought you meant the other woman in the bridge killings. See? Roldan, a victim. And Wilkes the other victim. I figured that was what you were telling me."

"Yikes. And we're supposed to be in the communications biz." Jane shrugged. "Doesn't matter. She is who she is. If Tuck comes up with something for my story, great."

She yawned, the last of her adrenaline departing. She needed coffee. Food. Sleep. How many hours had she slept? Like, four? "Now, if Kenna Wilkes gets murdered by the Bridge Killer, that'd be the ultimate worlds-collide. Anything new on that? I gotta admit, Arthur Vick isn't my favorite person on the planet right now."

Alex slapped his laptop closed.

Gave her his full attention, *thank you so much*.

"Nothing new I know of. Tuck's out now. Talking to—" He paused. "Whatever she does. Anyway, Jane. She'll handle the Bridge Killer. Unless you've decided to give us more on Sellica?"

"Alex—"

"Kidding. Anyway. You've got other fish to fry."

"Fish?"

"Remember I told you the Gable people called? They're saying the interview with her has to be today. So head over to Beacon Hill. Ellie Gable will be waiting for you."

Jane slumped back into the flat cushions of Alex's couch. "You know I'm happy to," Jane said. "I really am. But look at me. I'm a mess. I've been wearing this same outfit for two days."

"You look great," Alex said. "As always."

"I drove all the way to Springfield," Jane went on, ignoring the had-to-be-manipulative compliment. "I stayed up till whenever writing the story. Then drove all the way back. I'm wiped. My brain is fried. There's no way that Gable can—?"

"Your six-month tryout is now five months and three weeks," Alex said. "Happy anniversary. And here's your present. The Gable interview's not till five. So, go home, take a nap. Then show up at Gable's and get us the scoop."

"Kenna? Ah, nope." DeLuca's voice crackled over the phone, sounding confused. "No, Harvard, the victim's name's not Kenna. Listen, you at your desk? I'll be there in ten."

He hung up without waiting for Jake to reply.

Jake closed his eyes briefly. Whew. Tuck had almost sucker-punched him, for sure. She'd gotten some tip, one of dozens probably, decided to try it out on him. Who knew how that girl's brain worked. She wanted there to be a Bridge Killer so desperately, she'd do anything to keep it in the headlines. And keep her name on the front page. It was as much about her career as it was about the truth.

He crumpled Pam's "says urgent" note off the pad, wrote the name Kenna Wilkes on a clean page. He'd get someone to check it. So far, the name wasn't anything that would blow up his life. *Damn, Tuck.*

Jake took a swig of coffee, lukewarm. He put his feet on the desk, pulled his computer onto his lap, opened the folder marked PERSONAL, then the file he'd labeled BRIDGE.

Stared at the screen.

Longfellow was first. The first no-ID body. The one that started this whole Bridge Killer deal. Now DeLuca said they'd gotten a possible name for her. She'd shown no signs of trauma, no tattoos. Cause of death, drowning, according to Dr. Archambault. No shoes. Did that mean anything? No connection with Arthur Vick. So far. Maybe the name would help make the connection. But if she was connected with Vick, that'd be a horse of another color. They'd have to bear down on him. Three for three. That was no coincidence.

Three for three would mean there was a Bridge Killer, and his name was Arthur Vick. Jake scratched his head with both hands, squinching up his eyes. Why would Vick kill—?

Jake thought about Patti Vick, sitting in her suburban living room. Talking about her "best friend." She'd be rethinking that assessment if they nailed him for this. Wonder if she'd stand by him, all that "good wife" stuff.

He clicked to his next page of notes.

Charlestown, victim two, Amaryllis Roldan. A week later, another Sunday. They'd gotten her ID from the tattoo guy. She'd had bruises, face and back. Cause of death, drowning, again. Sellica's mother said she'd never heard of Roldan, but Vick certainly had. And that pitiful Beacon Market clerk Olive Parisella.

Sellica Darden. Body three. Not a Sunday. No ID on her, but Sellica Darden had gotten her fifteen minutes of fame. She didn't need ID. Did the killer know that? Or not? Jake sighed. Cause of death, drowning. But the roofies in her system were outliers. Date rape drug. Who had been her date?

If the killings weren't connected, maybe no other women were in danger.

If they *were* connected—well, still, whoever it was might be done.

Or not.

He buzzed his intercom. "Hey, Pam? I've got a name I need you to run."

"Ready, boss."

"Kenna Wilkes." He spelled it.

"Loud and clear," Pam said. "Gimme a few."

Jake stared at his computer screen, unseeing.

It was Sunday again.

Three dead bodies. And though it was his job to find answers, there were none.

40

Holly walked out of the post office, minus the package, Matt noted. Wonder what she'd mailed? She popped in her earbuds again, pulled off her cap, and messed around with her hair. She yanked the cap back on. Then readjusted her earbuds.

Geez. Get on with it.

He waited for her to get back in her car so he could follow her. His plan seemed eminently reasonable. He'd see if she went anywhere interesting or useful. Lassiter HQ, for instance. If so, play it by car from there.

If she simply went home, also useful. Because in that case, he'd leave. He knew where she lived, right? He could go back to his hotel, catch a nap, shower, and come back in the morning. See where she went. It wasn't like she was gonna leave Boston overnight.

Shit. Instead of turning right to get to her car, still parked in that spot by the fence, she was coming his way. He ducked, as if he were looking for something on the floor. He reached for the glove compartment, flipped it open, fingered out a map, unfolded it in front of his face. Sitting up, he sneaked a look around it.

Holly stood by the water, one ankle raised on the waist-high railing between her and the canal below. He saw her head bend to her knee, bob a couple times. Then she switched legs. Head to knee again. Stretching? *Duh.* She was going running.

Matt peered over the map, watching Holly put her slim body through a series of stretches and curls. Almost as if she were dancing for him, showing off in her skin-tight running suit, moving to the music he imagined must be on her iPod. She raised each leg, one after the other, slowly, excruciatingly slowly, lowering her head to her knee. She leaned back against the metal-railed fence, arms straight, arching her body toward him; then she turned and arched the other way. She turned her back to him. . . . *Is she teasing? Does she know I'm here? She can't*— Then she touched her toes, palms flat to the ground. She put her hand on one heel, then stretched her leg out, in full splits, standing right there, not twenty feet from him, no idea he was watching this performance.

Matt could almost hear her music. Almost forgot to hold up the map. Holly's head lolled back as she stretched her neck, eyes closed; then she rolled her head from side to side. She was drinking it in, enjoying it. She must be. The sun on the water, the seagulls, her body.

She thinks she's alone.

Holly unzipped the hooded jacket she was wearing and shrugged it from her shoulders, revealing a sleeveless black top. Made of that same stretchy stuff as her pants. She adjusted her earbud string and tied the jacket around her waist. He could see her chest, the swell of her curves more maddening than he remembered.

With a shake that was almost a shiver, Holly jogged along the sidewalk away from him and turned right across the bridge.

Matt could hardly breathe. She was—dangerous.

Another plan began to form. A new plan. A better plan.

He'd be ready for Holly when she returned.

"So we made it through Saturday night at least, ya know?" DeLuca's silhouette appeared at Jake's office door, a Dunkin's extra large cup in one hand. His partner raised it, toasting. "No new bodies. Maybe the Bridge Killer's decided to fold his tents."

Pam's voice buzzed through the intercom. "Jake, De-Luca's here." D never waited to be announced.

"You're a sick person, D. And there's no Bridge Killer." Jake typed the name Kenna Wilkes into his BlackBerry. Just in case. Looked up at DeLuca as he sent it to himself.

"Can't believe you're here plugging away." DeLuca lounged in the doorway. "You can't work all the time."

"You can if there's a serial killer on the loose," Jake said.

"Well, that's the thing. Maybe there isn't . . . a serial killer."

Jake looked up, watched DeLuca take a long pull of coffee. "You have two seconds before I—"

"Kylie Howarth. Is the Longfellow vic's name. But she's a suicide."

Jake stood slowly, closing his laptop. He sat down again, his metal chair creaking a complaint. He stared at DeLuca, calculating what that would mean. Longfellow had been the first body. The first domino of the so-called bridge killings. The beginning of the hysteria. Suicide?

I knew it. There was no Bridge Killer.

DeLuca came into the room, flipped around Jake's swivel guest chair, sat with one leg on each side. Draped his leather-jacketed arms across the back of the seat. Plunked his coffee on Jake's desk.

"We think," DeLuca said.

Jake slammed his palm on his desk, sloshing a mini-puddle of coffee onto the wooden surface. "You kidding me? What're you talking about, D? You on drugs? There's no room for *maybe* in this business."

DeLuca made the time-out sign. "Is there room for 'probably'? Hear me out. Her parents called. Kylie Howarth, *K-y-l-i-e,* is their daughter. They're from— Louisville. St. Louis. Someplace like that, it's in my notebook. Wife's, like, a city councilor. Husband's rich. Anyway, they'd been out of town in, ah, you know, Europe. Switzerland, someplace like that. Skiing. So they didn't get the letter. Till they got back."

"The—?" Jake wrote down the name Kylie.

"Letter. She's sorry, she let them down, she can't face it all anymore. Apparently she had some problems. She'd run off to Boston, poor-little-rich-girl type of thing, they hardly heard from her. So it didn't concern them when, you know. They were out of touch. So she sends them this letter. Saying she was gonna 'fly.' Didn't know they were gone. Apparently."

"But how did they, I mean why—?"

DeLuca blotted the spilled coffee with a handkerchief, stuffed it back in his jeans pocket. "The letter was postmarked Boston. They called the cops. Kurtz took it. She told me about it. I told her I'd fill you in."

Jake's intercom buzzed again. "Jake? Cadet Kurtz is—"

"Send her in, please," Jake said. "So how do we know it's her? Kylie How—?"

"Howarth. We don't," DeLuca said. "Description matches, though. Everything matches. Description, timing, 'flying'—you know, off a bridge. The parents are getting a plane A-sap, bringing the letter. Could be here today, they'll let us know. Then they'll have to see Dr. A in the ME's office. ID the body."

"Bad news for them," Jake said. "Hate that. But guess it's good for us."

"Yup." DeLuca nodded, swiveling the chair slightly back and forth. "Thing is."

"Thing is what?" Jake said.

"Detectives?" Cadet Kurtz, also carrying a Dunkin's cup, peered around Jake's door. She held out a sheaf of papers, but looked at DeLuca. "So you told him? I was going to call you, sir, but Paul—uh, Detective DeLuca— said that—"

"All set," Jake said. He motioned her to hand over the documents. "Good work."

DeLuca raised his cup at her. "Kurtz, I was about to tell Detective Brogan what you said the Howarths told you about their daughter's employment history. Where she'd applied for a job."

Jake began to read. He held the pages, midair.

"No way," he said. He looked at DeLuca, then at Kurtz, then back again, trying to read their faces. "You two are frickin' kidding me."

41

Two missed calls, a text, and an e-mail. Jane clicked her car door open, alone in the *Register*'s parking lot, turned on the key to get the heat started. *I have to sleep.* She would see who'd called, drive to her apartment, then answer, if she absolutely had to, when she got home. Then, sleep.

She clicked in her access code. If she didn't got some rest, she'd never make it through the Gable interview. Lucky she had already done her research. Lucky she didn't have to look good on camera for it.

Voice mail. *"You have two new calls. To listen, press one."*

"Jane Elizabeth?"

Her father's voice. Was something wrong?

There was a pause. Her dad hated leaving messages. Something must be wrong. Lissa? Her wedding? His health? "Your sister showed me the article in the *Boston Register* this morning. Online."

Another pause.

"Nice job, honey," her father said. He coughed, cleared his throat. "I wish your mother could have seen it."

There was a beat of silence, then a click. Her father never said good-bye on the phone. Why did she always feel tears, hearing his voice? She was tired. Just tired. She pushed 1 for the other message.

This caller's voice was so shrill, so tense, she almost didn't recognize it.

"We have to talk, Jane," Moira's recorded voice said. "Owen just got home. Now he says—well, first he told me he was in Springfield, but now he's saying he spent the night in Worcester. *Worcester!* That's more than forty-five minutes from here. Why not simply come home? Why not? I'll tell you why. He actually had that girl in the car. *In his car.* I saw her, she got out, preened herself in front of me, all that hair and . . . ah. That incredible b—"

Jane could hear Moira stop for breath, imagined her trying to calm herself. Did she hear the clink of ice?

"We need to talk, Jane. Did you see this person in Springfield? Why did Owen go to Worcester? It's terrible, Jane, it's terrible. You're an outsider, reliable, the only one I can trust. You know someone is going to notice. And when they do, it'll be too late. Call me, please."

Jane stared at the phone. Hit the Save button. And stared again. So much for Jane's feigned ignorance. Sounded like Moira, too, had seen the other woman.

She turned off the ignition. She had to go back upstairs and tell Alex.

She turned on the ignition. She had to get home. She could call Alex later and they could figure out what to do. If Moira was drunk, or delusional, or scheming, or sincere, or whatever all the other possibilities were. Nothing more was going to happen today. Nothing she could do anything about, anyway.

Who'd texted? She clicked a few buttons. Amy. "Another Sat nite by URself? How 'bout Hot Alex? CL me." If Amy only knew. And she hadn't even told her about Alex's on-again, off-again wedding ring. If she did, Amy'd be on the hunt for bridesmaids' dresses.

Jane yawned, her whole face stretched with the desire for sleep, her eyes closing. She covered her face with her palms, then batted her cheeks to wake herself up.

Next, the e-mail. From Jake.

Shoot. She clicked it open. Stared at it. Two words: *Kenna Wilkes.*

It was cold, and beautiful, and it felt like she was flying. Holly stretched to her longest stride, the music filling her head, a blast of salt air filling her lungs and making her so powerful. She was running and running, not away from anything, not anymore, but toward her perfect future. The post office had been open on Sunday, perfect, package number two now on the way.

Odd that Jane hadn't mentioned the first package. Maybe the mail had messed up. Maybe it hadn't arrived? She knew the address was correct, she'd chosen Jane carefully and copied her address at Channel 11 from the Web before she'd moved to Boston. She'd even written the mailing labels in advance.

Holly took a deep breath, trying not to fret. She'd only mailed it—when? Like, the other day. Maybe Jane hadn't seen it yet. Maybe Jane was ignoring it? Testing her? Or maybe she didn't recognize her from the photos. At the rally, Holly'd been so excited to see Jane! And thought she'd come on purpose, hoping Holly would be there. Funny, she didn't have a cameraman with her. TV reporters usually did.

Holly let it go, the wind whistling past her woolen cap, and she made the turn back to the post office. The muscles in her legs and her lungs had that nice burning sensation, so she knew she'd pushed to the limit. And a little beyond.

Her car was there, right where she'd left it. The lot had

been pretty empty when she parked, only a couple of cars. There were more now, now that it was—she looked at her black digital watch—a little after noon. A guy stood by the railing, a folded newspaper sticking out of his back pocket. She watched him toss bread crumbs or whatever into the water, swooping seagulls snapping them up.

Holly kept running, slowing down, following along her iPod selections in cool-down mode. She'd programmed them specially for her run, starting off slowly, then getting faster and faster, then perfect running music, the Cars, Gaga, Katy Perry, Flo Rida; then the cool down. She was almost through her favorite Sting, so one song still to go before her timed run-list finished. And she had to be back at the car, perfectly, when the downloads ended.

She'd make it. She always did, even if she had to hurry up or slow down a little to make it precisely right.

She leaned both palms against the hood of her car, her hands feeling the chill of the metal through her knitted gloves, and let out a long cleansing breath exactly as the cool-down music ended. The stretching music started. *Alanis.* She carefully lifted one leg behind her, then the other. She looked up. The guy was watching her.

She squinted in the October sunshine. Ignored the music's orders to continue stretching. Was the glare on the water playing tricks with her vision? Did she want it so much that it seemed to appear? She stopped, mid-stretch, staring. Blinked, twice, but the same man was still there. And she knew who it was. She *knew.*

No. Not possible.

The man was walking toward her. Could it be?

She pinched her own arm, hard. "Ow!" she cried. Like one of the seagulls skirling across the sky. But she felt it. She didn't wake up. It wasn't a dream. It was real.

The man came closer. Closer. Closer.

She heard him say, "Hollister?"

42

"Wake up, Hollister." Matt draped Holly onto the passenger seat of his car. She hadn't exactly fainted, but he'd arrived right in time to catch her as her knees gave way. He pulled off her stretchy cap and tossed it into the backseat. She still looked terrific, that was for sure. Though he figured seeing him would be a shocker, he never expected she'd totally lose it like this. Well, it could work for him. "Holly? You with me here?"

"Is it really you? Matt?" She turned to him as he got behind the wheel, one palm under her cheek like a groggy little girl. "How did you know—?"

"Let's not talk about that now," Matt said. "You look kinda woozy. Do you need some water?"

Holly shook her head slowly, staring at him. She reached out with one hand, didn't quite touch him. "No, no, don't leave. No water. I'm fine. It's only—Matt?"

"Yes, it's me."

"You called me Hollister. I knew you would, I knew it. Knew if I . . ." Her voice trailed off. She closed her eyes.

Geez. A complete wack. Matt felt her car keys in her pocket and clicked her car locked through his open window. Meters not in effect Sundays, that was a big plus.

Even if she didn't move her car tonight, she wouldn't get a ticket until the next day. Holly's earbuds had fallen out, and he'd looped them around her neck. He could hear the buzz of some music coming from them.

"The world works in mysterious ways." From somewhere he pulled out a line Holly used to throw at him. He rolled his eyes, knowing she'd never notice. "I guess I was meant to find you."

"Mmmmm," she said. Keeping her eyes closed. "Tell me the story, though. The whole thing."

"Tell you the . . . ?"

Holly sat up, tucked one ankle under her, wide-eyed as a kid asking for another fairy tale. "The whole story. How you found me."

Nip this puppy in the bud, Matt thought. Hell, he needed to stall for time, but he'd tell her the truth, kind of, then move on. "Well, I saw your picture in the paper. The Boston paper. I read it for the Red Sox, you know?"

He tapped the newspaper on the console next to him. "I don't get the print version back home, so I check out the *Register* online. And there you were, in a story about—"

"My picture's in today's paper?" Holly's eyes sparkled. She sat up straighter, grabbing for the Sunday *Register* he'd purchased outside the post office. "Let's see!"

Matt had to laugh, watching her scan the front page. "Not today's paper," Matt said. "It was . . . a couple days ago. So I flew in to see if I could find you."

He expected—he didn't know what he expected. But not this. Holly had the newspaper in front of her face. Like she'd completely forgotten about him.

"Holly? Hollister?" *What the hell?*

"Jane Ryland works for the *Register*?" Holly's voice was hollow, and her finger pointed at something on the front page. "She's a reporter for the *Register*? I thought she was television. A television reporter. Doesn't she work at Channel Eleven?"

She turned to him, her face crumbling. Was she about to cry? The woman was certifiable. Holly looked back at the paper, running her finger down a column.

"Jane what?" Matt said. "Who's she?"

Holly folded his newspaper so the article she was reading was the only thing showing.

"I have to go," she said.

Are you friggin' kidding me? "Ah, Holly, Hollister, no, not now, not now that we finally found each other again." Matt scrambled to get back the advantage. Whatever just happened, he had no idea. "Whatever it is about this Jane, whoever that is, I know I can help you. I'm here to help you. But, Holly, it's a beautiful Sunday, and we're together, and there's nothing you can do right now about whatever is . . ."

Matt put himself in full-speed-ahead sales mode, trying to gauge Holly's reaction.

"Let's go for a walk, the way we used to. Or sit in a café, and you can tell me everything." He was not going to let her escape, not until he found out what she was up to. Maybe this Jane thing was something he should know about.

Reality hit. *Shit.* Jane. *Reporter.*

"Hollister," he said. Was she planning to tell what she knew? Was she stalking some newspaper or television person? That could be a disaster. He put his hand on her shoulder. Last ditch. "Come to my hotel room. Be with me."

He watched as she lowered the paper. She turned to him, smiling.

And we have a sale, ladies and gentlemen. Time to

close the deal. "I'll bring you back to your car later," Matt said. "Unless you have other plans?"

"My Matt," she said.

Jake's car? In front of her house? As soon as she turned onto Corey Road, Jane recognized that undercover Jeep he sometimes used, dark blue, tinted windows. The bright morning had softened into gray afternoon. Sparse trees and empty sidewalks, fading piles of fallen leaves, even the rows of brownstones made her street a rainbow of neutral. End-of-October neutral. She caught a glimpse of Jake in the front seat. Why was he here?

Jake was out and beside her before she turned off the ignition.

"I need to talk to you, not on the phone," he said as she got out. He moved close to her, his hand grasping her arm. Pushed her car door closed with his hip. "How are you?"

She could smell peppermint on his breath, and coffee. "Hey, Jakey," she said. She left his hand there, didn't move away from him. No one was watching them. And if they were—well. They weren't. "I'm good. Except for being exhausted. Drove back from Springfield after all that, then had to go to the paper. And I need to take a nap before I die of sleep deprivation."

She stopped. Tried to read his face. "Jake? What happened? Is this about Kenna Wilkes?"

Jake gave her a funny look. Frowning. "Kenna Wilkes? Why would—?" He cocked his head toward her building. "Can we go in?"

Jane's eyebrows went up. "Sure, I guess. Is everything okay?" He was scaring her a little. But it had to be about his e-mail. After her initial bafflement, she'd figured he must have gotten the name Kenna Wilkes from Tuck. But why would he e-mail Jane about that? Unless Kenna— somehow—was connected with the bridge killings. Or maybe with Arthur Vick? She tucked her arm through Jake's, clicking her car locked.

She couldn't decide if she felt safer with him here, or more afraid. Maybe she was simply exhausted.

"Come in for five minutes. You can tell me what's going on. Then I have to sleep. I've got an interview at five with—well, a work thing. But is everything okay? Are *you* okay?"

"Sure," Jake said. "Everything's fine."

They climbed the series of narrowing concrete steps to her brownstone in silence, neither of them letting go of the other. Jane turned the lock in the outer door, scooped up the newspaper from the black and white tiled entryway. They climbed two flights of wood-paneled stairway, arm in arm, silent.

"Nice place," Jake said when she opened the door.

Jane gave her apartment a quick once-over look, relieved she'd put most of her stuff away before she'd headed out to Sellica's funeral. Gosh, only yesterday. Not too many magazines and newspapers piled on the glass coffee table, only one coffee mug on the end table, only one blazer hanging over the back of a dining room chair. *Presentable.* She glanced at the cocoa-brown leather couch in her living room, still half-expecting Murrow to leap from her spot and greet her at the door. Poor kitty. She'd had a long and good life.

"Thanks," Jane said. Weird he'd never been here before. She'd gone to *his* apartment. That once. That night. She plopped the newspaper on the dining room table and shrugged off her coat. Remembered she was still wearing the same black skirt and turtleneck as yesterday, and hardly had on makeup. Jake was already sitting in the taupe-striped wing chair by the fireplace, fussing with the zipper on his jacket.

What is this all about?

"Listen, Jane," Jake began. "I'd get nailed for talking to you about this. I just yelled at Tuck for ditching protocol."

"What did she—?"

"Doesn't matter," he said. "But we got some info about one of the victims. A Bridge Killer victim. I mean, not the Bridge Killer. *Look*. Off the record?"

Jane plonked her head against the back of the couch, hugging a paisley throw pillow. "Jake Brogan. You show up at my apartment. E-mail me a name with no explanation. Tell me about some Amaryllis person without saying why. I think we're way past off the record, dude."

"Yeah, gotcha. But, Jane, this is for you, not for the paper. I want you to be careful of Arthur Vick. Seems like all the victims are connected to him. Seems like he's not a good guy to have as an enemy. And if he's coming after—"

The doorbell rang, an insistent buzz that cut through Jake's words. Jane stood, knocking her pillow over the coffee table and onto the tight design of the rug. Her eyes widened, and she shook her head: *No idea . . .*

Jake was already at the door. He cocked his head. Made his hand into a puppet. *Ask who it is*, he mouthed.

43

"Yes?" Jane leaned closer to the door, peering through the peephole. Nothing. Was someone hiding? Flattened against the wall? Crouching? Did they know Jake was there?

"It's me," a little voice piped through the door. "Eli."

Jane collapsed against the doorjamb, holding her head in her hands, trying not to laugh, waving Jake off.

"Hey, kiddo," she said, swinging open the door. Eli was much too short to show in the peephole. She burst out laughing as he came into the foyer. "What on earth?"

"I'm a zombie anchorman, for trick or treat tomorrow!" he said. "Listen."

He furrowed his forehead, narrowed his black-rimmed blue eyes, and spoke into what looked like a paper towel roll with a tennis ball on top. "And now, the news of the dead," he intoned.

"Very cool. Especially the bloody microphone," Jane said. *Halloween*. She'd have to ask Mrs. Washburn to do Twizzler duty again. "This is my friend Jake. Jake, this is Eli. Eli's a pal. Jake's a police officer."

"Hey, Eli," Jake said.

"A real police officer? Do you have a gun?" Eli had

apparently forgotten about the news of the dead. "Did you ever shoot anyone?"

"Someday, you wanna come tour the police station?" Jake asked. He'd dropped to a crouch, eye level with the little boy in the open doorway. "I'll show you how we do target practice."

"Eli! Are you bothering Jane again?" Eli's mother was tramping down the one flight of burgundy-carpeted stairs, baby Sam balanced on her hip, his pudgy hand grasping the strap of her rock-star tank top.

"It's fine, Neen," Jane called out. "He was just showing . . ."

Arriving on the landing, Neena Fichera hitched Sam to her other already-slim hip, checked out Jake unabashedly. "Hi," she said, throwing Jane a look. "Are you—?"

"Neena, super of the building, Jake, um, work colleague of mine." Jane's brain was about to fry. Jake was showing an enthralled Eli his handcuffs, chatting as if they were old pals.

Neena raised an eyebrow, gave a quick thumbs-up.

Jane stuck out her tongue. Neen thought Jane was missing the motherhood boat, too. *This whole day is out of control.* And Eli seemed to have a new hero. How did that happen so fast?

"Come on, Eli, Jane's *busy,*" Neena said, scooting him out the door. Sam gurgled, sticking one bootied foot into a pocket of Neena's cargo pants.

"See you later, Eli," Jane said. "Great costume."

Eli turned, ignoring Jane, saluting Jake. "You promise? To show me?"

"Ten-four," Jake said.

By the time they'd gone, and Jane had closed the door, the afternoon was evaporating. She was exhausted. And craved sleep. But here was Jake, and he was so damn—

"He's a funny kid," Jake said, clicking his handcuffs back into place. "He adores you."

Jake paused, took a step closer. "I see why."

Jane didn't move. She could hear him take a deep breath, see him seem to consider . . .

He reached out a hand, touched her shoulder. "You know we could . . ."

She had to get this afternoon under control.

"No, we can't." She took a step back. "You know that, too, Jake. And you were warning me, I think, about Arthur Vick. That's why you're here, right?"

That ought to change the mood. For better or for worse.

"You really think he killed Sellica?" she continued. Determined. "Is he under arrest?"

Jake paused. Stuffed his hands into his jacket pockets.

"I see," he said.

The room was silent. Upstairs, a door slammed.

"Okay," Jake said. "No. No arrest. We talked to him. He said the L-word. Lawyer. So we're moving carefully."

Jane leaned against the white-painted wall, trying to kick her weary brain into gear. "And you said—all three victims? Are connected to him?"

Jake nodded. "Seems like it. Sellica, you know about. The second victim is Amaryllis Roldan. She worked at a Beacon Market. And the first victim had applied for a job at Beacon. But it's all—it's still not public. A next-of-kin thing."

"So Vick could have—," Jane began. She gestured him back to the living room. Might as well sit down. Sleep seemed unlikely at this point.

"Yeah. So. We don't know." He sat on the couch, next to her.

She picked up a paisley pillow. Made it a barrier between them.

"Janey, here's my point." Jake leaned toward her, elbows on knees. "If it *was* Arthur Vick—well, I thought you should—be aware. Cautious."

Jane stared at him, her fingers sliding through the pillow's silky fringe.

"Tuck's already sniffing around him," Jake went on. "Listen, are they gonna put Vick's name in the paper as a suspect? After what he did to you?"

"No idea." She blew out a breath, considering. It'd be interesting to see what Alex decided about that. "But—wait. Tuck. Did she ask you about Kenna Wilkes? Is that why you e-mailed me that name?"

"E-mailed you the name Kenna Wilkes?" Jake looked confused. "I never e-mailed you. How do you know that name?"

"Well, first off, because—" Jane pushed up the sleeves of her turtleneck, checked her watch. *Doomed.* "Listen. You want something to drink?"

The sugar maple outside her kitchen window had given up the last of its leaves, and a fat squirrel scuttled up a bare branch. The redwood bird feeder she'd rigged up was empty. Jane sighed. *The bird feeder was more for Murrow than for me.* She took the silver kettle to the sink, turned on the water. "Tea? Yes, no?"

Jake sat at the round table by the window, elbows on the yellow-checked tablecloth, examining her little terra-cotta pot of delicately blooming paperwhites.

"Sure. But Kenna Wilkes, Jane."

"Well," she said over the running water. "First, you e-mailed me the name. But I figured—" She turned off the water and turned on the stove. "—I figured Tuck asked you about her. Thing is, I had asked Alex to find out about her. For a whole nother story. He apparently misunderstood. But then, when you e-mailed me, I thought there might be something more."

"Like I said. I didn't." Jake pulled out his BlackBerry.

Jane found two chunky mugs, rummaged in the cabinet for tea bags. "Sure you did. Too late for English Breakfast. How about Calm?"

"Damn," Jake said.

"Huh?" Jane said. She pulled out two colorful boxes. "Okay. I have other kinds."

She turned to show him, but he was staring at his BlackBerry.

"I meant to send the name to myself," Jake said. "I guess I hit *JA*, then screwed up when DeLuca came in. Hit the wrong button. And it got sent to you. The next one on my contacts list."

The teakettle whistled. "Funny," she said, pouring steaming water into the mugs. "You had me thinking she was involved in the bridge killings. That'd be weird."

She put a mug in front of Jake, added a spoon and a folded napkin, pushed the sugar bowl toward him. She leaned against the kitchen counter, holding her own mug with both hands.

"Well, Kenna Wilkes doesn't exist, far as I can see," Jake said, stirring.

"Sure she does," Jane said. "I've seen her."

Jake took a tentative sip. Put his mug back on the table. "Well, you saw *someone*. But there is no Kenna Wilkes. Not that my assistant can find, anyway."

"Really? You looked her up in your woo-woo secret police files, whatever you guys have? Why?"

"Yup. We did. What's she to you, anyway? When Tuck mentioned her name, I thought she was a Bridge Killer victim. So I—"

"Kenna Wilkes isn't a Bridge Killer victim. She isn't dead."

"Well, whatever. That's what I thought at the time. So we checked out the name, and there's no record of her. Registry of motor vehicles, social security, criminal history. Nothing."

Jane watched the steam twirl up from her tea. Watched Jake, one arm draped over the ladder-back of her kitchen chair, legs stretched out on the hardwood floor. Just the two of them. A Sunday afternoon. If the world were different, they'd be luxuriating, reading the papers, watching an old movie, sharing a bowl of popcorn. Or ripping each other's clothes off, if wishes came true. But here they were talking about murder, and danger, and now he was telling her an impossible thing. That Kenna Wilkes didn't exist.

"I talked to her. Last night. In Springfield." Jane mentally replayed their conversation. How Kenna seemed to recognize her, but didn't know she'd been fired. They talked about the election. She pretended she wasn't involved with Lassiter.

Hey. Jane had taken her photo! She could simply show that to Jake. All she had to do was grab her camera from her purse, and—she stopped. That wouldn't prove anything about who Kenna was. Or her role in this election.

The election. There *was* a way to find out about Kenna Wilkes.

"Jake? Did your person check voter registration lists?"

Jake shook his head. "Doubt it. Why?"

"Kenna Wilkes told me she 'couldn't wait to vote for Owen Lassiter.' She said, 'I wish I could vote for him a million times.' So she must be registered. And that's public record. I'll look her up tomorrow at City Hall."

She toasted him with her tea, pleased with herself.

Jake nodded. "Nice going, Brenda Starr. Hope it works for your story. But, you know, she's not part of this case." He took a last swig, walked past her to put his mug in the sink. "Thanks, Janey. I'd better let you get some sleep."

She joined him at the sink, put her empty mug next to his on the stainless steel. They stood, shoulder to shoulder, looking out the little curtained window overlooking the courtyard. A cardinal, a flare of crimson, swooped into the bare branches in front of them.

Jane felt Jake's arm slide around her waist. Felt his warmth. Felt him breathe. Felt the slightest touch of his hair on her cheek.

She turned to him, barely. Not wanting to move. Wanting to move.

"Want some company?" Jake whispered. "For your nap?"

Yes, Jane thought. *Yes, yes, yes.*

He looked down at her, lifting her chin with one finger. "Janey," he whispered. "Tell me again why we decided . . ."

"It's hard to remember, right now." Jane could barely hear her own voice. Barely knew her arm slid under Jake's leather jacket, barely realized her cheek nestled in the soft wool of his sweater.

"You there, Jake? Over." A voice crackled through the portable radio clipped to Jake's belt.

She heard Jake sigh, felt his chest rise and fall. She kept her eyes closed, wrapping herself in the moment, marking it. It would soon be gone.

"I hear you, D. Over," Jake said into the radio. His arm tightened around her waist, one hand slipping under her sweater. His hand was cool, and warm, and soft, and strong.

"The Howarths got plane tickets. They're on the way. Meet at Logan in an hour? Terminal B. Over."

Jane opened her eyes. Saw the cardinal fly away.

"Roger that," Jake said.

"That's why," Jane said.

44

Thank goodness for my little tape recorder. Jane had made it to Eleanor Gable's office, right on time at five. Running on adrenaline. Gable was already talking faster than Jane's frantic note-taking could possibly keep up.

The candidate catalogued her personal history in nonstop bullet points: flossy childhood on the North Shore, boarding school, college, trust fund, escapades, law school. Women's rights, volunteer work, politics, change the world, do her part, take a stand.

Ellie Gable came out from behind the pale green antique desk in her opulent Beacon Hill study and paced, all broad gestures and unrelenting eye contact, in front of the tartan-silk curtains draping the bay window.

Wonder how many Chanel suits the woman has, Jane thought. *Not that there's anything wrong with that.*

"So when we finally got enough signatures to get on the ballot"—Gable was wrapping up the push-for-the-nomination chapter in her political life—"we knew we were on the way." She refilled a crystal goblet with the last of her Diet Coke, lifting the empty plastic bottle to signal a conservatively suited young woman standing near the doorway for another. The links of Gable's gold charm bracelet glinted in the light of the crackling fire. "And now with the election less than two weeks away—well, it's all been the most exciting, the most compelling—"

Wonder why her people called this an "interview." Jane dutifully took notes as Gable continued. It was more like a performance. A monologue. The world according to Ellie. Jane was too weary to try to stop her. It wouldn't work anyway.

"We've matched Lassiter dollar for dollar in contributions," Gable was saying. "And I'm sure you know all the polls—thank you, Frannie, you can leave us now." Accepting another Diet Coke, she unscrewed the plastic cap with barely a pause. "All the polls have us neck and neck. And Lassiter trending down. Isn't that what the *Register* says, Jane?"

Jane looked up from her notebook. "Is that what your internals are showing?"

"Well, yes, they do. But we won't know until election day, will we? That's why our get-out-the-vote organization—"

Jane eyed the photographs covering every flat surface and tabletop in the study as Gable continued. Silver frames, smiling faces, beaches and monuments and infants and christenings and graduations and inaugurations. Nantucket, again. Washington, D.C. *Wonder why Gable never married.* Maybe she had? Nothing in her bio about it. But that was proof of nothing.

"Is it difficult to run by yourself?" Jane's question came out almost before it was fully formed. "Most candidates these days have a spouse, a partner of some kind, to be a—you know, touchstone, companion, a reliable buddy on the campaign trail."

"More likely to be killed by a terrorist than get married after forty? Like that old *Newsweek* article? That where you're going with this?" Gable said. She took a sip of soda, smiling. "Nope, Jane, I'm a one-woman show, always have been. Looking for love? Well, of course, in the back of my mind. Aren't you? You're not married, right? But there are so many things I need to get accomplished. Marital bliss will have to wait."

Gable tucked a strand of ice blond hair behind one ear, revealing a filigreed onyx and gold earring.

"Is this the part of the story where you compare me with Moira Lassiter?" She put her hands out, raising and lowering, like a scale. "Married, not married. Family woman, single woman. Good wife, bad girl."

Jane started to protest. "You're hardly a—"

"What does Moira say about me, might I ask? And what does she say about being MIA?"

"Missing in action?" Jane asked. Interesting. The chic candidate was suddenly gossip girl.

"Not to mention the fiasco at the Springfield rally," Gable went on. Her voice lowered. "A mess, huh? I heard all about it. You're the reporter, Jane. But seems as if something's going on over there. Moira suddenly off the map. Campaign appearances canceled. Off the record? If you ask me, it's out of control." She gave a little smile. "Perhaps it's just Gable momentum. We'll see."

Gable placed her goblet onto a leather coaster atop a sculpted wood end table, ice clinking as it settled in the glass. "Let me ask you something, Jane. In the story you write, are you going to mention Lassiter's first wife? Or have you media people decided to leave that out?"

Jane knew she hadn't kept the surprise from her face. First wife? She racked her memory, going over the research in her file. She was zonked, *so tired*, but she'd have remembered that. There was nothing.

"I see you aren't aware of this," Gable said. "Well, some are, some aren't. It was . . . heavens, twenty years ago? Or more. Before he ran for governor. Before he got anywhere near politics. I simply wonder why it's never discussed."

Kenna Wilkes? Could Kenna Wilkes be Lassiter's first wife? Jane quickly calculated, estimating and subtracting. *Impossible*. Kenna—whoever she really was, if Jake was right—looked way too young for that. Ellie Gable herself would be closer to the right age. Now *that* would be a story.

"What happened to her? Do you know her name?" Jane asked.

"Katharine, something, I think," Gable said. "I'm not sure what happened to her. If anything 'happened,' you know? It would be easy enough to dig up the answers, I suppose. She certainly hasn't appeared at *my* front door, I can tell you that. More's the pity."

Strange that Moira never mentioned this. Or—Jane mentally shrugged—maybe not so strange. Everyone was divorced.

"Katharine what?" Jane asked. "Is her last name still Lassiter?"

Gable took a sip of her drink, examining the glass before replacing it on the coaster. "Oh, goodness. Those hotshots running Owen's campaign, I'm sure they know. Kiernan? Is that his name? And that Maitland. What's his name? Roy?"

"Rory," Jane said.

"That's right," Gable said. "Rory. I'm sure he decided it wasn't important. Times change, voters change. Ronald Reagan, Newt Gingrich. Rockefeller, Joe Kennedy. They all had first wives. Who knows who else. Everyone gets divorced."

"Except for you." Jane smiled. "Or do you have an ex-husband who's not in your campaign literature?"

"Me?" Gable said. Her charm bracelet flashed as she waved a hand. "Ask me anything, Jane. The Gable campaign has nothing to hide."

45

"I've never ever been happier. I knew you would find me." Holly draped Matt's jacket across her shoulders, stared at him, drinking him in. It had been two years and four months, but she could never forget the shadow of his cheekbones, the bulk of his shoulders, the lift of muscle as his arm encircled her waist. He'd brought her here to the Spinnaker Café, pulled out the wrought-iron chair for her. Finally the waitress left them alone.

And here, looking out over the harbor, on the second-story redwood deck, Matt was sitting right across from her! Just like that day in B-school by the river, the two of them, connected. She knew this would happen. She'd willed it to happen. It was supposed to happen. It was perfect.

She took a sip of her coffee, creamy and steamy in a thick white mug. He'd ordered it special for her, with Irish whiskey and whipped cream. Her white plastic straw was coated with sweetened liquor and sugar. She licked it like a satisfied cat, tasting the sweetness and feeling the warmth course through her.

He was talking to her, so charming and so Matt, but she barely heard his words. She watched his mouth, the way his jaw worked, the way the last of the sun twinkled on his curly ginger brown hair, the way he watched her. Wanting her. She knew he was, she knew it, even with his eyes hidden behind those sunglasses. He couldn't hide from her. He didn't want to. Didn't today prove that?

He found me.

She stroked the lapel of his jacket as if it were his skin, feeling the weave of the wool, inhaling the scent.

And when she'd finally get to tell him her plans— when she told him! She was sure he would never leave her again.

Matt watched her across the table, off in her own wacko Holly-world. She seemed to simply accept his being here, instantly buying his half-assed story, hardly questioning where he'd come from or how he'd found her in the post office parking lot or why he was in Boston. The woman was a total nutcase.

He smiled at her, ignoring his clenched stomach, trying to compose his face into whatever she wanted to see. Trying to say what would sell her whatever she was willing to buy. He watched her lick that little straw from her Irish coffee—he'd ordered a double—wondering if she thought using her tongue like that was sexy, making him want her or something.

God forbid. He took a sip of his Harpoon. All he wanted was to know what the hell was going on.

"So enough about me," Matt said. It was freezing here on the damn deck, but he didn't want people to see them together. He would pay in cash. He would keep his sunglasses on. Maybe her showing up around Lassiter meant nothing. Maybe he'd overreacted. Maybe he could go back to normal.

"Tell me more about you. Why you came to Boston."

"I know you, Matt," she said. "I know what you need. I've always known."

Play it cool. "That's so interesting, Hollister," he said. "Ah, what is it that you know?"

Good one, idiot. Subtle. But she didn't seem to notice his stilted, awkward question. She was yanking his jacket around her shoulders, like—petting it. Smelling it. Disgusting.

"Even when you went away, I knew why," she said. Her eyes narrowed, and she leaned in, closer to him. "It wasn't about me. It was you."

Hell it was. It was about you, sister. "Me?" he asked.

"Can I get you anything else?" A scrawny little waitress, black T-shirt and black apron, arrived at their table with a black leather bill flap.

Matt took a twenty from his wallet, tucked it in the flap without saying a word. Handed it back to her with a smile, like, *we're fine.*

"Thanks," the waitress said. "Have a nice evening."

"Oh, look," Holly said. "It's so beautiful!" She clapped her hands like a kid at the circus, then pointed to the harbor. A cruise ship, draped from bow to stern with garlands of glittering white lights, sailed silently past them, so close that Matt could see passengers lining the decks, waving. As the sun dimmed, each waterfront building seemed to disappear, showing only as an outline of twinkling lights, each reflected on the water below.

Holly leaped up, ran to the edge of the deck, leaned over the wooden railing. She turned to him, waving him to come. "Come see it with me," she said. "It's like the buildings are wearing beautiful jewelry, necklaces of diamonds and pearls."

It's more like you're a total wack job. The lights and the water and the cruise ship were actually kind of cool looking, but that's not what he cared about now. *Hell with Boston*. He wanted this over. He wanted his life back.

"I have an idea," he said. He put his arm around her waist. Felt her crowd into him. "I know I need to get you back to your car, but should we walk down there for a minute? Get closer to the lights?"

"Oh, I'd love to," Holly said. She looked at him. *My Matt*. Then she had an idea. Would she dare put on his jacket? She would. Giggling, she jammed her arms into the sleeves, as if the jacket were hers.

"How do I look?" she asked. She posed like a fashion model, then twirled in front of him. She still wore her extra-tight running pants, and—bad Holly, she gave her body a little extra shimmy as she turned to face him, posing. Her face felt flushed from the cold and the warmth of her drink and the rush of being with Matt again.

"You look great," he said.

He was so cute, acting awkward and tongue-tied. Maybe because she was so close.

She risked it, then, putting her arm—wearing his jacket!—through the crook of his elbow. "You know best," she whispered into his ear.

A long wooden ramp, like a sidewalk, stretched out in front of them. It led to a little park, and she could see the lights of a carousel twinkling in the distance.

"Oh, Matt, a merry-go-round! Shall we go see it?"

"Lead the way," he said.

Was he pulling her even closer? He was, he really was. She could smell the beer on him, just like he used to smell, and wondered if she smelled like sweetness and sugar and whiskey, and whether he liked that.

"You haven't told me why you're in Boston," Matt said, interrupting her thoughts.

She looked up into his eyes—*those eyes, I remember them so perfectly*—then down at her feet, biting her lip, trying to figure this out. They were close to the merry-go-round now, and the lights were on, all sparkly on the colorful horses and bejeweled elephants and curlicued carriages. Holly's thoughts were almost like a merry-go-round, she realized, spinning too fast for her to catch.

She would tell him when they got to the carousel, she decided. Maybe they could sit on a bench by the water, the two of them, and she would tell him the whole thing.

Yes. She would.

46

"**Let the record** show it's Monday, October thirty-first, at nine twenty-seven A.M., and this interview is taking place in the law offices of—" Jake paused his tape recorder, checking the stiff white business card in his hand. He took his finger off the Pause key and continued. "—law offices of Macording, McMurdow, Rothmann, and Lunt, 90 Canal Street, Boston. Present are myself, Detective Jake Brogan, as well as Detective Paul DeLuca, attorney Henry Rothmann, and Mr. Arthur Vick."

"And me," came a bleating voice from the beige leather couch.

"And Mrs. Patricia Vick," Jake continued. "This interview is being conducted with the consent of Mr. Vick, who is being represented for these proceedings by Mr. Rothmann."

Jake pushed Pause again. "Anything else?"

DeLuca, leaning against the closed office door, circled a weary forefinger. *Roll tape.*

Henry Rothmann, lawyer-perfect in tailored navy blue and no-doubt-pricey tie, posted himself behind Arthur Vick's leather club chair, testy and protective as a wing-tipped pit bull. His client, in chinos and a monogrammed crew neck sweater, rubbed a smudge from his tasseled loafers. "For the record, my client is not under arrest and is free to go whenever he chooses." He placed one defending hand on his client's shoulder.

Vick shrugged it off. "Let's get the show on the road," he said.

Jake hit Record. "And Mr. Vick is not under arrest and is free to leave. Now, Mr. Vick. We have previously discussed your employee Amaryllis Roldan. Where were you on the night of—"

"You asked him this already." Patricia Vick, balancing a yellow spiral notebook on her lap, brandished a stubby black Sharpie at Jake, then pointed it at Rothmann. "Didn't they, Henry? And we told him, Artie was home the night that girl was killed. With me. And listen, Mr., um, Detective. He was with me on the nights those other girls were killed, too. You wanna know where he was *every* night? Fine. Last night, my birthday party. At my studio. Any other nights you'd like to hear about?"

"Mrs. Vick, you're only here because your husband insisted that—," DeLuca said.

"Actually, my client's wife is correct here, gentlemen," the lawyer interrupted. "Asked and answered. Let's move on."

"This isn't a court proceeding, Mr. Rothmann," Jake said. *Lawyers.* "We can ask anything we want. However often we want."

"I was with my wife." Arthur Vick made a dismissive gesture. "Next question."

"Okay," Jake said. "Are you acquainted with an Amaryllis Roldan?"

"Henry!" Patti Vick's voice hit the ceiling. She plunked down the bag, spilling out a black plastic compact and a battered package of tissues. "Are you going to let them—?"

"Mr. Vick?" Jake ignored the woman.

"As you well know, she was a Beacon Market employee," Vick said. His voice dripped elaborate boredom. "I have hundreds of employees. Obviously. Do I know each and every one of them? Obviously not."

"But did you know Miss Roldan?"

"I did not."

"How about Kylie Howarth?" Jake said. "Does that name ring a bell?"

"Who? How do you spell that?" Patricia Vick's pen hovered over her notebook. "Like, Howard?"

"Mrs. Vick? We're fine here, we're on tape," Rothmann said. He remained at his post, standing sentry beside his client's chair. "Arthur? You don't have to answer that."

"Hell I don't," Vick said. "Never heard of her."

"She didn't try out for—?" Kylie's parents had told them yesterday at the airport that their daughter's suicide note indicated she'd applied for a job at Beacon Markets, wanted to be in the company's commercials, but became despondent because she hadn't been called back for a second audition.

"What part of *never* don't you understand?" Vick said.

"Fine. Never. Interesting. Noted." Jake checked the tape recorder. Rolling. "Sellica Darden," he said.

"And we're done," Rothmann said, brushing his palms together. "Thank you, Officers, but—"

"What about Sellica Darden?" Vick's mouth twisted into an almost-smile.

"That woman," Patti Vick said. "Should have gone to jail. That woulda saved her. No offense."

"Jake?" DeLuca's voice came from the doorway. He was looking at his cell phone screen. "I need a moment in private." He slid his phone back into his inside jacket pocket, then cocked his head toward the door. *Outta here.*

Jake hit the Off button, stopping the tape recorder, then looked up, trying to read his partner's face. But De-Luca, hand on the doorknob, was giving him nothing.

"Five minutes?" Jake said. "Okay with everyone?" He surveyed the room. Patti, her Sharpie clicked closed, was punching little pieces of gum from a crackling cellophane and foil package. Vick actually yawned, then pulled out an iPhone.

Rothmann shrugged, smoothing his tie. "Do what you gotta do."

"What the hell?" Stashing the recorder in a pocket, Jake followed DeLuca down a side hallway, striding to keep up with him. His partner stopped in front of the men's room door, looking both ways down the corridor.

"Dammit, we need an empty office or someplace," DeLuca said.

"Paul, whatever it is." Jake crossed his arms, done. "Rothmann's waiting for us. Vick's gonna bail. Just tell me."

"May I help you?" A bearded guy in a pin-striped suit emerged from the men's room, adjusting his tie. He considered the two of them. "Are you gentlemen looking for someone?"

"Just the can," DeLuca said. He caught the heavy wooden door with the flat of his hand, stopping it before it closed. "Thanks."

"This had better be good," Jake said. Once inside, DeLuca clanked open each metal stall door. No one else was in the room. The glaring fluorescent lights banged off the white-tiled walls; the place smelled of spearmint and lemon. Jake caught a glimpse of himself in a long polished mirror over a bank of fancy stainless steel sinks. He looked baffled. "You 'bout ready to do this? Before I—"

"That was the supe on the phone." DeLuca stared at his feet, not at Jake. Then crossed his arms over his chest. "It's bad. We got bridge victim four."

Jake was afraid to check the mirror again. No reason to see what screwed looked like. "Water? Bridge? Woman? Sunday night? No ID?"

"You got it," DeLuca said. "Total cluster f—"

The door creaked open. DeLuca, lightning, slammed it closed before whoever it was could enter. "Out-a-order," he called out. He leaned against it, bracing his feet on the elaborately tiled floor. "Come back later."

"What's the rest?" Jake would find out eventually, might as well be now.

"Found her this morning, some joggers or something. ME says drowning. No bruises, no trauma. By that lobster place, ya know? By the post office."

"Killed overnight, they think?"

"Yup. TV's all over it. Newspaper. It's a shit-storm. Supe's calling a press conference for this afternoon. Says you and I gotta know something by then. As if."

"Vick," Jake said.

DeLuca crossed to the sink, pumped out a pink ribbon of soap, put his hands under the faucet. Cranked his head around to look Jake in the eye. "You think? He's the Bridge Killer?"

Jake heard the hiss of the water, the buzz of the paper towel reeling out from the motion-activated dispenser. Saw DeLuca hit the wastebasket for two.

"No," Jake said. "Vick's an asshole, and he's lying about something. Maybe about a lot. But a serial killer? Naw. He's just—not a candidate."

"So who—?"

"Hell if I know."

* * *

"And you got up to my office *how*?" Rory Maitland was up and out of his chair before Jane got halfway to his desk. Three televisions, sound up full, showed the CNN, HLN, and Channel 11 morning news.

"Elevator," Jane said, smiling. She raised her voice over the TV sound. "I got here by elevator." Might as well try a little humor. Maybe this wasn't the greatest idea, barging into his campaign office unannounced, but too late now. "There was no one at the front desk downstairs, or in your outer office, so I took a chance and—"

Maitland punched a red button on his phone console, yelling into the speaker. "Deenie! You out there? Where the hell is everyone?" No response. He puffed out an annoyed sigh, giving up on the phone, then held out both palms, dramatically mystified. "Enlighten me here, Miss Ryland. You ignore the rules, ignore the protocol, ignore Sheila King, ignore security, you sashay up here like a— Where's the regular *Register* guy, anyway?"

"Mr. Maitland?" *Apologize first, hit him with the Gable bombshell later.* She put on her best beseeching look, contrite. "I'm so sorry, there was just no one to ask, and Sheila didn't answer her phone, and I really need to talk with you." She eyed the door. "Privately."

"Oh, now I get it." Maitland clicked a silver remote at the television sets, one after the other, jabbing their screens to black. "You're still dogging us about that pitiful Springfield rally. Listen. Advance team blew it, the candidate is not happy. Old news. You want to find out what happened? Ask those hotel people."

"No, I—" Jane took one step into the room, testing.

"We have a campaign to win." Maitland waved the remote at Jane, as if to turn *her* off. "We're interested in tomorrow, not yesterday. You can quote me. That do it for you, Miss Ryland?"

"Well, it's not about the rally." Jane took another step into the office. "You're right. Old news. It's just—you know I've been trying to get permission to do an interview with Mrs. Lassiter."

"No can do." Maitland flipped a palm at her, *forget about it*. "As Sheila King told you. Moira's exhausted. Taking some time off."

Sure she is. Jane nodded, wide-eyed, as if buying his line. "So I hear. But while waiting for her to, uh, come back, I did a little research on her, you know? Now I have a couple of quick questions. About her background."

Big smile. Notebook out. Wait.

Maitland's face changed, then changed again before Jane could catalog the emotions morphing by.

He lowered the remote, eyes narrowing at her. "Moira's background? What about it?"

"Well," Jane said. "It's actually less about Mrs. Lassiter, and more about the candidate himself."

"Have a seat. *Jane.*" He pointed to a tweedy upholstered chair in front of the bank of still-dark TVs. "Now. What's this really about?"

"Katharine," Jane said.

Maitland took off his rumpled sport jacket, draped it across the back of his desk chair. He unbuttoned the cuffs of his shirt and rolled back his sleeves. Once, twice. He glanced at a chunky Rolex.

He's stalling, Jane thought. *Love it.*

"Who?" Maitland said.

"You know who I mean," Jane replied. Keeping it polite. "Owen Lassiter's first wife. Why is she never mentioned? She's not in any of your—"

Maitland placed both palms flat on his desk, leaning toward her. His yellow-striped tie flapped forward, the ends touching a stapled pile of documents. "Where are you going with this, Jane?"

Jane put a hand up, conciliatory. "Look. It's only that I'm doing a profile on Moira Lassiter. If there was another wife, a first wife, that means Moira—"

She stopped, midsentence, realizing exactly what it might mean. It flashed through her mind, fully formed, clear as a memory. It might mean, back then, Moira and Owen had been—having an affair. It might mean that still-married Owen cheated on his wife with Moira. It might mean Moira was now recognizing the signs of Owen's infidelity because she had seen them firsthand. When Moira was the other woman.

Or, not.

"Excuse me," Jane said. She pretend-scratched her head. "Lost my train of thought. Anyway. If there was another wife, I was wondering why she's never mentioned. And where she is now."

"Jane." Maitland sat back in his chair, steepled his fingers. "Divorce is hardly an earthshaking event in politics these days. Times change. I mean—Ronald Reagan. Newt Gingrich. Rockefeller. Everyone gets divorced."

Jane almost burst out laughing. Exactly what Gable had said. *Politicians.* "Yes, Mr. Maitland. I'm aware. So are you telling me Owen Lassiter and Katharine—what was her last name? Are divorced? And if so, when and where? And why? And where is Katharine now?"

"Mr. Maitland?" A voice from behind her. A young woman in a green turtleneck and unfortunate shoes hovered in the doorway holding a brown paper carton of precariously tipping Dunkin' Donuts cups. "I went for your coffees, and—"

"About time, Deenie," Maitland interrupted, waving her in. "I'll take those. Where is everyone? Why is Kenna not at the desk downstairs?"

Kenna? At the desk downstairs? Jane's brain blasted into hyperdrive, calculating the possibilities. Maybe she worked here? Maybe she had an appointment? Either way, Maitland knew Kenna Wilkes. Jane thought about the photos in her bag. She could— *Wait,* she told herself. *Wait.*

The woman hurried into the room, frowning at Jane. As she placed the flimsy tray on Maitland's desk, it caught on the edge, knocking over a supersized coffee, the white plastic lid popping off, spilling a stream of steaming brown liquid. Maitland yelped, jumping back. "Jesus *Christ*!"

"Oh, Mr. Maitland, I'm so—" Deenie grabbed a stack of napkins from the tray, blotting and wiping and trying to stop the flow of spreading coffee. The cup had knocked over a gold-framed photograph, clattering it from the desk to the floor. It landed facedown, milky liquid dripping on the velvet-covered backing and splashing onto the carpet.

As Deenie and Maitland scrambled to clean up, Jane grabbed a wad of tissues from a box on a side table and picked up the photograph, blotting it dry. *Pretty photo,* Jane thought, putting it back on the desk. Umbrellas on a beach. The muffled trill of her phone came from her tote bag next to the swivel chair. Whoever was calling would have to wait. She had to find out about Katharine, then about Kenna Wilkes. Nothing could be more important than that.

By the time Deenie backed out of the room, carrying a sodden pile of documents and paperwork, Jane's phone had rung twice more. Annoying, but she couldn't answer it. She stood by her chair, waiting.

Maitland looked disdainfully at the blotches now scattered across his yellow silk tie and once-white shirt. "So much for this," he said.

"Yeah," Jane said. "Mondays."

Maitland checked his watch. "So. Excitement over. We done here?"

Jane couldn't help but smile. *Good try.* "No, actually. You were about to tell me about Katharine, Mr. Maitland. Where is Owen Lassiter's first wife?"

47

Matt stared at the ceiling, biting his thumbnail, mind racing. Flopped on the white chenille spread of his hotel's king-sized bed, still wearing his running shoes and the jacket he'd managed to retrieve. At two in the morning, after carding open his hotel room door, he'd slugged down the entire five-dollar bottle of fancy water on the nightstand, then filled it with tap water from the bathroom. He'd never been so thirsty. He hadn't slept since then, not at all.

What to do? Now, the morning light through the window blinds made slashes of shadow above him. *Like bars in a prison cell.* The heater kicked on, humming. *I have to figure out what to do.*

There'd been no cops banging on his door—why should there be? No accusing phone calls from—whoever. Why should there be? Far as anyone in Boston was concerned, he was no one, with no connections. And certainly no connection with Holly Neff. Or whatever name she'd been using.

He almost dumped Holly's little purse in the water after she'd gone in. Then worried—maybe it'd float, or wash ashore. He'd stuffed it under his jacket. Her keys, too. But like that old movie, there'd be no reason for anyone to link him to her. He was a stranger in town, and so was she.

What if the waitress in the bar remembers me? The guy selling newspapers at the post office? Are my fingerprints on her car? What if they are? No one has my fingerprints to compare them to.

His brain ached. *Do they?*

He'd spent the last five hours talking himself down from the ledge. It had all been an accident, right? An accident.

He flopped over, punching an oversized pillow into place, and stared out the window, unseeing. The movie of what happened kept playing in his head, over and over and over.

They had sat side by side on that molded-metal bench by the merry-go-round. He felt uncomfortable, awkward, the bench hard and cold and unyielding. Night gathered, making the wind chilly over the harbor. Seagulls squawked overhead, airplanes roaring their descent to Logan. *Did anyone see the two of us there?* Countless office and hotel windows overlooked the park, but who would have cared about the two figures by the water?

Holly had been clinging. Crowding him. Suffocating him. "You're still not married," she said. Putting her face too close to his. "And I know why. That's why I'm here. To take care of everything. To make you happy. This is all for you. For you, Matt."

She outlined her plans—and he listened to her explanation with escalating dismay and increasing alarm. She was completely nuts.

He had made one frigging bad choice. Back in B-school, he'd told Holly the truth. And now, this was his payback? Maybe he could talk her out of it. Convince her not to do it. Pay her off. Everyone had a price. But she kept talking and talking.

"Your father killed your ability to love." Holly said this, solemn and sincere, her voice trembling with the strength of her belief. "He left you, deserted you, deserted your poor mother. That's why you couldn't love me. That's why you can't love."

He couldn't breathe. What was she, friggin' Dr. Phil? She was—crazy. Wasn't she?

"Your mother died because of him, and your life was taken away. Your family was taken away. Your father. And then your mother. That's exactly what you told me that day by the river. You could have been the governor's son," she said. "That's what you told me. Instead, you were the throwaway child. The child whose father destroyed everything."

It was true. It was true. That's what he'd said, probably. He could almost hear his own mother telling them that. But it was long ago. Long ago. Now, after all these years, he only wished to be a son again. He wanted his father back. Someday he could make it work. But he wasn't about to tell that to Holly.

"I couldn't let that happen to you," Holly persisted. "He ignored you, he erased you. You said that word, *erased*. He killed your mother. Didn't he? Didn't he? So what do you think he deserves in return?"

Matt's stomach lurched. He couldn't take his eyes off this nutcase.

"But now, I have the power. The power to give you back your life. The power to destroy Owen Lassiter."

What was he supposed to do? Call the cops? "You're not planning to—"

Holly's laugh, brittle and crystalline, floated out across the deserted park. "Don't be ridiculous," she said. "I'm not crazy. This is all so we can be together. You found me, and that proves it's meant to be. But let me ask you—he does what he wants, takes what he wants, leaves his family behind. Does he just—get away with that?"

Matt couldn't find the words to answer. Thought of his mother. His poor baby sister, who'd found her. But—

"When the time comes," Holly continued, "the good Owen Lassiter will not be going to Washington. Oh, he won't be dead, my darling Matt. He'll just wish he were."

She had rubbed up against him, her eyes shining.

"You'll be free of him. We'll be together. Won't that be perfect?"

A double rap on the hotel room door jolted him from his memories. *Holy shit. The cops. How did they find me? And why?* He bolted to his feet, yanked off his jacket, mussed his hair, calculated excuses and alibis and denials.

"Maid service," an inquiring voice came through the door.

"Later," Matt called back. His voice didn't sound like his. He was dizzy. Couldn't feel his feet. Could not breathe. "Come back later."

He collapsed back on the bed, struggling to tame his thoughts.

What made it worse, if that was possible—Holly's plan was still under way, even with what had happened. She went public to that reporter, she had crowed, and the result was only a matter of time. To stop it all, now *he'd* have to go public somehow. Wouldn't he? And when he did, the story would come out anyway.

Either way, disaster. Either way, he was trapped.

All of a sudden he could hear the sound of his own breathing. Maybe the sound of his own heartbeat. He'd gotten himself into this. Now he had to get himself out. He'd spent his days working the system, right? Market up, market down. Assess, calculate, make his move.

He sat up. Taking back control. Taking action. *He had to*. Maybe he could use this. Get his life back. The life he deserved.

He ran a hand over his face, thinking it through.

First he'd have to find the reporter, that Jane Ryland, and somehow convince her the story Holly was selling wasn't true. She absolutely could not print it.

He'd also have to warn Owen Lass— He felt his fists clench and stopped himself mid-thought. *No*. He would say it.

He'd have to warn his father.

He stood, went to the window. Seeing the morning. A sense of peace came over him, a certainty. He'd already saved his father's political life, hadn't he? If you looked at it that way? Maybe he should let him know that. Matt felt his shoulders go back, his chin come up.

Maybe he should let Governor Owen Lassiter know, after all these years, what his own son had sacrificed to save him.

Yes. That's what he would do.

48

Jake stared at the crime scene. Sun glint on the water, rocky shoreline, office buildings, bridge. No footprints, no evidence, no nothing. Murk and obscurity. Just like this case. Silent ripples lapped close to his boots, then slid away into the depths of Fort Point Channel. The ME's office had long since taken away her body, whoever she was. Victim four. "Fort Point," Jake would call her, until she had a name. He patted his pockets for his gloves. Cold by the water. *Colder in it.*

He swiveled his head, scouting. Perhaps not the wisest move, strategically, for him and DeLuca to leave Vick and company mid-interview, but there was no alternative. And if Patti was telling the truth, Vick had a pretty damn good alibi for this killing. A birthday party, for chrissake. Someone else had killed victim four. Whoever she was.

If she worked at Beacon Market, though, all bets were off.

The yellow crime-scene tape cordoned off the Monday-morning lookies who pointed, gawking, over the railing from the bridge above. The post office parking lot was already filled with side-by-side news vans and satellite trucks and hovering reporters. He'd nearly decked that Channel 11 chick who ventured down here, ducking in under the tape in those rubber boots, all hairspray and lipstick and ridiculous questions. *Jane would never have* . . . He checked his watch. Half an hour till the damn news conference. Why the supe decided to hold it at the post office—

"Harvard, you there?" DeLuca's voice came over his two-way radio.

"I hear you," Jake said, punching the Talk button. "Whatcha got? You up in the parking lot?"

"Ten-four. Supe just got the sketch of number four. Wants you to see it before he hands it out."

"Copy that," Jake said. So now she would have a face. It was his job to find the someone, somewhere, who would recognize her. He looked again at the water, at the shoreline, at the buildings lining both sides of the channel. Hotels, offices, the museum, studios in the boho-chic Fort Point Channel artists district. *Studios.* He blinked in the late-morning sunshine, a memory punching its way to the surface.

Where is Patti Vick's studio? In Fort Point? Could be Arthur Vick's alibi wasn't so airtight. His wife kept insisting he was "with me," but had she said they were at home? Not last night. Jake clicked on his BlackBerry, checking his notes.

Exactly. She'd said—the birthday party was at the studio. What's more, Sellica's body had been found, what, three blocks closer to the harbor from here? Down by the Federal Courthouse. What if Patti Vick's studio was around here? What if Vick used it to shoot those commercials, luring in women, then killing them?

Okay, seemed like he hadn't killed Kylie Howarth. But maybe she, the first victim, was the outlier. Maybe Vick killed Amaryllis Roldan, and Sellica, and now this one. What if there *was* a Bridge Killer? *Dammit.* What if it was Arthur Vick? What if he had three victims, not four?

And Jake and DeLuca had just left Vick in some lawyer's office.

"Shit," he said.

"You ever been married, Miss Ryland? Divorced?" Maitland reared back in his chair, crossing one ankle over a knee. The hem of his jacket, still draped over his chair, touched the coffee-spotted carpeting.

Jane blinked, taken aback. "What difference does that make?"

Maitland scratched his head, as if pondering a baffling dilemma. "Precisely my point. Maybe I should know that about you, your past, your marital status, before I go talking to you. Maybe it makes you—I don't know. Biased. You think?"

"Don't be silly, Mr. Maitland." Jane smiled, humoring him. "That's irrelevant. But it *is* relevant for Owen Lassiter. Will it matter to voters? Who knows. But *they* need to decide. Not you."

"And I suppose you're the one anointed to tell 'em? You and your newspaper?"

"Why not just tell me the truth?" Jane said. "If you don't, you certainly must be aware, it's going to appear there's some big secret."

She leaned forward, half-serious. "*Is* there some big secret?"

"You reporters are all alike, you know that?" Maitland clanked his chair to the floor, got to his feet. Stabbed a forefinger toward the office door. "You see some ex-wife beating down my door to make trouble for the governor? When Owen announced, it got big national coverage. Everybody and his brother knew about it, the entire country. Don't you think if there was something 'unacceptable' in Owen's past, some mistake, some skeleton, some ex-wife wouldn't have already made that pretty darn public?"

"I'm looking for the truth," Jane said. She watched Maitland's face harden, his ears turn red. Good. The higher the bluster, the more possibility of a big story. In her tote bag, her phone was ringing again. *Damn. Not now.*

"Oh, bull. Don't insult me with that BS about your search for 'the truth.'" Maitland rolled his eyes, making air quotes around the words. "You're only about the scandal, all of you media types. The dirt. Poking into the past, digging for something where there's nothing. Some news that when it turns out to be wrong, you'll run some pitiful correction, if you even bother to do that, while someone's reputation goes down the tubes. But you've got to get your story. Make yourselves the new Woodward and Bernstein."

"Mr. Maitland?" Jane kept her voice even, as if calming a five-year-old in the midst of a temper tantrum. "What about Owen Lassiter's first wife?"

"What about her?" Maitland shot back.

"Is she hiding for some reason? Are you hiding her?"

"Hiding her?"

"Where is she?" Jane continued.

"Where is she?" Maitland echoed.

Jane struggled not to laugh out loud. Maitland was clearly losing it, repeating her questions like that. She was about to win this round. What would happen when she pushed him about the mysterious Kenna?

"Yes, Mr. Maitland, where is she?"

"I'll tell you exactly where she is." Rory's eyes did not match his smile. "Where she's been for the past two years. Cambridge, Massachusetts."

"She's in—"

"She's a resident of Poplar Grove Cemetery."

49

Today had not gone as planned. Ten minutes to go, but Jake could see the news conference was already packed. The media clumped together outside the post office, microphones, tape recorders, cameras. Coffee. Klieg lights. Soon would come the inevitable questions. Jake had zero answers.

Today was supposed to have been a big score for the good guys. The headlines were supposed to have been Kylie Howarth. Now that her parents had identified their daughter, the supe planned to call the press to the BPD media room, disclose the victim's identity, reveal she was a suicide, reassure the public, and stop the manufactured clamor to catch some mythical Bridge Killer.

Then they'd found the fourth victim. Now they were out in the miserable windy cold, getting ready to deliver bad news in a damn parking lot. The Kylie story would be buried. The vulture patrol would care only about Jake's failures, and about stampeding people into thinking some serial killer was on the loose. *There must be a better way to sell newspapers.*

A tap on his shoulder. "Detective? Supe wanted me to show you this."

Pam, the homicide office clerk, held up a manila envelope.

"Hey, Pam." He gestured at the still-growing crowd. "Quite the turnout, huh? Whatcha got?"

The clerk reopened the metal-pronged closure and drew out a piece of paper. "It's the sketch of the—"

"Come over here for a sec." Jake could tell the Channel 5 reporter was edging closer. Trying to eavesdrop, see over his shoulder. *Vulture.* He turned his back, motioned Pam to do the same. "So what've we got?"

"Sketch guy just finished," Pam said. "Supe called me in to hand these out. Also, DeLuca's at the Suffolk County Jail. He says there may be a collar in the Roldan case. Says he'll call you."

Jake took the sketch. And there she was. *Fort Point.* Jake stared at the postcard-sized drawing, mesmerized. A bulleted description was typed in the lower right: *Hair: light brown. Eyes: blue. Distinguishing marks or tattoos: none. Age: approx. 25.*

What the bullet points didn't say was—she had been beautiful. The colored-pencil sketch was something more suited to a magazine than a morgue. Long curly hair, model cheekbones, full lips. Some sort of little necklace. Young, gorgeous, and dead.

Did she die because I suck at my job? Did she die because I refused to believe her killer existed? Is she as much my victim as the Bridge Killer's?

He thought about Arthur Vick. About Vick's connection with Amaryllis Roldan, and with Sellica. And Kylie. Kylie Howarth, the confirmed suicide who ruined the whole case. Or solved it.

"Thanks, Pam," he said. He slid two copies of the sketch into his jacket's inside pocket. Then he had an idea. "Hold one up for me, okay?"

Jake took out his BlackBerry and snapped a picture of the picture.

A flurry of activity—a siren, a car crunching through the gravel, a door slamming. Lights flicked on; photographers scrambled to their cameras.

"Supe's here," Pam said.

Jake slid his BlackBerry back into his jeans pocket. "Showtime."

"Okay, okay, okay, I just have to get into this parking space."

Jane tried to keep her phone between her cheek and her shoulder while she backed into a too-small almost-space near the post office. The parking lot was crammed with trucks and vans and news cars, staffed by reporters who'd answered their phones in time to arrive *before* the news conference started. How was she supposed to know it had been Alex on the phone? How was she supposed to know there was another Bridge Killer victim?

Plus, she'd had to run out of Maitland's office before she could ask about Kenna.

Damn. After this morning's unpleasantly contentious encounter, it would be a real challenge to even get near Maitland again.

She inched as close as she could to the gigantic pickup mooching too much space in front of her. She tapped its fender, wincing. "Yeah, yeah, Alex, I'm here. I'll let you know when Tuck arrives. Where is she, anyway? She owes me, big-time."

She was talking to air. Alex had hung up.

A hulking black Crown Vic four-door blurped its siren at her in warning, turning across her path as it slid into the post office parking lot. A BPD decal on the side of the car said SUPERINTENDENT.

Thank goodness. Jane, out of breath, reached the pack of reporters before Rivera stepped to the lectern's bristling bouquet of microphones. Jane eyed her colleagues—ex-colleagues, some of them. Maybe it was good she was late. She wouldn't have to chitchat, pretend to like them. She pulled out her spiral notebook, wrote *11:45 A.M.* at the top of a clean page.

A gaggle of cops surrounded the podium. Superintendent Rivera, wearing dress blues and his hat yanked down over his forehead, towered over the rest. Laney Driscoll, the PR guy, hovered next to him, clutching a thick manila envelope. A few uniforms stood stationed along the fence, eyes hidden behind identical dark Ray-Bans.

Jake.

In those jeans and leather jacket, almost with his back to the crowd, talking to some woman in a black police-issue pullover. *Poor Jake. Another victim. He must be . . .*

The woman was holding up a piece of paper, and Jake seemed to be snapping a photo of it. As the woman walked away, Jake turned around, now facing the reporters but not making eye contact.

Jane shifted position, willing him to see her. *Come on, Jakey.* She sent him ESP messages. *I'm here.*

But everyone's attention was on the superintendent. He marched toward the podium, face grim.

"Jane Ryland?" A voice behind her.

Someone wanted to talk to her. *Who?* The news conference was about to start.

The man stepped closer. Not someone she recognized, not a reporter, no notebook in hand. Not a cop. Maybe some young business exec on a day off, wandered by the news conference, got curious. Good-enough looking, mid-twenties, athletic-ish, hair mussed and a hint of stubble. Running shoes. Water bottle.

"Yes?" she said. She glanced deliberately at the podium, to make sure this guy knew she had no time for interruptions.

"Jane Ryland from the *Register*? Who had that front-page article in yesterday's paper?"

Jane nodded, needing him to hurry up. But he'd asked about her article. Maybe he knew something about the rally?

"My name is Matt. Uh, let's leave it at that for now," he said. "I think I have a story for you."

"About the rally?"

"Rally?" Matt said. He gave a little shrug. "No, it's . . . well, it's really a long story."

She smiled back, trying not to be one of those pretend-reporters who weren't open to possibilities. You never knew where the next big story would come from. Still, it probably wasn't from here. She gestured to the podium, where Laney Driscoll was adjusting the microphones.

"I'm assigned to cover this," she said. "Can I give you my card?"

Then she realized she didn't have a *Register* business card yet. "I'll give you my private number at the paper," she said. She scrawled it on a page of her notebook, ripped it out, and handed it to him. "Call me later today."

"Ladies and gentlemen," Driscoll was saying. "The superintendent will have a brief statement, then take a few questions. There's a handout which we'll distribute. No one-on-one interviews, no live shots, nothing more today. We clear?"

"I want to hear this, too," Matt said. Jane saw him stash her number into the pocket of his jacket. "I'm gonna get closer. I'll call you later."

"Great," Jane said, giving him her best pretend-sincere smile. *Adios*.

The man squeezed past the camera in front of him, threading through the journalists until Jane could see only the top of his head and a jacketed broad shoulder. He stopped at the edge of the group, toward the front.

I should have at least taken his phone number, Jane scolded herself. *Maybe I'll get it after.*

"My name is Francis Rivera." The voice came from the podium. "I'm Superintendent of the Boston Police Department. We're here today to . . ."

Jane tried to focus her attention on Rivera, but where the heck was Tuck? This was *her* deal, and Alex promised she'd show up. Now it was looking like Jane would have to handle this herself. Which was a drag, since she was hot on the trail of the other women in Owen Lassiter's life.

She'd track down Katharine, maybe with records from Poplar Grove Cemetery. As for Kenna Wilkes? Jane smiled. *Woodward and Bernstein, huh?* As if breaking big political news were a bad thing.

"Hey, roomie." Tuck, ponytail bobbing, trotted up beside her. "Thanks for covering for me. Supe say anything major yet?"

"Hey, Tuck," Jane said. "Nope, just started." Up at the podium, the PR flack was dumping papers out of a big manila envelope.

"Great," Tuck said. "You're clear from this location, Alex says, just check in later. I've got this now. There's more big news about to break."

"Yeah, I know. Great." Jane flapped her empty notebook closed. Tuck could have this story. Jane had her sights set on Katharine, whatever her last name was, and Kenna Wilkes.

Kenna Wilkes. *The other woman.* No mistake about that.

So what if she was a little late getting to campaign head-quarters today. It's not like there was any big deal. Kenna Wilkes parked her stupid rented hybrid and strolled up the manicured front walk of Owen Lassiter's ritzy house. Owen, she knew, was off at a conference, some union thing. But it was not Owen she was here to see.

She flipped her hair out from under the collar of her white wool coat. Extravagant, yes, and ridiculous in the Boston grime. But it looked so good with her hair. And, according to the article in *House Beautiful*, Moira loved white.

The doorbell binged. The door swung open. Moira herself, *imagine that.*

Kenna switched her stack of brown envelopes and file folders from one arm to the other, held out her hand, polite as could be.

"Mrs. Lassiter? I'm Kenna Wilkes, from the gover-nor's campaign office? They did call to tell you I was coming, right? Mr. Maitland sent me with some photos for you to sign?"

Not exactly true, but close enough. She could fix it all later, get everyone's stories straight. She saw the wom-an's famously elegant face twitch for a moment, in fear. Or anger? Or defeat? Didn't really matter. This was merely Kenna's inaugural get-to-know-you visit.

"They didn't, no." Moira didn't budge from the door-way.

"I'm so sorry, ma'am," Kenna said. *Ma'am.* She al-most burst out laughing. She'd said it on purpose, as if Moira hadn't noticed the difference in their ages. It had been a long time since they'd last crossed paths. A long, long time. Not that Moira could possibly realize that. "Could you autograph these? Then I'll get back to the campaign. You know how busy we are now!"

She smiled, so enthusiastic, handed Moira the envelope. Inside were a stack of eight-by-ten photographs she'd snagged from Sheila King's press office.

Moira took the envelope in one manicured hand, clearly reluctant.

"What a lovely home you have," Kenna said, peering around Moira's shoulder. Kenna patted her hair, reprising the same gesture she'd used the day before in her little driveway drama. She gestured to her own white coat. "I love the all white. As you can see. Would you like me to wait outside while you sign the photos?"

"Oh, no, no, of course not." Moira seemed to remember where she was. "Come in. Of course. Miss—?"

Kenna stepped into the foyer, taking in the flowers and the affluence and the ease and the privilege. "Kenna Wilkes," she said. "Please call me Kenna. Everyone does. I'm new."

"Ah," Moira said.

"It must be so difficult that your husband is so rarely home these days," Kenna went on. *That'll get her*. "I only mean, you know, the campaign and all. I'm sure Owen—I mean the governor—misses you out on the campaign trail. Of course, he's always surrounded by fans and voters and staff. He's so charming."

"I'll only be a moment, signing these," Moira said. "Who sent you here with these, by the way?"

"Wasn't that terrible about that rally thing in Springfield?" Kenna continued, ignoring her question. "It's lucky you weren't there, you know? And then we had to stay overnight in Worcester, gosh, not exactly the garden spot. Although the hotel was lovely."

"I'll get a pen," Moira said. She patted the pockets of her tailored wool slacks and, finding nothing, pulled out a drawer in an ivory-glazed Parsons table.

The gilt-edged mirror above the table, polished and reflecting the sparkling crystal chandelier overhead, also reflected Kenna's own smile. And, Kenna noted, Moira's clearly growing discomfort.

Moira opened a sleek silver pen, clicking the cap to the end, and sat in a white velvet side chair. She pulled the glossy photographs from the envelope and arranged them on her lap.

"I could never keep my house this perfect." Kenna took a few steps into the foyer. She couldn't resist pushing it. "My little Jimmy is four now. Do you have children? It's the best. I can't imagine life without my son."

Moira's pen clattered to the cream and white tiled floor, rolling to a stop against a white-lacquered pot bursting with white chrysanthemums.

"Oh, let me get that for you," Kenna said. She hurried across the entryway, then stopped, picking up the pen. It probably cost as much as her rent once had, Kenna calculated. It was about time for her luck to change. And she was going to be the one to change it.

She handed Moira the pen, flashing her best smile. "Almost election day, isn't it exciting?"

"Very." Moira didn't look at her as she answered, but with a final flourish of a signature, stacked the photos into an even pile and slipped them back into the envelope. "There you are, Miss . . ."

"Kenna."

"Kenna." Moira stood, brushing down her slacks, then took a step toward the front door. "Could you ask Mr. Maitland to call me, please?"

"Certainly, ma'am," she said. *Not a chance.* They arrived at the front door, but Kenna turned for another look at the opulently upscale surroundings. No wonder this woman was . . . Well, it was only a matter of days, now, until it all changed. If all went as planned. Which Kenna was increasingly certain it would.

Kenna paused, relishing Moira's attempt to keep her composure. She patted the package of photographs. "Thank you so much for this. I'm sure Mr. Maitland will call you right away," she said. Big smile. "You take care now. And I'll be sure to tell the governor you said hello!"

50

"That's impossible. Impossible." Jane watched the drawing gradually emerge on Alex's computer screen. Tuck had e-mailed it to Alex from the news conference—still under way—but Jane didn't need to see the whole thing. "I know who that is, Alex. I know her."

"What are you talking about? You know victim four?" He hit Print, and the paper popped from the printer.

Jane grabbed it before it landed in the bin. Stared at the face in the police sketch.

"And you know her, too, Alex. Look, look, look." She flapped the picture at him, her heart racing with certainty. "It's Kenna Wilkes. You know. Kenna *Wilkes*!"

Jane stabbed at the paper so hard, her fingernail tore the page.

Alex took it from her, lifting his glasses to his forehead, examining it. "You think?"

"Are you kidding me? Positively. She's the woman in the red coat. Lassiter's girl. Kenna Wilkes. The one I talked to Saturday at the—" Jane clapped both hands to her head, slowly lowering herself to Alex's couch.

Jane ticked off the points on her fingers, thinking faster than her words could keep up. "I mean, we have the archive photos of her. We have lots of photos of her. I got another one that day at the Esplanade, too. With Lassiter! Then, like I said, I just talked to her at the Springfield rally. And her picture from there—with Lassiter!—is still in my camera, too. So that proves she was connected to the campaign for, like, weeks now. Unbelievable."

Alex's eyes were still on the photo. "Let's stay calm for a moment. Consider all the possibilities. She might have been, you know, a Lassiter supporter, a fan. A political junkie, who happened to be in a few of the photos. Like I told you on day one."

"No, no, that's what I'm trying to tell *you*. That's why I ran up here as soon as I could get away from the stupid news conference—"

"Tuck," Alex said. He reached for the phone on his desk. "Gotta call her. She'll need to—we'll need to add this to her coverage of the—"

"No!" Jane leaped to her feet, planting her fists on her waist. *Tuck?* "This is mine, Alex. If anyone's going to break this story, it's got to be me."

Alex raised both palms, gesturing Jane back to her seat on the couch. "There's enough story for everyone, Jane, okay? If you're right about this. We need to think it through."

"If I'm right?" Jane instantly wished her voice hadn't gone up so high. She willed it back down, willed herself to stay calm. Alex hadn't meant anything. He was only being careful; that was his job. "I mean, yeah, okay. But listen, listen, that's why I came in here in the first place. Why I needed to talk with you. According to the voter registration office, there's no Kenna Wilkes registered to vote in Massachusetts."

"But couldn't she be—?"

"There's more. I went to Rory Maitland's office at Lassiter headquarters this morning. Trying to find out about Lassiter's first wife, Katharine, what Gable told me, remember? But then—well, short version. Kenna Wilkes works at the campaign office. For sure. Absolutely. No question."

Alex leaned back against his desk, staring at her. "She works there? Did you see her?"

"No. And that's exactly the point." Jane felt her own eyes get bigger as the realization dawned. Her mind began to juggle what lay ahead of them, and who she'd have to call, and who she'd have to tell, and what this would mean for—*Jake*. She'd have to let him know she recognized the victim. Wouldn't she? She yanked herself back to the moment. Kenna Wilkes.

"That's how I got up to Maitland's office. She was supposed to be at the front desk this morning, like a receptionist, and she wasn't there. And people were confused about where she was."

"And you think she was absent because she was—"

Jane nodded slowly. "Yes. Because she was dead."

Standing on the fringe of the press conference, Matt listened to some black cop talking about the "progress" they'd made in a different murder. Apparently some victim they thought was murder turned out to be a suicide. The cops seemed pretty happy about that.

"Kylie Howarth, that's *K-y-l-i-e*," the big guy was saying. "And her next of kin have confirmed . . ."

The wind off the harbor was picking up, making it harder to hear. The reporters edged up to the podium, scribbling in notebooks they held close to their faces. A couple of squawking seagulls swooped in, perching atop the metal posts studding the railing along the water.

Freaky to be standing here, knowing he was the guy the cops were looking for, waiting to hear if the cops knew it. He'd heard on TV, breaking news, something about them finding another body. That the cops were holding a news conference by the post office. Now he could find out what they knew. If anything.

They hadn't brought up Holly yet, the discovery of her body. He surveyed the place, wondering if they'd checked all the cars in the parking lot. Holly's was there, over by the wall. He had the keys. Should he come back later, move the car? What if someone saw him? There were probably surveillance cameras everywhere. Were there?

"At this point," the cop continued, "we're considering the Howarth case closed. Not connected to any of the other recent deaths in the city of Boston."

Other recent deaths? *That* what this was about?

"So now there's *three* bridge killings?" some reporter yelled. A slinky brunette took a step closer to the podium, holding a microphone, her cameraman beside her. "Sellica Darden, Amaryllis Roldan, and *our* sources say there's now a new victim. Is that correct?"

A lackey in a pullover tried to step to the microphone, but the big cheese waved him away. "There's no Bridge Killer, Miss Wu. As we've repeatedly told you. The other cases are under investigation, and—"

"*Our* sources also say there's a new victim, can you confirm that?" Another reporter pushed to the front. "That hardly means the city is any safer."

Whatever, Matt thought. Soon as this was over, he'd find Jane Ryland again. He had something even bigger for her.

"Guys? Superintendent Rivera has another statement for you." The PR flack stretched toward the bank of microphones, leaning in front of his boss. "Hold your questions until he's finished. Otherwise, we're done here, and I'll return your calls as soon as I can manage the time. But it probably won't be before your deadlines. You catch my drift? Are you ready for the statement?"

Here we go. Matt's eyes suddenly burned; hot sweat broke out across the back of his neck and behind his knees. Thirsty. *Thirsty.* He flipped up the plastic top of his water bottle, took a swig.

"What's this about? You know anything?" A guy with a tape recorder on a shoulder strap muttered at him, adjusting dials on his equipment.

"Uh, no," Matt said. "You?"

"Nope." The guy shrugged. "All I know is, some new victim. It was all over TV. Guess we're gonna hear."

"At approximately oh-five-thirty this morning," Rivera said, "three joggers along the Fort Point footpath discovered the body of a young white female, approximately twenty-five years old, that's two-five, in the waters by the Fort Point overpass. As of now, we have no identification, but—"

"So it's true? Another Bridge Killer victim?" The brunette reporter again. "You think you're burying the lead here? That makes three victims! And you're still telling us there's no serial killer targeting unidentified young women and dumping them in the water near bridges?"

Serial killer? Matt's mind raced. That's what they'd been saying on the TV. If the cops thought Holly was a victim of a serial killer, he was home free. Right? Whenever the other killings happened, he sure hadn't been in Boston.

A window of hope began to open. An escape route. The beginnings of a smile pulled at his mouth, the first time he felt happy since he'd seen Holly's photo in the online *Register*.

He might win this round. All he had to do to reclaim his birthright was figure out how to keep Jane Ryland quiet. And thanks to this news conference, he might have been handed the perfect way to do it.

51

"He's in there, Jake. He's yelling for a lawyer. But he's guilty as sin." Paul DeLuca flipped on the lights, illuminating the dingy interior of room 3, fourth floor of the Nashua Street Jail. Behind the one-way glass, Jake saw a fidgeting train wreck of a man sitting at a long metal table. The suspect took a slug of Mountain Dew from a can, one scrawny leg jiggling, eyes darting ceaselessly from ceiling to floor to window and back. His other leg was shackled to a circular eye-bolt in the floor.

"That guy's in great shape," Jake said. "Cranked up?"

"Bad thing to be a junkie," DeLuca said.

"Worse to be a murderer." Jake flipped open the red-coded file of documents his partner handed him, scanning photos and arrest records. "You'd think it'd be a problem being a tattoo guy by day and a druggie at night. Think it would make your hands shake, you know? So he did Amaryllis Roldan? Her tattoo?"

"His specialty was the Celtic vines, so says his junkie pal. The one who ratted him out for Roldan when he realized they were both facing twenty-five to life for distribution. Whoever talked first got the deal."

"That's what friends are for," Jake said. "Supe know?"

"Yup. Laney Driscoll even told him about it, but he

didn't want to mention it at the news conference. Not till it's signed and sealed. Your pal Tuck has it, though. God knows how she finds this stuff out. She was here when I got here."

"He confess?"

"In a manner of speaking," DeLuca said. "He insisted he didn't kill Amaryllis Roldan. Problem was, we hadn't accused him of anything yet."

"Gotcha." Jake closed the file.

"That's exactly what I said to him," DeLuca said.

So this was the guy who'd killed the girl Jake had once called Charlestown, "the punk Ophelia," left her under the bridge battered and bruised, left her to drown. But this guy hadn't killed Kylie Howarth, of course. Kylie'd done that herself.

Jake watched the suspect yank at the collar of his white T-shirt, then fiddle with the snaps on the front of his orange jail-issue jumpsuit.

"How long's he been in here? In custody?"

"That's the first thing I asked, too." DeLuca tapped the file. "Since last Thursday."

"So he's got a perfect alibi for Sellica. And for yesterday."

"Yeah," DeLuca said. "You're looking at an asshole who's probably not going to see the light of day for a while. He killed Amaryllis Roldan. But if there's a Bridge Killer, it's not him."

"All I have to do is call and say, 'May I speak to Kenna Wilkes, please?'" Jane pointed to the phone on Alex's desk. "I bet they'll put me off. Transfer me to Sheila King's office. They must have seen the sketch the cops are handing out, it's got to be on TV already. They'll have to make a statement. I mean, the Bridge Killer's fourth victim works for the man who's running for Senate. And might be his lover! It's like—the headline of all headlines. Beyond amazing."

Jane couldn't sit still on Alex's couch one more second. She paced to his closed office door, then back to his desk, arms flailing. "She's gorgeous. She's dead. And we can prove she had a . . . a . . ." She looked at Alex, needing a word.

"Relationship?" Alex said. He rolled a pencil between two palms. "I have to call Tay Reidy. The publisher has got to be in on this. And the lawyer. And maybe the police."

"We need to interview Moira." Jane rooted through her tote bag. She needed to make a list. "We need a reaction from Eleanor Gable. *Damn.* May I use that pencil?"

Alex swiveled his chair, handing her his pencil with a flourish. "You know, Jane, I've got to say. The fifth floor is really pleased with you. I am, too. The way you've thrown yourself into this. Team player." Alex raised an eyebrow, inquiring. "Are you okay with it? Transitioning from your old life?"

Jane blinked, surprised at the personal question. "Well, sure, I'm . . ." She paused, thinking for a beat, considering precisely what it was she was sure about. "Thanks, Alex. Yes, I'm—feeling like a reporter again."

"Well, you've knocked this one out of the ballpark," Alex said. "I'm thinkin' no more six-month tryout. We'll have to keep the networks from grabbing you away from us, when this thing hits the fan."

The room was silent for a moment. "It's a big story," Jane finally said.

Alex's intercom buzzed. "Victoria on line two," a woman's voice squawked through.

"I'll call her right back," Alex said into the speaker.

He gave Jane a look. Then held up his left hand. "My wife. Soon-to-be ex-wife."

"Oh, I'm—" Jane scrambled for the appropriate response. Sorry? Happy? She couldn't help but look at his fourth finger. *Nothing*. Hot Alex was suddenly soon-to-be available. Amy would go ballistic. Send her a subscription to *Brides* magazine.

"Anyway." Alex waved away the moment, changing the subject. "Back to Kenna Wilkes. We need to work this out. We need to be careful. The election is only eight days away. We can't accuse—"

"Like I said, we should call the campaign first." Jane nodded, relieved to be back on track. "See what they say. And *who* they're going to say she is."

"Well, they'd never admit she's—"

"The other woman," Jane said. She took out her cell phone. This was such a crossroads. "I know. Amazing. I can't wait to hear what they do say. I'm calling. Right now."

52

The shower had been a great idea. Steaming soapy water, coursing over his shoulders, washing away the fear, washing away the memories, washing away that morning's news conference, washing away everything but his determination. Matt had used all the towels from the hotel's racks, wrapping himself dry, rubbing away two days of craziness. He'd called in sick to his office, grabbed a take-out lunch from the hotel coffee shop. Now well fed, clean shaven, in pressed Levi's, shirt and tie, and leather jacket, he knew what he had to do.

He stood in front of Lassiter headquarters, one gloved hand ready to push the revolving doors. He couldn't make himself do it.

A gaggle of laughing campaign types swarmed ahead of him, young girls with Lassiter buttons on their puffy vests, one wearing a hat with two Lassiter buttons on wires, sticking out like political antennae. "Don't forget to vote next week," one girl called as she pushed against the door.

The door revolved and campaign headquarters swallowed them up, leaving Matt standing outside. He reviewed his plan, one more time. Go in. Maybe that

Deenie person who'd told him about Springfield would help him. He'd find Owen. Go from there.

Besides, he was here with good news, right? He decided he would promise Owen—his father—he'd keep quiet about their relationship until *Owen* wanted to make it public. He wasn't here to create problems. The way he'd dealt with Holly proved that, right? He wasn't going to mention that, of course.

He would finally be Matthew Lassiter again. No longer left behind, no longer forgotten, no longer erased from his family. His mother, bitter and divisive, had moved them to Philadelphia and changed their names to Galbraith, but he was really Matthew Lassiter. And he was part of the solution.

He put his hand on the glass and metal door, ready to push through. Then he stopped.

Maybe he should—forget it. Go to one campaign event, get one close-up glimpse of his father, call it even. Maybe now wasn't the right time to show himself. Election day looming, a tight race, maybe Matt's very existence would ruin it all, and where would that leave their relationship? Someday they'd meet properly. Someday his father would accept him. Treat him as a real son.

He patted his pockets, wishing for cigarettes. Instead, he felt Holly's car keys. And the paper with Jane Ryland's phone number. Reminding him of what happened.

With that, Matt straightened his shoulders, pushed on the metal bar, and stepped inside as the glass door began to turn. *Turning point,* this is what they mean by that.

The fluorescent lights in the headquarters lobby glinted on the polished marble floors; march music blared through unseen speakers; red, white, and blue bunting draped across the ceiling and looped down the walls.

Huge posters of Owen and Moira Lassiter lined one side of the lobby. But it was the front desk that commanded Matt's attention.

The woman at the front desk was not Deenie Bayliss.

He stared. Felt his heart threaten to break through his chest. Felt every memory of every year of his life and every year of his loss flood back over him, swallow him, suffocate him, overwhelm him.

His lips went dry; he knew his voice would never work.

What was *she* doing here?

He took a step closer, put both palms on the reception desk. Tried to think of what to say.

"Cissy?" He heard his voice rasp, didn't sound like himself.

The woman lifted her head.

She had her mother's eyes. Same as his.

"Hello, Cissy," he croaked again.

The woman stood slowly, not taking those eyes off him. "No," she said. "No."

"Yes," Matt said. "But—"

She ripped off the telephone headset, put her hands to her mouth, scanning the room. They were alone. She darted from behind the desk, clutched Matt's arm with a vise of manicured fingers, hissed into his ear.

"You idiot. Get out of here."

She pulled him through the lobby, stumbling once in her high heels, pushed him into the revolving door, herself right behind him, the door moving fast, spilling them onto the sidewalk. He still towered over her.

She jabbed a forefinger into his chest. Her eyes narrowed; spots of color flamed her cheekbones. "Get out of here. Now. Leave. Oh, my god, you'll spoil everything. What in hell are you *doing* here?" She turned away, as if to go back inside, then whirled to face him. "No. I don't even want to know. Just—go. You didn't see me, you don't know me. Good-bye."

"Five minutes." He grabbed her arm, thin under the soft black sweater, stopping her. "That's all. We have to talk. You need to know that—"

She rolled her eyes. "I don't need to know anything."

But she let him draw her into a little alleyway next to the building, into a shadow, out of sight. Cissy needed to know about Holly Neff. What he'd done. Everything. Holly's plan. It was just as dangerously destructive to his little sister as it was to Owen. Cissy needed to know they were all in it together. A family again. Their father just didn't know it yet.

With a start, Matt realized what *he* needed to know.

"Hey," he said. He didn't let go of Cissy's arm. "What are *you* doing here?"

"See, Jakey? I told you. She's not there. She's supposed to be at the front desk, and she's not. Look," Jane whispered, pointing at the window fronting Lassiter headquarters. The *Register*'s lawyers had insisted Jane call the police with what she knew about Kenna Wilkes. She and Alex had protested, a united front, arguing about breaking news, headlines, and the separation of journalists and law enforcement. Alex had been terrific, supportive, genuinely on her side. Still, they'd lost. And now she was in a position she shouldn't be in—cooperating with the cops. Making a deal.

With Jake.

Quid pro quo. They'd reveal the identity of Kenna Wilkes, the newest murder victim; the police would give them the exclusive. Not the most desirable situation, but the cards had been dealt. It was a great story, that was for sure, and gave her massive brownie points at the paper. And getting such a good lead on the case might make Jake look good to his superiors. *She* was the one helping *him* now. It evened the score.

"So did you call?" Jake peered through the window, cupping his hands along each side of his face to block the light.

"I wanted to. But Alex insisted we come check it out in person. I guess he's right. Better to gauge the reactions face-to-face."

"Pretty empty in there," Jake said. "Guess everyone's still at lunch. Interesting, though. We know Kenna Wilkes must be a fake name."

"Yeah." Shoulder almost touching Jake's, Jane put her face close to the window, wanting to see inside again for herself. "She pretended to be registered to vote. She was hiding something, that's for sure. So either she was fooling the heck out of everyone here at Lassiter headquarters—or they're complicit in whatever she was up to."

"Or both," Jake said, turning to her. "Could be her intentions wound up making her some enemies."

"Which means—you think someone in the Lassiter campaign killed her?"

"That's what we're here to find out, right?"

"I love it when you talk cop. Shall we get this show on the road?" Jane smiled, bursting with excitement at what was about to unfold. It was sad, of course. Someone was dead. But in journalism and in law enforcement, you couldn't ignore the satisfaction of getting to say, *case closed*. "I can't believe we're working on a story together."

"I could get used to it if you can, Janey. Maybe we could arrange a little after-hours research—"

"Jake, you read me?" DeLuca's voice crackled over the two-way.

"Loud and clear," Jake said. He shrugged at Jane. "Two seconds."

"You someplace secure?" DeLuca said.

"Not exactly." Jake's eyebrows raised. "Stand by one, D."

Jane pointed to herself, then to the front door. She mouthed the words, *I'll go in*.

Hell, no, Jake mouthed back. He grabbed her wrist. Letting go, he put a finger to his lips, signaling her to keep quiet.

"Go ahead, D," he said into the radio.

"You know that search warrant you asked for? For Patti Vick's studio?"

Patti Vick? Jane leaned in, eyes widening. They'd searched Arthur Vick's wife's studio? Jane knew from her stories it was in one of the Fort Point buildings. Near where Kenna was found. She struggled to make sense of it. Was Arthur Vick connected to Kenna Wilkes, too?

"Why did—?" she whispered.

Jake glared at her, warning her to keep quiet. "Copy that."

"You have the address?"

"Ten-four."

"Then you better get over here."

53

"She threatened me," Matt said. Standing in the alley, he held out both hands to his sister, pleading his case. Trying to make her understand. The October sun barely filtered through the narrow space between buildings. Cissy must be freezing in that thin sweater. She was calling herself Kenna Wilkes, she'd said, but she was Cissy Galbraith to him.

He told his sister, fast as he could, about Holly, and B-school, and what he'd revealed to her, and what happened after he saw Holly's photo in the paper. "She was going to ruin my life. And yours, too, Cissy. And, most important, our father's life."

"So you killed her? Are you crazy?" Cissy ignored his explanations, frowning with disbelief. She put her hands on top of her head, took a few steps away from him, farther down the alley, then turned back, hands outstretched. "Please tell me it was an accident. We can go to the police. We can tell them you snapped, or she threatened you, or she tripped, or she—"

"Yes, yes, of course it was an accident." *She has to understand.* "I didn't mean to. I hadn't planned to. I only wanted to stop her. She was sabotaging our father's campaign. She was going to ruin him, make it look like he was having an affair with her. And I couldn't have that happen. I couldn't!"

"You idiot," Cissy said.

Her head was shaking back and forth, like their mother's used to whenever she was upset. He hated that. He wished she would stop it. He wished she would listen to him. "Cissy, that's not all."

"Oh, dear god, what else?" Cissy looked at her watch. "I've got to get back inside. They'll be freaking, wondering where I am. And I have my own—ah. So what, Matt, what now?"

"She told a reporter. Jane Ryland, at the newspaper. Mailed her a bunch of stuff, incriminating-looking stuff, about Holly and our father. Holly has photos. Of the two of them together. And now Jane Ryland has them."

"Holly Neff? And Owen Lassiter?" Cissy's forehead furrowed, as if she were deciphering a secret code. "Jane Ryland?"

"Yes, and so you've got to be ready. Any time now, this Jane Ryland could show up at Lassiter headquarters. When she does, it means all hell's about to break loose. We have to stop it."

"Holly Neff? And Owen Lassiter?" Cissy said the names again, deliberately, syllable by syllable, like she couldn't quite make them compute.

Matt raised his hands, frustrated. *Doesn't she get it?* "The pictures aren't real, you know? They never really—I mean, he didn't even know her. Let alone have a torrid affair with her. But she said the media would buy it all, instantly, and wouldn't get to the real truth until it was too late. And she's right, you know? The more he denied it, the more they wouldn't believe it. The headlines and speculation alone would— What?" Matt stopped, mid-sentence, baffled. Cissy was suddenly smiling. "Why are you looking at me like that?"

He saw his sister take a deep breath, then look up through the narrow band of still-blue sky. "Let's go inside," she said. "It's cold out here."

"So you have to leave? Right *now*?" Jane stamped a foot, annoyed. Bad enough to have to take Jake with her as she revealed the identity of the city's newest murder victim and political paramour. Now Jake wanted her to wait?

"See?" She patted her tote bag. "Now *my* phone's ringing. But am I answering it? *No.* So I don't see why you—"

"Search warrant. I've got to be there. There's no way I can—"

"Oh, no, Jakey, we're doing this," Jane insisted. Her phone stopped ringing. *Good.* "And *then* you can go do your search warrant thing. In fact, I might go with you. Arthur Vick won't get any less guilty if we wait fifteen minutes. Then I can go write my page-one, blockbuster-headlined, Channel-Eleven-can-eat-my-dust career-making story, and you can go catch the bad guy. Okay?"

"Sorry, Janey, there's no choice." Jake zipped up his leather jacket.

Jane retied the black wool belt of her coat, girding for battle, and poked a finger against Jake's chest. "Jacob Dellacort Brogan. Listen to me. You and I are going in. *Now.* We're going to prove Kenna Wilkes is the victim, and, soon, we're going to find out why she was killed. Big, big, big news. Whatever your guys found in that studio can just—"

She stopped, mouth open. Two people were walking around the corner, coming out of that little alley between the buildings. Even half a block away, she recognized one of them. That guy from the press conference. Matt. What was he doing here?

The other was a knockout blonde. She'd obviously spent a bundle on boots and hair-care products, but she clearly needed a coat.

Jake stepped aside to let them pass, turning away as his phone trilled. He raised a finger, *back in a second*.

The Matt person stopped in his tracks, staring at Jane. "Jane Ryland? From the newspaper?" he asked. He gave the woman beside him a look Jane couldn't translate. The blonde took his arm, tucking herself behind him.

"Well, yes, we met this morning at the news conference, didn't we?" This was all Jane needed. She cut to the chase, *let's get this over with*. "You were going to call me, right? But you didn't, right?"

"Is he with the newspaper, too?" Matt waved a hand toward Jake, who was leaning against the building, back to them, away from them, still focused on his phone call.

"No." Jane stepped in front of him, blocking the view. End of chitchat. "He's a friend."

"Matt was just leaving." The blonde smiled, waving Matt away. "Weren't you?"

As Matt headed down the sidewalk, the woman took a step forward, holding out a hand to Jane. "I've heard so much about you," she went on. "I'm such a big fan of yours. It's lovely to finally meet you."

Jake returned to Jane's side, joining them.

Jane smiled, acknowledging the woman's attention, shook her hand. *Always good to have a fan*. "Jane Ryland," she said.

"Oh, of course I know that," the blonde said. "And I'm Kenna Wilkes."

54

Jane stared at the woman. She'd never seen this person in her life. Not at the Springfield rally. Not at the Esplanade event. Not in Archive Gus's photos. How could she have gotten this wrong?

She put out a hand, touching the thick glass of the headquarters window, grounding herself.

"You're—?" Jane's voice was out of order. Not working. *There's an explanation.*

"Kenna Wilkes?" Jake finished her question.

"But I thought—" Jane's brain struggled to remember. The hotel clerk had shown her the name on the computer screen, clearly, unmistakably. Kenna Wilkes. She was registered there. Jane had talked to her, taken her photo, for gosh sake, and the woman—*not Kenna?*—had answered to that name. Hadn't she?

How could she have gotten this wrong?

Oh, god. *Alex.* Her story. The paper. Her job. Her career. She would forever be Wrong-Guy Ryland.

"Do we know each other?" the woman said. She looked at Jane, inquiring, then at Jake. She caressed her hair back from her forehead with one hand, let her curls fall into place again.

"Jane?" Jake said. His voice was wrong, too. Cold,

cop-ish, and not-Jake. "Do we need to be somewhere else? To—talk?"

"No, no," Jane said. Now she'd not only blown her own career, but Jake's, too. "I mean, no, we don't know each other. Sorry. I'm just—distracted."

"Don't give it another thought," the woman said. She wrapped her arms across her chest, hugging herself. "But, brrrr. I need to go inside. Lovely to meet you."

Jane watched the woman's back revolve through the glass headquarters door, a burst of tinny march music spilling out.

She was determined not to burst into tears. "I don't know, Jakey, I mean—there's just no way that—she was absolutely—I mean, I saw, I talked to—"

Jake zipped his jacket up and down. "I guess it's a good thing you didn't do a front-page story about the beautiful and mysterious Lassiter campaign staffer who was done in by the elusive Bridge Killer."

She was going to lose it. "But I *know* that she—"

He reached out a finger, lifted her chin. "Janey? You going to be okay? I really have to go. But no harm. I mean, we're lucky. Right? No confrontations, no embarrassments, no headlines. You just—got it wrong. She's the wrong woman. Everyone makes mistakes."

Jane watched him click open the door of his unmarked cruiser. He gave her a final look—pity? disappointment?—before he got in and drove up Causeway Street, siren blaring. She stared after him, unseeing.

Her phone rang, its muffled trill struggling out from inside her tote bag.

"Shut up," she told it. Then dug it out, clicked it on. "This is Jane," she said. *Whatever*. At this point, how bad could it be?

"Is this Jane Ryland?"

A familiar voice. A man. But not—

"This is Samuel Shapiro."

The lawyer for Channel 11. A flitter of hope struggled to emerge. Maybe this was some kind of good news. The million-dollar judgment was overturned, or Arthur Vick admitted he lied. Maybe she'd won the appeal? Could it be?

"Oh, hi, Sam." Jane perched on a masonry ledge along the front of the building, feet braced on the sidewalk. Sam was a good guy, defended her every moment of that horrible trial, stood shoulder to shoulder with her on the courthouse steps on verdict day. "What's up?"

"It's about your appeal," Sam said. "We're pushing the deadline. It's fish or cut bait time. If you can prove you weren't wrong, let's hear it. You got anything from your source? Any confirmation? Anything at all?"

Sellica was dead. And she couldn't say a word about their relationship. Her ex-employers would have to fork over a million bucks. "No, Sam. Not any more evidence than I had at the beginning. I mean—you know this. My source is impeccable. Vick was lying."

"Yeah, well, we told that to the jury. And look what happened. Now, frankly, we're somewhat disturbed that at this juncture you're having a difficult time proving what you told your employers is the truth."

"But—"

"We need to have a brief meeting of the minds, Miss Ryland."

Miss Ryland? Sam never called her that.

"We're, shall we say, of the opinion that we're not actually the ones with the liability here. If you were—and I'm not saying you were, but merely *if* you were—not totally honest with Channel Eleven, then legally, it's you who are liable for the judgment. I've been instructed to inform you, you might want to retain your own counsel."

Jane felt the blood drain from her face. She took the

phone away from her ear, briefly examining it as if it were an alien being. Taking a shuddering breath, she tried to answer.

"Retain my own—?"

"Exactly. Because if the judgment is primarily a result of your negligence, Miss Ryland, then Channel Eleven feels they should not have to pay it. Here's the bottom line: You're the one who's answerable for the million-dollar damages. Not Channel Eleven. It's not our responsibility to pay that judgment. It's yours."

55

"So who are these women, Mr. Vick?" Jake dealt a hand of five-by-seven photographs across the oil-paint-spattered table in Patti Vick's studio. Ground level, triple-sized sliding windows showed off a panorama of the Fort Point Channel, with a perfect view of the post office parking lot where the supe held his press conference a few hours earlier. "Fort Point"—*the victim who isn't Kenna Wilkes*—had been found in eyeshot of here. So had Sellica. That proximity, combined with Vick's connection to three of the victims, was why the judge had quickly granted Jake's request for a search warrant for the place.

Jake didn't recognize any of the faces. The photos DeLuca'd just found in a desk drawer had no names on the backs, no photographer credits. Just twenty-something women, smiling and not-smiling, all in a row. No Roldan, no Howarth, no Sellica, no Fort Point. De-Luca had whispered that disappointing info to him. Jake's own examination confirmed it.

"You're asking me? About photos you found in my wife's studio?" Arthur Vick barely turned his head, not moving from his post at the window, voice oozing boredom. "How would I—?"

"Detective Brogan?" Henry Rothmann, his gray pin-stripes a counterpoint to Vick's pressed jeans and mono-grammed crew neck sweater, sidled up in front of his client, as if to prevent Vick from seeing the photographs. "I must interrupt here, because—"

"Well, your wife's paintings, the ones in your living room, are somewhat, shall we say, nonrepresentational?" Jake ignored the lawyer's attempts to derail his questioning. "Not portraits. So I'm wondering if you'd know why she'd be collecting photos of young women. Any thoughts? And, since she is your wife and all, I'm curious as to whether you know any of them. The girls in the photos."

Two uniforms were posted outside. Two veteran detectives from Jake's unit worked the back rooms, continuing the search. Stacks of canvases leaned against beige cement-block walls. Tubes of paint lined an industrial metal-and-bolt wall-unit of shelves. Bouquets of paint-brushes soaked in liquid-filled containers. The place reeked of turpentine and oil. So far, nothing unusual for an artist's studio. Nothing incriminating.

Still, Jake was intrigued by the photos. Because they were in Patti Vick's studio didn't mean they were hers, obviously. But what had Sellica Darden's mother told him? *All those other girls wanting to be in commercials.* Something like that.

"Detective Brogan." Rothmann was moving closer to Jake and signaling Vick to stay back. "As a show of good faith, my client is willing to stipulate that some of those women may have auditioned for his television commercials. But he doesn't know how the photos got here."

Rothmann ran a hand across his forehead. "Now. Let me ask *you*, Detective. What if these *are* girls from the ads? Any of them reported missing?"

Which was, of course, the problem. If there had been

a photo of the Fort Point victim—*who is not Kenna Wilkes,* Jake remembered with another pang of regret—or of Roldan, or Sellica, this would be the slam dunk, and Jake could pull out his handcuffs. But so far, so nothing.

"We done here?" Arthur Vick made a big show of pulling out a cell phone and thumbing some keys.

"We're not, as a matter of fact," Jake said. Pompous ass. "You ever have, say, 'auditions' here? Bring any of the commercial wannabes to this studio? Do you have keys to the place?"

"Detective Brogan?" Darrell James, a veteran homicide cop the squad called "Humpty," appeared in the hallway. A black vest of body armor, emblazoned PO-LICE, covered his big-and-tall sports jacket. He'd ripped open the Velcro side-straps so the vest hung on him like a bulky bib.

Between two purple rubber-gloved fingers, Humpty dangled a clear plastic Baggie. "Jake? You might want to take a look at this."

"Jane? You okay?"

How long have I been sitting like this? Jane's legs were almost numb from balancing against the building. She stood, smoothing her coat, every muscle complaining.

"Oh, hi, Trevor." She was so bummed about the lawsuit, she'd let it distract her from the Kenna thing. *What am I missing?* "I'm fine, thanks. Just, ah, thinking."

"Are you scheduled for a meeting?" Trevor said, arriving at the front door. His canvas briefcase slung crosswise over his navy pea jacket. "Something I can help you with?"

"Well, no, I . . . well, wait. Yes, actually. You can." *Trevor. The campaign insider. Kenna. The campaign mystery woman.* "Do you know a Kenna Wilkes?"

"Kenna Wilkes?" Trevor gestured toward the lobby. "The woman who sometimes sits at the front desk? Receptionist? Sure. I know her. Kind of."

He glanced at the lobby again, then back at Jane. "Why? Is there a problem?"

"Oh, no, of course not. I just met her, she's very nice, and I was curious—" Jane had to untangle her thoughts. Every link in the chain so far reassured her this was, somehow, still a story. The name Kenna Wilkes was on the hotel register. Gina, the hotel clerk, had said Wilkes was with the campaign. But Jake's research had proved there was no real person named Kenna Wilkes. Trevor might provide the next link. "—Do you know how she connected with the Lassiter campaign? And when?

"I'm researching," she added, trying to come up with something Trevor might believe, "you know, a possible story on campaign volunteers. Who they are. Why they care. The new politics."

Trevor's face relaxed, as if this was something he could buy in to. "Oh, okay. Yeah. I was with the candidate when they met. Part of my neighborhood meet and greet project. She's like a—war widow. Pretty sad." Trevor aimed a forefinger at Jane, as if she'd had a brilliant idea. "You know, she'd be a great story. Has a little son, volunteered to help, very enthusiastic. Patriotic. And come to think of it, Jane, Channel Eleven was covering the campaign in Deverton that day, maybe you could— Oh, sorry."

Trevor grimaced. Fumbled with his jacket buttons. "You don't work there anymore. My bad."

Perfect. Now I have the upper hand.

"No, that's okay," Jane said. Kenna Wilkes didn't exist on paper. But in real life, she did. So who was she? "You get her name from a list of registered voters?"

A trio of college kids wearing Boston University

sweatshirts trooped up the sidewalk, each holding a grease-spotted fast-food bag. "Hey, Trev," one said. "You coming to the get-out-the-vote thing?"

"Yup, be right there. Hold the fort."

"She's on the voter registration list?" Jane repeated as the kids went inside. "Or how'd you find her?"

"Well, that's easy enough to check." Trevor unzipped his briefcase, pulled out a clipboard. He flipped the creased pages of a yellow pad, muttering. "Here it is. Notes from that day. I have her at 463 Constitution Lane."

Jane wrote the address in her notebook as Trevor continued.

"Let's see. Nope, she wasn't on my voter list. Turns out Kenna Wilkes was—Jane? You with me here?"

But Jane had already closed her notebook. She could see straight again. And she was seeing a good story. She needed her camera.

"Just a sec, Trevor. I need to ask you something."

Yanking it from her tote bag, she clicked through the photos, searching for the best one of the woman in the red coat—okay, she wasn't in the red coat in these pictures, but whatever. Maybe her name wasn't Kenna Wilkes. But she was connected to the campaign. She'd been at all those campaign events.

Now she was dead. That was a story, no matter what her name was. What's more, someone in Lassiter headquarters must know it.

And might already be working to cover it up.

Jane flashed through the photographs as fast as the camera would change shots—*the Esplanade, I haven't looked at that one recently*—until she hit the Springfield rally and the picture of the woman falling into Lassiter's arms. *Whoa.* That snap was going to make a knockout front page.

"See this woman, Trevor?" She held up the camera, angling it to keep the little square screen out of the sun's glare. "Do you know who she is?"

"Whatcha got, Humpt—I mean, Darrell?" Jake waved the detective over, watching Vick take a step or two backward toward the studio's sliding glass windows. He saw DeLuca straighten, sidle closer to the suspect.

"We'd like to see what you think you found, Detectives." Rothmann moved toward Jake. "We're allowed to examine whatever you remove."

"Like hell you—," DeLuca muttered.

"Mr. Rothmann?" Jake interrupted his partner, even though he agreed with him. "We allowed you to be here during the search. We didn't have to, as you are well aware. But under no circumstances are you allowed to 'examine' what we collect. You've got plenty of experience with this. You were given a copy of the warrant. You'll be able to see the evidence at the appropriate time. Which is—not now. Are we clear on that?"

Jake took the Baggie from the detective, turned his back on Rothmann, and peered through the clear ziplock bag, smoothing it over the brown plastic container inside. A medicine bottle, white screw top, with a typed prescription label from the CVS pharmacy indicating the contents were for PATRICIA A. VICK. FLUNITRAZEPAM. TAKE 2 PRN FOR SLEEP.

"We're done, Henry." Arthur Vick grabbed a leather jacket from the back of a paint-speckled chair. "I'm out of here."

"Not so fast." Jake gave back the Baggie, nodding in salute to the officer. He kept his voice low. "Make sure this is listed properly on the return, then let's get it to the lab A-SAP. The rest of us will finish up here."

"Will do, Detective." Humpty took the evidence bag and headed out the door. Jake saw him give a behind-the-back thumbs-up to DeLuca.

"As for you, Mr. Vick?"

"As for me, what?" Vick pulled a plaid muffler from one of the jacket sleeves, looping it around his neck. He shoved his arms into the jacket and gestured a hand at the lawyer. "You coming?"

"*You're* coming, Mr. Vick. Downtown." Jake reached under his jacket and unclicked his handcuffs from the carrier. "Whether your attorney comes along is up to you. But, Arthur Vick? You're under arrest for the murder of Sellica Darden."

56

Trevor Kiernan had insisted he didn't recognize the woman in the photo on Jane's camera. Which was either the truth, or the beginning of the big lie. Now Jane had another plan. She had to talk to Alex, of course, but he'd been on the phone, so she headed for her desk at the *Register,* hoping Tuck wasn't there. She needed some alone time.

No Tuck. *Score one for Jane.* She sat down, flipped open her laptop, punched up the Deverton assessor's office. Affluent communities had property info online, thank goodness, so what Jane needed to confirm would be a few clicks away. While her computer was thinking, Jane dug out her notebook and found the page with Kenna Wilkes's address.

"You avoiding bill collectors or something, roomie? You've got mail."

Tuck stood at the cubicle entrance, one arm around a stack of brown envelopes and magazines.

"Hey, Tuck." *So much for alone time.* "Mail?"

Tuck plopped the pile of mail on their desk, a few stray envelopes sliding onto the floor. "Yeah, it's like e-mail, but it comes on paper. Through the U.S. Postal Service.

Goes to the mailroom. Where you're supposed to pick it up. Unless your cubemate is nice enough to get it for you. Which she is. Once."

Jane scooted her laptop to one side and rolled her chair back, giving Tuck some space. "Mailroom?" She shrugged, thinking back. She picked up a few of the envelopes, examining them. *Junk.* "No one told me about the mailroom."

"Now they have," Tuck said. She dragged a rolling chair from an adjacent cubicle. Swiveled it backward and straddled it, one cowboy boot on either side of the seat, her short jeans skirt climbing up her thighs. Today she wore a Bruins cap, her ponytail swinging behind. "So, you must be psyched."

"Psyched?"

"Yeah, roomie. About your pal Arthur Vick."

"Oh, yeah, they're searching his wife's studio. Pretty interesting." *May he rot in hell,* she didn't say. Jane picked up another stack of mail. Junk, junk, junk. No wonder no one had told her about the mailroom, she didn't need to know. No one used mail anymore. She looked up. "What? Did they find something?"

"So you don't know? That they arrested him for Sellica's murder?"

Jane dropped her head into one hand, propping it up with one elbow on the desk. She turned to Tuck, disbelieving. "Are you—?"

"Horse's mouth," Tuck said. She wiggled her fingers toward the desktop computer. "Can I get in here, roomie? I need to write the story about the studio, the proximity to the crime scenes, and Arthur Vick's connection to three of the victims. The cops found roofies there, too. But that's off the record. Bummer. But bye-bye, Arthur, don't you think?"

An e-mail popped up on Jane's computer. From Alex. Jane read the subject line: NOW.

"Ah, Tuck, listen, I've got to go talk to Alex." She flapped her computer closed. *Alex can wait thirty more seconds.* "They found roofies? In Vick's studio?"

"So says my source. Remember, the ME found them in Sellica's tox screen?" Tuck nodded, lofting one leg over the chair back and taking Jane's place at the desk. "Mrs. Vick had them as sleeping pills, apparently. They're saying her husband must have used them to knock Sellica out before he killed her. But I'm not allowed to go with it. They're keeping that tidbit back."

Jane clutched her laptop to her chest, trying to remember to breathe.

"Roomie? You okay?"

"Yeah. I'm just thinking. . . ."

Tuck, smiling, put a palm up toward her. "High five, sister. If Arthur Vick killed Sellica Darden, that pretty much also kills his testimony that he had no relationship with her."

Jane held up her own palm, slowly, and touched it to Tuck's. Exactly what she'd been thinking but afraid to say out loud. Could it be true?

From the sliding glass window of Patti Vick's studio, Jake could see the blue and white cruiser, Arthur Vick in the backseat and two uniforms in the front, crossing the Harbor Street bridge on the way downtown. Behind them, at the wheel of his ridiculous sports car, a probably still-fuming Henry Rothmann.

"The happy couple," DeLuca said.

Jake stared across the water, remembering the parking lot press conference mere hours before. He squinted at the parking lot. "D?" he said. "I have a thought."

"Alert the media," DeLuca said.

"Come with me." Jake ignored the wisecrack. "Vick and his pal can stew downtown for a while."

It was two minutes away, less. Jake turned his Jeep into the post office parking lot, driving past the cars parked along the railing.

"What're you thinkin'?" DeLuca asked from the seat beside him.

Jake jammed the shift into Park, flipped on his wig-wags. "I'm thinkin'—that one."

Opening his door, he pointed to a white car with several orange parking tickets under the windshield wiper. The car had been there, with one ticket, during the press conference. It was still there. *Why hasn't the owner moved it?*

"It's what happens in the news business, you know?" Alex said. "Until it's in the paper, it's not wrong. It's reporting. Right?"

Jane nodded. Alex was taking the Kenna Wilkes thing pretty well. She perched on the edge of his couch, tentative, almost afraid to say anything for fear of upsetting the balance. The Arthur Vick arrest had just about steamrolled everything else in her mind. She had to call Sam Shapiro, because Arthur Vick's arrest was proof she was right. Right? Vick would have to admit he and Sellica had a connection. Exactly the opposite of what Vick had testified under oath. Wouldn't the judge be compelled to grant their appeal? Overturn the judgment?

Wouldn't he be obligated to make it all go away? Her million-dollar albatross?

Alex glanced at his computer monitor, then adjusted

the screen so Jane could see it. "Tuck's already got the Arthur Vick story working. Here's her draft for the e-version. 'Grocery Magnate Arrested for Call Girl Murder.' That'll be the headline. We're putting it up as soon as we get another confirmation."

Alex leaned against the side of his paper-strewn desk. "How are you about this, Jane? Seems . . ." He blinked a few times, thinking. Toasted her with his striped paper cup of coffee. "Pretty huge. For your appeal."

Jane put her elbows on her knees, chin in hands, staring at her own black leather boots. Ten minutes ago, she'd been trying to unravel the identity of a murder victim, trying to keep her job at the *Register,* trying to figure out how she was going to pay for a lawyer to defend herself against a million-dollar judgment. With the Vick arrest, everything changed. Didn't it?

"One step at a time," she said aloud. She stood, picking a bit of couch lint from her black wool skirt and adjusting the stretchy black belt over her turtleneck. "We'll see about that. The appeal. But the Kenna Wilkes situation—"

"Yeah. As you said, we still have the photos of whoever the victim actually is." Alex paused, contemplating. "Someone at the Lassiter campaign must know her, right?"

"You'd think." Alex was talking about what happened *next*. So Jane's job was safe. He really was a pretty thoughtful guy. He'd stuck by her. Trusted her.

Alex took a sip of coffee, then gestured his cup toward the door. "So, ace reporter, why aren't you on your way over there to find out who the victim really is?"

57

"N-e-f-f?" **Jake said** the letters out loud, indicating De-Luca should be writing them in his notebook. Jake used one hand to drive, the other to hold his cell phone. "First name, Holly? *H-o-l-l-y?*"

DeLuca nodded, writing. "Got it."

"Is there an address on the application? A local address?" Jake pulled up to a stop sign, listening to the rental company clerk. It had taken three phone calls—one to the Registry of Motor Vehicles, one to the Budget Rental Car main headquarters, one to their local of-fice—to track down the name of the person who'd rented the white car parked in the post office parking lot. The first ticket had been issued today at 9:35 A.M. for violation of the thirty-minute meter. Several more orange tickets had piled up on top of that one. But one was all Jake needed. Sunday, he knew, the meters were not in effect. What if the victim had parked there Sunday? And didn't pick up her car—because she was dead?

"55423 Harborside Drive." With a glance, he con-firmed DeLuca was getting it. That address was less than a mile away, in a sprawling yuppie complex near the harbor. Lots of newcomers, postgrads with financial district jobs. Dogs. Hot tubs. "Apartment forty-three. Phone number?"

Jake hung up, then punched his lights and siren as DeLuca wrote the numbers he'd rattled off.

"Call her," Jake said. "Maybe she's, I don't know. Shacking up with someone. Shopping at Downtown Crossing. Having lunch at Quincy Market. Left her car at the P.O. because a ticket is cheaper than a Boston parking lot."

"We'll soon find out," DeLuca said. He thumbed cell phone buttons as their car powered through a red light, made the turn onto Hanover Street. "It's ringing. No answer yet."

"Voice mail?" Jake asked. Half a mile to go.

"Nope," DeLuca said. "Nothing."

Jane stuffed the legitimate-looking mail into her tote bag and tossed the junk into the wastebasket. Tuck, fingers flying over the keyboard, hardly acknowledged her. Jane grabbed her coat from the hook, wrapped it closed. "See you—"

"Hey, roomie." Tuck gestured to the floor. A stray envelope. "You dropped one."

Jane picked it up, the postmark from four days ago, noticing it had been forwarded to her from Channel 11. *Nice of them.* No return address. And not the same awkward handwriting as the creepy letters. Those had stopped, thank goodness.

Almost without thinking, she ripped it open.

"Jane? What's wrong?" Tuck turned, one hand still on her keyboard, and stared at her, frowning. "You made a weird noise."

"I did?" Jane looked back at the envelope. What she'd pulled from inside. She couldn't take her eyes off it.

"Yeah, like you'd seen a ghost or something."

"Yeah." Jane blinked at the snapshots she held in her hands. It *was* a ghost. A person who was now dead. *Kenna W*— Well, not Kenna Wilkes. But it was the woman in the red coat. With Owen Lassiter. A recent photo of the two of them. And another, and another, and another. And then, what looked like a . . . a picture of a shrine to Lassiter. A whole wall of photographs of him, decorated with Lassiter balloons on ribbons and Lassiter buttons. Photos of rallies, wide shots of speeches, the exterior of his headquarters. Moira. At the bottom of the pile, a current photo of what looked—from the posters on the wall—like Lassiter's own office, the candidate smiling behind a massive desk.

"I guess that's kind of right," Jane said. She wouldn't have recognized her own voice. "A ghost."

By the time she got back to Alex's office, her brain was working again.

"Boston Police Department, official business," Jake called through the door marked number 43. He'd knocked several times. No answer.

DeLuca was shaking his head as he walked up the hall. "No one at the front desk," he reported. "There's a phone, looks like a house phone. But no one picked up."

"No one answered the manager's door, or the doors on either side," Jake said. "No one's answering Holly Neff's door, either."

DeLuca patted his pockets, took out a wallet, extracted a thin piece of plastic from between two bills. "In about three seconds I can get us in there," he said. "Take a look around."

"In your dreams," Jake said. "Let's see if we can find the super."

"I'm serious," DeLuca persisted. "Exigent circumstances, right, Harvard? The law says if we think there's something—"

"I'm familiar with exigent circumstances." Jake gestured his partner toward the elevator at the end of the hall. "You know as well as I do, it's a probable cause thing. Problem is, we don't genuinely believe Holly Neff may be bleeding to death inside that apartment. That's because we genuinely know she's already dead. And inside the morgue."

"But what if, uh, uh, the guy who killed her is in there?" DeLuca stopped, beseeching Jake with outstretched palms. "What if he took her keys, ya know? How about that? We know she didn't have them on her when she was found. What if he snagged them, and he's inside right now. Maybe he dragged his next victim there, and if we don't get inside, he might—"

"Good try, my man. But no way," Jake said. "We gotta get a warrant to go into that apartment. Or whatever we find would get thrown—"

A rumble sounded within the walls, and a ping of the aluminum elevator. The doors swished open. And a menagerie emerged. Jake recognized two corgis, a pug, and one of those yappy poodledoodles, each with a Halloween jack-o'-lantern decoration on its collar. His own Diva would have eaten them each in one golden retriever–sized chomp. Holding the ends of all their leashes, one of those women-who-look-like-their-dogs. Bug eyes, button nose, a halo of curls, pumpkin dangly earrings. She wore a denim jacket over a denim work shirt over a denim miniskirt. Sneakers.

"May I help you?" she said. "I'm the manager of this building. Live here, too. Barbara Bellafiore." Each dog yanked her in a different direction, but she looked at Jake, then DeLuca. Chose Jake. "Puppies, no! You're cops, right?"

"Yes, ma'am," Jake said. "Detective Jake Brogan, Boston PD. This is my partner, Paul DeLuca." Jake pulled out his BlackBerry. Clicked to the photo he'd taken that morning, the sketch of the Fort Point victim. "Do you recognize this person? Does she live here?"

A snuffling pug fell in love with DeLuca's shoes. The corgis sniffed each other. The woman stared at Jake's BlackBerry screen.

"Holly Neff, apartment forty-three, one of my month-to-months," Barbara said. "Puppies, no no no!"

"You sure?" Jake and DeLuca asked her at the same time. DeLuca shrugged, gestured with a palm. *All yours*.

"Oh yes," Barbara said. "I think she's a . . ." She stopped, shrugging.

"A what?" Jake said. "Has she been home this weekend?"

Barbara let the dogs drag her a few steps down the hall. The corgis, yapping, seemed to be tracking some invisible prey. Jake and DeLuca followed, DeLuca making a surreptitious *cuckoo* gesture. They stopped at apartment 43.

Barbara looped the leashes over one wrist, pulled a jangling collection of keys from a pocket of her denim jacket. "Easy way to find out," she said.

She banged on the door with what looked like a brass whistle on the key ring. Waited a beat. No answer. She sorted through the keys, then brandished one. "All righty then."

"No, ma'am, don't do that." Jake took a step forward. This could ruin everything. He almost wanted to close his eyes. "We can't—just tell us whether—"

But she had already swung open the apartment door.

58

"I know who the other woman is. I know her *name*!" Moira Lassiter's voice over Jane's cell phone speaker, insistent, cut through the rumble of evening rush hour traffic. Jane navigated Boston's zig-zag side streets, one hand on the steering wheel and the other digging into a bag of Cool Ranch chips she'd snagged from the *Register*'s ancient vending machine.

"She was here, at our home, Jane. Flaunting her little tight-jeaned self like I was someone's dotty grandmother and she was Queen of the May. I told you, Jane. I told you. I knew it."

A parking place. Jane licked the salt from two fingers. "Mrs. Lassiter, hold on one second, okay? I'm just parking." Jane eased her Audi into a too-small spot on Canal Street, turned off the ignition. If Moira knew who the other woman was, that meant there *was* another woman. And that meant Jane had been right about this story from moment one.

What if the other woman Moira's talking about—the one who'd been at the Lassiter home—is the victim now lying in the morgue? Moira said, "I know her name*!"*

Maybe she was about to hear the key to the whole deal.

"Okay, I'm back." Jane ate the last chip, trying to chew softly so Moira couldn't hear. "So you said—you know her name?"

"Absolutely." Moira's voice was certain. "Kenna Wilkes."

"Oh, no, Mrs. Lassiter . . ." Jane's shoulders sagged, and she rested her forehead on the steering wheel as Mrs. Lassiter described how flossy "Kenna Wilkes" looked and how inappropriately the young woman behaved.

Moira was apparently as confused as Jane had once been. At least Jane now knew the other woman—Red-Coat Girl—was *not* named Kenna Wilkes. Kenna Wilkes was a receptionist.

And, more important, not dead. Kenna Wilkes was not the woman in the pictures. And that's what had to come next on Jane's agenda. Finding the identity of the woman who *was* dead. And finding who had sent those photographs to Jane.

"Mrs. Lassiter?" Jane took a chance, interrupting mid-tirade. "Listen, I have some ideas about this. In fact, you might be— Well, do me a favor. Let me do some investigating. Can you give me some time? Sit tight? And I'll be back in touch?"

Jane clambered out of the car, clicking it locked. Headed down the sidewalk toward Lassiter headquarters. Moira continued to vent.

"They'll lie to you, Jane, if you ask about it. Be careful. I need to know what the truth is. That's all I can think about. I don't believe that Rory person even comprehends what 'the truth' means. And as for Owen, he's—"

"I'll call you, okay?" Jane arrived at the campaign HQ. She had to go in. Right now. "I promise. Today."

As Moira hung up, Jane pushed through the revolving doors. Pushed away thoughts of Moira, for the time being at least, and focused on the photo mystery. No one was at the reception desk. *Hmm. Wonder where Kenna-whatever-her-name-really-is went?* But not having to talk her way inside certainly made Jane's life easier. She yanked her tote bag securely up and over her shoulder, then poked the elevator button with one finger. She poked it again to make sure.

Poor Rory Maitland. He was not going to be happy to see her again.

"I think I saw a movement in the back. Inside the apartment. Could be trouble." DeLuca took a step toward Holly Neff's open door. "We better check it out."

"You did not," Jake said. He didn't move from his spot in the hallway.

"You saw something?" Barbara Bellafiore shepherded her pack of lapdogs toward the door. "Is there gonna be a problem? Do I need to call the—? Oh, right, you *are* the cops."

She turned to Jake, the dogs wrapping themselves around her legs. "Is Holly Neff in trouble?"

Jake watched DeLuca edge closer to the door. A god-damn open door, an open door to the apartment of the latest victim in a string of murders that—even though unconnected, he was certain—had made his life miser-able for the past month. He was as tempted to go into that apartment as anything he'd ever been tempted to do in his entire life.

Yet, it would take only one phone call to get the war-rant allowing them to look inside, legally. Anything in-side now would still be there after they got a judge's signature. Anything they saw before that would get tossed out of a murder trial. That made the decision a no-brainer.

"DeLuca, I mean it." Jake knew his partner was craning his neck, trying to look inside without looking like he was looking.

"Officer?" Barbara touched his arm with a key. "About Holly Neff?"

The dogs had gone quiet, looking up at their mistress. Her eyes were wide as the little pug's.

"Holy shit," DeLuca said. He winced. "Sorry, ma'am."

"Don't even—" Jake turned to him, frowning. What if DeLuca actually did see something wrong? "What? This had better be good."

"The place is full of Lassiter stuff," DeLuca said. "Like—"

"Oh, I can help you with that," Barbara said, perking up. "You should see what's inside her apartment! You wouldn't believe it."

All Jake needed to hear. A witness describing what was inside? *That* was legal.

"Ma'am?" Jake took out his BlackBerry, cued up his notes. Turned his back on the door, waving DeLuca to do the same. "How would you describe what's inside?"

"She must be some kind of photographer," Barbara said. "There's ten million pictures of Owen Lassiter. And lots of 'em with him *and* her. Okay, not really ten million, but lots. Holly and Owen Lassiter."

DeLuca scratched his cheek with two fingers. "Was Owen Lassiter himself ever here? You ever see him?"

Barbara shook her mass of curls. "No. But I suppose—"

"Don't 'suppose,' ma'am," Jake said. "Just what you know for sure. You never saw Owen Lassiter here, correct? Did Miss Neff have a boyfriend at all?"

Barbara's curls bobbed again, this time up and down. "Oh, yes, she did. But he was never here. That I saw. She

said he was . . . I don't know. 'Away,' I think she said."
She brightened. "But she has his picture, you know? Inside. I could show you." She took a step toward the door,
arm outstretched, dogs jumping to all fours to follow.

"Bingo. That's a suspect." DeLuca took a step toward
the open door. "Probable enough cause for me. Thanks,
Miss—"

"Those pictures ain't going anywhere," Jake interrupted. *Have to give D credit for trying.* "Go call Judge
Gallagher. Now. Tell her the deal. She'll give us the warrant. Then we can go in. Signed, sealed, and legal."

"Boy Scout," DeLuca said. He flipped open his phone,
dialing.

"I'll go to the car, report this to the supe." Jake gestured at the open door. "And the identification of Holly
Neff. Ma'am? Can you lock the door again, please?
Absolutely no one is to go inside. Detective DeLuca will
stay and make sure."

By the time Jake got to the car, he'd filled in the supe,
promised to head back to HQ for the follow-up paperwork, and been told Arthur Vick was in holding room 6,
conferring with his lawyer. "Sadly," as the supe had put
it, no bail hearing could be scheduled any time soon.
Jake signed off, smiling. Then he punched another number on his speed dial.

He had to talk to Jane.

Only that afternoon, at Lassiter headquarters, Jane
was certain the fourth victim was a person calling herself Kenna Wilkes, a woman connected to the campaign.
Meeting Kenna Wilkes, indisputably alive, blew that theory to hell. Now, it appeared that Jane was wrong about
the name but right about everything else. The victim *was*
connected to the Lassiter campaign. That escalated Holly
Neff's murder into a complicated political nightmare.

Damn. Jane's voice mail.

He couldn't risk leaving a detailed message. Or any message at all. He heard the beep.

And he hung up.

Why does my phone always ring at the worst times? Jane let it go to voice mail, ignoring it as she faced down Rory Maitland. She stood on one side of his glass-topped desk, extending her arm, a photo of the girl and Owen Lassiter between two fingers. She'd been given ten minutes, so she didn't even take off her coat.

Rory stayed barricaded behind the desk, as if repelled by what he saw. This picture was of the woman and Lassiter at some outdoor rally, his arm around her shoulder, sunlight spotlighting her obvious pleasure.

The rest of the photo collection still lay in Jane's tote bag, still in the manila mailing envelope, safely beside her on the floor of Maitland's office. She didn't need to reveal her whole hand at once.

"So?" Jane said. She moved the photo closer to him, offering it, but he made no move to take it. "You've seen, what, six snapshots now? Of this woman with the candidate?"

"So?"

Jane could tell he was struggling to keep a poker face, but she saw his nose twitch briefly, as if he smelled something unpleasant.

"Mr. Maitland? Let me put it this way. I'm writing a story about this for the paper. This woman is clearly connected to the campaign."

"I'm not sure I'd use the word *clearly.*" Maitland crossed his arms over his pale blue oxford shirt, his red-striped tie crinkling underneath. "Or, *connected.*"

"Whatever word you'd use," Jane said. "Our story—"

"Story about what?" Maitland interrupted. "You wanted to show me photos. I agreed to see you, you've shown me. So what? Is this about the volunteer story you pitched to Trevor Kiernan?" He pushed the red button on his desk intercom. "Deenie. Ten minutes is up. What's my next appointment?"

Jane laid the photo on Maitland's desk, face up. Then dug into her tote bag.

"Mr. Maitland? Before you call in the troops? Let me show you this." Jane placed another picture on the desk. "This is the police artist's sketch of the fourth bridge victim. Released just a few hours ago. I'm sure you've seen it on all those televisions of yours. Look again."

She pointed her forefinger at the sketch, then at the snapshot. "Look at this. And then this. Now do you see why I'm asking?"

Maitland stood, placing his palms wide apart, flat on his desk. His eyes on the pictures.

"Deenie's gone for coffee, Mr.—" A voice from behind, at the office door. Jane turned to see who was interrupting.

Kenna Wilkes.

59

Jane Ryland is in Rory's office. That could not be a good thing. Luckily Kenna had been in the press room when the reporter showed up. As soon as she heard who'd arrived, she raced upstairs, sent Deenie for coffee, and staked out Rory's office for herself.

Jane had to be showing Rory the photos Holly sent, just as Matt predicted. She couldn't believe her brother's crazy ex—or whatever she was—had geeked herself up as that mousy Hannah woman, gotten inside that way. But she, Kenna, was the only one besides Matt who knew that. So no problem there, at least. Matt, now packing to leave town, told her Holly had never been to Lassiter headquarters as herself.

"Kenna, come in. This is Jane Ryland, a reporter for the *Register*. Jane, this is—"

"We've met," Kenna said with a smile, entering and standing in front of the bank of darkened televisions. She looked at Rory for direction, got nothing. "Hello, Jane."

"Kenna, Miss Ryland is preparing a story on campaign volunteers. Pitched it to Trevor. And she asked him whether you'd be interested in participating. Tell why you're involved in the Lassiter campaign."

My, my. One door closes, another opens.

Kenna's smile was genuine this time. "Well, of course," she said. She perched on a chair, crossing one leg over the other, flapping closed the front slit of her black pencil skirt. In full interview mode. "This close to the election, I'm delighted for the public to hear how wonderful Owen Lassiter is. How beneficial he'll be for Massachusetts. Much more effective than that Eleanor Gable. And I think—"

"So, Jane, let's arrange for you two to connect at some point, *later*." Rory cleared his throat, interrupting. He came out from behind his desk, moving toward the door.

Ah. Got it. Kenna stood quickly and turned in the same direction. "Miss Ryland? Come to my desk downstairs and arrange a time. Maybe at—" She looked at Rory. "My house?"

"One moment, please." Ryland was frowning. Holding that piece of paper. "I was asking you, Mr. Maitland, about this sketch. So since Miss Wilkes is here, let me ask her, too. Do you recognize this woman?"

The reporter held up what looked like one of those police drawings. Pencil. Black and white. She'd never seen that face before. Still, she feared it had to be the real Holly Neff.

The truth was one thing. What Kenna needed to say was another.

"Just *if* you've seen her before," Jane said, moving the picture closer to her. "Around the campaign. Or anywhere."

"I've never seen that woman, no," Kenna said. True-ish enough.

Besides, what did it matter what she told a stupid reporter? It wasn't like it was the cops. She'd have to talk with Matt. Get their stories straight.

"How about this person?" Jane held up a photograph.

Now what? This was clearly one of the photos Matt warned her about. The same woman with Owen Lassiter, smiling, arm in arm. Ryland had apparently received Holly's little gift. The reporter was "sharing" it, exactly as Matt feared. But Kenna just might have figured out how to make it all work. Because, thanks to big brother Matt, she knew what to expect.

The fly in the ointment, potentially, was Rory. How he'd handle this. But *his* truth was, he'd never knowingly met Holly. Hannah didn't count.

It was up to Kenna. She took the photo from Jane. *Holly and Lassiter at some rally.* "No," she said. "I've never seen her."

"How about this one?" Jane held up yet another photo.

Holly and Owen arm in arm on the Boston Esplanade. Funny, she and Rory had been there that day. Her first day on the job. "No," she replied. *Oh, so baffled.* "Who is she?"

"Miss Ryland, I don't know where you're going with this." Rory stepped in front of Kenna, as if to steer her out of the room. "I told you, that person is not connected with the campaign. Every photo you've shown includes dozens of people, they're clearly taken at public events. The candidate is on his way to one of them this very minute, in fact. We hope there'll be Lassiter supporters there. We actually invite them. We even encourage them to take photos."

Kenna stood back, taking it in. Rory's sarcasm was making this even better.

"Someone's sent you pictures of the candidate at public events. That's pretty darn newsworthy, Miss Ryland." Maitland held out an arm, dramatically showing Jane the door. "I know where you can get a whole lot more, exactly like that. In the newspaper. Every day. We done?"

I hope not, Kenna thought. *We're just getting to the good part.*

"You're so right, Mr. Maitland, they *are* public places. But look at *this* photo," Jane said. She pulled out another snapshot. Showed it to Maitland, then to Kenna, then back to Maitland. She was taking a chance with the next question. "It appears to be in the candidate's office. Lassiter's personal desk. Doesn't it? That's hardly a public place."

Jane waited, taking in the silence. Maitland and Kenna—*who is she, anyway?*—exchanged glances.

"Look here, in the reflection of the glass display case. You can see the person taking the photo. Hard to tell, certainly, but it could be the same woman."

No one was correcting her.

"And since it *is* the governor's private office, who took this photo? And how did the person who sent it to me get this photograph without having some connection to the governor?"

Maitland gave a snort, dismissive. "I beg you. The number of people who are brought to his fourth-floor private office to meet—"

"Exactly," Jane said. "Who brought her? Cards on the table. This woman is dead. She's connected to the campaign. She knows Owen Lassiter. If you don't know who she is, I'm sure someone on your staff does. Whoever took her into the governor's fourth-floor office. I'm not leaving until someone tells me her name."

Kenna was edging toward the door. Maitland raised a hand to stop her, gave a half shake of his head. *What is that about?*

"And while you're considering that, one more thing."

Jane displayed the picture in front of her, one hand holding the corner, the forefinger of the other pointing to a certain place on the photo. "See this big book on the governor's desk? There's a Magic Marker circle around it. Why?"

60

"**Do you have** any idea who this man is?" Jake showed Barbara Bellafiore the framed photo from Holly Neff's dresser. It showed Holly with a youngish guy, both wearing gray Red Sox sweatshirts and navy baseball caps. "Did Miss Neff tell you his name?"

" 'Scuse me, Jake?" Darrell "Humpty" James knocked on the doorjamb of apartment 43. He was already wearing his purple nitrile gloves. Humpty's search team—Officer Kim lugging her trace evidence kit and Big Joe laden with his camera equipment—trooped behind him into Holly's living room.

Humpty scanned the array of photographs covering two walls, shot Jake a *mother-a-gawd* glance. "Okay if we start? We looking for anything in particular?"

"DeLuca's in the back." Jake cocked a thumb toward the first bedroom. "He'll give you the lowdown."

The building manager, two-page warrant now in hand, watched the search team tramp through. "At least she didn't die here," Barbara said, almost to herself. "Won't be a problem to rent the place again."

Jake figured that didn't need a response.

"Ma'am? We don't have much more for you. Just

this." Jake held up the framed photo again. Hard to see the guy's face, his baseball cap low on his forehead, mirrored sunglasses. His arm looped over Holly's shoulders. Background looked like a park or something, a lake. *Could be anywhere.* Before Jake removed the framed photo from Holly's dresser, he'd taken a snap of it with his phone. "Just confirming. Miss Neff told you he was her boyfriend, but didn't say his name?"

Barbara shrugged, folded the warrant into thirds, and stuck it into the waistband of her skirt. "Wish I could remember," she said. "But—no, I don't think so. Names, you know. Why would I remember?"

"I understand, ma'am. If it comes to you—" Jake handed her his business card. "—you call me, okay? Or if anyone comes by asking you about her? You'll let me know."

"I could stay, you know. Help." The building manager craned her neck, looking toward the bedrooms where DeLuca and the others would be digging through drawers and burrowing into closets. Joe's flashbulbs popped. "Maybe they need—"

"We're fine, ma'am," Jake said. Death always had a strange effect on the living. Barbara had been shocked, of course, initially. Took her about ten minutes to start rerenting the victim's apartment. Now she wanted to poke through Holly's personal property. Jake put a hand under the woman's elbow, escorting her to the door. "We'll inform you when we've completed the search. Thank you so much for your help. I'm sorry for the loss."

"The? Oh. Yeah." Barbara looked as if she'd just remembered why they were all here. Touched the warrant in her waistband. "Thank you."

Jake reached for his BlackBerry as the woman—eyes glued to the search team—backed toward the door. *Peo-*

ple. He cued up his photo of Holly and the boyfriend. Punched in Jane's e-mail, typed a message. "U recognize?"

He paused, thumb over the Send key, considering.

Jane faced the corner of the Lassiter headquarters lobby, trying for privacy on her cell phone call.

"I know, Alex, but what was I supposed to do? I tried, but I can't demand to go upstairs into Lassiter's office with them, you know? To see what's in that book that was circled?"

Not many people were around. Jane had watched the curved streetlights glow into intensity, glaring now through the lobby's front windows. Headlights flashed by on Causeway Street.

"Maitland promised to tell you what was in it?" Alex said. "Oh, like that'll happen."

Her face probably reflected the same skepticism. *This stinks.*

"Yeah, I agree. Whatever's in there, they're never going to tell me. Like I said, they're insisting they have no idea who the woman is." Jane shrugged, even though Alex couldn't see her. "I say, we go with this no matter what. We have the photos, we have the sketch. They match. If the campaign bigwigs insist they don't recognize her, then fine, we quote them. We're running the sketch of her on the Web site already, right?"

"Yup. We put it up after the news conference."

"No one's called in to say they recognize her?"

"Nope."

"I wonder about that. I mean, if she's from around here—"

"Jane?" Alex interrupted. "Hang on a second."

Jane kept the phone to her ear, examining the now-quiet

headquarters lobby. The reception desk, empty. A phone console and a chair. Where Kenna sat. Empty.

Jane's fingers itched to open a desk drawer or two. See what she could find out about Kenna. *Find out about Kenna.* A memory struggled to emerge, something about . . . *Oh.* She clamped the phone between her ear and shoulder, pulled her laptop from her bag.

Since Kenna was upstairs, no reason why she couldn't use her desk, right? She perched on the edge of Kenna's chair to indicate she was not really sitting there, just visiting. Flopped open the laptop, punched in her code. She hadn't found a second, yet, to look up the address Trevor gave her. This was a perfect time. The site flickered open.

Town of Deverton. Assessor's office. *Click.* 463 Constitution. Last sale, five years ago. *Click.* Current assessment. *Click.* $567,000. Owner. *Click.* The screen flashed.

And she saw the name.

"Jane? You still there?"

"Alex, yeah, I'm here. Listen to this. You know that—"

"Wait, Jane, let me tell you something first."

"But this is—"

"Jane? They've got the ID of the victim. The police. They have the ID of the Fort Point body. Tuck found out."

The computer screen popped to black. Jane hit Enter to bring it back, staring at it, unseeing.

Was this a good thing? To have the victim's identity? No matter what Tuck knew, Jane had the line on the campaign connection. The photos were sent to *her*, not Tuck. The Lassiter relationship story—whatever it was—also belonged to *her*. Not Tuck. Or was Tuck about to pull the whole rug out from under her? Would Alex let that happen?

"What's her name?" Jane managed to ask. At least she was right here at campaign central. Once she knew the name, she could quickly ask about it. *Someone* here would have to recognize her. Have heard of her.

"Don't know. Tuck's on her way to get it," Alex said. "She's not sure how long it'll take."

"Are we running a story that there's an ID? In the online edition?"

"Not yet," Alex said. "Got to have one more source. Tuck'll call as soon as she has it. Jane? Wait. My other line. Maybe this is her. Hang on."

Jane pressed her lips together, chin in hands, elbows on desk. Nothing to do now but wait.

And think. *Jake knows about this. He has to. And he must have realized the same thing I did.* This victim, whatever the heck her name turns out to be, is connected with the campaign. *The minute I hang up, I'm calling him. On his cell. Forget protocol.*

"Nope, not Tuck." Alex was back on the line. "Anyway. Jane. Your turn. What's happening on your end?"

Jane watched the elevator lights come on. Heard the mechanism clunk and slide. On the way down. Could be Kenna and Maitland. If so, that meant right now, instantly, she and Alex had to figure out how to handle her discovery.

"Alex. Listen. You remember I told you Kenna Wilkes—"

"Or whatever her name is," Alex interrupted.

"Yeah, yeah, that's the point." The elevator whirred, the sounds getting louder. *Closer.* "That Kenna Wilkes or whatever-her-name-is was not registered to vote in Massachusetts, but yet Lassiter met her at some house in Deverton, where she supposedly lived? Where Trevor Kiernan thought she was registered to vote?"

"Yes, sure, I remember."

The elevator doors slid open. Jane leaped from the chair, grabbed her laptop, ready to make excuses. But no one got out. The doors slid closed again. Heart rac-ing—*what am I afraid of?*—she picked up where she'd left off.

"Here's the scoop: I looked up the owner of that ad-dress. And the house belongs to—" Jane checked the screen one more time. The indisputable key to Kenna Wilkes was still there, clearly shown in digital black-and-white. Jane took a deep breath. "—Eleanor Gable."

61

Kenna followed Rory up the rickety metal stairway. She'd punched the button for the elevator, but Rory had waved her off, saying the back elevator was broken, repair guy was coming tomorrow. *Fine*. Almost there.

"So you really have no idea about the book on Owen's desk?" Kenna said. Such a pain to climb steps in high heels. Men had no clue.

"No." Rory turned to look back at her over his shoulder. He frowned. "Do you?"

"No, of course not," Kenna said. That was basically the truth. She was as curious as he was about where this was going.

Rory stopped at the landing, halfway up. Narrowed his eyes at her. Questioning.

She waved him to keep climbing. "Really. No."

He grabbed the railing, taking two more steps. "But I'm thinking about that woman," he said, stopping again. "No idea who the frig she is. But she's dead, and if she's somehow connected with the campaign, so's Lassiter. Dead, I mean."

"I guess it's not politically correct to have a murdered girl connected to the candidate." Kenna's heel caught on an opening in the latticed metal of a step, and she yanked it out with a muttered curse. "Gary Condit. Didn't do much for his career. Even though he had nothing to do with Chandra Levy's death."

"Owen's going to flip," Rory said. They were on the landing. "He'll be back in his office after tonight's event. I'll wait till then to tell him."

Rory clanked open the door, waving Kenna through. The long hallway had been walled off with temporary barriers to keep Lassiter's office private and secure. "We'll have to call Sheila King to handle the press. This is a new one, I gotta say. Right before the election. Incredible."

Kenna knew it was frumpy Hannah who'd taken the private-office snapshot. She'd been in the room that day. Maitland, too, though he obviously didn't realize it. But what was the deal with the book? Matt hadn't told her about that little surprise.

They entered the private office. And there it was. Just like in the photo. Owen's desk, and the big book on the corner.

Kenna watched as Rory picked up the thick leather-bound volume. It looked like an old law book or some such, pale yellow binding, cracking spine, raised red and black letters.

"You think there's a legal decision about Owen, something like that?" Kenna tried to figure what Holly might have known. "Maybe it's marked? Why would Owen keep that particular book on his desk?"

"Christ if I know. Mass Code of Laws." Rory turned the book over, examined the back. Turned it right side up again. "Let's see if there's anything obvious, then decide how to handle it."

She watched Rory open the front cover. Nothing. Open the back cover. Nothing. He held the book by its binding, shaking and flapping the pages above the desk.

A piece of paper floated out, slipped off the edge of the desk, and onto the oriental rug.

Kenna moved to pick it up. Rory was faster.

He stood, paper in hand.

"My, my," he said.

She couldn't stand it. "What is it?"

Rory turned the page to face her.

Her eyes widened. This was— She never would have predicted.

A photograph of a woman. The same woman in Ryland's pictures. The same woman in the police sketch. Holly Neff.

Except in this photo, she wasn't dead. Far from it.

Here, it was only her. And not much else. She was skin and lace and legs and hair and gloss and breasts and pouting lips. Oozing lust. Oozing promise.

And on the photo, across one extended leg and just touching a scrap of black lace lingerie, an inscription.

Kenna took the photo in hand, read it out loud.

"'To Owen, with all my admiration and gratitude . . . after a wonderful afternoon. Here's to many more.' Then it says, 'xoxo. Holly Neff.'"

Kenna looked at Rory.

"*Xoxo*," he said. "Who the hell is Holly Neff?"

She handed him the photo, shrugged like, *who knows?* "Jane Ryland is waiting downstairs."

"Let her wait," he said.

I have a better idea, Kenna thought.

"Eleanor Gable? That house belongs to Eleanor Gable?"

Jane closed her laptop as she listened to Alex's astonishment.

"Yes. Can you believe it? Eleanor Gable's the owner. Even though we know she lives on Beacon Hill—I was just there, you know? The assessor's records prove she's owned the Deverton house for years."

The lobby was still deserted. After seven o'clock, people must be at dinner, or home. The elevator doors had opened again once or twice, but no one got out. That meant Kenna and Maitland were still upstairs. With whatever they'd found. "So, Alex, why was Kenna Wilkes at Gable's house? And who the heck is she?"

"Here's what you do," Alex told her. "Go to Gable headquarters. Don't call. Just go. See what she has to say."

"Okay. . . ." Jane stared at the scuffed floor. Was that the way to handle it? She stowed her laptop, hefted her tote bag to her shoulder, paced to the front window, then back to the desk. "But Kenna and Maitland are supposed to come down here. Tell me what's in the book."

"Oh, forget *that*," Alex said. "You think for one minute they're going to? If they do show up, it'll only be to inform you there was nothing in the book. No question. We'll never know the real deal."

That part she agreed with. "True. But I think we should see. This woman's dead, after all. Gable's house in Deverton is going to be there whether we confront her about it tonight or tomorrow. And what's there to confront her about, really? Someone who happens to volunteer for the Lassiter campaign is living at her house? So what?"

Each was silent for a moment. She could almost hear Alex thinking about her question. But she couldn't stop thinking about Lassiter's book. *What could be in it?*

Maitland and Kenna promised to tell her. If they weren't coming down, she would go up. She strode to the elevator, confident. Nodding in solidarity with her own decision, she punched the green button.

"Alex? I'm going to push them about the book. But the Gable house—don't we have to go to Lassiter first?" *And someone else has to be told. The candidate's wife. She thinks Kenna Wilkes is the other woman. That means—* "And tell Moira? That someone working in the campaign could be in cahoots with Owen's opponent?"

Jane heard the elevator's gears and pulleys shift into motion.

Go with what you've got. That's what she learned in journalism school. What they had were multiple photos of a dead woman with Owen Lassiter, and a photo of a book in Lassiter's private office that someone—whoever mailed her the photos of Red Coat—had circled. If the campaign mucketies insisted they'd found nothing, and the murder victim had no connection with the campaign or the candidate, fine. Say so. Readers—*voters*—could decide who was telling the truth.

Elections had been lost after the smallest of scandals. This one could be massive.

"One thing at a time," Alex said. "Call me as soon as—"

Jane poked the Up button again.

And jumped back, startled, as the elevator doors began to slide open.

"You listening?" Kenna had hissed into her cell phone. "I've got zero time. I'm in an elevator at Lassiter headquarters. Jane Ryland is down in the lobby. She's asking questions about Holly Neff, but she'll be leaving soon. Out the front door. Then meet me here at headquarters at eleven tonight. Fourth floor. Got me?"

"I understand. Did she say Holly's name? Does she have the photos?"

"Yes, she has the photos. No, she apparently doesn't have her name."

The elevator bell pinged at floor one and eased to a stop. She clicked off the phone.

"Yet," Kenna said.

62

Jane saw Kenna slap her cell phone closed. The woman stepped out of the elevator, alone. She looked both ways, then at the front door, then at Jane. The elevator doors swished closed behind her, framing her black-sweatered curves in glistening burnished silver.

"Alex? Gotta go. Call you right back." Jane hung up and looked at her expectantly. "Hi, Kenna. So? What did you find? Where's Rory?"

"I'm sorry, Miss Ryland," Kenna began.

Her voice, almost a whisper, seemed uncertain. Unhappy.

What is all this about?

"Mr. Maitland says to tell you . . . ," Kenna continued. She stopped, looked at the floor, moved her black patent toe along a line in the pattern of the tiles. When she looked up, her eyes were welled with tears. "I'm sorry. He says to tell you there was nothing in the book. It was—a law book, the Massachusetts Code of Laws. It was just a book. And he says . . ."

Jane crossed her arms, waiting. Hiding a smile. Exactly what she and Alex predicted. This woman was the personification of lying. A terrible actress giving an absurd performance. And why was she living in Eleanor Gable's house?

"And he says . . . ," Kenna repeated.

Then Kenna's face hardened. She took a step forward, then another, her eyes darting, side to side. She grabbed Jane, putting one hand on each arm.

"Miss Ryland. I can't do this," the woman whispered, leaning close. When a wave of hair fell across her face, she flipped it away, fidgety. "Come outside with me. Just for one moment. Please."

Suddenly letting go, Kenna hurried through the revolving door. Jane scooped up her belongings and followed. *What the hell?*

Kenna turned right, then right again down that little alleyway between the buildings, Jane trotting behind. A lone spotlight illuminated the latticed fire escapes zagging up one side and down the other. The headlights of passing cars flashed, intermittent pulses of light, as Kenna headed deeper into the alley.

Not a chance, Jane thought, stopping short. There's no Bridge Killer, that was clear, but she wasn't stupid enough to walk into a dark alley with anyone. Even a knockout blond source with tears in her eyes.

"Kenna?" Jane stayed in the light, one foot on the sidewalk, in full view of anyone on the street. Safe. Illuminated. She beckoned with one hand. Kept her voice low. "Let's talk out here, okay? No one's around."

"Maitland," Kenna said. Almost a whisper. She didn't move.

Maitland? Jane looked up, scoping out the place. "There's no windows from headquarters overlooking out here," she said. "We're fine."

Kenna took a step, hesitant, closer to Jane. Then stopped, hands clasped in front of her, forefingers together, pointing. "I'll say this once. And if you ever, ever tell, I'll deny it."

Jane nodded. *What on—?* "Of course. What?"

"We did find something. But Rory will pretend we didn't." Kenna's chin came up, resolute, as if she knew she had irrevocably crossed some line. "He's lying, Jane. He's protecting Owen Lassiter. And I can't . . . can't . . . condone it. I signed up with Lassiter because I thought he was a good guy. An honest, trustworthy candidate. But he's—I can't work for someone who—who—" She gulped, the torrent of her words suddenly seeming to catch in her throat.

"It's okay, I understand." Jane said. *Yikes.* Now Jane was looking around, checking for Maitland. Or anyone. But they were alone. "What was in the book, Kenna?"

"It was a photograph of that same girl," Kenna said. "The one you showed us. Only this one was— provocative."

Jane's eyebrows went up. Across the street, someone honked, and someone else honked back, battling for a parking space or something. *Shut up.* She didn't want any distractions. She didn't want Kenna to change her mind.

The woman's lower lip trembled, and her now-mournful green eyes didn't meet Jane's. She touched her fingers to her mouth, as if it were difficult for her to let the words out. "You know. Sexy. Lingerie. Lace, that kind of thing. And the photo was signed. It said, 'To Owen, with all my admiration and gratitude . . . after a wonderful afternoon. Here's to many more.' I saw it. I guess Owen was . . . keeping it close to him. But Rory will never let on. He'll never tell you. He left by the side door to avoid you. And that photo, he's probably already destroyed it. He'd do anything to win this election. Anything."

"Signed?" Now it was Jane's turn to whisper. "With what name?"

A car whizzed by, then another, raking Kenna with headlights. She darted back into the shadows, then emerged. One step, then another. She looked into the street, wary, watching a car that eased by.

"What name?" Jane repeated. *Come on, honey.* Rory was already gone. And this woman—whoever she really was—was about to bolt.

"Holly Neff. *N-e-f-f.*" Her hand darted forward, grabbing Jane's arm again. "I know you can keep a secret. I read about you. I know you protect your sources. Now you have to protect me."

63

Who the hell is Holly Neff? And who the hell is Kenna Wilkes? Talking on the phone while driving a stick shift in Boston evening traffic. Fine, she could handle it. She had to call Jake. And Moira. And damn it, she had to find out about the Deverton connection. Maybe Kenna didn't even know who owned the house. But she had to call Alex first.

Jane punched in the number, pulled out of her space, waited two rings, filled Alex in at light speed.

"*N-e-f-f,*" she repeated. She pictured Kenna. Her pleading eyes. "I can't say how I know. I'm on my way to the newsroom, so I'll start checking her out when I get there. Can you stand it? Sexpot photos of a murdered woman, the campaign connection, Lassiter's involvement. The package of photos. Amazing. See you in, like, ten."

She shifted into second, making the curve onto Merrimack. Frowned. Alex was telling her to—*what?* She weighed the pros and cons as she listened to her boss. The light turned red. Now he was talking about—*what?*

"Sorry," Jane interrupted. "Traffic. You said they're appearing together? Gable and Lassiter? Where?"

The light changed as Alex explained. Traffic snarling,

drivers snarling, maybe the Boston Garden had basket-ball tonight. "I'll never get all the way to Porter Square in time," Jane argued after Alex finished his instructions. "Traffic sucks, it's starting to rain, it's going to be a mess."

Jane turned left, heading over the Charles River on the Longfellow Bridge, its salt-and-pepper turrets illuminated against the now-dark sky. Kylie Howarth's body was found down there. *Poor Kylie.*

Alex's voice buzzed through the car. Lassiter and Gable, some Chamber of Commerce thing. The *Register* had a reporter there, covering it, but Alex's brilliant idea was—

"Wait," she interrupted again. "Say I go to this event. Am I supposed to confront Gable about the Kenna house? Or confront Lassiter about the sexy photo and his relationship with a murdered mistress?"

Alex didn't answer right away. Jane's tires clunked over the metal reinforcements as she reached the end of the bridge, her headlights too close to the guy in front of her because someone else was hugging her tail. It was misting now, not really rain, but she flipped on her windshield wipers. *A mess for trick-or-treaters.* Checking her rearview, she saw her own face mottled light and dark in the flickering shadows. Gable as saboteur? Lassiter as philanderer? The candidate connected to a murder? *Some election this is turning out to be.*

"I see what you mean," Alex said. "We have this, exclusive, right? I guess if we have to wait on this story, we have to wait."

"What about our deal with the police? This means we actually do have a confirmed identity of the dead—"

"Get yourself to the event, let me know when you're there," Alex said. "I'll call Tay Reidy and the lawyers, then call you with an update. It's touchy. What we can say, what we can't. The victim's name. The political angle."

"Gotcha," she said. "Moron! Pick a lane!" Jane slammed on her brakes, yanked the wheel. "Sorry, Alex, it's just—Boston drivers in the rain. Tailgating as a way of life. You know. Anyway. Call me."

She barely clicked off the phone when it rang again.

"Hey, Janey."

She touched a hand to her hair, remembered Jake couldn't see her. "Hey," she said.

"Hey, *you*."

She could almost feel his touch. How could that be?

"You driving?" he said.

"Slowly," Jane replied. "I'm headed to cover a political thing. It's in Porter Square, but I'm only by the Science Museum, and it's raining. It's like a contest for who can drive the slowest."

With a start, she remembered what she knew. What she had to tell him.

"Listen," she said. "About this morning. The Fort Point victim."

"Yeah," Jake said. "That's why I'm calling. You listen, okay? I need to e-mail you a photo. But don't look at it while you're driving. Can you pull over?"

"Photo?" It could not possibly be the Holly Neff lingerie shot. That would be— She looked at the dashboard clock. Almost nine. She would never get to Porter Square in time. "Of what?"

"Pull over, okay? I'm sending it to you by e-mail. You'll see why."

"Two seconds," she said, eyeing the road in front of her. She knew a strip mall with a parking lot—and a Dunkin' Donuts—about two blocks ahead. "But while whatever it is flies through cyberspace, let me tell you what I've confirmed. First of all, the Fort Point victim turns out to be a woman named— Listen, do we still have our deal? I tell you the name, you give us the story?"

Silence on the other end. Had she blown it? Maybe the cops were about to have a big news conference, reveal the scoop, before Jane could get the big byline. But Jake couldn't know about the Lassiter connection. Even if the cops gave out Holly's name, only Jane would have the political angle.

Moira would—

"Janey? How soon till you can pull over?"

"Getting there." She flipped on her right blinker, crossed in front of a battered Honda, turned into the Dunkin's lot. A couple of other cars also turned in behind her, probably on a caffeine hunt. She pulled under a light, her wipers sloshing in the now more-than-drizzle, left the engine running. "Okay, all set. I'll hang up, check the photo, call you back. What am I supposed to be seeing?"

"Just look at the picture," Jake said.

Where the hell is she going? Matt almost said the words out loud. He yanked the steering wheel, careened into the parking lot, banged a hard left as Jane Ryland's car turned right. She couldn't get out of the lot without him seeing her.

He chose a spot in the corner by the exit, clicked off his headlights, left the motor running. The radio, low, played some impenetrable jazz. Matt's fingers drummed on the steering wheel. He'd checked out of the hotel. Put his suitcase in the trunk. If he had to, he could take the late train to New York. Get an early plane home from there.

Jane was still in her car, interior light making her a fuzzy silhouette. Looked like she was—texting. Or looking at something. Wasn't going for coffee.

Cissy had told him to follow her, right? But what was he supposed to do when she got where she was going? Cissy'd hung up so quickly, and didn't answer when he called her back.

He had to plan.

Number one, if Jane still had Holly's photos with her, the ones of Holly and Lassiter, he could get them back. Did she bring all of them? Had she copied them? *Problem*. He'd figure that out when the time came.

Two, Jane would connect the woman in those photos with the Fort Point victim—that's what police called Holly at this morning's news conference. So Jane knew she was dead. *Problem*.

And three, because of Holly's deceptive photos, Jane would definitely assume the dead woman was connected with his father. Eventually with Matt himself. *Big, big problem*.

He squeezed the steering wheel with both hands, not taking his eyes off the woman in the front seat of the Audi.

Matt had to stop Jane Ryland. He was certain Cissy would agree.

64

Jane stared at the minuscule photo of a photo, frame partly showing, off center and canted slightly in her phone screen. Her windshield wipers slapped and clacked across the glass, the heater fogging her windows, her engine idling in the still-crowded parking lot. Outside, the rain intensified, one of those muggy-wet Halloween nights that was half summer, half fall. Inside her car, Jane couldn't take her eyes off the couple in the picture.

She clicked into phone-mode so she could call Jake. It rang before she could dial.

"Yeah," she said as she answered. "That's amazing."

"What's amazing?"

It was Alex, not Jake.

"Oh, nothing, Alex," she said. "What's up?"

"Change of plans," Alex said. "The Lassiter event is over. Our reporter just called. Everyone's gone. Come back to the newsroom. Or head home if you want. Nothing more we can do tonight. No story tomorrow, Tay Reidy says."

"Really?" That seemed wrong. "But we know the victim is named Holly Neff. We have the photos. We should go with that, at least."

"Can't confirm it. Tuck says it's a next of kin thing.

Police are giving out nothing until tomorrow. What's more, our lawyer's worried the pictures you have could be Photoshopped. Fake. So we're waiting. Publisher's orders."

Jane frowned, considering. "You think they're phony, Alex? I don't. And what if Holly sent copies to every newsroom in town? What if they're on Channel Eleven tonight? What if we're totally scooped?"

"What can I say?" Alex paused. "Look, Jane, don't kill the messenger. It'll all work. See you tomorrow. Okay?"

"Okay." He was just doing his job. As she had to. "See you tomorrow."

She clamped her phone closed, leaned against the headrest. *That's that.* Then she sat straight up, remembering. She had something that certainly wasn't fake. The photo from Jake. Jane opened her phone and hit speed dial.

"It's me," she said as Jake answered. "It's amazing."

"Took you long enough," Jake said. "So that's her? You confirm that's the woman in the photos you got? You said there were pictures of her with Owen Lassiter."

"Huh? Sure, that's the same girl. I know her name. But where'd you get that photo?"

"Initials HN?" Jake asked.

So he also knew. Which blew her leverage for an exclusive. But wherever this came from, Holly Neff wasn't what shocked her about this photo.

"Yes, yes," Jane said. "But Jakey? That's not what—"

"You don't happen to know who the guy is, by any chance? According to the landlord, that's her boyfriend. He's now suspect one."

Jane rolled her eyes. "If you'd let me talk," she said.

"Talk," Jake said.

She spilled it, the whole thing, as fast as she could. "And he was at the police press conference. Oh, my gosh. He came up to me, saying he had a story. Matt, he said his name was. No last name. How'd I know he—? Anyway, then, later, Jakey, you saw him, too. Today. At campaign headquarters. When that woman . . . you know, said she was Kenna Wilkes."

Silence on the other end. "No, I didn't see him," Jake finally said. "Wait. Was it when I was on the phone? The person who walked away?"

"Yes, that was him. That guy!" Jane said. "So now we know exactly how to find him. Because even though we don't know his last name, or where he is, we know who does. Even though according to your research, she doesn't exist."

"Kenna Wilkes," Jake said.

"Exactly." *This could work.* Jake nabs Kenna, she gives up Matt, Jake arrests Matt, big scoop, everyone wins. "Are you going to Lassiter headquarters to find her? The campaign thing is over. I'll meet you there."

"You'll do no such thing," Jake said. "Go home. Nothing's going to happen tonight with the elusive Kenna Wilkes. I'll call you."

Kenna Wilkes, who hosted Owen Lassiter at 463 Constitution Lane in Deverton. "Wait, Jake. Listen. She might be at—"

"Janey?" Jake's voice had softened. "I have to go now. Go home, okay? Please? And be careful."

She was leaving. *Finally.* Matt watched as Jane eased her car into traffic, turn signal blinking him her plans, turning right, away from Boston. *Where's she going?*

He waited until two other cars slid in behind her, then edged out onto the rain-puddled street, keeping his eyes on the red glow of her taillights. He could see her perfectly, even in this shitty weather, it was like his eyes were tuned in to her, riveted on her. Jane Ryland was going to ruin his plans. Ruin his life. Ruin his father's life. Never. *Never*. It was his turn to win. His turn to have a life. It didn't matter where Jane Ryland was going. Or how long it took. He'd be right behind her.

Her taillights flashed, taunting him.

Talk about ruined. *This is all on Holly*. She'd ruined his life, ruined it from the moment he met her. From the moment he'd first talked to her. From the moment he'd f—

He shuddered out a sigh. Whatever.

At the next stoplight, Jane flipped open the center console. Fumbled inside through her stash of peanut butter crackers and emergency flashlight and emergency batteries and parking meter change. Keeping her eyes on the light, she fingered the power cord for her cell phone, jammed the plug into the charger. Her battery was about shot, and she still had another call to make. Maybe two. No matter what Jake and Alex said.

The light turned green.

She'd go home. But not quite yet. She couldn't go all the way to Deverton. But the Lassiter home, that was much closer. Hours ago, she'd promised to call Moira Lassiter. Now, thanks to Jake, Jane had a photo of Holly Neff together with the person named Matt. Maybe Moira would know who he was, and where to find him.

Jane checked the glowing numbers on her dashboard. Pushing nine thirty. Lassiter was out, of course, so maybe Moira would invite Jane to chat. After all, now they had something to discuss. Holly Neff as the other woman. Holly Neff as the *dead* other woman.

Moira's number rang, kept ringing, echoing through the car. No answer yet. Waiting, Jane reached into the console again. Grabbing the crackers with one hand and steering with the other, she ripped the cellophane with her teeth, yellow crumbs dropping on her coat. She was starving, but this would have to hold her for a while.

Still no answer. The voice mail picked up. *Rats.* Jane clicked off the phone, left it to charge. So much for that idea.

Next time she could make a left, she'd turn around. Go home. Get some real food. Regroup. Try Moira again. Wait for Jake to call.

She scanned the road beside her. No side streets, no way to change direction, only an unbroken stand of lofty sentinel poplars, side by side, flanked by a scrollworked metal fence. The rain had stopped, but the iron spikes of the fence posts still glistened as she passed, misted with the night's fog. Looking to make a U-turn, she was going just fast enough to catch a glimpse of what lay behind the fence, behind the trees, illuminated by hazy spotlights. Rows of headstones.

Jane's brain clicked. Poplar trees. A grove of poplars. Poplar Grove. Poplar Grove Cemetery.

Where Katharine Lassiter was buried.

Jane munched her peanut butter cracker, its oily crumbles sticking to her gloves. She could check it out right now. Might not even have to get out of the car. Find Katharine Lassiter's headstone, see what she could learn about Owen Lassiter's first wife. Gravestones were a wealth of info. A date of birth could lead Jane to Katharine's birth certificate, which would give her parents' names and occupations, their hometown, her maiden name, her doctor, the hospital where she was born. Lots of leads. She'd looked up the cemetery after Rory mentioned it the other day, knew it had gravesite locator charts near the front gate.

It would only take a minute.

65

Jake gunned his cruiser, banged a U-turn in the middle of Hanover Street, hit the lights and siren. Headed for Lassiter headquarters. *Sorry, Janey. This is police business.* He felt bad about lying to her. But this might be dangerous.

Until the Kenna thing, he'd planned to go downtown, where Arthur Vick and Co. were cooling their heels. Still, Jake figured the wait might give the guy some time to get religion. Or for his lawyer to spell out the facts of life. Vick's breaking point would come soon enough, once he realized he was no longer Mr. Big. Now he was simply Mr. Suspect. Poor Patti Vick. *Till death do us part?* More like life. Without parole. It would feel great to put this sucker in the "solved" column.

At least Vick was safely in custody. The other man, Matt No-Last-Name, was still in the wind.

"DeLuca?" Jake clicked the button on his radio, driving bat-outta-hell with one hand as traffic slowed, moving over to let him pass. "You read? What's your ETA?"

"In two."

"I'm pulling up now," Jake said. He saw an empty parking place right in the front. Good sign. No lights on inside the headquarters. Bad sign. "Looks deserted. Lights off."

"Copy."

Leaving his unmarked cruiser running under the glare of the streetlight, Jake trotted to the front window, where only this afternoon he and Jane discovered Kenna Wilkes was not dead. But now, that woman seemed the key to something. Jake had to find her again.

"Sir? May I help you?"

A mousy young woman in a baggy jacket stood beside him, looked up from behind her glasses, questioning. She carried a clacking array of what looked like card-keys attached to a webbed lanyard.

She took a step away, eyeing the cruiser, then looked back at him. He saw the light dawn.

"Are you a po—?" she said.

"Detective Jake Brogan, Boston PD. Are you with the Lassiter campaign?"

She held up her yellow lanyard, both hands fussing, flapping the cards against each other.

"Deenie, um, Denise Bayliss," the woman said. "Yes, I work here. Is everything okay?"

"It's fine, Miss Bayliss." Jake jabbed a thumb toward the headquarters door. "Anyone inside?"

"No, sir, not right now. I just locked up." She displayed her collection of plastic. "They might be back later, though. After the governor's event. But he uses the side entrance. Do you need me to call—?"

Jake recognized the rumble of DeLuca's cruiser. Heard his car door slam.

"My partner, Detective DeLuca." Jake pulled out his BlackBerry, punched up the photo of Holly and the man Jane called Matt. It wasn't that clear a shot, a Black-Berry photo of an old picture, but it was all he had. "Let me show you this photo, Miss Bayliss. Do you recognize either of these people?"

The woman peered at it, lifting her glasses, her nose

almost touching the screen. One car whispered by in the rain-dampened street, then another. "No, Detective, I don't think I've ever seen them before."

"One more question," Jake said. "Do you know a Kenna Wilkes?"

She looked everywhere but at Jake. "She's a volunteer. New. Like, a receptionist. Sometimes. But . . ."

"But?" Jake kept his voice noncommittal. Encouraging. "You were saying?"

"Nothing," the woman said. "She—goes places with the governor. You could ask him about her. I guess. Or Mr. Maitland. But I . . . don't know anything about her. Why are you asking me this? Is everything okay?"

"It's fine, ma'am, all we need," Jake said. He handed her a business card. Nothing for him here. "We have your name."

By the time Deenie Bayliss was out of sight, Jake had opened the door of his cruiser, and sat, one leg out the driver's side, radio crackling. "Repeating now?" he said. "We have a BOLO for a white male, approximately twenty-five years of age, brown hair, eyes unknown, first name Matt, last name unknown, who might be in the company of a younger white female, age approximately twenty-three, hair blond, eyes green, who may be using the name Kenna Wilkes. Please do not apprehend, but contact . . ."

DeLuca rested one arm on the top of the cruiser as Jake dictated his be-on-the-lookout bulletin. "We rock, gotta admit," he said as Jake signed off. "Howarth solved, Roldan solved, Vick in custody for Sellica Darden. And now—"

Jake clicked the radio mic back into place, moved DeLuca out of the way as he pulled his leg in and closed the door. He buzzed down the window.

"—and now," DeLuca repeated, cocking his head toward Lassiter headquarters, "all we gotta do is find some dish who's apparently got an inside with the candidate, and have her give up the guy who killed Holly Neff. And we are four for four."

"Told you there was no Bridge Killer," Jake called as DeLuca headed for his car. "See you downtown, D. Time for you and me to rain a little reality on one Mr. Arthur Vick."

DeLuca peeled out, full speed ahead, beeping his horn in salute. But Jake sat in his front seat, staring out the windshield, more than Arthur Vick on his mind.

Matt No-Last-Name. Approached Jane at the news conference. Showed up at Lassiter headquarters exactly when she did. Now he was whereabouts unknown.

Who the hell is Matt? What if the guy who killed Holly Neff was now looking for Jane?

So near but yet so far. Jane sat in her front seat, car in Park, engine idling, staring at the CLOSED sign in front of Poplar Grove Cemetery. She'd devoured the last of her peanut butter crackers and was starting on a pack of gum unearthed from the bottom of her tote. She tried Moira again. Nothing.

Now she was contemplating the tiniest bit of trespassing. No locked gate in front of her in the driveway, no gate at all. No chain, no barrier, no nothing. Above her a massive cast-iron arch loomed, twisted metal letters spelling POPLAR GROVE. Beside her, a very small plastic sign with press-on letters spelling CLOSED FOR HALLOWEEN.

What if I hadn't seen it? Jane tried out a few excuses:

It was dark. I was looking the other way. The sign is smallish.

But what if there were some alarm thing, that as soon as she crossed some barrier would trip, blaring bells and sirens, announcing her illegal entry to some goons lurking who knew where? Unlikely, though, in a cemetery, right? People were *supposed* to go in. That was the whole point. And the place was lit up—sorta. She could see a winding tree-lined lane, a fork in the graveled access road leading up each side of a grassy rise. Spotlights revealed curving rows of headstones and grave markers, shadowed statues of angels and crosses and sleekly marbled obelisks. *Like Mom's,* she thought, then pushed it out of her mind. That lectern thing a little beyond the arch must be the locator map. The place was actually kind of—peaceful. Not creepy-scary. Just empty.

Empty.

Traffic whizzed by behind her. No one cared. No one was stopping. All she had to do was pull in. She wasn't going to hurt anything. It wasn't *that* illegal.

Matt drove half a block past the gate, turned into a side street, and made a U-turn. At the cemetery entrance, he stopped. Turned off his lights. He was freezing. Sweating. Having a heart attack. His chest hadn't felt so tight, so constricted since—since the last time he was here. Cissy was enraged he'd added "Lassiter" to the headstone on the Galbraith family plot. Hadn't spoken to him at the funeral, or after, because of it. But Lassiter was his birthright. It was their history. It was the truth.

He'd visited the grave only a few times since, walking up that little hill, using the big angel as the landmark. His mother's headstone, pink marble, stood in the shadow of the angel's wings. He owed her a visit, he knew. But this was too . . . too much.

His chest clutched again. What was Ryland doing here? Exhaust plumed from her tailpipe. Her car didn't move. And then it did.

66

So far, so good. Jane drove in, creeping along, gripping the steering wheel, shoulders tensed for the blare of alarm bells. But nothing happened. She did a quick scan for security cameras, saw nothing. It was easy to check the locator. Easy to see the diagrams in the dimly warm lights tucked into trees and staked along the paths. Easy to find the name Katharine Lassiter. Section D, Row 23.

When she arrived at the right place, one frustrating glitch. She couldn't see the headstone from her car. But this would take only two seconds.

Leaving her car running and door open, Jane crunched through fallen leaves and gooshed through mud, glad she'd kept her rubber wellies stashed in the backseat, a leftover-from-TV habit.

Row 23. Up two rows, then down three headstones, picturing the map at the entrance. She carried the flashlight from her console, all powered up and batteries fine. Her cell phone, not so much, still charging in the car. *You can't win them all.*

The night air hit, hazy and sodden with leftover rain. Clammy. She pulled her coat closer. Tree branches bowed and bent in the light wind; wisps of clouds scudded across the navy sky. Alone in a cemetery. On Halloween.

Shut up. She wouldn't think about scary stuff; that would be stupid. She could still hear occasional cars on the road. Her own, ready to roll, was right there.

She mentally whistled a happy tune. Not afraid. She'd be here only two seconds.

If he drove in right behind her, she'd hear the car. Matt watched Jane's brake lights go on, then off, saw her Audi pull in through the arched gateway, stop at the locator. Watched her get out, check the diagrams, get back in the car.

Where was she going? It was an incredible coincidence that whoever's grave she was visiting was in the same cemetery as his mother's. Still, that could leave Matt alone with her. He hoped his mother would understand what he needed to do. He needed his life back. *Damn Holly*, he thought again. But family came first. Time to prove he was a real Lassiter.

He watched Jane turn left, toward his angel, then head slowly up the rise. Matt shifted, touched the gas pedal, eased into the cemetery driveway.

Her car was a couple hundred yards up the access road, still heading toward the angel. *Where the hell is she going? Will she get out of the car?* If he followed in his car, she'd hear it. He stopped, backed up, pointed his car's nose toward the exit. Turned off the ignition and opened the door. Closed it as quietly as he could.

What was that? Jane stopped at the end of Row 23. Stood absolutely still, muscles taut across her shoulders. She didn't want to use her flashlight—what if someone saw the beam? Plenty of light without it. The flashlight was merely backup, in case she needed to read something. The moon, almost full, appeared through the tips of the waving poplars as the rain clouds parted. Constellations glistened into view, Orion. The Dippers. The sound didn't happen again. Probably a squirrel. An owl.

Three headstones to go. Jane took one step, her dark green boots barely crunching in the close-clipped brown grass. Paused. Nothing. The first headstone was for a Walter Galbraith, born . . . it didn't matter. She took another step. Paused, eyes closed, listening as intently as her ears would manage. Opened her eyes. Nothing. Another step.

What was that? She stopped, one hand to her throat. For sure, that was an owl. *Go.*

The third headstone was the one she cared about.

It looked like marble. Polished, pink marble. Lighter than its neighbors, waist high, gracefully curved across the top, almost glowing a bit in the combination of moonlight and spotlight. One more step and she could read it. She paused. Listened. Nothing.

She took the step.

And there was the inscription. KATHARINE FLANNERY GALBRAITH LASSITER, it said, the elegant letters etched deep into the stone.

BORN OCTOBER 21, 1956
DIED APRIL 14, 2010

Smaller letters below. Jane risked the flashlight, played the thin yellow beam across the words carved into the pink stone.

BELOVED MOTHER OF SARAH (BORN 1989) AND
MATTHEW (BORN 1987)

Jane stared at the names.
Then she heard the sound.

* * *

It can't be. Matt took one last stride, crouched behind the big angel, sneaked his head around the curve of her alabaster wing to watch Jane take a few tentative steps toward his mother's grave. She took one step, then stopped. Then another. *She looked right at him.* Didn't she? He darted into the cover of the lofty wings, forehead pressed against the deep grooves in the sleek white stone. Had she seen him?

Jane looked away. She hadn't. She took another step. *That reporter is visiting my mother's grave. She knows.*

This friggin' clinched it. Ryland had Holly's damn photos. Of course, she figured Holly was sleeping with his father. Having an affair. No one would ever believe it wasn't true. No matter what anyone said. His father would be ruined. *Ruined.*

He put one hand on the angel's cool skin, trying to stay calm.

If this woman had half a brain, she would soon know exactly who he was. But in a few minutes, it wouldn't matter. His father's future was at stake.

The carved pink marble of his mother's headstone still seemed different from the other headstones, somehow. Stood out from them, always had. Secretly, he'd thought it his mother's light shining through.

Jane was taking another step.

Matt could see her car, just down the lane, door open. Holly's photos had to be in there. He'd seen the manila envelope under her arm when she left Lassiter headquarters, and she hadn't gone anywhere else. Matt pursed his lips, calculating time and distance and weight.

Jane took another step.

Matt knew exactly what she was about to see. His name. It was time.

67

"Unacceptable. Unacceptable!"

Henry Rothmann practically frothed at the mouth. In interrogation room C, Styrofoam cups littered the yellowing burn-pocked table and Arthur Vick did not look like a happy camper. His lawyer, tie askew and once-slick hair now tufted above each ear, was also a member of the unhappy camp.

Jake knew the news he was about to deliver would make them even more unhappy.

"Mr. Vick? Your wife is here," Jake said. He nodded at Rothmann. "I'm afraid we'll have to get your statement before we allow you to see her, however."

"Unacceptable! You arrested my client at approximately one P.M. today. It is now ten P.M. You—absurdly—charged him with murder. According to case law, *Commonwealth versus Rosario,* my client must be arraigned before a judge or magistrate, without unnecessary delay, and clearly this is—"

"Ah, yes," DeLuca said. He leaned against the wall, dramatically dismayed. "Thing is—"

Jake shot him a look. "Mr. Rothmann, you are, of course, correct. However, by the time we all arrived here at headquarters, and we contacted the magistrate, it was well past closing time for the court. As a result, your client is scheduled to be arraigned in Suffolk Superior Court at nine tomorrow morning. That, I'm afraid, is the best I can do."

"That's—" Rothmann flapped his yellow legal pad at Jake. "Preposterous. And a clear violation of the speedy trial decision."

"Feel free to explain that to the judge," Jake said. "Tomorrow. As for your client, we've got him on motive, means, and opportunity. He knew the victim, he had access to the drugs that incapacitated her before her death, he had proximity to the location of the deceased."

"I didn't kill anyone." Arthur Vick's voice growled, rising from deep in his throat. His shirt had come untucked. His eyes, red-rimmed and bloodshot. A splotch of coffee stained his once-pristine sweater. "This is bull. Complete bull. I never did anything."

"I'm so interested to hear your story, Mr. Vick, all you know about Sellica Darden," Jake said. *How the mighty hath fallen.* He flipped open a folding chair and sat down, facing the defendant. "You're facing life without parole, you know. In Cedar Junction. Maximum security. Where your clothes will still be monogrammed. But with *DOC*. Department of Correction. In case your lawyer has not informed you."

"And your colleagues will not be pretty girls," DeLuca put in. "Though they may think *you* are kinda cute."

Rothmann planted himself in front of his client. "Not a word, Arthur," he said. "Do not. Open. Your mouth."

Jake smiled, pleasant, infinitely patient. "Your call. No problem. I'll go see what *Mrs.* Vick has to tell us."

Jane could hear her own breathing. The muck of the soft ground under her boots, the tips of her fingers cold even through her gloves. *Matthew.* Matt. The guy from the news conference was Katharine Lassiter's son. Owen Lassiter's son.

Why was that a secret?

She snapped off the flashlight, tucked it under her arm, and crouched low to the ground, flapping her coat underneath her to keep it from dragging in the mud. Stared at the headstone. She reached out, touched the letters. So not only had Owen Lassiter been married once before, but he also had kids. They'd be Moira Lassiter's stepchildren. Certainly standard practice these days—everyone had stepkids. Why were they out of the picture?

And why did Matt—was he Matt *Lassiter*?—show up at the police news conference? He'd said he had a story for her. And then—he'd been with Kenna Wilkes.

"So now you know."

Startled at the voice, Jane stood, too quickly, wobbled off balance, falling against the pink marble. Crying out, she tried to catch herself, one rubber boot sliding in the slick grass, one hand clutching at the air, the flashlight dropping from under her arm.

No use. Her ankle wrenched under her weight. She landed, hard, on the ground, splotches of cold dampness instantly soaking through her wool coat. Breaking her fall with one hand, her wrist slammed the hard stone of the next grave.

She looked up to see—*Matt?*

Matt was making no move to help her. He stood, looking down at her, his hands stuffed in his pockets. "And since you *know,* that's a problem," he said. "Even my father doesn't know. That I'm here. Who I am. And he's not going to know. Until *I* tell him. Not *you.*"

"Matt?" She smiled, trying not to act as terrified as she was. *Lassiter doesn't know he has a son?* Wait—"doesn't know—that I'm here," Matt had said. So Lassiter knew Matt existed, just not that he was in Boston.

Why does that matter to him? What in hell is this guy doing at the cemetery? How does he know I'm here? He must have—followed me?

She eyed her car. *Time to get out of here. Fast.* "What a surprise. Guess I lost my footing there."

Matt stared at her, silent.

Not good. *Not good.* She was down, and small. He was up, and big. And not talking. She leaned forward, planting her glove in the wet grass, trying to clamber to her feet. She could see well enough. Her flashlight was right over there.

Her car. With her phone. *Over there.*

She heaved herself to her feet—but Matt was already moving forward, fast, pushing her back. Both hands, strong, angry, pushing her, and she fell back again. Cold cold cold and hard. *It hurts, my head, oh, no* . . . tears came and a jag of lightning in her head, and—

"Why are you—?" But her voice wasn't there, she needed help, this wasn't good, *he is Lassiter's son* and now he . . . why would he—? The news conference. *Holly Neff?* The woman in the photo. *His girlfriend,* Jake had said. But maybe that was wrong. *What if Matt killed Holly Neff?*

Her phone was ringing, in her car. She had to, had to, *had to* get up . . . or—

"Matt." Her voice struggled to be heard. But he was coming at her again, his face hard and angry and focused and not seeing her, not seeing her . . . she had to get him to—she shifted, gritting everything, raising herself on one elbow. She felt something crawl across her hand, her hair was cold, her head *splitting*, she had to *think*.

He was Lassiter's son. And Matt was angry; she knew that. Why? *Maybe because of Holly's death?* Would he figure Jane suspected him, since he'd approached her at the news conference? But the cops had never said Holly's name. He couldn't know she knew it. So the best thing—would be to pretend she had no idea about Holly. Change the subject. Take away his fear.

"Matt!" Her voice was so loud now, so strident, so shrill, it hurt her own ears. Her head was throbbing, *it hurts so much*. She struggled for calm, needing to reach him, distract him, misdirect him. Talk fast. *Convince him*. Otherwise, she would be his next victim. *And no one knows where I am*.

"Yes, you're so right," she told him. "But, listen, Matt, I already knew who you were. That's why I'm here, confirming it. It's not a secret, it's wonderful! And, listen, Matt. I've already told your father. Less than an hour ago. Kenna heard me. She was there for the whole thing. I told your father—'your son is in Boston.' So he already knows. He *knows*!"

68

"I'm afraid your husband won't be coming back for . . . a while," Jake said.

Patti Vick, legs crossed and clutching a bulging pocketbook, didn't get up as Jake greeted her. She'd settled in the armchair in the duty officer's room, filling the gray upholstery with coat and shawl and purse, not an inch of chair visible. Tattered "Wanted" posters and a calendar, last month's, were the room's only decoration.

A white-bordered clock, slow, Jake noticed, ticked reluctantly over a pitted wooden desk. Just after ten.

"What will happen now?" Patti Vick snapped open her purse, took out a little pink notebook. She clicked open a bright green ballpoint pen. "Does he have a chance?"

"Have a chance?" Jake hadn't heard that one before. Some spouses of murder suspects went ballistic, furious at their partners for screwing up, getting caught, or leaving them all alone. Others sobbed uncontrollably, shocked, sad, terrified, lost in confusion or surprise or, sometimes, a haze of drugs.

Patti Vick was a new one.

"Let me ask you." Jake leaned against the cinder block wall, arms crossed, in front of a poster showing a guy he'd captured. He'd give this a try, why not? Even though Patti Vick would probably clam up. Certainly that lawyer had filled her in on the three rules of talking to police: don't, don't, and don't. "What do you think about Sellica Darden?"

"She was such a—" Patti Vick shrugged, her purple shawl tipping off one sweatered shoulder. "I mean, in that world she lived in? Probably dozens of people had her in their sights. It coulda been anyone. You know what she was."

"What was she?" Jake asked. Not his place to warn her about "could be used against you." Patti Vick wasn't under arrest. She could make her own decisions.

"Puh-leeze," the woman replied. She fingered one of her hoop earrings. "My husband is no killer. Okay, he's no saint. I know that. I live with that. All those girls, the commercials, I know what goes on. Who knows how far she pushed him. Maybe someone else was there, you know? Tried to rip my Artie off. Some sleazy friend of hers. Roofing her up. Now my husband's up the creek for it."

Jake paused. One name on his mind. *Jane Ryland.* And the trial that almost cost her her career. *Jane was right. I knew it.* He kept his voice casual, not wanting to lose Patti Vick. "Must have been difficult for you. How long had your husband 'known' Sellica Darden?"

Patti slid one arm through the strap of her purse, holding the voluminous leather bag to her ample chest. He could almost see her calculating dates.

"I don't know." She swallowed. "Not before the reporter trial. Of course."

"Of course." *Bull,* Jake thought. "So, you let him use your studio? Did he have a key?"

Patti shrugged, looked relieved. "He paid the mortgage."

Jake blinked. Remembering the search. Remembering

what they'd found. "You ever paint portraits, Mrs. Vick?"

"Huh?"

"Why were there photos of women in your studio?"

"Oh, those." Patti closed her notebook. Waved him off. "Arthur's. From his commercials. He gave them to me. I paint from them sometimes."

"I see. And you have trouble sleeping?"

"Oh, yes, it's terrible." Patti raised a plump hand to her forehead, *woe is me*. "Sometimes not a wink."

"You ever sleep at the studio?"

"At the studio?"

"Yes, ma'am. I asked if you slept at the studio. We didn't see a bed there."

"Well, um, I suppose I . . ."

Jake's phone didn't ring. But he pretended it did. "Excuse me for a moment, ma'am."

He took the BlackBerry from his jacket, pushed a random button, put it to his ear. "Detective Brogan," he said. He paused, nodding, as if someone were telling him something portentous. "Yes, I'll tell her. Okay. I'll be right there."

Tucking the phone away, he shook his head, so very full of regret. "Bad news, I'm afraid, Mrs. Vick."

Patti stood, eyes wide. Her shawl fell to the chair. "Bad news?"

"Your husband's confessed," he said. "If you'll wait right here? We'll come back and get you. I know you'll want a moment to say good-bye."

"He—?" Patti sank into her chair, blinking furiously, one hand fluttering to her throat. "But . . ."

"Stay right there. I'll send someone to sit with you," Jake said. "And then I'll be back. I promise."

* * *

"He knows?"

Jane—freezing, wet, heart pounding—watched Matt process what she'd told him. She could see his brain at work. Assessing. Deciding. What she'd said was not true, of course. But sometimes the only way to suck the power from a secret is to tell it.

Jane shifted one leg carefully, knowing she might have only one chance to get to her feet. She had to get away. He'd certainly killed Holly Neff. He'd certainly kill her, too. The chunky black flashlight was almost within her grasp. Her only possible weapon. If she could reach . . .

She waved a hand to distract him, get him used to motion. Trying to engage him. "I'm a reporter, Matt, right? I find out things. I dug out birth records, you know? This is such good news, isn't it?"

She kept her eyes locked on his, adjusting her arm underneath her. *I have to get up. Without startling him into action.* The back of her head throbbed; her neck and shoulders ached. Not only with pain, but also with the tension of pretense.

"In fact, I was hoping to bring you two together. A big wonderful family story, like a reunion. You know? Right before the election. Father and son. Didn't anyone tell you? Maybe your . . ." Jane paused. The letters engraved on the headstone. *Two* children. "Your sister?"

She saw him swallow. Both hands—empty—came out of his pockets.

"Tonight at headquarters, his private office," Matt whispered. His eyes looked off in the distance. "At eleven. Is that when you—?"

"Yes, yes, exactly." Jane nodded. *Whatever.* "When Governor Lassiter gets back from his event. It'll be wonderful. So we really have to—"

"No," Matt whispered. "No." A cloud floated over the moon, deepening the shadows on his face. He pointed to

Jane, one accusing finger. "I know you had photos. She told me you showed photos to—"

"Oh, gosh, ridiculous, huh?" Jane was almost on her feet. Smiling. Lying. Playing for time. "My editor thinks those are Photoshopped, can you believe it? Fake as can be. Wherever they came from, who knows. What some people won't do to get attention."

Matt took a step back. Considering? Believing her?

Jane put one hand on the pink marble. Slowly, slowly, hoisting herself to her feet. Thinking, for a yearning fraction of a thought, of her *own* mother. How much she still missed her. Loved her. Maybe—

"You must have loved your mother very much," she said. Hoping she was right. Watching his eyes. Hearing his ragged breathing. Cars murmured past on the street outside the cemetery. A tentative wind rustled through the bare branches.

Matt was nodding.

"She'd want you to be happy," Jane continued. Keeping her voice quiet. Not wanting to break the spell. "Tonight at eleven. Right? I can help you—"

"Do not move!"

The voice split the darkness, blinding lights blasted her, the glare so instantly intense she staggered backwards, almost falling again, grabbing the grave marker behind her, scraping one hand on the rough stone.

"Do not move, do not move, stay right there." A grating voice bellowed over—over what?

Jane struggled for balance, shading her eyes, squinting, looking for—loudspeakers? Her hand was bleeding now, she could feel it, but that was okay, whoever this was would protect—

Footsteps, running, movement in the trees, more shadows. "This is security, we see you, do not move! We see you, and you're now under arrest. Damn kids! Put your hands in the air! Now! Now! Now!"

The loudspeaker voices continued, threatening, commanding, piercing the quiet. Two silhouetted figures, men, came into view. One ducked behind the angel, as if taking cover. The other approached, cautious, holding something in his hand. A gun?

Matt gave her a terrified look. Whirled. And bolted.

"Yes, yes, I'm here, don't shoot!" Jane yelled, waving both arms. Both guards were headed right for her. She pointed at Matt, still running, now almost to a car parked by the exit. "Stop him!"

69

Matt hit the accelerator almost before he got his car door closed, powered out of the cemetery, under the archway, away from the voices and the guards, away from Jane Ryland. What she'd told him. Could it be true? *My father knows?* That's what Cissy was planning for tonight? He shifted, gears grating, turned onto the street, ignoring the stop sign, heading toward Boston.

He patted the seat beside him, risked a fast look under the dash. Where did he put his damn phone? His car swerved, crossed the yellow line, edging into the other lane. He steered back to safety, headlights flaring—*too close!*—in his side mirror.

"Asshole!" he yelled at the night as some jerk honked at him. *Christ.* He had to calm the hell down. He was fine. It was fine. He was out of there. And Cissy had told him to be at Lassiter headquarters at eleven.

For a family reunion?

He felt the beginnings of a smile. His first real smile in a long while.

He would make it. Just in time.

* * *

"Ma'am? Do you realize you're trespassing?" The stocky man, wearing a dark nylon jacket marked PG-SECURITY, growled at Jane, aiming his flashlight in her face. Her rear end and gloves soaked with mud, head throbbing, she'd watched the other guard race after Matt. He now trotted up beside his partner.

"Lost him," he said. "What's the status, McCray? Ma'am, we're going to have to call the—"

"Oh, thank goodness you came," Jane cried, holding out both hands, damsel in distress. There was the trespassing issue, sure, but she could explain. At least she was alive to explain it. And these two, pudgy and pudgier, weren't so intimidating without the loudspeaker. Seemed they didn't have guns. Only flashlights. "I was visiting a—"

"You not see the closed sign? It's Halloween, ma'am. We're closed." The taller one pointed behind him. What looked like a microphone was clipped to his jacket, a miniature loudspeaker strapped over his shoulder. "You can't be here, miss."

"Oh, really?" Jane widened her eyes. Talking fast. "I thought it was open all the time. I was looking at the headstone, it's so beautiful, in the moonlight . . . and then that guy came in, and I didn't know what he was doing, and it was so scary, and then I tripped, you know, and—"

"Yo, McCray, check it out. She's Jane Ryland," the shorter one said. He waved his long-handled flashlight at her. "But with shorter hair. You're on the news, right? What're you doing here?"

"Leaving. Right now." Smiling, smiling. "Like I said, I was visiting a friend's grave. Is that okay? I'm so sorry. I mean, I didn't know it was closed, and . . ."

The two guards exchanged glances. One shrugged, then the other.

"Don't do it again," pudgier said.

* * *

"Bad news, I'm afraid, Mr. Vick." Jake put on a somber face as he entered interrogation room C. Arthur Vick, still seated in a folding chair, arms crossed on the long table, slowly raised his head. His eyes were rimmed with red, his drawn face the picture of defeat. Coffee-stained Styrofoam shards now littered the table. Someone had torn the cups into pieces, lining up the bottoms in a row of grubby polka dots.

"Huh?" Vick said. He squinted at Jake, blinking as if he'd been asleep. "What happened to the other cop?"

"Shut up, Arthur." Henry Rothmann leaped to his feet, his metal chair banging against the wall. "What bad news, Detective? Bad news for *you*, maybe? You admitting this whole thing is a farce? You going to let my client go? The way you should have hours ago?"

Jake closed the door behind him, then stood in front of it. Vick lowered his head back down onto his arms.

"Maybe so," Jake said. This was risky, and if the whole thing went to hell, there'd be Miranda violations out the ass. It would kill a murder case against Arthur Vick. Jake hoped that wouldn't matter.

She was roofed up, Patti had said. How'd she know that? The cops kept that secret. Either Vick told his wife he drugged Sellica and killed her, which was pretty damn unlikely, or Patti Vick—scorned wife of the hooker-hiring grocer-about-town—killed the other woman herself.

Vick's head lifted ever so slightly, only his eyes showing.

"I'm aware that I can't direct my statement to Mr. Vick, since he's Mirandized," Jake continued. "And on the record here, I am not asking him to respond. However."

He paused, giving his strategy one last gut check.

"However, Mr. Rothmann. And I remind you all conversations in this room are taped. Patricia Vick has just confessed to the murder of Sellica Darden."

"Answer the phone, answer the phone," Jane said to the darkness as she drove over the Longfellow Bridge, alert for speed traps, headed as fast as she could back to Boston. She'd found a stash of paper napkins in her glove compartment, cleaned off her coat as best she could, wrapped a couple of them around her now barely bleeding hand. It stung like crazy, and she really needed an Advil for her head. She could already feel the lump behind one ear. But she'd live. Which, for a couple of moments there, she'd wondered about.

Those rent-a-guards might call the police about Matt. Good news and bad news—really nothing for them to tell.

Her call kept ringing, the speaker filling the car with the sound. "Come on, Jakey, pick up, pick up. . . ."

The names on that headstone.

Two children. Matt—Lassiter's son. Could Holly Neff be Lassiter's daughter? The ages were about right. What was she doing at the campaign? Why was she using a phony name?

Still. Had Matt killed his own sister? But Jake had said—girlfriend. *Maybe that's wrong. Maybe everyone just assumes that. Or believes that.* Maybe Holly Neff was Matt's sister. *Owen's daughter.*

The phone rang again. Jane hit the red light at the Charles Circle rotary. Watched the late-night traffic battle for right-of-way around the rain-slicked loop to Mass General and Beacon Hill.

Or. Maybe not. Maybe not Holly. Would she send such a sexy photo—to her own father?

Maybe Owen's daughter was the *other* woman.

Jake's phone went to voice mail. "It's me," Jane said after the beep. "I think I know where to find Kenna Wilkes. Matt, too. Call me. Right away. Call me."

70

"Bull. Shit." Henry Rothmann poked the air at Jake with each word. "What a cheap, worn-out cop trick. Pitting the Vicks against each other. I demand to confer with my client's wife. Confirm she really confessed. We've been here nine full hours. My client is exhausted. And this is simply—"

"Henry?" Arthur Vick raised a palm.

"Shut up," Rothmann said. "She had no lawyer, she was coerced, you tricked her, nothing she said will hold up in court. And, Detective Brogan, you just presented my client with an indisputable chunk of reasonable doubt. So they'll both go free."

"No." Vick stood, smoothing his sweater, tucking in his shirt. "No way. Forget it. I'm not going on trial for a murder I didn't do. I'm not going to rot in prison for this. I didn't kill Sellica. *Yes.* My wife did. And I can prove it. What else do you need to know?"

"Arthur, I order you to stop talking," the lawyer tried again. "They're trying to—"

"She was jealous of you and Sellica?" Jake's phone was ringing, vibrating in his jacket pocket. He couldn't answer it, not now that Vick was spilling. "Your relationship? So your wife was, what, out for revenge?"

"I suppose. Sure." Vick shrugged. "Patti hated the commercials, hated my life. Swiped those photos from my computer. We were supposed to have a deal: I let her paint. I could do whatever."

"You agree to testify against her?" Jake asked.

"No, a husband cannot testify—" The lawyer tried to interrupt again.

"Can't be *compelled* to, as you well know, Mr. Rothmann," Jake said. "But voluntarily? No problem."

"Yes, I'll testify against her," Vick said. "If I can go now."

"Not quite yet," Jake said. "So you had a relationship, a financial relationship with Sellica Darden? Prior to her murder?"

"Yes, yes. Like I said." He looked at the door, fists on hips. "Can we go now?"

Jake tilted his head back and forth, as if considering. He was actually considering how gratifying this was about to be. He had taken an oath to protect and defend. To seek the truth. And here it was.

"Ah, in fact, no, you can't go," he said. "Arthur Vick, you're now under arrest for perjury. For your false testimony in the Jane Ryland defamation trial."

"Kenna?" Governor Owen Lassiter, back from the Chamber dinner, stood in the open doorway to his private office, one hand on the doorjamb. He took a deep breath. "The back elevator's broken again."

Smiling prettily, Kenna looked up from her place behind Owen Lassiter's important-person desk. Sitting in Owen Lassiter's important-person chair. She'd dressed for the occasion, formal in a black blazer and sleek white silk blouse, lace camisole, pearls, charcoal pencil skirt, and pricey suede pumps.

"Hello, Governor," Kenna said. "Yes, we know. And Mr. Maitland says to tell you he'll be here momentarily. We have something to discuss with you."

Lassiter turned, looking behind him at what Kenna knew was the empty corridor. She knew Rory was elsewhere, otherwise occupied. And would be for some time.

"This is somewhat of a surprise, I must say," Owen said. "It's rather late, Kenna, close to eleven. Couldn't we chat tomor—?"

Kenna stood, her fingertips touching the glass desktop. She waited, eyeing him, wondering if she ever crossed his mind.

"I'll take only a moment of your time."

The governor came into the room, took off his suit jacket, held it by a finger over one shoulder. Gave a half smile. "Well, what can I do for you, Kenna?"

"Something we need to discuss." She kept her hand on the desk to keep herself from floating away. "You're dropping out of the Senate race."

Almost there. Matt made the light at Causeway Street, found a space, locked the car. His heart raced; his face felt hot. He was about to face his father. Face his future.

His life was about to change. About time.

He trotted up the sidewalk toward Lassiter headquarters, dodging a couple of beer-toting Celtics fans wearing numbered green jerseys over their jackets. Boston Garden. *Someday my father and I might—*

The headquarters lobby was dark. He pushed the revolving door with the flat of his hand. It didn't budge. He tried again, his eyes filling with tears of frustration. Locked? *Locked?* And the lobby was empty. Silent.

No. No. He had to get inside.

71

Kenna watched, almost—entertained, by the slideshow of emotions across Owen Lassiter's face.

Disbelief. Confusion. Disgust. Fear?

Finally, he seemed to decide on derision. Laughing softly, he draped his suit jacket on a mahogany hanger, fastidiously adjusting the shoulders, taking time to straighten the lapels, setting it into a curved bracket of a wrought-iron stand by the door.

"It's late. You're tired. I'm sure you understand this is not amusing." Owen's voice was cool. "I'm not quite sure what your goal—"

Kenna interrupted, drinking it in. "Here's the thing, Owen." She drew out his name, dropping the title she'd always been careful to use. "You have a problem with women. Yes, indeed. Sadly. And your wife knows, of course. I suppose that's why she's been in hiding all this time. Soon, even more sadly, everyone will know."

"Will *know*?" Owen looked at the door, at his desk, at the phone. "Are you—drunk? High? In one second, I'm calling security."

"Our little fling was fun while it lasted, wasn't it?" Kenna continued. He wasn't calling anyone. And if he made a move against her, she was prepared to stop him. She gave her voice an edge of drama, as if reciting a movie plot. "I mean—you invited me to your hotels—I even took souvenirs from the presidential suites we shared."

She reached into her pocket, pulled out a pink vial of body lotion labeled PRESIDENTIAL SUITE. Dangled it in front of him.

"I was so enamored with you. Rory knows how often we were together, of course. The hotel people, too. The room service I ordered for us. You were so loving, so charming. You said it would be just the two of us, as soon as you were elected and you could get rid of that silly social-climbing wife of yours. But now—it seems you were unfaithful to me, too. Taking up with that *Holly* person."

Owen crossed his arms, brow furrowed, eyes narrowing. "Holly? Are you cra—? Who the hell is Holly?"

She held her expression, wide-eyed, lashes fluttering.

"Oh, gosh, I think you know. And when you dumped me for that little tramp, and then she turned up dead, well, I just couldn't allow someone with your—shall we say—questionable morals to ascend to a seat in the highest echelons of government, now, could I? I mean, did she get in your way? What if you killed her? And what if I'm terrified that I'm next?"

Poor man. He was crumbling in confusion. It was all she could do not to laugh.

"So, there you have it," she said. She pointed toward the phone with the lotion bottle. "Better call the secretary of state's office. Her private phone number from your Rolodex is right there. Tell her you're dropping out. Maybe—here's a good one—say you want to spend more time with your family."

"There's just one phone call I'm going to make, Miss—," Owen sputtered, brushing her off, wiping his palms as if to clear away her demands. "And that's to security."

She ignored him. "And oh, in case you have any second thoughts? Allow me to show you one more thing." She drew a manila envelope from her black suede purse. Handed it to him. Smiled.

He sneered, dismissing it with one hand. "There's nothing you can—"

"You think not?" She slid the photograph out of the envelope, slowly, slowly, teasing. Poor stupid Holly. *Her* plan hadn't worked as she'd hoped, but it certainly played into Kenna's hands. Matt had said Holly was nuts, anyway.

Kenna held the photo toward Owen. "We—Rory and I—found this in a book on your desk. Jane Ryland—the reporter?—knows all about it. And I know the inscription on this little gem by heart. 'To Owen, with all my admiration and gratitude . . . after a wonderful afternoon. Here's to many more. *xoxo*. Holly Neff.'"

She pretended to be perplexed. "And now she's dead, correct? Do the police know about your relationship?"

This time Owen was silent. He smoothed his red-patterned tie. Did it again.

"So?" Kenna danced the photo at him, taunting. "The call?"

Owen yanked the slick photograph from her, stared at it. "I've never seen this before. Absurd. Anyone could have— This is—extortion. Blackmail. Pitiful. And—"

"Oh, dear. Such ugly words. And the truth—gosh, whatever that is, will certainly come out. But probably not until after the election. Which you, no doubt, will lose. In humiliation, and embarrassment, and there'll never be a time where someone won't wonder—*did he, really?* And I'll be long gone. So, fine, if you don't want to drop out of the race, lovely. Your decision. How-ever—"

"Kenna, you're upset, you've misunderstood—something," Lassiter interrupted. He put the picture down, then held up both palms, conciliatory. "Let's talk this out. You're not thinking clearly, you're—"

She felt one curl slide onto her cheek, brushed it away. "Yes, I am. Thinking clearly. And, I should tell you, it's not Kenna. It's—Sarah."

She wasn't answering her cell. Matt couldn't call the main campaign line—it was dark inside Lassiter head-quarters, and he could see no one was there. But she had told him to arrive at a specific time. That was now. What was he missing?

And then he saw it.

A little white button in the metal siding of the door. He pushed it, heard a buzz, and after a second, the door clicked open. She was waiting for him. He was expected. It was all going as planned. He pushed the elevator but-ton. Looked at his watch. Just after eleven.

He would make it in time.

72

"**Sarah Lassiter. Your** daughter. Remember me?"

Kenna soaked up her father's shock, wrapped herself in it, delighted in the slack of his jaw, the pain in his gray eyes, the way the man staggered a step, gripping the back of a striped wing chair. *Yeah,* she thought. *Hurts when someone pulls the rug out, right?*

"Sar—" Lassiter's eyes widened, he stepped toward her, one arm reaching out to her. Then he stopped, took a deep breath. "Sarah? Is that what this—this—photo thing, this hotel thing, this *Holly* thing—is all about? Why would you threaten me with—?" His chin came up. Wary. "Is your mother behind this?"

Oh, please. Sarah—yes, she'd call herself that now, why not—could not believe this. He was bringing up her *mother*?

"And you have a little boy?" Owen continued. His voice went soft. "My grandson? Why would you—?"

Sarah burst out laughing, the brittle sound ringing in her ears. *Jimmy, the rent-a-kid.* She put a hand over her mouth, pressing her lips together. *No.* She would handle this carefully. Quietly. It would be such fun to tell him everything.

"Why would I?" Sarah raised an eyebrow, enjoying

her scorn. "Let me remind you, *Governor,* of when we last saw each other? I'm not quite sure I remember it exactly, my being, what, two years old? But Mother told us all about it. Again and again. You discarded us. Deserted us. Left us! To—to fend for ourselves while you ran off with . . ."

Sarah stretched her fingers, tried to keep her voice calm. No need to yell. He'd hear her out. "*You* were happy. With that other woman? And that's all that mattered to you."

"It was, complicated, Kenn—Sarah. More complicated than just . . ." Owen lowered his arms slowly, his shoulders sagging. "I know I—your mother and I—your brother—is he—?"

"Let me finish," Sarah interrupted. Had to. "When my mother killed herself—"

Lassiter's face went white. "She killed herself? Katharine?"

See, that's just what I mean. "Of course you never knew. You never cared. Not for our mother, not for us."

A buzzer sounded. *Perfect.* Sarah hit the black button under Lassiter's desk.

Lassiter collapsed into the wing chair, pressed his hands together, placed them near his lips. "Kenna. I mean—Sarah," he said. "I can't believe you're sitting there. It's—it was the most difficult thing I've ever done, leaving you both. Please try to forgive me. This picture thing, this hotel thing, this—*Holly*—is absurd, ridiculous, you know it is. Why don't we—may I just explain?"

Sarah waved a hand. *Let him talk.* What could he possibly say?

"Your mother was—well, Katharine screamed. Insisted, demanded, demanded everything. I mean, Moira—wanted you. Wanted to love you both." His face softened;

he searched her eyes. "But you couldn't have known that, of course."

Moira? *Impossible.* He was lying. "Of course," Sarah said. "But funny, if we were all so lovey-dovey, why did you just—dump us?"

"I never—we didn't . . ." He sighed, leaning forward, hands on his knees. "Because I left, your mother got sole custody. I came to visit, again and again. You were just a baby. And Matt a toddler. You couldn't remember. Then your mother took you—and vanished. Must have changed her name. And yours. To—Kenna Wilkes? She wrote me, said you both hated me. I tried to find you. I did. *We* did. She must have worked hard at it, to make it so impossible."

"Oh, I beg you." Sarah's eyes burned, so angry, her skin tingled. Her hands clenched into fists, nails jabbing into her palms. "Don't insult me. You became governor, for God's sake! You could do anything you wanted! But finding your own children? Simply *not* on your busy agenda."

She saw his shoulders flinch, as if she'd tried to hurt him. Well, she had.

Owen stood, reaching out both arms, pleading. "I tried. But your mother told me—well, I wish you could understand how hard I tried. I've never forgiven myself. I wish I could make it up to you. What can I do to—?" His hands dropped to his sides.

"Do? Ah. That's an easy one." Sarah gestured to the phone. "It's my turn to take something from *you.* The only thing *you* really love. End your campaign, or I'll end it for you. Your choice. Make the call. Or I—go public with the photos. And oh, so many more. Not to mention—"

"But, Sarah. Why? Now you're here. We can start over. Isn't that right? Sarah? And is Matt—?"

"Oh, you remember his name, how charming," Sarah said. "Just what I was about to mention. I *do* have some news about him. Which, given the events of the past few days, I'm quite sure will speed your decision. And in fact—"

She paused, then turned toward the open door. Where her older brother, just arrived, now stood. "In fact, let me introduce you, *once again,* to Matthew Lassiter Galbraith. Who, you may remember, is your son. Perhaps he'll tell you the news himself."

73

Jane held her cell phone in one hand, talking as she opened her car door, kicked off her wellies, and slid into her tall leather boots. "Jake? Oh, my gosh, I am so glad you answered. Where have you—? Watch it!" Some guy in a Celtics jacket and Halloween mask almost ran into her car door, waving a cup of something. The game was letting out, judging by the crazies on the street. "Anyway, I'm at Lassiter headquarters. Did you get my other message?"

"I've been a little busy," Jake said.

Whatever. "Okay, so get over here, okay? It's Kenna Wilkes. And Matt. I think they'll both be here. How long will it take? For you to get here?"

"You sure this time? Matt's there? No mistake?"

Jane started across the street, biting back a crack. Last time she'd asked Jake to meet her here, they'd met a woman she'd promised him was dead. "I'm sure," she said. "And listen. His name is Matt *Lassiter*. I'm almost at the front door."

"Stop!"

Jake's voice was so commanding, she actually stopped. In the middle of the street. Rolling her eyes, she continued toward headquarters.

"I'm using the crosswalk," she lied.

"What? No, listen, stop. Do *not* go in there by yourself. I'm in the car now, I'm headed to you. Lights and siren. Listen for me. I'll turn them off when I hit the corner of Causeway. Don't want to spook anyone. Two minutes. I'll be there. Do not go in, Janey. Got me?"

"Got you." Jane clicked off the phone.

She peered through the front windows. Saw the lights off, lobby empty. She listened for Jake's siren. Nothing. Looked at her watch. Five after eleven.

Forget it.

She was going in.

Matt couldn't move. Could barely believe it. He stood in the office door, seeing the back of a man's head. The man was seated in a big chair, gray hair just showing over the top, a white shirtsleeve on the armrest. Saw Cissy, her face flushed and angry, yelling at him about "finding your own children." Saw the man stand, slim, tall—his father—take a step toward her.

What Jane Ryland had said was true. *My father knows.* But why was Cissy acting so mean? This was their time to be together.

Cissy pointed right at him. "Your son," she was saying.

His father turned.

Matt saw the tears come to his father's eyes, felt the same in his own.

"I—we—"

"Matthew?" Lassiter came toward him, glanced back at Cissy, then stared at him.

"Father?" He couldn't help it, it was crazy, but even after so many years and so much unhappiness, he still loved him. He was a Lassiter. Nothing could change that.

He fell into his father's arms, feeling the tears, feeling the man's chest rise and fall, feeling—

"Are you kidding me?" Cissy was beside them, using both her hands to yank them apart. She punched Matt in the arm, her eyes slits of anger. "He ruined our lives, remember? Remember? Mother killed herself!"

She whirled, pointed a finger at their father. "Because of you! You might as well have murdered her!"

"Sarah, Matthew, I'm so sorry—"

"See, Cissy?" Matt interrupted his father, needing to help. Maybe he could make this better. *We're here to surprise dad, right? Reunite as a family.* "Our father loves us. Can't you see that? Life doesn't always work the way we hoped. But we can still be a family, can't we?"

His father put a hand on Matt's shoulder, the weight of it feeling like years. Their eyes met, father and son. Matt pressed his lips together to keep from crying, seeing the love in his face. It would all be okay. Even despite Holly. He had to say something now, talk to him, let him know how much he had sacrificed for—

"You decided what was best for *you,* Governor." Cissy's voice cut through the silence. "Now it's about what's best for *us.* You're dropping out of this race. Your political life is over. Every action has consequences—and this is it. Make the call. Now."

Matt saw her hand go into her jacket pocket. And pull out a—

"No!" Matt yelled. "Cissy! He's our father. You have to stop!"

74

A white button in the molding of the front door. Jane pushed it with a finger. She heard a buzz. Tried the door. Nothing. It was locked. *Dammit.*

And then she heard the siren. She scooted away from the door as if she'd never tried it. He'd never know.

"Jane!" Jake's voice came from a few yards away. "I told you not to— Hey. You're covered with mud. Are you okay? What the hell happened?"

"I'm fine. Tell you later about the mud. But I bet this door's locked," Jane said. "And they're supposed to meet at eleven." *I think.*

Jake rattled the door handle. Smiled. "So observant of you. Come with me." He trotted down the sidewalk, beckoning her to follow.

"Down this alley," he called over his shoulder.

She caught up with him, jogging alongside, their footsteps echoing against the brick buildings on each side.

"But why are we—?"

"There's another door," Jake said. "Gotta be. The secretary—Deenie, whatever her name is—told me the governor uses the side. Maitland, too. Maybe we can get in that way."

"Look," Jane said. A lone bulb illuminated a black

metal door set flat in the side of the headquarters building.

They reached for the battered metal knob at almost the same time.

Jane got there first.

"Our *father*?" Cissy almost spit Matt's words back at him. "He decided he didn't care about us. He killed our family. You know what? You know what? We shouldn't let him get away with it. It was all about money, and power, and ambition. And Moira. Our mother wasn't good enough for him, so he dumped her. And us."

Matt stared at the gun glinting in his sister's hand. A gun pointed at their father. *Why? We're supposed to*— "Think for a minute, Cissy. You'll never get away with it. All I have to do is yell. Somebody's out there."

"Yell away," she said. "By the time anyone arrives, it'll be over."

"You don't want to do this, Kenn—Sarah." Lassiter stepped toward her. "Matt's right, we can be a family. I'll make the call. Just like you asked."

Make the call? What were they talking about? But his father was courageous. Strong. Matt could be the same. He held out his hand, gesturing for the gun. "Come on," Matt said. "You don't want to do this."

He couldn't understand the look on his sister's face.

"You don't want *me* to do this, Matt. But maybe *you* did it." She waved the gun at him. "After all, you're already a killer. You killed Holly Neff."

"What?" Lassiter looked at him, taking a step back. "Who the hell is this Holly Neff?"

Matt had to explain. Fast. He struggled for the words. "She was—she was—she was going to ruin you, Father. She was setting it up to look like you were having an affair. She was telling the reporters a big lie. She thought I would love her for it, want the revenge. I needed to—"

But Cissy was still talking. Holding that gun. Pointing it at his father.

"This can go either way, brother dear. Because I can say *you* killed your father. And when the cops get here, you'll be dead, too. I'll have killed you, trying desperately, though, alas, not successfully, to protect the candidate."

Cissy was actually—smiling.

"I'll be a hero," she said. "The valiant campaign staffer who tried to save her boss. No one knows who we really are, do they? By the time they figure it out, if they ever do, I'll be long gone."

"Sarah, honey, you—" Lassiter threw Matt a glance. Eyes wide, hand to throat, stutter-stepping backward. Matt knew he was pleading *help me*.

They were in this together. They could get out of it together. Matt would protect his father. That's what a son had to do.

"Dammit. This elevator's not working." Jake punched the button again and again, but there was no light, no sound, no clanking. "We'll have to go to the front—"

"Stairs," Jane said, heading for a metal doorway. "Fourth floor."

"You're either in it with me, brother, or you're dead," Cissy said. "And don't you see? I'm trying to protect you! If he quits the campaign, right now, that means no one will ever know what you did! It means you and I leave town together. Or—we don't. Your call."

With a roar that came from his very soul, Matt threw

himself at his sister, knowing about the gun, knowing it was a risk, knowing he might—

"No!" Sarah saw her brother's body come toward her, his bulk and his arms and his hands, waving, he was trying to stop her, but she'd just been tormenting Owen, wanting to scare him. She would never have actually shot—

"No, Matt, stop! I wasn't really going to—"

Her body recoiled with Matt's weight—she saw the bookshelves tilt by, then the ceiling, shuddered from the recoil of the gun, too, suddenly hot in her hand, then felt Matt heavier, heavier on top of her, and he wasn't moving anymore and—

She scrambled to her feet, frantic, panicked, suffocated, pushing Matt's body away, saw her father come toward her— *Is that my own scream?*

Then he was—her arm was twisted, *twisting?*

He was taking her gun? *No!* She needed to get it back. This wasn't supposed to—

And it fired again.

75

"You hear that?" Jane yanked open the stairwell door, Jake not two steps behind her. She was winded, running up the three flights in high-heeled boots. Hearing the sound—unmistakably a gunshot, then another—propelled them both down the hall.

"Nine-one-one, what's your emergency?"

"A speakerphone?" Jane frowned even more, confused by the sounds coming from an open doorway. They were steps away. Breathing hard, she showed him a door, whispering. "That's Lassiter's private office. The only office on this floor."

From inside the room, a man's voice, anguished, called out. "Send an ambulance, now! Someone's been shot! I'm trying to—"

Jake grabbed her, whirling, pinning her flat to the corridor wall, her back pressing tight against the bricks. "Do not move," he whispered, his mouth close to her ear. She saw his gun come out of his jacket. "I'm not kidding, Jane. Do. Not. Move."

Two more steps to the door. Jake needed to call for backup. But there wasn't time. Still, if someone inside was calling 911, they weren't afraid of the cops. One good sign, at least.

Weapon drawn, Jake pressed himself against the brick wall directly outside the open door. He cocked his head at Jane. *Get back. Get back!*

He could hear cries from inside. A man's voice. A woman's. "Ambulance is on the way, sir." The flat monotone of the operator crackled over the speakerphone. "Two minutes."

Jake pointed his gun into the room and immediately stepped inside. "Police, freeze!" he yelled, scanning the wood-paneled room in an instant, corner to corner, ceiling to floor. Windows, closed. Desk, empty. Glass-fronted shelves. Lassiter posters. American flag. "Police! Do not move!"

Two bodies on the floor. And Owen Lassiter, kneeling. No one else.

"Hello? Sir?" The dispatcher's voice, concerned, crackled through the silver speaker of the desk phone. "Is someone else there?"

The candidate, his white shirtsleeves splattered red, bent over a woman lying face up on the jewel-toned pile of the oriental rug, a cascade of blond across her face, pearls dangling, bare legs stretched out toward the door. She wore one black shoe. Lassiter held tan cloth of some kind against the woman's chest, the light-colored fabric rapidly changing to crimson.

A man's body lay nearby, splayed, motionless. White male, no gun in anyone's hand, Jake catalogued. A desk blocked Jake's view of the man's face, but he could easily see the darkening bloom in the center of a once-pale-blue shirt. The man's khakis were streaked with mud. *Mud?* His loafers were muddy, too.

Did Lassiter shoot two people? Where's the damn gun? Jake kept his weapon on Lassiter, yelling toward the speakerphone on the desk. "Detective Jake Brogan, Boston PD on the scene, Dispatch. Requesting backup. And medical. We have a person down. Two. Do you have a twenty on this location?"

"Copy that, Detective," the voice came back. "On the way. Are you secure?"

"Help me, Detective. Please help me." Lassiter wiped his forehead with one hand, leaving a dark trail across his skin and staining his gray hair. "She's bleeding, too much, too fast. I'm using my suit jacket to—"

"Detective?" The dispatcher's voice. "Please respond. Over."

"My son is dead." Lassiter's voice was a pitiful croak. "My daughter shot him, and now she's dying. It was an accident. An accident. But it's all my fault. I tried to take it from her—"

A once-shiny silver gun—a .22—lay in a dark stain on the rug, almost under the couch.

Jake kept his weapon chest high, edging farther into the room. He kicked the .22 out of Lassiter's reach. "We are secure, Dispatch," Jake called out. "Repeating the request for backup. And a medic. Pronto."

"Copy," the voice said. "ETA is in one minute."

"Black button under the desk," Lassiter said. "Opens the front door. Lets them in." He didn't take his eyes off the woman. Tears streamed down his face, landing on hers. "I was trying to take the gun from her. It was an accident."

"Jane!" Jake called, loud as he could. He needed to unlock the front door for the EMTs. Needed to check on the man, whoever it was. And to see if he could assist Lassiter. "Janey! Need your help in here."

The woman on the floor stirred, then with a thin gasp, opened her eyes.

Christ. Jake wasn't ready for that. He aimed his

weapon at her, then lowered it. The amount of red on the rug meant she was unlikely to fight back.

"All your selfish fault," the woman hissed at Lassiter. Her eyes closed again.

"Kenna Wilkes." Jane's voice from the doorway. "That's Kenna Wilkes."

"My wife," Lassiter whispered. "I need to call my wife."

76

"It's so quiet in here. It's usually blaring some Sousa thing, you know?" Jane, whispering, leaned closer to Alex. The lobby was crowded with sleepy-eyed reporters and photographers, some clutching paper cups and Tuesday's morning paper, others lugging lights and tripods. "The campaign posters and stuff are still up, though."

"You think he's going to quit?" Alex also kept his voice low. "I had to see this. Quarter to eight. Can you believe they called it for this early?"

Three rows of folding chairs faced a portable lectern set up in front of the elevators. Behind them, a wooden riser for television cameras. The reception desk was empty. A week before the election, and the front-runner's headquarters reeked of bad news.

She and Alex had done it. Scoop of the year. Both had stayed in the *Register* city room till dawn, side by side, slugging down coffee and banging out the front-page wall-to-wall blockbuster. Now both were running on caffeine and adrenaline, Jane's coat still spotted with mud but the lump on her head tamed with Advil.

She craned her neck, checking the competition. "See everyone reading the *Register*?"

Sliding into the seat next to Alex, Jane pulled her own copy of the morning paper from her tote bag. Banner headlines—biggest the paper had used since the mob thing—proclaimed ELECTION TRAGEDY. Underneath, CANDIDATE'S ESTRANGED DAUGHTER CHARGED WITH MURDER IN ASSASSINATION ATTEMPT.

According to sources close to the story, Matthew Lassiter Galbraith was killed in an attempt to prevent the now-hospitalized victim, Lassiter's estranged daughter, from murdering their father. Lassiter campaign officials insist . . .

Jane knew every word by heart.

Tuck had the byline on the sidebar story. CANDIDATE'S SON SUSPECT IN BRIDGE KILLING, with the subhead—"Now Victim in Lassiter Shooting." Archive Gus's photos of Holly Neff were arrayed across the jump page. Exclusive.

Police have no motive in the slaying of Holly Neff, age 25, who recently moved to Massachusetts from Pennsylvania. Sources say Neff's apartment contained numerous photos of Senate candidate Owen Lassiter, estranged father of the deceased Matthew Lassiter Galbraith, as well as several photographs of Neff and her alleged murderer. The Register's *investigation proves the victim was a regular attendee at Lassiter events, although campaign officials insist . . .*

Jane dropped the paper to her lap, crumpling the pages, and jabbed Alex with an elbow.

"You know what kinda kills me, Alex? It's really *my* investigation, you know? So funny, after all that, Tuck winds up with the woman-in-the-red-coat story." Jane flipped the newspaper to the front page, pointed to the headline. "But there's no Bridge Killer. And I still don't agree with 'assassination.'"

"It's exactly what happened," Alex said. He turned toward her, draping his arm across the back of her chair, keeping their conversation private. "Like the cops said. Lassiter thinks Kenna—Sarah, whatever—had lured him to the office to kill him, after years of being taught to hate him. That's assassination."

Jane risked a bit of an eyeroll—they were pals now, after all. Practically. "We'll see, though, if she recovers enough to talk." She read her story yet again.

Lassiter campaign officials would not comment on the incident, or on the candidate's relationship to the woman known as Kenna Wilkes—who reportedly worked as a campaign volunteer. Sources do confirm the woman is actually Sarah Lassiter Galbraith, the candidate's daughter from his first marriage. She remains in critical condition and under police surveillance at Mass General Hospital.

Jane looked up from the paper. "What's wrong?"

Alex, now on his feet, was scanning the room. Frowning. "Five minutes till the press conference. Our photog isn't here." He patted his jacket pockets, found his cell.

"I've got my camera." Jane unzipped her tote bag. "Worst comes to—damn. Memory card full. I've got to delete some stuff."

Good-bye, pigeons. Good-bye, Amy in Nantucket—*yikes, I have to call her*. The guy who wasn't Fabio in front of Saks. Her car parked at the broken meter. Good-bye—*wait*.

Jane clicked the little zoom lever, pushing the snapshot into a close-up. It was that day at the Esplanade rally, when Trevor took her backstage, and she'd seen the red-coat girl in the crowd. She'd managed only that one snap before Trevor cut her off. She hadn't needed to look at it again. And now . . .

"Hey. Check this out." Jane held the camera with both hands, showing him the screen.

Alex clicked off his cell. Muttering. "The guy's looking for a parking place. I mean, every place is a parking place if you're press. What, Jane?"

"It's a photo I took. At my first Lassiter rally. There's Holly Neff, right? But look who else is in the shot." She clicked the photo to a tighter close-up. "The woman? That's Kenna—I mean, Sarah Lassiter. And the guy with his arm draped around her? That's—"

"Ladies and gentlemen, are we ready?"

Jane looked up at the lectern, where an exhausted-looking man in a tweed jacket and rumpled chinos, ID cards dangling from a webbed lanyard, adjusted one of the microphones.

"That's Trevor Kiernan at the mic," Jane whispered. "Alex, before this starts. See who's with her in this photo?"

"We'll have a brief statement, but we will not be taking any questions." Kiernan placed a clipboard on the lectern. A barrage of megawatt television lights clicked on, spotting the podium and glaring on the art deco elevator doors behind it. "We will not be doing any interviews."

Looks like a guy emceeing his own funeral.

"Understood?" Kiernan locked eyes with Jane for a split second, then glanced across the crowd. "Statement, then good-bye. Got me?"

"Trevor!" A guy in the front row stood, holding up a hand. "Where's Governor Lassiter? Is he going to stay in the race?"

"Any word on his daughter's condition?" The woman next to him wasn't going to be scooped. "Why was he estranged from his own children?"

That started the torrent.

"Is Lassiter under arrest?"

"Is Owen going to drop out?"

"Has Eleanor Gable called you?"

"So much for 'no questions,' " Jane whispered to Alex. "But I must say, I can't wait to talk to Gable. The Kenna—I mean Sarah—connection. The Deverton house. You know?"

Alex, ignoring her, had Jane's camera almost to his nose, his glasses balanced on his forehead. Staring at the photo.

The burnished silver of the elevator doors vibrated, the lights pinged to green, the doors slid open.

"But this is—," Alex said. He turned to Jane, pointing a forefinger at the photo.

A man emerged from the elevators, into the spotlights. Took his place at the lectern.

"Rory Maitland," Jane whispered.

"Rory Maitland," Kiernan announced, "will now read the candidate's statement. Then we're done."

77

"Why didn't she just kill her husband, you know, Harvard? If she thought she could get away with it?"

Jake and DeLuca stood at the end of a dim hallway at the Nashua Street Jail. The women's unit—different from the men's only because of the sign—held mostly punks and angry crank heads. Patti Vick would not enjoy this slumber party.

This was the end of the line, Jake always thought. Layered with fear and wrong decisions.

The last of Patti Vick's obscenities floated down the jail hallway, her shrill voice bouncing off the walls. Two matrons, one on each side, ignored her protests as they led her away. The woman had confessed. Jake got the whole damn thing on tape.

Her husband was out on bail. Facing a complicated and unpleasant future.

"Well, she told me she'd thought about it," Jake said. "Killing him."

"Yeah?" DeLuca stuffed his fists into his jacket pockets.

"Yeah. But she figured it'd be too obvious if she killed him. It's always the spouse, everyone knows that. Plus, if her husband was dead, she thought she'd lose the million bucks. From his judgment against Jane, you know? She thought if he was in Cedar Junction for life, she'd still get the money. Vick had Sellica's private phone number, of course. So Patti pretended to be some secretary, told Sellica her big-shot boss was auditioning for a photo spread, they'd heard about her via the grapevine, they were shooting it at the studio—you can figure out the rest. And Sellica had never seen Patti, you know? Clever Patti wrote some nasty notes to Jane, too, after the trial. Figuring they'd make her husband look guiltier."

"So Patti does away with Sellica, sets up her cheating husband, and keeps the money." DeLuca pursed his lips, nodding. Then he frowned at Jake. "Is that even how it works?"

"Nope," Jake said. "If he died, she *would* get the money. If Vick were found guilty of Sellica's murder, the missus probably wouldn't. How dumb is that? Guess Patti could have asked a lawyer for clarification. But that'd be one iffy conversation."

The two stood in silence for a moment. In the distance, a clang of metal.

"Jane know about this?" DeLuca finally said.

The day's second bright spot.

"Nope." Jake took out his phone. He wished he could tell her in person. He'd love to see that smile. Then he'd inform Leota Darden. "I'm calling her right now."

"Owen Lassiter says he's staying in the race." Jane caught Eleanor Gable as the candidate walked up the front path of her Beacon Hill home. "So there are a couple of things I need to ask you."

Instead of continuing the interview on the sidewalk, neighbors peering from brownstone windows, Gable invited Jane inside. "Five minutes," she declared.

But standing in her high-ceilinged foyer, Gable made no move to invite Jane any farther inside. Five minutes. An interview in the entryway. Fine with Jane. She had only three questions. First, the easy one.

"We're still working on your profile piece, of course. But because of last night— Well, I'm sure you heard Owen Lassiter's statement," Jane said. Her tote bag hung from her shoulder, the tape recorder rolling in an outside pouch. "I'm taking notes by tape, okay? So Lassiter said 'tragic personal circumstances beyond my control do not diminish my public responsibility to stay in this race.' What's your reaction?"

"The voters will decide about that, Jane." Eleanor Gable slouched off her camel-hair coat, turned her back to hang it in the hall closet. She didn't offer to take Jane's coat. "And now if you're finished?"

"Two more questions," Jane said. "There's a house at four-six-three Constitution Lane in Deverton. You own that, correct?"

Gable, minus her usual hail-fellow demeanor, glanced upstairs, as if she wanted to get away. She tossed her head, her pale hair swinging across one cheek, then back into place. "Yes, if that's the address of my family's Deverton property. One of many. I'm sure you know that, Jane. That's hardly a random question."

Ball to Jane's court. Fine.

"And do you have a tenant in that house now?"

An almost-laugh. A glance at a thin lizard-strapped watch. "Jane, please. If you have a question, just ask it."

"Owen Lassiter visited a woman at that house."

"Visited? A woman?" Gable raised an eyebrow. "Perhaps you should discuss that with him."

"Well, I could, I suppose, but he's at the hospital with her right now. Kenna Wilkes. As I'm sure you are aware."

"His daughter. 'Long-lost daughter,' as your article

THE OTHER WOMAN 413

this morning so eloquently described her." Gable glanced up the stairs again, a double-tall mulberry-walled gallery, silver-framed photographs covering it floor to ceiling, edges aligned and almost touching. "Miss Ryland, do you have a point?"

Jane followed Gable's glance upstairs. Was someone up there? Or was she just signaling Jane to leave? The photos on the wall reminded Jane of—*coffee?* Why? She must really need sleep.

"I do have a point," Jane said. "And you know what it is. Why was Owen Lassiter's estranged daughter, who infiltrated his campaign without his knowledge and later apparently attempted to kill him, living at a home you own?"

"Jane, I'm sure I have no idea." Gable turned to the front door, placed her hand on the polished brass knob. "And if you have any further questions, please contact my—"

A creak from the top of the stairs.

"Ellie?" A voice called down.

A man.

"Just a moment," Gable called back.

Oh. No wonder Gable was uncomfortable. She had a guy upstairs. So much for the—

"Ellie?" the voice came again, louder.

Jane turned toward the sound. Gable did, too.

"Jane?" Gable took Jane by the arm, ushering her out. "Any more questions, please call my office. It's been a long day. The election is right around the corner."

Jane had one foot in the foyer, the other on the front step. And the door began to close behind her.

78

Jane straight-armed the door. Keeping it open. She turned to look inside. *Coffee*. The picture. She knew where she'd seen it. And she recognized the voice on the stairway. No way she was leaving.

Rory Maitland stood, one hand on the banister, frozen midstep. No longer rumpled and polyester, he now sported khakis and a turtleneck. Beacon Hill casual.

Eleanor Gable whirled to face him, then turned back to Jane. Her nose went up, and she waved toward the stairway. "I'm sure you know Rory Maitland," Gable said. "We're discussing whether our campaigns should contact the secretary of state's office to inquire about postponing the election. Given the ramifications of these difficult events."

Rory Maitland? At Gable's house? *Discussing?*

"Did you find the powder room, Rory?" Gable smiled, gracious hostess.

"I noticed a photo on your wall, Ms. Gable. That one. Third from the bottom." Jane was not buying Gable's preposterous explanation. "A beach in Nantucket? The same photo's also in your campaign office. Funny, there's one exactly like it on Mr. Maitland's desk. I blotted spilled coffee from it the other day. Remember, Mr. Maitland?"

"Jetties Beach?" Gable said, eyeing the photograph. "Hardly exotic."

"You've been there, too, Ms. Gable?" Maitland said. He'd almost reached the bottom of the stairs. Loafers with no socks. "Not surprising. Who hasn't?"

"She was 'Ellie' when you called down a moment ago," Jane said. "And Ms. Gable? I was here before you arrived. Remember? You invited me in? There was no meeting under way. Mr. Maitland was already here. Upstairs."

"I—," Gable began.

"We—," Maitland said at the same time.

Jane rummaged in her purse for her camera. "Let me show you this," she said, finding the camera, for once, on the first try. She clicked the button. "This is a Lassiter campaign rally on the Esplanade a week ago, remember? There's Holly Neff, the woman Matthew Lassiter apparently killed. And here's—see? With his arm around the other woman?"

Jane held up the camera, first to Gable, then to Maitland, who'd moved closer. They examined the screen, then exchanged glances.

Gable spoke first. "And what this has to do with me is . . . precisely what, Miss Ryland?"

"So? I knew her as Kenna Wilkes," Maitland said. He shrugged. "A campaign volunteer. One of many."

"How did you know where Katharine Lassiter was buried?" Jane persisted. "Kenna told you, didn't she? She hated her father. You two were in it together."

Jane paused, looking at Gable, then Maitland. Statues. Ice and icier. "Or more likely—you *three*. Now I see. Ms. Gable, I bet Sarah approached *you* first. Maybe offering a ready-made scandal? And then *you* lured in Maitland."

Maitland crossed his arms in front of his chest. Rolled his eyes. All drama. "That's ab—"

"Good-bye, Miss Ryland." Gable put her hand on the front door. With a flourish and a grand gesture, she yanked it wide open.

A puff of chill, Beacon Hill revealed, now almost in darkness. The bustle from Pinckney Street filled the entryway: taxis honking, car door slamming, a distant siren. The old-fashioned wrought-iron gaslights glimmered in the dusk, then glowed bright.

Lights. Jane put her fingers to her lips, realizing. She ignored the open door. "Mr. Maitland? It was you who turned off the lights at the Springfield rally, wasn't it? Pulled the alarm? Turned up the thermostat? You who put the campaign in such disarray? I'm right. It all makes sense. Because you were working—" Jane pointed at Gable. "—for *her.*"

Jane shook her head, struggling to grasp this level of deception. "Political consultant, huh? You used Ms. Gable's Deverton house to insinuate Kenna—I mean Sarah—into the campaign. You both tried to manipulate Moira Lassiter into believing her husband was having an affair. And making it public. When *you* were the ones who were actually cheating."

Jane paused, seeing the final possibility. "Was it personal, too? Or only politics?"

Maitland took a step up the stairs, then seemed to think better of it. "You could never prove I was here."

Gable moved in front of him, blocking him. Hands on hips, charm bracelet jangling. "You'll hear from my attorney, Miss Ryland. I know your reputation. So does everyone. There's nothing between me and Mr. Maitland. No one will believe a word you say. And we'll insist this whole conversation never happened."

Jane's eyes narrowed. She thought about greed and corruption and power. Thought about her tape recorder, still rolling in her purse. Thought about how quickly she'd need to get the hell out of here if they came at her together.

"I write the facts, Ms. Gable. The truth. And the truth is, your campaign dirty tricks resulted in two horrible and unnecessary deaths. And put your pawn, Sarah, in critical condition. And I think readers—or should I say, voters?—will be fascinated by that whole story. We'll let *them* decide what the truth means."

79

Why didn't Jane pick up her damn messages? Jake propped his BlackBerry on the Jeep's steering wheel, the heater humming, the shift in Park. He hadn't even gotten to give her the word on the Vicks. He hit Redial. "It's me. Again. By now you've heard. Call me."

Should he head directly to her apartment? He tipped the BlackBerry back and forth on the wheel. Maybe yes, maybe no. Jane was certainly not in danger—Matt was dead, Sarah Lassiter hooked to a bunch of beeping monitors with two cadets and DeLuca guarding her hospital room. Not talking yet, but they'd buzz him if she came to.

She might live, doctors were saying. *If she does, maybe she'll get Patti Vick as a roommate.* Jake had to smile. So much for the Bridge Killer.

End of story.

He shifted into Drive, eased out of the cop shop parking lot. *Jane's apartment.* Why not?

That's odd. Alex's door is closed.

Jane had dashed up the three flights to the city room, unable to wait another moment for the exasperatingly slow elevator. Her head was full of her story—Maitland a turncoat, working for Lassiter's opponent, Gable as the other woman—well, she couldn't actually write all that, not yet.

Now, fidgeting in the waiting area outside Alex's office, she waved both hands, signaling, trying to get his attention. He had the desk phone to his ear, cord stretched to the limit, pacing. Gesturing. Frowning.

She decided to go ahead, write what she had, a first draft. She had to call—who? Lassiter, of course. And the secretary of state, she was in charge of elections. Could she postpone the whole deal?

And Moira. Who so far wasn't returning Jane's calls. Would she play the good wife in all this?

Jane dug in her tote bag for her phone. *Damn.* Still on mute from this afternoon. She clicked it back on, turning the ringer to extra loud.

The city room was deserted, tomorrow's first deadline past and the night shift not due for half an hour. She would have some quiet to get her thoughts together.

She rounded the corner, hoping Tuck wasn't occupying their chair.

Great. Empty.

She plopped into the swivel in front of the desk, then quickly stood again. She was in the wrong cube. No Bridge Killer crime scene photos pinned across the bulletin board, no Snickers wrappers in the wastebasket, no bulging manila file folders taking up all the room on the desktop.

Jane paused, confused. But her own stuff was there, where she'd left it last night. Her envelope of photos. Her campaign brochures. Archive Gus's file.

Only Tuck's possessions were gone. Maybe Jane's scoop snagged her an office of her own?

A footstep in the corridor. A cough. And then Jane's phone beeped. A message. *Has to be from Jake.*

"Jane?" Alex appeared at the cubicle entrance. He draped one arm over the low fabric-covered divider.

Had she ever seen him in a suit and tie before? *Hot Alex,* indeed. Her phone beeped again. Extra loud.

"Hey, Alex, listen," Jane said. She stood quickly, smiling, eager to tell the story. Describe every detail. "You won't believe what I just—"

Alex put up a palm. The twinkle was gone from his eyes. "Two things," he said. "First, good news. You know about Patti Vick, right? Police released it, five minutes ago."

"Patti? Vick?" Jane tried to figure out where this was going. *Arthur Vick's wife?*

"Confessed to killing Sellica Darden. Revenge. For her husband's—affair. You see what that means."

Jane sank back into her desk chair, one hand on the smooth metal desktop, needing to keep her balance. Her knees were not to be trusted.

"Didn't Jake call you? You don't know?"

Jane glanced at her phone. It beeped again. Alex had a funny look on his face.

"No, I—" Jane tried to think. She'd clearly missed Jake's call. *Patti Vick?* She couldn't wait to hear every— *Wonder if Leota Darden knows.* Jane reached for the cell.

"Before you pick that up," Alex interrupted. "The bad news. We had to fire Tuck. She was seeing Laney Driscoll, the police PR flack. Turns out, he leaked her those crime scene photos. And a lot more. The superintendent just fired *him,* too. It's a bad deal. All around. We trusted her, we printed it, we'll back her in court. First Amendment, all that. But sleeping with a source? Any kind of inappropriate behavior? The *Register* will not tolerate that."

Jane's hand hovered over her cell phone. It beeped again. Insistent. And, since Alex obviously suspected who was calling, potentially career-ending.

80

Her car wasn't there. Jake trolled Corey Road for the third time, barely touching the accelerator, just to be sure. Past ivy-covered brownstones, leafless trees, a fedora-wearing geezer walking an overweight collie. No Audi. He drove through the narrow alley in the back of her building. No Audi. She wasn't home. Maybe at the *Register*?

That little boy, Eli, was scuffing through piles of fallen leaves on the front sidewalk. His mother stood beside him, pushing a stroller back and forth. But no Jane.

He checked again. No messages on his cell.

Jake flickered a rueful glance at himself in the rearview. *She's got ya, bud, doesn't she?* he thought. *And what of it?* he answered his own question.

He'd buy her flowers. Deliver them to her in person at the *Register*. As congratulations on her scoop.

What woman wouldn't appreciate that?

Should she pick up the phone? If her voice mail was from Jake—and of course it was—she'd have a hard time hiding it. But Alex knew they were pals. Jake had recommended her for this job. Suddenly that wasn't such a good thing.

Tuck's empty bulletin board proved why.

But Patti Vick? *Confessed? That means Sellica's death was not a result of her TV story. And that means . . .*

Alex's cell phone interrupted. He pulled it from his jacket pocket, glanced at the screen. "It's Ellen. The *Register* intern. At the hospital. I've got her staking out Sarah Lassiter."

"Is she—?" If Sarah died, they'd never find out what really happened. Owen and Moira Lassiter were at the hospital, been there since last night. Gable and Maitland—who knew. Maybe hiring lawyers.

"Okay." Alex was checking his watch as he talked to Ellen. "Ten minutes."

"Sarah Lassiter is awake," he said. "I need you to get over to Mass General."

"On the way." Jane scooped up her belongings. If Sarah was talking, they were about to get some answers.

Jake pulled into Casswell Boulevard, headed his Jeep in the *Register*'s direction. He shouldn't have let Jane talk him out of—being together. A relationship. She'd been terrific, last night, in that chaos. No freaking out. No crying. Efficient, competent. And she was the one who'd figured out the Matt thing.

She was a knockout. All there was to it.

A clay pot of white tulips wrapped in crinkling clear cellophane teetered on the seat beside him, trailing a pink ribbon to the floor. She loved tulips.

He stopped at the red light, good cop. He'd never told Jane anything the supe could criticize. They'd simply have to agree to keep their professional and personal lives separate. They could be careful. It could work.

He missed her.

"Brogan? You read?" his radio interrupted.

"Brogan," he said, pushing the button. He hit the accelerator as the light changed. "Loud and clear, D. What's up?"

"Sarah Lassiter. You better get over here."

Jake eyed the flowers. Then he flipped on the lights and siren and banged a U-turn across two lanes of traffic.

Maybe Jane will be at the hospital, too.

"What did Sarah Lassiter say? Where's Trevor now?" Jane grabbed Ellen by the elbow, recognizing the elaborate braids and wire-rimmed glasses of the *Register*'s intern. Jane had parked in the Mass General garage, run down two flights of water-stained stairwell, raced past a couple of waiting ambulances, pushed through the glass front doors. Almost got to the elevator. When a security guard stopped her.

Now she was trapped in a windowless holding room with every reporter and photographer on the planet. At least Ellen had made contact with Trevor Kiernan.

Ellen pulled a spiral notebook from the back pocket of her jeans. "Sarah Lassiter? A nurse ran out of her room, freaking. Then all hell broke loose and I got booted down here. Owen Lassiter's in Sarah's room, and his wife, too. And about a million cops. I told Trevor Kiernan you were on the way."

"What'd he say?" Jane had to talk to Lassiter. And Moira. Tell them what she knew. Warn them. They didn't know about Gable. The *other* woman.

Ellen shrugged. "He said—thanks. Now, we wait."

Outside Sarah Lassiter's room, two uniform cops stood sentinel. Jake knew DeLuca was inside.

Owen Lassiter, arm across his wife's shoulders, slumped on a low bench against the wall. She must have brought him a change of clothes—last night's blood-spattered shirt was gone, replaced by a dark blue turtleneck. A tweedy guy holding a clipboard leaned close to Mrs. Lassiter, whispering.

All three looked up at Jake's arrival. Faces drawn, exhausted.

"Detective," Lassiter said, standing. "My daughter's dead. She said she never meant to kill me—she was just—I don't know. Trying to scare me. But she said I took her mother's life. And, I suppose, I did."

Moira made a soft sound, not quite a sob. Her head dropped into her hands.

"And my own son sacrificed his life for mine." Lassiter's shoulders went back, a muscle in his jaw working. He reached out a hand, almost caressing his wife's hair. "We could have worked it out. Now it's too late."

Jake remembered that boisterous rally on the Esplanade. Candidate Owen Lassiter. Confetti and crowds and music and adulation. Confident, powerful, promising to save the world. Now he stood only in sorrow, facing a future of second-guessing and certain regret.

"I'm sorry for your loss," Jake said.

81

Jane punched the green button before her cell finished the first ring. She'd heard Jake's messages, finally. Incredible about the Vicks. But if this was him calling back, she'd have to nip this whole thing in the bud. Right now. She wasn't going to be the next Tuck.

"Jane Ryland," she said.

"It's Trevor Kiernan."

Oh. *Terrific.*

"Don't say a thing. Don't say it's me. Come to room 415. It's a private sitting room. The cops will let you by. Now."

Trevor, waiting in the hallway, opened the door as Jane arrived. Someone had cracked open the room's tall windows, revealing a wide-shot view of the Charles River, lights of Cambridge glimmering across the water, gauzy curtains shifting in the evening breeze. Moira Lassiter was a silhouette, framed in the gathering night.

"I'm sorry for the . . . intrigue," Moira said. She came into the light, smoothing her already-smooth hair with one hand, adjusting a plush gray sweater across her shoulders. "But I owe you, Jane. I want to clear things up. Off the record?"

Jane nodded. Waiting. A matching floral armchair and

love seat flanked a low glass and metal coffee table. A paper cup, tea bag string dangling, bore a print of Moira's plum red lipstick.

"I'll leave you two," Trevor said. The door closed after him with a soft click.

Moira sat on the love seat, tucking the charcoal pleats of her skirt underneath her, and gestured Jane to the chair. "Please."

She's already been through so much. Moira and her husband don't even know the rest. Jane wished she didn't have to tell them about Gable and Maitland. A knockout story for her. A knockout punch for the Lassiters.

Moira took a tentative sip from her cup, holding the tea bag string with one finger. She looked past Jane, past the flutter of curtains, into the night.

"This all started with me," she said.

"When you called me." Jane remembered that day, Moira and her maybe-vodka, the request to find "the other woman."

Moira shook her head, her lips tight. "No, Jane, long before that. Years before that."

Jane nodded, transfixed.

"We were—in love. And just trying to be happy," Moira said. "Owen had a miserable marriage. His wife was a constant battle. She'd . . . Well, who knows what she might have done. When he finally left, he was distraught. Inconsolable. But it was out of necessity, you know? Then, it got worse. She kept the children from him. Every time he tried to see them, she'd prevent it. Threatened him, sent him away. One day she just disappeared with them. Owen was devastated. She'd told him, again and again, Sarah and Matt loathed him. Apparently, Sarah actually did."

Moira moved a hospital-issue paper napkin on the

table, set her teacup on top of it. Her chest rose, then fell, her sweater draping as her shoulders momentarily sagged.

Jane had a thousand questions. But this wasn't the time to ask them.

"Sarah—Kenna, she called herself." Moira crossed her legs, crossed her arms, protecting herself. "All this time she was—taunting me. Making me suspect my own dear husband. That whole Springfield charade, Owen told me all about it. Last night in her hospital room, even with all those tubes, Sarah said she wanted to hurt me, and then hurt Owen. The way we hurt her."

She took a deep breath, let it out slowly.

"But during the campaign? Owen never, ever did anything wrong. Now, both his children are dead. Because of me. Because all those years ago, I was—the other woman."

She reached out, touching Jane's arm with one graceful hand, her brown eyes brimming with tears. "You can choose your sin, Jane," she whispered. "But you cannot choose your consequences."

82

"This one belongs to you, Jane." With a flourish, Alex handed her the first copy of Wednesday's morning paper. "It's a long way from Wrong-Guy Ryland, I must say."

Jane stood up from her spot on Alex's couch, bowing dramatically as she accepted the bulldog edition. Both of them were wired on two lattes each after yet another all-nighter in the *Register* newsroom.

"Talk about wrong," Jane said. "The cops found an incredible stash of photos in Holly's apartment. Apparently, she'd been stalking Lassiter for weeks, putting together her own political campaign to humiliate him, make him look like a womanizer. And I just found another batch of them in my mailbox, forwarded from Channel Eleven. From her, I guess. Her scheme could have worked, I bet. If Matt Lassiter hadn't—ah."

Jane sank back on the couch, folded newspaper in hand, leaning her head against the worn upholstery, propping her blue-jeaned legs on the coffee table. Thinking about Moira. "And Lassiter did absolutely nothing wrong during the campaign, you know? It's terrible. Greed. Deception. Power. The whole thing."

"But a helluva story," Alex said.

"Got to admit." Jane opened the paper, held up the front page.

Jane's story, headlined SENATE RACE SCANDAL— CONSULTANT CONS CANDIDATE IN ELECTION DOUBLE- CROSS, covered the entire front page above the fold. Below, the follow-up to Patti Vick's arrest—minus Tuck's byline—rated one paragraph and a jump. *Jake was right. There is no Bridge Killer. Or, actually, there are four.*

Alex plonked his feet on his desk, tilting in his chair. "Secretary of State Doniger insists she can't call off the election. So next week, people will either choose a sleaze for senator, or vote for a dupe who can't tell that his closest ally is actually working for the other guy."

"The other woman, you mean." Jane read her story yet again, scanning for the highlights. It was *all* highlights. Seduction. Betrayal. Murder. Jane had worked through the night, trying to make sense of all that had happened. Choosing exactly the right words so her story could explain it, clear and objective.

"The dupe—I mean Lassiter—is gonna win, at least," Jane said. "Trevor'll get to go to Washington, if he hasn't quit, you know? But Gable's jeered wherever she goes now. Talk about toast. Got to love Maitland's quote, though, that he and Gable 'did nothing illegal.' "

"He can tell that to the grand jury." Alex, as usual, started reading his e-mail while he talked. "Our court guy says the target letter's in the mail. Maitland's finished, you know? His backroom double-dealing led to murder, after all. And Gable's already turning on him. Alleges he was stalking her, sending her love notes. Which she destroyed, of course, conveniently. *Geez.* When he rats her out, can you imagine the mess?"

He suddenly leaned closer to the computer screen. "Oh. Holy shit. Body in a hotel room."

"Where? Who?" Jane's phone trilled from the pouch of her fleece hoodie. She flipped open her cell. Didn't get a chance to say a word before the whisper on the other end.

"Janey? It's me."

Jake. Just hearing his voice, Jane knew she must look guilty. But Alex was deep into a phone conversation of his own. She'd have to let Jake know the score.

"Yes, this is Jane Ryland, what can I do for you?" she said.

Jake watched Humpty unspool the yellow plastic tape across the hotel room door. Penthouse of the Madisonian. High-class, high-priced, and now, a crime scene.

He could tell from her voice Jane was not alone. De-Luca had filled him in on the fiasco with Laney Driscoll and Tuck. Jane must know about it, too.

"I understand, Miss Ryland," Jake said. Telegraphing, *I get it.* "And we'll have to follow up on that. But to let you know. Body was just discovered at the Madisonian Hotel. Looks like suicide. It's Rory Maitland."

A sharp intake of breath on the other end. He could picture her, twisting her hair, mind racing, assessing who might hear her.

"I know you can't talk," he said. "But, Jane? On the way out? Check the *Register*'s front desk. Something there for you."

He clicked off the phone.

Janey would finally get those tulips. And, Jake hoped, she'd understand the card he'd tucked inside.

"Dead body in a hotel room, our stringer reports," Alex said. He had flipped open his laptop, now talking to

Jane and typing at the same time. "No ID? *Damn.* Hang on a second, Jane. I've gotta find someone to cover this thing."

"I'll go," Jane said. *Thanks, Jakey. How can I stay away from him?* She stood, brushing down her jeans. "Got my trusty notebook, got my trusty tape recorder, cell phone all charged. Who knows what story may be unfolding. Right?"

"No mistake about that," Alex said. He paused, slowly closed his laptop. "Jane?"

He looked at her so intently, she took a step backward. His eyes were softer than she'd remembered. And that smile was one she'd never seen.

"Yes?"

"Jane, listen. I want to tell you—you've really rocked this." He swallowed, adjusted his glasses. Smiled again. "We're a good team, you and I, don't you think?"

Hot Alex. He only means "a good team" professionally, right? I won't mention this to Amy.

Not a bad way to start the day. Seven in the morning, a front-page exclusive, and praise from her boss. Her dad would be proud, too, wouldn't he? She couldn't wait to tell him. Maybe her sister's wedding would even be—fun. Now another big story was in the works. After that? That was the joy of reporting. And of life. You never knew.

Mom was right. One door closes, another door opens. Maybe I can even help Tuck find a new job. Kind of— karma. I know what it feels like to get the rug pulled out.

"Thanks, Alex," Jane said. "Yeah. We *are* a good team. And I'm really—"

Her cell phone was ringing. Extra loud. She couldn't ignore it, not with Alex watching. *Wonder what Jake left at the front desk?*

"Go ahead, pick up," Alex said, gesturing. "Might be—"

"Jane Ryland," she answered.

"Jane-ster. It's Bart Finneran at Channel Eleven. Congratulations on that story. You're really knocking 'em dead."

"Ah," Jane said. She stared at the floor.

"What?" Alex said.

"Here's the scoop, kiddo. With the Vick arrest?" Finneran continued. "Lawyers tell me it's a done deal now. Appeal over. Judgment vacated. Like it never happened."

"Ah," Jane said again. *Kiddo. What a creep.* But the judgment was—gone? The whole million-dollar mess?

"What?" Alex said again.

"I guess you're speechless, huh?" Finneran said. "Don't blame ya, kiddo. It's all over, Jane."

Jane remembered his studio-trained voice, his movie-star face, how he'd lied to her as he fired her. Her hand clutched her phone. Her voice was not working.

Alex watched her, waiting.

"Anyway, Jane"—Finneran was still talking—"we're hoping you'd like your job back. Like none of this ever happened. You'll be our superstar. Big-time. What do you say?"

My job back. Exactly what I'd thought I wanted.

But I was wrong.

Jane paused. Waited a beat. What to say? The perfect response would be wry and knowing. Brief and memorable. So cleverly dismissive, Finneran would go back to his overstuffed office and his overpaid cronies and say, *That Ryland. I offered her the moon, and you know what she told me?*

Jane could think of that perfect line. She would. Maybe while drinking a latte at her city room desk, maybe while hashing it over with Amy, maybe while sharing a clandestine glass of wine with Jake.

But she knew what the line would mean.

"What I say is—no thank you," she said. Then, she couldn't resist. "I'm afraid you've got the wrong girl."

With one decisive click, she hung up.

"*What?*" Alex said. "You okay?"

"Yup." And it was true. She was fine. "That was Channel Eleven. They want me back."

She saw Alex's eyes widen. "But you—we—"

"I know," she said. Jane smiled as she picked up her tote bag. *I have a story to cover.* "They obviously made a mistake."

ACKNOWLEDGMENTS

Unending gratitude to:

Kristin Sevick, my brilliant, hilarious, and gracious editor. Thank you. The remarkable team at Forge Books: the incomparable Linda Quinton, indefatigable Alexis Saarela, and Seth Lerner for the cover of all covers (and I know I'll never beat you in Scrabble). Copy editor Eliani Torres, who had me laughing all the way through the copyediting with her yellow highlights. (Sometimes, I repeat words. Thank goodness she noticed.) Talia Sherer, who shares my passion for libraries. Brian Heller, my champion. The inspirational Tom Doherty, who makes it all happen. What a terrifically smart and unfailingly supportive team. I am so thrilled to be part of it.

Lisa Gallagher, a wow of an agent, a true goddess, who changed my life.

Francesca Coltrera, the astonishingly skilled independent editor, who lets me believe all the good ideas are mine. Editor Chris Roerden, whose infinite care and skill and commitment made such a difference. You both are incredibly talented. I am lucky to know you both—and even luckier to be able to work with you.

The artistry and savvy of Madeira James, Charlie Anctil, Patrick O'Malley, and Nancy Berland. The expertise, guidance, and friendship of Dr. D. P. Lyle and Lee Lofland and Cathy Pickens. And the wizardry of Carol Fitzgerald.

The inspiration of David Morrell, Mary Jane Clark, Jim Huang, Marianne Mancusi, Suzanne Brockmann, Kaye Barley, Carla Neggers, and Robert B. Parker.

Sue Grafton. And Lisa Scottoline. And Lee Child. Words fail me. (I know, a first.)

My dear posse at Sisters in Crime. Thank you. And at Mystery Writers of America, the dolphin gang: Reed Farrel Coleman, Jessie Lourey, Larry Light, and Margery Flax.

My amazing blog sisters. At Jungle Red Writers: Julia Spencer-Fleming, Hallie Ephron, Rosemary Harris, Roberta Isleib/Lucy Burdette, Jan Brogan, Deborah Crombie, and Rhys Bowen. At Femmes Fatales: Charlaine Harris, Dana Cameron, Kris Neri, Mary Saums, Toni Kelner, Elaine Viets, and Donna Andrews. At Lipstick Chronicles: Nancy Martin and Harley Jane Kozak, who brought us all together.

Ken Schanzer and Jim Flug and Tom Sussman and Terry Straub, my political mentors from way back.

My dear friends Amy Isaac, Mary Schwager, and Katherine Hall Page; and my darling sister, Nancy Landman.

Dad—who loves every moment of this. (Mom—Missing you, and using cucumbers.)

And Jonathan, of course, who never complained about all the pizza.

(I've tweaked Boston geography a bit to protect the innocent. And I love readers who read the acknowledgments. Thanks to you all.)

www.hankphillippiryan.com
www.jungleredwriters.com
www.femmesfatales.typepad.com

Turn the page for a preview of

THE
WRONG
GIRL

HANK PHILLIPPI RYAN

*Available in September 2013 from
Tom Doherty Associates*

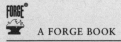

1

"Listen, Jane. I don't think she's my real mother."

Jane Ryland took the phone from her ear, peering at it as if it could somehow help Tuck's incomprehensible tale make sense. *Real mother?* She didn't know Tuck was adopted, let alone looking for her birth mother. Why would Tuck call *her*? And spill this soul-baring saga of abandonment, adoption agencies, then meeting some woman in Connecticut? Jane and Tuck were barely friends, let alone confidantes, especially after Tuck had—

The doorbell?

"I'm in your front lobby." Tuck's voice buzzed over the intercom at the same time it came through the phone. "Sorry to show up at your apartment on a Sunday, you know, but I couldn't come to the *Register,* of course."

Of course. It'd be humiliating for Tuck to visit Jane at the newspaper where they'd shared a cubicle as "news roomies" only months ago. Once a hotshot reporter, Tucker Cameron had been fired from the *Register* for sleeping with a source. The Boston Police public relations officer, of all dumb choices. In the months since, according to the nonstop newsroom gossip, the two pariahs,

Tuck and Laney, had dropped off the map. Until now. But that was Tuck. *Never a dull . . .*

Jane pushed the red button in the intercom box, retied the drawstring on her fraying weekend sweatpants, and opened her front door, making sure Coda didn't streak through her legs. The calico—a kitten, really—had arrived on the downstairs stoop a few weeks before, tiny paws icy with snow. All Humane Society intentions disappeared after the shivering fluff nuzzled into Jane's shoulder, but neither of them was quite used to the other yet.

Jane heard the entry door click open, three flights down, and Tuck's footsteps climbing the hardwood steps as she talked into her cell. "So what am I supposed to do now, roomie? I'm not a reporter anymore. No one will talk to me. Laney's looking for a job. I'm like a—well, you're the only one who can help me. The only one who was even nice to me. After."

Tuck's head appeared around the landing, a black knit cap over her dark ponytail. A puffy snow-flecked black parka emerged, then her black jeans. She paused, one leather glove grazing the mahogany banister, the other raised in tentative greeting. Tuck's trademark swagger—her outta-my-way confidence—was missing.

"Tuck? You okay?" Just another February at Jane's. First a stray kitten, and now—was Tuck crying? *Tuck?*

"I guess so." Tuck stomped the last of the snow from her salt-stained boots, punched off her phone, stuffed it into her parka pocket. "I'm trying to be angry instead of miserable. But I can't let this go."

She swiped under her eyes with two gloved fingers, wiping away what could have been snow. "It's my whole life, you know?"

"Tell me inside. Get warm. Dump your boots by the

door." Jane took Tuck's soggy parka and cap, draped them over the banister, then ushered her visitor into the living room, pointing her to the taupe-striped wing chair by the bay window. Slushy snow pelted the glass, the wind clattering bare branches, the last of the afternoon's feeble gray light struggling through. Coda slept on the couch, almost invisible, curled on a chocolate-and-cream paisley cushion.

"Tea? Beer? Wine?"

"Wine. Thanks. This has really kicked my ass." Tuck plopped into the chair, then twisted one leg around the other. "The lawyer I contacted at first was worthless, then the agency got my hopes up, but now, well, this is worse than not knowing. Which is why I'm here."

Which made no sense whatsoever.

They'd been office mates for only about two weeks. Jane was dayside, covering politics. Tuck worked the night shift, seemed to care only about her sensational front-page Bridge Killer stories. Their paths crossed only when their stories did. Now for some reason Tuck seemed to think she needed Jane's help, so here she was. That was Tuck.

"Hang on a sec, let me get your glass." Jane padded to the kitchen, grabbed the wine from the fridge, twisted it open. *What would it feel like, not to know your own mother?* As a kid, she'd thrown around adoption like a threat. "When my REAL mother comes to get me, you'll be sorry," a petulant eight-year-old Jane taunted her parents. She and BFF Laurie, slumber party faces smeared in beauty goo, speculated in late-night whispers whether Jane's chestnut hair and hazel eyes meant she might really be adopted, might really be royalty or Bono's girlfriend's abandoned daughter.

Jane *did* know what being fired felt like. It happened to her last summer and the sting hadn't quite gone away. So if Tuck needed her for something? She held out the glass and sat cross-legged on the couch. Least she could do was pour some wine and listen. "Okay, all ears."

With Coda's purr a rumbling underscore, Tuck spilled the details.

Jane's reporter training switched into gear, assessing what could be wrong, or a coincidence, or a mistake. She ticked off her questions, finger to finger, as she did with every story she covered.

"So back at the beginning. You called the agency. Your mother told you which one?"

"Yes. 'The Brannigan,' they call it. Brannigan Family and Children Services. Ten years ago, when I *first* called, they told me all the records were sealed until my birth mother gave the okay to open them. A closed adoption, you know? Then I guess I tried to forget about it. I mean, I was eighteen, she might have been dead. Plus, I knew my mom—adoptive mother—wouldn't love that I was looking."

Tuck paused, rolled her eyes. "She'd have said, in that snarky voice she uses, 'Why do you need *another* mother, Tucker dear? Am I not enough for you?'" She shrugged. "She'd probably still say that, even in her . . . condition. But she lives in Florida, she stayed in their condo thing after Dad died. So she'll never know."

"Condition? She's . . . ?" Jane searched for a way to ask. She missed her own mother every day. *Poor Tuck*.

"Yeah. Doctors say it won't be long, and ah, I don't know. I'm trying to deal with that, too. It's hard." She puffed out a breath, shook her head. "*Anyway*. Last week, after all that time, the Brannigan called to say they'd found my birth mother. It felt perfect, you know? With me and Laney serious, thinking of kids, and the last of my adoptive family almost gone? But now . . ." Tuck pulled the stretchy band from her ponytail, then twisted it back on. Took a sip of wine, carefully replaced her glass on the coaster.

She looked at Jane. "But now, even though I'm not at the paper anymore, I think I may be on to the story of my life."

2

"Kurtz got here first. She's got the two of 'em in her cruiser. See 'em? Parked out on the street?" The beat cop, a grizzled veteran Jake didn't recognize, cocked his head toward the Roslindale triple-decker's inside stairway. "Lucky my new partner likes kids. Looks pretty bad upstairs, gotta warn you, Detective Brogan. DeLuca's already up there. Back room on the left, second floor. Crime Scene's on the way. The ME. And family services. Snow enough for you?"

"It's Boston, right?" Jake's words puffed in the chill. He brushed now-melting flakes from his police-issue leather jacket, pulled out his BlackBerry for taking notes. He looked to the top of the stairs, scanning. Sniffed. Nothing. The entry door behind him was open, letting in the cold. Any smell was long frozen away.

"Door open when you got here, Officer Hennessey?" That's what the cop's badge said, R. Hennessey. Looked old enough to be a lifer, still on the beat.

Hennessey nodded. "They're canvassing, seeing if anyone saw anybody leaving. So far, no."

"And there are two kids? Whoever called nine-one-one wasn't clear. We know who that is yet? I have the kids as last name—" Jake checked his BlackBerry short-hand. His phone always ridiculously auto-corrected. "Is it Lussier?"

"So says the nine-one-one caller." Hennessey, a stocky fire hydrant zipped into foul-weather gear, flapped his leather gloves against his BPD navy parka. "Wish we could close the damn door."

At least Hennessey knew enough not to touch the scarred wooden doorknob of 56 Callaberry Street. There was barely room for the two of them in the cramped square of dark-paneled foyer. The dusty bare light bulb overhead didn't cut it, and the one on the first landing was out.

"So, the kids? Don't they know their mother's name?"

"We asked. 'Mama,' the boy said. Their own names, he knew. Phillip and Phoebe. What kind of a name is Phoebe?"

"Hennessey?" Commentary, he didn't need. "How many kids? The nine-one-one call indicated—"

"Apparently two. Maybe the caller meant three people resided here, ya know?" Hennessey shrugged. "We found a boy and a girl, approximately one and three years of age. Weren't crying or anything when Kurtz brought them down. Guess maybe they don't know. Victim's their mother, looks like, white female, age approximately thirty. Checking her ID now. Cause of death, looks like blunt trauma. No weapon so far. Like I said. Ugly. Frying pan, something like that."

"So says—?" Jake raised an eyebrow. It wouldn't have been Kurtz, the officer who had the kids in her cruiser. She was new on the street, just promoted from cadet, now evidently partnered with Hennessey. The ME was still on the way.

"So says your partner, DeLuca." Hennessey lifted his plastic-covered cap with one hand, propping it while he scratched a bristle of gray hair. "Guess he'd know. You two the big-time detectives and all."

Here we go. All he needed. Yes, his grandfather, Grandpa Brogan, had been police commissioner. Yes, Jake got his gold badge at thirty, three years ago. Jake had aced the academy, probably gotten higher scores than this guy. Still, even cracking last fall's Bridge Killer case, getting the commendation from Superintendent Rivera, hadn't stopped the sneers from the old-timers. "The Supe's fair-haired boy," they called him. Whatever.

Jake ignored the bait. "So the nine-one-one caller? Any ID? I know we'll have it on tape, but anything else I should know?"

"Yo, Harvard, that you?" Paul DeLuca's voice boomed down the stairwell. "You planning on coming up here anytime soon?"

"Chill," Jake yelled back. Jake's college history and Brahmin mother were a constant source of amused derision for his partner, though after a few close calls together and a couple of massacres on the basketball court, their relationship had matured into respect and good-natured banter. Jake held two thumbs over his phone keyboard. "So, Officer Hennessey? Anything? Sign of forced entry? Anyone else live in the apartment? Husband, boyfriend, the nine-one-one caller?"

"Nope. Nobody's owning up. Neighbors all say it wasn't them. Mighta been a blocked cell, ya know?"

Calling from a cell phone, Jake knew, didn't give dispatchers a GPS location. Enhanced 911 often worked only from a landline.

"Cell phone nine-one-ones are a bitch," Jake said. "Keep at the canvass, though, right?"

Hennessey's eyes went past him and out to Callaberry Street, where a gray-and-blue cruiser idled, plumes of exhaust darker gray than the darkening afternoon.

"Poor kids," the beat cop said. "They're screwed."

3

"**The woman from** the agency said my name is Audrey Rose Beerman, can you believe it?" Tuck laced her fingers together, clamped them on top of her head. "It's an okay name. But I don't feel like an Audrey Rose Beerman."

Jane took a sip of her Diet Coke, not quite sure how to react. What did Tuck want *her* to do?

"Maybe it's all about what we're used to. How we see ourselves." Plain Jane, Jane the Pain—the nicknames Jane'd been saddled with as a bookish kid in the relentless social hierarchy of Oak Park Junior High had sent her to name-fantasy world. *Anything but Jane.* For a while she'd wished to be Evangeline, courageous girl of the forest. Then Hyacinth, all flowy skirts and poetry. Her mother chose "Janey" when affectionate, "Jane Elizabeth" when making one of her pronouncements. As in "Jane Elizabeth Ryland is a perfectly good name. Evangeline is ridiculous."

Hey, Mom, Jane sent a message upward. *You were right. Miss you.*

But today was about Tuck. "So you didn't know your real name? Before?"

"Well, yeah. I did. That's one of the weird things, and tell you about it in a minute. But anyway, my—adoptive mother, I guess I'm supposed to call her—told me the agency always said my birth mother—" Tuck stopped mid-sentence, slumped her shoulders. "It's impossible. 'Real' mother? 'Birth' mother? 'Adoptive' mother? I mean, the woman I called my mother took care of me and changed my diapers and let me stay left-handed and yelled until the softball coach let me be the pitcher. She's kind of a whack job, at times, but what mom isn't, right? My biological mother, who conceived me, carried me for nine months, gave birth to me—she left me at the Brannigan."

Jane's eyes widened, she couldn't help it. How would it feel to take something from yourself, a helpless new human, and give it away? That child was now twenty-eight. Twenty-eight, bitter and confused. And, somewhere, was a woman grieving the loss?

"I'm so sorry," Jane almost whispered. "But your poor mother. It must have been horrible."

"Not so horrible she couldn't dump me at—well, whatever. My life has turned out fine. Even after the shit hit the fan, Laney and I are okay. He insists everything will work out." Tuck fiddled with the fringe on the chocolate-and-cream afghan draped over the chair. Jane's mother had crocheted it in her hospital bed, the last afghan she made. "Not feelin' it so much today, you know?"

Today was turning out to be quite the Sunday. Jane needed to get this talk back on track. Whatever that track was.

"So, Tuck. What is it you want me to do? You got a call from the Brannigan. They said they found your birth mother. You drove to Connecticut, and then what?"

"Long story short." Tuck folded the afghan over the arm of the chair. "I go to Connecticut. We meet at Starbucks. She's great, she's terrific, I'm in a Hallmark card or a Lifetime movie. I've never been so happy. I'm crying, she's crying. We each order a triple venti nonfat latte— exactly the same thing!—and we start crying again."

Tuck pressed her lips together, closed her eyes briefly.

"'Audrey Rose. You're so beautiful,' she says. 'I knew you'd be a knockout.' She said that, 'knockout.' 'You have my dark eyes,' she says, 'so skinny, and my crazy hair.' We spend two days together. I'm thinking—I have a biological family. I have a history. I have a story."

"Well, that sounds wonderful, Tuck. It sounds like—"

"No." Tuck slugged down the last of her wine. The timer behind the couch clicked on the bulbs of the brass lamp beside her. Jane was shocked to realize it was almost dark outside. February in Boston. It wasn't even five.

"I'm telling you, Jane. She's not my mother. She expected her long-lost daughter. But I'm . . . I'm not her."

"You're not—why would you think that? Come on, Tuck, why would they—?"

"I don't *know*. That's why I'm here. You're the reporter. My only—you've got to find out for me."

Tuck stood, tears welling, tumbling a throw pillow to the floor. Coda opened her tiny green eyes at the sound, looked up, then dropped her head back into her paws.

"Imagine how she'll feel? When she finds out?" One tear rolled down Tuck's cheek, and she swiped it away. "After all the plans? The calls? She looked so happy. But I know it. I *do*. They sent that poor woman the wrong girl."

Forge

Award-winning authors
Compelling stories

· ·

Please join us at the website
below for more information
about this author and other great
Forge selections, and to sign up for
our monthly newsletter!

 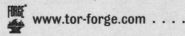

© LYNN WAYNE

A former U.S. Senate staffer and political campaign aide, **HANK PHILLIPPI RYAN** is the investigative reporter for Boston's NBC affiliate. She has won twenty-eight Emmys and ten Edward R. Murrow awards for her reporting. The bestselling author of four mystery novels, Ryan has won the Agatha, Anthony, and Macavity awards. She is on the national board of directors of Mystery Writers of America and Sisters in Crime. Visit her on the Web at www.HankPhillippiRyan.com.

36913

UPC

⚠ S

0 37145 00799 1

Jane Ryland was a rising star in television news . . . until she refused to reveal a source. Now a disgraced newspaper reporter not content to work on her assigned puff pieces, Jane finds herself tracking down a candidate's secret mistress just days before a pivotal Senate election.

Detective Jake Brogan is investigating a possible serial killer who may be hunting Boston's young women under the city's bridges.

As the body count rises and election day looms, it becomes clear to Jane and Jake that their investigations are connected . . . and that they may be facing a ruthless killer who will stop at nothing to silence a scandal.

Seduction, betrayal, and murder—it'll take a lot more than votes to win this election.

$7.99 ($9.99 CAN)

ISBN 978-0-7653-6913-0

50799

EAN

9 780765 369130

Cover photograph © Andy & Michelle Kerry / Trevillion Images

Tom Doherty Associates, LLC
www.tor-forge.com
Printed in the USA